FIREDRAKE

Nihilan smiled.

'On Moribar we unearthed the means to wreak our vengeance.' He pulled the scrolls to his side. 'On Scoria we enabled its realisation, whilst striking a stinging blow to our enemies.' This time he looked at Ramlek, who returned his lord's admiration without emotion. 'Old Kelock had no idea of the power he had chained. Scoria was nothing, a tenth of our strength. Now, we will harness all of it. Our Spear of Retribution is almost ready,' he announced to them all. 'And with it we shall tear out the heart of a world.'

Nihilan thrust out his clawed gauntlet in a fist.

'Death to Nocturne.'

The others followed suit, punching their knuckles together and forming a ring of red ceramite.

'Death to the Salamanders,' Nihilan concluded.

FIREDRAKE

Nick Kyme

BLACK LIBRARY

*To Big Mikey, the strongest man in the room, and
Laura Lizard for taking it through a whole new door.*

A BLACK LIBRARY PUBLICATION

First published in Great Britain in 2010 by
BL Publishing,
Games Workshop Ltd.,
Willow Road, Nottingham,
NG7 2WS, UK.

10 9 8 7 6 5 4 3 2 1

Cover illustration by Cheoljoo Lee.

A CIP record for this book is available from the British Library.

ISBN13: 978 1 84970 005 4

Distributed in the US by Simon & Schuster
1230 Avenue of the Americas, New York, NY 10020, US.

See the Black Library on the Internet at
www.blacklibrary.com

Find out more about Games Workshop
and the world of Warhammer 40,000 at
www.games-workshop.com

Printed and bound in the US.

IT IS THE 41st millennium. For more than a hundred centuries the Emperor has sat immobile on the Golden Throne of Earth. He is the master of mankind by the will of the gods, and master of a million worlds by the might of his inexhaustible armies. He is a rotting carcass writhing invisibly with power from the Dark Age of Technology. He is the Carrion Lord of the Imperium for whom a thousand souls are sacrificed every day, so that he may never truly die.

YET EVEN IN his deathless state, the Emperor continues his eternal vigilance. Mighty battlefleets cross the daemon-infested miasma of the warp, the only route between distant stars, their way lit by the Astronomican, the psychic manifestation of the Emperor's will. Vast armies give battle in His name on uncounted worlds. Greatest amongst his soldiers are the Adeptus Astartes, the Space Marines, bio-engineered super-warriors. Their comrades in arms are legion: the Imperial Guard and countless planetary defence forces, the ever-vigilant Inquisition and the tech-priests of the Adeptus Mechanicus to name only a few. But for all their multitudes, they are barely enough to hold off the ever-present threat from aliens, heretics, mutants – and worse.

TO BE A man in such times is to be one amongst untold billions. It is to live in the cruellest and most bloody regime imaginable. These are the tales of those times. Forget the power of technology and science, for so much has been forgotten, never to be re-learned. Forget the promise of progress and understanding, for in the grim dark future there is only war. There is no peace amongst the stars, only an eternity of carnage and slaughter, and the laughter of thirsting gods.

'Remember your purpose.

Remember, brothers, why we were born in Vulkan's forge.

Remember the anvil and how we are tested against it.

Not merely through war and the fires of battle.

To endure the cauldron is every warrior's lot.

We are not every warrior.

We are Fire-born.

Our purpose is to be a bulwark against oppression.

Our purpose is to protect the weak and those who cannot protect themselves.

We live amongst the people, because we are their champions.

We learn humility from their example.

Remember your purpose.

For in the darkest hours when the hammer strikes hard and the anvil is unyielding against your back

That is when you will need it most.'

– attributed to Tu'Shan, Chapter Master of the Salamanders

PROLOGUE

The serpent dwells in a frozen black sea fractured by diamonds. It hovers, asleep, defying the atmospheric pull of the red orb below it. It is a sentinel, a fell guardian. Slowly, a morsel ship glides towards it on cones of fire. Silently, covertly, the vessel closes on one of the serpent's many mouths. Deep space augurs do not detect it. Yet its signature is recognised by the serpent, and it starts to stir.

It is a small ship, but one that has travelled a great distance and seen much of this galaxy and the one that shadows it. No icons regale it; no markings identify its origin or allegiance. At first, the serpent only watches. Its eyes are open and aglow. The other heads do not move and still sleep. A few hundred metres away and the morsel ship comes level before this gargantuan beast. Now, its neck is extending, reaching for the unremarkable vessel. It is a piece of flotsam to this mighty creation, with its body of *solar-scarred granite and cratered flesh. Upon its back and long neck are spines. Other vessels are impaled on them, some many times larger than the morsel ship. Slowly, so, so slowly, the serpent opens its maw.*

Such artifice and craft is evident in those metallic jaws. Its scales are smooth. The metal is dull and hard, almost black like onyx. The eye-slits, burning like embers of violent potential, are viewports. Tiny, dark insects bustle within them like miniature irises in the grip of fever. The maw, though it is fanged and a tongue lies flat inside, is not a mouth at all. The morsel ship, its outer lamp arrays snuffed, flies within on engine gases. Stanchions, clawed like the feet of some predator-beast, extend with careful inevitability and the vessel lands on the serpent's tongue.

It is not a tongue, though. It is a deckplate, one scratched by alighting gunships and other, much larger, vessels. The serpent's head is empty, barring this one, unassuming ship. The deckhands busy themselves with automated protocols, ritually cleansing the ship in lapping fire. Atmospheric pressure has already been restored in this vast chamber of dark metal and fiery brazier-lamps. There is the reek of soot upon the air. The fuliginous environment only adds to the sense of old burning and fire.

Rituals observed, the side of the unassuming ship cracks open, severing its hermetic seals, and a single figure steps out. His footfalls are heavy, but not from fatigue. He feels the import of stepping upon the hallowed ground of this place. The serpent's head has swallowed him whole, accepting him back into its heart. Unclasping his battle-helm with a hiss of escaping pressure and lifting it off, he gazes upon his new accommodations for the first time in a long time. Breathing deep of the soot-soaked air, he smiles, and a flash of fire lights his blood-red eyes.

The automatons hurrying around him do not heed his

words. They are not meant for them. These words are for him and him alone.

'It's good to be home.'

STRIDING THROUGH GLOOMY corridors of lacquered stone and gunmetal, the figure took in all of his surroundings at a glance. He saw the brazier pans simmering dulcetly and the glow of fire-lamps overhead. He felt the heat in the air, prickling his skin. The scent of ash and cinder abraded his nostrils. He tasted metal and the acrid tang of burning. To some, this would be a hellish, diabolic place – the darkened, pseudo-subterranean lair of monsters. He knew it by another name:

Prometheus.

Even to think it as he trod its clandestine corridors, the conduits that led from the serpentine docking hangar to the inner sanctums, prompted a half smile. He had not felt this way for many years. He had not been here for many years, and yet he knew it like he knew his own honour-scarred flesh.

None barred his passage, for there were none abroad in the halls to witness it save the cleansing-servitors and they paid no mind.

It was as he wanted it to be. The Regent had orchestrated it this way, just as he had requested. Soon, he would meet him again. The throne chamber was not far. Such trust and confidence to dismiss his Firedrakes.

As he passed the pits of fire, burning lambently in alcoves of jet, a tremor of excitement ran through his armoured body. The wish to come back to the fraternity of his brothers was something he had repressed whilst on the quest for the Nine. Portents and signs had forced him to change his course. An astropathic message had gone out heralding his return to the Regent and the Regent alone. He'd locked the desire for the bonds of brotherhood deep within himself, but as he reached the great arch leading to the throne room he found he craved them again.

He wanted to pause before the mighty gate, to examine and appreciate the craft in the coiling dragons and the sigils of fire wrought around it. He had hoped to touch the artistry in the black lacquered doors, to detect the subtle variations in the many strata of volcanic rock upon their surface. But it was not to be. All these feelings, the sense of joy at reunion, the waves of nostalgia at familiar sights, he kept hidden. He sensed, though, as the great gate opened and the burning red eyes of the one upon the throne within alighted on him, that *he* knew. The Regent was wise. He possessed the shrewdness of the primarch. He could discern what was within the hearts of men and those that were something more than merely men.

Tu'Shan sat before him, deep in thought. He rested his broad chin on a slab-like fist encased within a gauntlet of green ceramite. The Regent of Prometheus had received the gifts of his primarch's prodigious strength and bearing as well as his wisdom. His armour was ornate and finely artificed with iconography of dragons, drakes and other saurian creatures of Nocturnean myth. His hulking pauldrons were fashioned into the image of two snarling lizards, and a thick cloak of salamander hide spilled from his broad shoulders.

'Welcome, brother,' said the Regent, acknowledging the visitor as he stepped into the room. His voice was deep and low, as if it had been dredged from the deep lava pits below Mount Deathfire itself.

He came to stand before Tu'Shan and knelt down, head low, helm clasped under his arm like an offering.

'It is I that should be kneeling to you.'

The penitent visitor did not move. The fiery light played upon the intricacies of his finely-wrought armour and pooled darker shadows in the scarification lines webbing his face.

Tu'Shan rose slowly from his throne, every movement deliberate, his step measured and powerful. He placed a firm hand upon the visitor's shoulder.

'Vulkan's fire beats in my breast,' he intoned, inviting the other to complete the litany.

The visitor lifted his gaze. His eyes were like flame-wreathed calderas.

'With it I shall smite the foes of the Emperor.' His voice was lighter, soft like a susurrus of ash drifting across a lonely grey plain. It echoed the isolationism he had embraced as part of his sacred calling to the Chapter.

'Kneel before me no longer,' Tu'Shan told him. 'Rise, Vulkan He'stan.'

CHAPTER ONE

I
Faith in Fire

A HARD CERAMITE finger jabbed into the map-slate, webbing its polished surface with small cracks.

'There,' said a dour, commanding voice, 'the South-East Capitol, Ironlandings. That will make a strong staging point.'

The light was low in the tacticarium-bunker, emanating from a single lume-strip. It deepened Agatone's frown. Despite the confidence in the brother-captain's voice, his physical demeanour betrayed him. The hard fire in his eyes flashed belligerently, turning his coal-black skin a ruddy orange, as another of the war party spoke out.

'It makes no sense.' The Salamander was larger than Agatone. His iconography denoted a sergeant's rank. His left shoulder pad, like his captain's, had a snarling orange drake on a black field – 3rd Company. With folded arms, he looked about as

15

immovable as a mountain, only craggier and clad in green plate.

Agatone's silence, and that of the other shadowy figures around the tacticarium-bunker looking on, invited him to continue.

'Dusk-wraiths don't hold territory.' He gestured to another chart, steam-bolted to the ferrocrete wall. Aside from a small entourage of humans in flak vests and ash-grey fatigues, the rest of the war council could make out a star map of the subsector in the gloom: *Gevion Cluster Worlds, Uhulis Sector, Segmentum Solar.* 'And an assault of this magnitude on an entire subsector of worlds…' The burly Salamander shook his head slowly. 'It's deeply out of character for them.'

'Dusk-wraiths?' one of the humans asked, a grizzled-looking veteran by the name of General Slayte, 156th Night Devils, the Emperor's Imperial Guard.

'Sergeant Ba'ken uses an old Nocturnean name for the dark eldar,' Agatone explained, turning his attention back to the other Salamander. 'I agree, but the fact remains, here on Geviox, we have the best chance to eliminate this raider threat. Out of character or not, we must liberate the South-East Capitol and all the slaver territories inbetween. I won't stand to let the citizens suffer another day. And there,' he punctured the map-slate with his finger again, at Ironlandings, and the web of cracks broadened, 'is where our hammer will fall hardest.'

Slayte spoke up. 'Which means you're sidelining the Night Devils, am I right?'

Agatone exhaled. He wasn't annoyed, just regretful. He gave Slayte a soldierly but paternal look.

'Your men have fought bravely during the campaign, general, but are spread thin. The bulk of your regiments are occupying and stabilising the lesser Gevion worlds. Your strength is depleted here.' Agatone's burning red eyes flashed with eager fire. 'Let my 3rd Company Salamanders do the heavy lifting. Support us, as you have done, gallantly, so far. The dark eldar are a vindictive, cowardly race. They will inevitably target the weaker formations. Your men would be at risk of sustaining high casualties. I can't allow that if it can be avoided.'

'So you consign us to corralling citizens and protecting aid stations?'

'It is noble work,' Agatone interceded genuinely.

Since the dark eldar had appeared on Geviox, a steady stream of refugees, those who had managed to escape the slavers' nets, had made for the outlands and the temporary Imperial aid stations there.

Slayte continued, unconvinced. 'We are warriors, like you, my lord. We want battle. We've earned that much.'

Any other Chapter would've dismissed the general at once, pulled rank and exercised authority. Salamanders, however, were cut were from a different cloth. It was a scaled, unyielding garment, like the one Agatone wore upon his back, but not so inflexible that it couldn't bend. The brother-captain placed his hand on the general's shoulder. It was like a giant soothing an intemperate child.

'I am truly sorry, General Slayte, but I swore an oath to preserve life wherever possible. Here, that means removing your men from the front line and preserving them for future wars in the Emperor's glorious name.'

Slayte appeared about to protest, before straightening his greatcoat and summoning his peak-cap from a nearby aide.

'Then our business here is concluded, my lord.' He saluted, but there was a hint of irony to it, visible even in the half-light.

Agatone opened his mouth to speak but changed what he was about to say. Nodding, he said instead, 'You'll receive your standing orders within the hour, general. In Vulkan's name.'

'For the Emperor,' Slayte added, before turning on his heel and leaving the bunker. The door slamming shut in his wake echoed around the chamber for a few moments before the Salamanders resumed.

Ba'ken was the first to break the silence. 'His pride and courage are an example to all. It feels like we're tarnishing his honour.'

'You mean saving his life,' a sibilant voice replied. Iagon stepped into the glow above the map-slate. His narrow eyes suggested cunning and an undercurrent of ruthless pragmatism. His perpetually sneering mouth suggested derision.

Ba'ken's slab-like face cracked with a snarl. 'Don't claim that's your concern, Iagon.'

Though he was much slighter and noticeably shorter than the giant Ba'ken, Iagon didn't flinch before his brother's anger. 'I'm not. I hold these humans in no greater regard than your bolt pistol – less so, in fact.'

'Well, you should,' Agatone intervened, his tone brooking no further argument. 'Human life is precious. We have a duty to defend it, sergeant.'

Iagon bowed his head contritely. 'As you wish, my lord. I was only asserting that our main concern is the Geviox people, those who cannot defend themselves from the slavers.'

Ba'ken's fists clenched. He was about to weigh in

again when he felt a scathing glance from the darkest recesses of the room and stopped himself, before Agatone had to.

'Don't lie to me, Iagon. Don't feign concern for a people you care nothing about,' Agatone chided. 'You've ridden high on the recommendations of your previous sergeant. Tsu'gan was most insistent as to your promotion. His own position affords him influence in this regard, but I still ratified the appointment. Don't give me cause to regret it,' he warned. 'Make war, kill our enemies, but do not pretend you are benevolent. Not to me.'

Iagon was rubbing the gauntlet of his left hand. He developed the affectation shortly after losing his organic one to an ork's chainblade on the long-deceased ash-world of Scoria – a bionic one, wrought by the Chapter's Techmarines, served in place of his old severed flesh now. Scoria was also where he bore sole witness to the death of the previous 3rd Company captain, N'keln, an event that had earned Iagon certain notoriety amongst some of his brothers.

'I meant no offence, Captain Agatone.'

Agatone wasn't looking any more. He surveyed the map-slate instead, the geographical surface of Geviox pockmarked with conflict runes and known enemy dispositions as well as friendly ones. The dark eldar were fighting a guerrilla war, a slow retreat into their slave camps where the Salamanders couldn't bring their full force to bear for fear of collateral damage.

It was a cynical tactic.

He addressed the assembled sergeants, most of whom had remained silent during the briefing.

'You have your orders,' he said. 'Light the flame. Prepare for battle. We make war in two hours, at dawn.'

The sound of clenched fists slamming against plastrons and the sporadic uttering of 'In Vulkan's name' greeted Agatone's announcement. He muttered the litany in return, but kept his gaze on the map-slate as if trying to scrutinise some hitherto unseen detail that had escaped his notice. He stayed like this for several minutes, the tacticarium-bunker having long since descended into silence.

'He's right, you know,' he said to the darkness, 'About this being out of character for the eldar. What do they want here?'

'What does any xenos race want?' the darkness answered, a cold breeze chilling the humid atmosphere in the bunker. A black shadow moved to Agatone's side. The whirring of its armour servos gave off a din like grinding bone. The warrior's power fist, slaved to his left arm, was louder still. Tiny drake heads adorned each of the knuckles. Wrought by none other than Forgemaster Argos, it was a magnificent weapon. 'They seek to usurp humankind,' he concluded. 'You can question their motives, try to explain their mores and their tactics, but the fact remains they are a stain to be purged, not understood.'

Agatone looked up from the map-slate at last and found the fiery glare of Elysius upon him. It was almost as if the Chaplain were *measuring* him. Agatone knew he was not the first to fall under that appraising stare. Nor would he be the last. Satisfied, Elysius continued.

'The creatures will do as they will. We must prosecute our duty, bathe them in Nocturne's fires until there is naught left but ash. They flee because they are weak. They use human shields because they are weak. They seek to confound us with obscure tactics because they are weak. *We* are strong, Captain Agatone. *You* are strong. Let that be how you are tested against Vulkan's anvil.'

Agatone bowed to the Chaplain's wisdom, but was still hesitant. 'It is not my resolve that I question, Lord Chaplain.'

Elysius leaned back, allowing the shadows to gather about him again. The Chaplain had ever been a warrior of the dark. Much was unknown about him. His skull faceplate showed only uncompromising, painfully mortal bone. Ever since he had been inducted into the Chaplaincy by none other than Xavier, the Salamanders' long-dead Reclusiarch, Elysius's face and true identity had remained a mystery. It gave him power but also made him shrewd about the secrets of others.

'Your bickering sergeants,' he said.

'Yes.'

'Legacy is a great and terrible thing. It can drive us to emulate and even exceed the great deeds of the past, but it can also debilitate and condemn us to repeat past mistakes. Let me lead our forces into Ironlandings,' he said. 'The south-west, over by the Ferron Straits, also needs strong leadership.'

Agatone was incredulous. 'You're suggesting I abandon my post here?'

'Not abandon, merely *relocate*. I will observe Ba'ken and Iagon, and see if the root of acrimony can be excised.'

'You will take the Capitol at Ironlandings yourself?'

'Indeed. It does not require both of us. Faith in fire, brother-captain – remember that. Either our warring sergeants will be re-forged in it, their bond assured, or they will burn. It is the Promethean way.'

Agatone nodded, but was reluctant.

The Chaplain's eyes widened as if seeing more than what was merely visible before him. Elysius was no Librarian. He did not possess witch-sight or the psychic gift. He did have incredible insight, however, instinct and subtlety to rival their Lord Tu'Shan.

'You wish to confess something more, brother?'

Agatone's jaw clenched, a vein tensing in his cheek.

'I do.'

'Then speak.'

'First Kadai, then N'keln. There is a feeling that the captaincy of the 3rd is a poison barb.'

'I didn't take you as one who believed in curses, captain. Superstition does not become you. Nor is it true to the Promethean Cult.'

Agatone's posture stiffened with barely restrained anger. 'I don't believe in curses. And I am not Kadai or N'keln–'

'That is true,' Elysius agreed, interrupting. 'You don't possess Kadai's charisma, but you also do not suffer from N'keln's doubts.' His penetrating gaze narrowed. The voice was cold from behind the mask. 'In many ways, you are the Promethean ideal: pragmatic, unswerving, loyal. These are laudable traits for a son of Vulkan.'

'Three years ago, I did not support my captain as I should have.' Agatone just came out with it, the long-harboured burden that he was constantly reminded of due to his position in the Chapter.

Now, Elysius seemed profoundly interested. 'And what should you have done, brother?'

Agatone dipped his head at first but then raised his chin defiantly. 'Spoken out against him. N'keln was not ready, and he died for it.'

'You're wrong. He was tested against the anvil. That's all any of us can really ask for. It is Vulkan's judgement, after all. Victory was won on Scoria, Captain Agatone, just as it will be won again on Geviox. Our brothers die – it is a fundamental fact of our existence. The 3rd has experienced more grief than most, but the blade that bears the brunt of the hammer's wrath in the forge and does not break will be the hardest in the arsenal.'

'What does not kill us makes us stronger?'

The Chaplain's intensity lessened. 'If you want to employ an ancient Terran idiom, then yes, I suppose so.'

Agatone paused, weighing up the wisdom of Elysius's words.

'I request a benediction, my lord…' he said at last.

'To purge the misgivings clouding your soul,' the Chaplain asserted. 'Kneel, Adrax Agatone. Vulkan's eyes are upon you now.'

The captain took a knee and Elysius drew forth the Sigil of Vulkan from his belt. It was a holy artefact, once a piece of their primarch's armour and thus named for him. It resembled a hammer, an icon of the Chapter and symbolic echo of Nocturne's atavistic heritage. Its purpose, besides being a venerated Chapter relic, was unknown. In solitude, Elysius had studied it often but despite many years of examination, even after consulting the Tome of Fire which contained all of their primarch's wisdom and prophecy, was no closer to unlocking its secrets. For someone obsessed with truth, it was an infuriating conundrum.

'Vulkan's fire beats in my breast…' Elysius intoned.

'With it I shall smite the foes of the Emperor,' Agatone concluded.

The Chaplain drew the icon of the hammer with the Sigil in mid-air above the captain's head.

'Arise now, brother.'

'In Vulkan's name,' Agatone returned with renewed purpose, his mind already cast to the fresh field of war presented by the Ferron Straits.

Elysius's voice was little more than a rasp, his rictus visage disappearing into shadow.

'May he watch over us all.'

RITUAL PYRES BURNED along the horizon, throwing harsh light over the ruddy Geviox hills. It was a small world, barely five million souls, but rich in ferrous ore. Grey banks of iron dust streaked a landscape festooned with silos and towers. Cities were two-thirds factorums, inhabited by a predominant labour force population. But Geviox was no forge world; it had no allegiance to the Adeptus Mechanicus. It was a processor-planet, where raw materials would be ground from its earth, its very lifeblood yoked until it was dry. Then the populace would move on, little more than labouring transients, to the next world in need of harvest.

In the firelight, veins of rust brought about by the hot steam of the purifying-plants shimmered deep, visceral red. A metal tang infected the air, filtered through Iagon's rebreather mask, reminiscent of blood.

He trudged up the iron hill, loose earth scattering down in his wake where his heavy boots displaced it. A ritual pyre burned for him, too. Just like his brothers, he'd built it himself, lit it and returned once it reached its apex. Reaching the summit, he cast around and counted almost fifty towering flames. Every Salamander waging war come the dawn was anointing their armour for battle, locked in solitude and focussed on inner reliance.

Iagon, however, was *not* alone. He saw his companion through the haze, a flickering outline obscured by flame and smoke.

Sitting opposite, he eyed the silhouette warily. White ash was gathering at the base of the pyre, into which Iagon dipped the gauntleted fingers of his right hand. His gaze never leaving his silent companion, he proceeded to draw the icon of the flame upon his left vambrace then the serpent on his plastron.

'Wrath and cunning,' he explained to the figure. The lambent light filled the crevices of his gaunt face, making it look hollow and dead. 'I will have need of such traits come the dawn.'

As if catching a gesture from his companion, Iagon regarded the sergeant's iconography on his armour. 'Ah yes...' he muttered in a thick drawl. 'Your scraps, for which I am *eternally* grateful.'

Like a snake snatching suddenly for prey, Iagon yanked off his left gauntlet and sent it tumbling across the ground. Beneath it, his fingers were made from wires and metal, plastek and servos. They whined and churned as he clenched them. Brandishing the augmetic hand at the figure, he spat, 'But the sacrifice does not seem to fit the reward, now does it!'

Surging to his feet Iagon leapt through the ritual flame, a cry of anguish on his lips. He seized the figure on the other side, lifting it bodily into the air.

'Betrayer!' he accused, casting his companion down into the pyre.

'Liar!' He smashed his armoured boot down onto the figure's torso. The flawed metal cracked and split immediately.

'Burn, you bastard. Burn!' Again and again, Iagon drove his foot down upon the hollow armour suit, which broke and crumbled against his rage.

His voice came between rasping breaths. 'I trusted… you…'

Mastering his composure, a cold detachment swept over the Salamander.

The anger had come much more quickly this time. Iagon pondered what that meant, watching as the effigy he'd fashioned was slowly devoured by ritual fire. It resembled a sergeant's battle armour, but some of the markings upon it were distinctive and unique. *He* wore different panoply now. *He* had snatched at it without thought for those who had toiled and sacrificed to bring it within his grasp.

'Selfish dog… Your promises are like ash,' Iagon hissed, feeling the wrathful serpent retreat within him again, coiling around his cankerous heart. 'I will not be discarded like some broken brander-priest,' he vowed, heading back down the hill. It overlooked a sparse landing field where a pair of Thunderhawk gunships and three transporters waited for the dawn. 'Nor will I be consigned to obscurity, a footnote in your great destiny.'

He bent down to retrieve his gauntlet – strange how after all these years he could still see blood on his hands, even the augmetic one – and replaced it with a savage twist.

'My destiny is written too. Yours will be short, traitor.'

'Brother?' The voice was deep, coming from the left. It was distant but as Iagon swung his gaze around he saw Ba'ken stomping towards him.

A patina of ash coated the hulking Salamander's

armour. His slab-like face carried faint traceries of white.

Iagon's sour glance held a challenge. Despite his brother's size, he wasn't intimidated. Ba'ken had a warrior's soul. Unlike Iagon, he didn't possess a cold-blooded killer's.

'Who were you talking to?' Ba'ken asked, casting a wary eye towards the ritual pyre.

Iagon's expression was cold and lifeless.

'The dead.'

He stalked away without another word, leaving Ba'ken to wonder at the dwindling shadow inside Iagon's ritual flame and what had transpired on the hill. He too noticed the landing field, where the Night Devils Valkyries and Chimera tanks had once idled, where now Astartes Rhino APCs were being made ready by a Techmarine and his coterie of mindless servitors. The pride of the 3rd Company armour, the Land Raider *Fire Anvil*, was anointed and ready. Ba'ken heard the slow-building fire of its machine-spirits as the engines were put through their final pre-battle routines.

Come the dawn, they would mount up and travel on armoured tracks to the battlefront. Come the dawn, they would enter the fires of battle where all of Vulkan's sons must be tested.

It was as it always was, as it always had been on countless missions, during countless campaigns. Yet this time, for Ba'ken, it felt different. It felt *wrong*.

II
Strongpoint

BA'KEN KEPT AS low to the ground as his frame allowed. Overhead, shard-fire turned the air into a razor-filled haze.

Reaching a partially destroyed emplacement strewn with dark eldar corpses, he snapped a pair of magnoculars to his eyes. He didn't need them to see the assault was going well, but the additional magnification, combined with the genetic enhancement of his occulobe implants, revealed intricate detail.

A broad field of flat terrain stretched before the Salamanders from the penultimate line of xenos earthworks. Spikes, wound tight with wire and hellbarbs, jutted from the ground at obscure angles. The dark eldar had also dug pits filled with corpse-bombs, human casualties packed with alien explosives. Brother Mulbakar had lost his hand and most of his forearm when he'd gone to the aid of one still twitching in the pits. After that, the Salamanders burned them.

They were crude, cynical deterrents designed to sting and frustrate rather than actually impede to any great degree. Behind them, through a squall of rust-red ore dust, a firing line of dark eldar warriors shrieked and cursed at the Astartes. Through the lenses Ba'ken discerned every sweep and curve of the aliens' segmented armour. Each barb, every blade, the grotesque daemonic mimicry of their coned helmets was made clear to him. The hated xenos. Ba'ken drank it all in and used it to fuel the fires of his wrath.

He estimated approximately sixty-three xenos defending the immediate area outside the gate to the Capitol sector and Captain Agatone's strongpoint. Of that garrison, five had heavy cannon. Though the xenos shard weaponry lacked the strength to penetrate power armour easily, the long lances in the firing nests were deadly.

'Stay low,' he growled into the comm-feed fixed into

his gorget. He stowed the magnoculars so he could replace his battle-helm. At once, the battlefield was drenched in a tactical-yellow film. Distances, dispositions, formations and geographical data swarmed across his retinal display, swallowed up by Ba'ken's eidetic memory.

The fire overhead was still thick, punctuated by arrowed blasts from the lance cannons that left the air hot and cleaved. Two squads including Ba'ken's were poised to advance down the centre but not before the heavy cannon were neutralised.

Blink-clicking a comm-rune on his retinal display, Ba'ken addressed a fellow sergeant.

'Ek'bar…'

The return came back fraught with static and the distant rumble of explosions. Sustained gunfire underpinned the cacophony of war in a raking drone.

++*Advancing*++

'I need those lances taking out.'

There was a short pause. More battle sounds filtered through. ++*Momentarily, brother. You have the patience of Kalliman*++

A wry smile crept onto Ba'ken's lips at the dryness of his fellow sergeant's wit. Kalliman was an ancient Nocturnean philosopher who had once spent forty days and nights in isolation to better learn the virtue of stoicism. Ba'ken was in no doubt that Ek'bar had meant the remark ironically.

On the left flank, the other sergeant made slow but certain progress, chewing up the dark-armoured xenos with strafing heavy bolter fire and well-timed grenade bursts. Ba'ken's urging had lent him aggression, though. A huge plume of dirt and debris went up where one of the dark eldar's cannon nests had been positioned. Ek'bar's squad swarmed over it, chain-blades cutting, bolters barking. Two lances down.

Clovius, granite-like and stocky, roamed the right flank. His troops were just as methodical, laying waste to the ravening skimmer-machines the xenos were attempting to use to deploy their warriors further into the Astartes ranks. The barb-like engines hovered via some depraved xenos anti-grav technology. It gave them manoeuvrability but the open-topped transports lacked armour and that made them vulnerable to sustained bolter fire.

It was a weakness the single-minded Clovius exploited to the full. Exploding shrapnel shredded the air as the whining vehicles were torn apart. A smaller squadron of grav-bikers retreated in the wake of the larger machines' destruction, howling and whooping. They circled the battlefield jeering and spitting threats, tantalisingly out of reach, before laughing and burning up the sky with their over-revved engines. With the swarm in full flight, Clovius was able to direct his attention to another gun nest, a well-aimed plasma beam reducing it to smoke and scorched metal.

Behind him, Ba'ken felt the presence of Ul'shan and the ever-dependable Veteran Sergeant Lok as they pounded the Capitol's outer gates with salvos from their Devastator squads. The heavy weapons had already cracked the walls. Bringing down the gate was only a matter of time.

Here, in the long to middle ground, the Salamanders reigned supreme. The gun nests and artillery emplacements the dark eldar had erected were not meant to last for long. They were not a static force. Grievously ill-equipped to hold territory – it was just as Ba'ken had asserted during the briefing.

'This is nothing. A blooding at best. The cauldron awaits us behind those gates,' shouted Chaplain Elysius. It was as if he'd read the sergeant's thoughts.

The sudden change in command echelon had surprised Ba'ken, but as much devotion and loyalty as he had for his captain, serving under Elysius was always a stirring experience. The Chaplain's zeal and fervour were contagious.

'We are ready, Lord Chaplain,' said Iagon, coldly despatching a wounded xenos half-buried in the sundered emplacement. The dark eldar seemed to shudder with pleasure as it died. According to Imperial data concerning the aliens, they relished all forms of sensation, even the painful ones.

'Aye, if the enemy are already half-slain,' muttered Ba'ken, unsure if he was more disgusted at the alien or his fellow battle-brother.

He didn't appreciate being so close to Iagon on the line – it was like having a bolt pistol pointed squarely at the back of his head all the time, but those had been Elysius's orders. The dispositions were clear, and so too were the Chaplain's methods. He was testing them both. Iagon had the wit to see it, too – Ba'ken suspected his fellow sergeant was a great deal cannier than he let on – and had performed exemplarily since the combat action had begun.

'The wall breaks, my lord!' Brother Ionnes pointed to the gates as they collapsed under the Devastators' incendiaries, throwing up clouds of dust and grit.

Four of the five cannons were down.

Elysius raised his crackling crozius mace into the air.

'Into the fires of battle, brothers!'

'Unto the anvil of war!' they cried back and stormed towards the shattered gate house. Beyond it was the

Capitol, a key defensive structure in Ironlandings, one of Geviox's factorum-bastions. With it, the Salamanders would hold a strongpoint to launch further sorties into the city and eventually cleanse it of the xenos taint. The mission and how to accomplish it was clear – it always had been. What didn't make sense was why the dark eldar had not cut and run already. They were raiders; this method of take and hold did not suit them at all.

Ba'ken felt a cluster of razor shards scythe his arm greave but kept on coming undeterred. A desultory burst from his bolt pistol took the head off a dark eldar warrior emerging from the earthworks to meet them.

The Space Marines ate up the metres between them and their enemy in a few short minutes. It was a brutal sight. The earth shook as several thousand kilograms of ceramite pounded over it. Emerging like green-armoured leviathans from a ruddy mist, the Salamanders laid into the remnants of the xenos vanguard with close-ranged fury.

Here is where we sons of Vulkan excel! Ba'ken revelled, crumpling a dark eldar torso with a blow from his piston-hammer as he leapt down into a shallow trench. The bespoke weapon, crafted by his own hand, rumbled eagerly in his grasp, smashing bone and pulping flesh.

Eye-to-eye is the Promethean way!

Tongues of fire lapped either side of the sergeant as the flamers went to work scouring the earthworks utterly. The dark eldar had crumbled against the determined Astartes assault, the few warriors that remained to defend the trenches throwing themselves at the Salamanders with suicidal abandon. Efficient and methodical, the Fire-born eliminated the rest of their opposition swiftly.

Stepping over the bodies of the dead, crushing their ashen remains underfoot, the Salamanders rolled on through the shattered gatehouse and into the Capitol itself.

A wide plaza opened out before them, strewn with human bodies.

'Name of Vulkan…' swore Sergeant Ul'shan, last through the gate as part of the force's rearguard.

'Stand fast,' ordered Chaplain Elysius, having brought the Salamanders attack to an abrupt halt. Smoke stacks, silos, processing towers and gravel-grey dorm-habs loomed over them silently. Corpses hung from ragged spires, attached by chains and swinging in an iron-tinged breeze. The charnal pit that had exploded across the bloody plaza rippled with bodies bloated by putrefaction.

But Elysius saw it for what it was. Tiny incendiaries were lodged in the mouths or sewn crudely into the stomachs of the dead.

It was a minefield.

Adopting defensive positions, the Salamanders waited and fought down their anger at such degradation. The dark eldar, or dusk-wraiths as they'd once been known on Nocturne, had ever plagued their home world. The sons of Vulkan despised all enemies of mankind, but reserved a particular hatred for the ravening dark eldar. It was an old enmity, one that went back millennia.

Several avenues, made tight by the structures clustered around them, led up to the Capitol and the strongpoint the Salamanders sought. It was a bastion-like building with high, flat sides and crenulated walls.

Here, Ironlandings's overseers would calculate and log production rates, feeding the data to their Imperial tithe-masters. On this day, with the inhabitants of the city either dead or incarcerated, the yield was low. Still, the industrial complexes ground on, obeying automated doctrina protocols that kept the great machine going.

Refineries filled the air with a low hum, a mind-numbing pseudo-silence that only racked up the tension further.

Chaplain Elysius showed no discomfort. 'Clovius and Ul'shan, keep our egress secure,' he said.

'Four points of attack, my lord?' suggested Sergeant Ek'bar in his usual clipped manner. It made tactical sense: one squad per route of assault, terminating in the final breach of the Capitol itself. It would be what Agatone would do, but Elysius was not the brother-captain.

'No. We are the hammer.' The Chaplain indicated the largest thoroughfare leading directly to the Capitol building's main entrance. It was essentially a roadway, littered with upturned ore-trucks and half-tracks. The vehicles had been left that way by their occupants when they'd fled the raiders. Judging by the gruesome display littering the plaza, it had availed them little.

'Lay down a curtain of flame,' ordered Ba'ken, now the plan was set.

Two of his battle-brothers stepped forwards and bathed the putrefied bodies with promethium. The hidden grenades and incendiaries detonated instantly and for a few seconds the plaza was consumed by violent explosions. When the conflagration had died down there were just ashen body parts and scorched earth barely visible under a veil of thick, dark smoke.

'Well, at least that will have got their attention,' remarked Lok after the last of the deep concussions. One of his eyes was bionic. It whirred and clicked, seeking out any lingering traces of explosives but finding none. Even without the lifeless orb in his socket, the veteran sergeant glared coldly across the devastated scene. A grim feeling was creeping over them all.

Ba'ken was eyeing the tall drill towers, looking for signs of snipers. He would have manned those towers, put a couple of those lance cannons in them. In the open ground, smoke or no, the Salamanders would be shredded. His sergeant's rank insignia did not sit easily on his armour but Ba'ken was as tactically shrewd and experienced as any in the 3rd.

Elysius had no such concerns about enemy snipers. He would defy bullets and razor-shot with willpower alone.

'That way, in force,' he barked, thrusting out his crozius again, 'Stoic and implacable, brothers.'

'In Vulkan's name,' the sergeants returned in unison and started out along the still burning roadway.

AT A SLOW run, it took approximately fourteen seconds to clear the roadway and enter the labyrinthine cluster of dorm-habs and stacks delineating the Capitol of Ironlandings.

The Salamanders adopted a diamond approach pattern down the main thoroughfare. On Ba'ken's tactical display, overlaying the right retinal lens of his battle-helm, a cluster of force icons showed his brothers keeping to tight squad coherency discipline and arrayed in a two-rank oblique line formation. Elysius had the lead, the diamond's tip. A bolt pistol, and not his crozius, was gripped in the Chaplain's armoured fist now. He was attached to Ek'bar's squad, one of its angled sides. Ba'ken was to his immediate right, the other front side of the diamond. Four metres of permacrete roadway separated the two squads as they hugged the abandoned vehicles either side.

Behind them making up the rearguard and the last two sides were Squad Lok and, of course, Iagon.

At least the viper at my back will keep me sharp, Ba'ken thought ruefully.

'Where are the rest of the populace?' asked Ionnes just over a minute into their advance. They'd slowed now, dropping down to a cautious walking pace. Ionnes's tone suggested the barren streets and conduits unsettled him.

'They hang from the rafters and the spires, brother,' Koto replied, his flamer nozzle burning quietly.

'That can't be all of them,' said Ionnes. 'Look at the size of this place.'

'Like dactylids with their wings spread for flight...' remarked L'sen dispassionately. With his bolter he gestured to the upper storeys where several of the dark eldar's victims were pinned into the rockcrete, their flayed flesh suspended under their arms in crude diaphanous membranes.

'Enough, brothers,' muttered Ba'ken. 'Maintain vigilance.'

++*They have a point, Sol*...++ Lok's voice came through Ba'ken's comm-feed on a closed channel. ++*Does this remind you of anything?*++

Cirrion, loft-city. Ba'ken didn't say it aloud. They'd lost their former captain that day. Everything had changed after that. Here, in the densely packed streets of Ironlandings, he was reminded again of war-torn Cirrion. It was a bad omen and Ba'ken drew the hammer of Vulkan across his breast to ward against it.

The ranks of bodies strung above them in the upper storeys seemed to thicken all of a sudden. A vague shifting of the light came from up ahead.

Ba'ken was only a second behind Elysius.

'Fire-born! Bolters and blades!' roared the Chaplain, strafing an explosive line of bolter shells through the hanging meat sacks above. Several of the wretched creatures survived the attack, launching themselves at the Salamanders despite sundered limbs and gaping torsos.

Ba'ken rammed his pistol into the gaping maw of a beast that had dropped beside him and blew what was left of its intelligence out the back of its skull. A *thunking* blow from his piston-hammer mashed the torso of another.

The things that descended on fleshy wings to attack the Salamanders had once been human. The evidence of it was still just discernible on their tortured bodies. Each time Ba'ken killed, the monsters dropping down around him with heavy *thwacks* of meat hitting stone, he saw the shredded semblance of a man. There were mine workers, labour-serfs, overseers, indentured citizens.

Flesh-bonded, mutated, sewn, cut and then re-sewn into horrific parodies of biology, they were now abominations. Vat-grown bone and chitinous layers of carapace had been grafted to drug-enhanced musculature. Some had distended maws filled with several rows of needle-like fangs. Dead-eyed with stimm-fuelled strength, they fought like chrono-gladiators or suicide-servitors whose lives were measured in minutes and seconds, whose only purpose was to kill and then be killed in turn. And there were hundreds.

But as Ba'ken hurled one of the wretched grotesques into the side of a broken down ore-truck, he knew their incoherent wailing pleaded for a single, irrefutable desire.

Mercy…

Time slowed, and the battle din became a dull, half-heard clamouring at the base of his skull. Around him, he knew his brothers had slipped into a similar state. Ba'ken's secondary heart surged into life, filling him with vigour, providing his limbs and organs with the relentless energy they needed.

One of the piteous human-grotesques reared up in his peripheral vision…

Turn thirty degrees – kill stroke to jugular administered by piston-hammer. Eliminated.

A split-second later, another lashed out from the opposite side…

Back a half-step, two shots point-blank into midriff. Torso destroyed. Eliminated.

A third, then fourth charged him from the front…

Lead with right shoulder. Disable foremost threat by shattering ribs and collarbone. Headshot with bolt pistol to second target. Cranium destroyed. Eliminated. Return to disabled primary threat. Downward hammer strike to shatter spine. Fully incapacitated.

Blood pounded in his ears as he killed, Ba'ken playing his part in his brothers' choreography of war.

In the initial rush the Salamanders were pushed into a tight cordon, their natural instinct to form a circle and defend outwards. Ba'ken felt the generator of his power armour slam against one of his brother's. It was like a rock, allowing Ba'ken to focus on his forward-facing enemies. Litanies to Vulkan, Prometheus and the enduring spirit of the Fire-born chorused in air rent by hellish, plaintive screaming. The creatures surged against them but the green bulwark of ceramite held.

Malformed by dark eldar torture-science, the beasts were formidable. Against any other opponent, deadly. But Astartes, especially those led by the burning rhetoric of their Chaplain, were superhuman and not so easily undone.

'Advance, for the glory of Prometheus!' bellowed Elysius, driving the Fire-born through the bulk of the grotesques with sheer willpower and aggression. Above the Salamanders, the railings and rafters were almost devoid of corpses. The avenue was slowly clogging with the bloodied and the slain.

The circle broke apart again and Ba'ken turned to acknowledge the battle-brother who'd held his rear-guard unshakeably.

He was surprised to see Iagon return his nod with a curt glance through the lenses of his battle-helm before dropping back with his squad to support Lok.

Ba'ken let it go. Ek'bar had fallen in behind their Chaplain, who was tearing his way through the mob with bolt pistol and power fist. Elysius heaved one grotesque – it looked vaguely like a woman but with a long serpentine tongue and rib-line spines jutting from her bulbous back – up in the air with his power fist. A flex of the weapon and the creature's screeching head popped, showering his armour with gore. The Chaplain cast the fleshy wreck aside and forged on, spitting diatribes against the mutant and the alien as he went.

Through his retinal display, Ba'ken judged the Capitol gate to be under a hundred metres away. A rapid structural analysis suggested they'd need breaching charges or a multi-melta to penetrate it.

++*Lok, how far away from our position are you?*++ Ba'ken lagged a few metres behind Ek'bar's squad, forcing a cordon through the abominations.

After a few seconds, the comm-feed crackled.

++*Enemy presence is intense back here. Press ahead and we'll link up as soon as it's clear*++ A short burst of static broke the feed before he added, ++*Wait. Something else is coming…*++

Just as a low drone filled the air behind him, Ba'ken saw another force hastily move into position ahead of them. Two lance cannons held the end of the roadway. In seconds, they were blistering the air with deadly fire.

A dark beam struck Ek'bar and put him on one knee. The brother-sergeant grunted but got to his feet again immediately, roaring at his warriors to advance with Elysius. Rippling shield returns blossomed around the Chaplain as his rosarius field protected him from the heavy weapons.

++*Keep it tight. Single file behind Elysius!*++ Ba'ken urged.

Ek'bar pulled his troops in at once, bolters flaring either side of the Chaplain's aegis, tearing up the street ahead with snapshots.

Ba'ken mirrored him, low and spear-like through the remnants of the mob now converging on the Salamander rearguard.

The Capitol gate was approximately seventy metres away; the dark eldar lance cannons another fifty. Eyes ahead, Ba'ken saw one of the crude barricades sheltering the cannons torn up by bolter fire. The gunners spun and collapsed against the fusillade. Part of the adjacent wall, weakened by sustained fire, collapsed on top of the bodies.

Fifty metres to the Capitol gate.

++*Krak grenades ready at my command*++ Ba'ken ordered, going to prime the explosives mag-locked to his belt when a shadow cut across them.

Something fast swept in low and without warning. Too fast for his retinal display to track, especially with the energy interference from the heavy guns ahead, Ba'ken could only watch as Brother L'sen gurgled and was lifted off his feet.

Reaching for his throat, where a red ooze was running down from his gorget, the Salamander dropped his bolter. He was hoisted a half metre before the almost invisible snare binding him was released and he collided into an upturned half-track.

In his tactical display, L'sen's rune blinked from green to amber.

Disabled.

The drone came again, this time from the front and then above them.

++*Find cover and stay down*++ Ba'ken fought to track the attackers but their speed combined with the distraction of the blistering cannon fire fouled his efforts.

Ahead, Ek'bar was having similar problems. His squad was hugging the walls, split either side of the roadway. In the centre, Brother Drukaar lay prone, a lance wound in his chest.

Another rune went from green to amber, but then to red.

Permanently incapacitated.

Ba'ken glanced behind him. Reinforcements were still far off. Lok and Iagon were mired in battle against the last of the human-grotesques.

++*Can you see them, brother?*++ Ek'bar barely kept his

anger checked. Drukaar had served at his side for over a decade.

Ba'ken heard the drone but their unseen enemy was still elusive.

++*Above somewhere*++ he said. ++*Using the stacks and towers as cover. They are fast*–++ A shadow passed across the roadway again. ++*Wait…*++ Ba'ken realised it presaged another attack. He turned to Ionnes, hunkered down behind him.

'Two frags,' said the sergeant, holding up two fingers.

Ionnes handed over the grenades from his belt. Ba'ken took them as he turned to Koto.

'Have you seen this?' said the flamer trooper.

Ba'ken quickly followed his gaze.

Elysius had broken cover and was charging the last fifty metres.

'You mad, courageous bastard…' Ba'ken muttered, then added in a louder voice to his troops, 'Our Chaplain is baiting them.' He showed Koto the two fragmentation grenades in his open palm. 'Burn them on my order.'

Koto nodded, looking to the sky as the drone intensified.

Elysius was sixteen metres out, barrelling towards the last cannon. He'd dropped his bolt pistol somewhere during the melee and wielded his crozius instead. Bright energy bursts shuddered against his rosarius field.

Ba'ken had his eyes on the ground where the shadows abruptly fled. Tilting his head up, he threw the frags high into the air above Elysius's position.

'Do it!'

Koto triggered the flamer, shooting a gout of

super-heated promethium into the grenades and cooking them explosively.

An expanding cloud of fiery shrapnel filled the air just as four dark eldar mounted on anti-gravitic boards and trailing razor-snares flew into the blast zone. In the brief moments before they were smothered by flame and smoke, Ba'ken saw their wild hair, heard them shrieking like hellions. Engulfed by the explosion, two of the xenos simply disappeared. The other two, lagging a half-second behind, tried to pull away but were buffeted by the shockwave.

'Take them down!' Ba'ken roared.

A fusillade of bolter fire answered and tore the last two hellions apart.

The Salamanders were already moving again, hurrying up the roadway, when Elysius reached the cannon and demolished it and the crew.

'Make me a hole, brother-sergeant,' he said as soon as Ba'ken had reached him. The pain in the Chaplain's voice was obvious.

Ba'ken battle-signed for his troops to advance, Brothers Ionnes and G'heb brandishing krak grenades and racing the final twenty metres to the gate.

After a pair of dense, deep percussions the gate was breached and the way into the Capitol was open.

Lithe silhouettes moved languidly in the shadows within, shrouded partially by the resulting smoke from the explosion.

For the first time, Ba'ken noticed a wound tract in Elysius's power armour scored by the dark lance. A glancing blow – anything else would've killed him – but painful despite that. The Chaplain paid it no mind. Regarding the last of the xenos defenders, he was emphatic.

'Bring them bolter and flame.'

Vulkan's name was on their lips as the Salamanders charged the breach and took the first real step towards the liberation of Ironlandings.

ELYSIUS HAD MADE his command post in one of the overseers' offices. It was a large chamber, grey and hard like the world around it. The low, squat desk – wrought-iron and heavy – had stayed, whilst the rest of the furnishings had been removed. Whereas before yield logs and processor reports had covered the desk, spattered with their old master's blood, maps and charts adorned it now. This was all that the Chaplain needed to prosecute his part of the fight on Geviox.

Cleansing the bastion, even the running battle up the roadway to reach it, had been easier than anticipated. Enemy forces had been light and swiftly subdued. He believed in the strength of his Fire-born, that wasn't the issue; he'd just expected sterner resistance.

Brother Drukaar had fallen into a sus-an membrane coma. That was lamentable. At least L'sen was walking, if not speaking due to his garrotted throat. Any other injuries sustained, including those he'd suffered himself, were negligible.

A vox-unit set up in one corner of the room crackled.

++...*status of Ironlandings... is... secure?*++

'Yes, Captain Agatone. We sustained a single casualty and will need an Apothecary at this destination, but the South-East Capitol is ours,' the Chaplain answered.

++*Praise Vulkan... send... Brother Emek... your location... Ferron Straits... still contested...*++

'Are there signs of a command echelon?'

It was one of several facts bothering Elysius. They

had yet to encounter any leader of the raiders, no slave-master or xenos lord.

++*Negative*++

'I'm instructing elements of the Guard to this position. Their time is better spent holding the Capitol. Squads Lok, Clovius, Ek'bar and Ul'shan will redeploy to the Ferron Straits, as per your orders. Thunderhawk carriers are already en route.'

++*Confirmed, Brother-Chaplain*++

'Ba'ken and Iagon will remain to secure the strongpoint until I'm convinced we are not needed here.'

There was a short pause presaging Agatone's next question.

++*Something concerning... Elysius?*++

'Nothing I can grasp at this time.'

Agatone seemed to consider that for a moment before saying,

++*In Vulkan's name, then*++

'Unto the anvil, captain.'

Elysius cut the vox-link and the chamber fell silent. Utterly focussed on a geographical chart that tracked the xenos troop movements, he forgot about the attendants in the room until one of them shuffled.

'Dismissed,' the Chaplain snapped, sending his attendants and armour serfs scurrying away.

'*Inexplicable...*' he muttered at the icons denoting the dark eldar.

A fire was burning in the labour-yard below. Its glow, seeping through the dirty plastek window of the office's south-facing wall, gave the chamber an eerie, orange cast. They'd found the last of the Capitol's staff within its walls. They'd suffered badly before they'd died – playthings for the xenos. Elysius had ordered them gathered and burned. The firelight was the only

source of illumination in the room. The rest of the
lights, old gas-burning lanterns, had been doused.

'My lord?' a voice uttered from the darkness.

The address held an implicit question.

'Not you, Ohm,' Elysius said to his brander-priest.
'My flesh is in need of scarification.'

'Shall I assist you with your battle-helm, lord?' Ohm
shuffled forwards into the fiery glow spilling into the
room from the labour-yard below.

He wore black robes, befitting his station as a
Chaplain's brander. The rod he clasped in his thin fingers was also a guide staff. For Ohm was blind.

Ever since Elysius had known him, it had been this
way. The scars across his eyes suggested an old pain, a
searing that left a dark band in its wake. It had not lessened Ohm's skill with the branding iron. His craft was
exemplary. As such, he had refused all optical aug-
mentation.

'Not yet, Ohm…' The Chaplain's voice tailed off in a
tired rasp. Certain he was alone, barring his brander-
priest, Elysius leaned heavily on the wrought-iron desk
and felt the pain in his flesh anew. The lance burn had
hurt him, but he could crush that with willpower. It
was another wound, an old itch really, that distracted
him.

'Here,' he added. 'My fists…'

Ohm reached out and helped the Chaplain remove
his gauntlets, laying them flat on the desk with the
utmost care and attention. Then he took the burden of
Elysius's left pauldron when he'd removed that too. A
loud clang resonated around the room as Ohm set it
down heavily on the metal.

'My apologies, lord. My strength is not what it
was.'

'It's all right, Ohm. You have strength enough yet for your duties to me.'

A power fist hummed beneath where the armour had been. Its couplings and linking-brackets were exposed and vulnerable.

'Step back,' said the Chaplain, and Ohm obeyed, affecting a low bow that dropped his cowl so it obscured his fire-ravaged visage.

Taking care to twist his torso so the weapon was braced over the desk, Elysius then set to disengaging the wires, unfastening the brackets and couplings. Muttering a litany to placate the machine-spirits within the power fist, he unfastened the shoulder joint and the heavy weight left his body. Beneath it, the iron desk groaned.

Exhaling his relief, Elysius massaged the scarred stump of his mutilated shoulder where the ork warboss had severed his limb, where afterwards Brother Fugis had stitched and seared him closed. It was the Salamander's last act as Apothecary. Something had happened to him on the mission to Scoria. They had spoken on it briefly, him and Elysius, but in the end Fugis had felt the Burning Walk was the only way to find spiritual peace again. Few returned from such a journey, and the Chaplain doubted they would see each other again.

On the battlefield none would doubt the fire in Elysius's heart. His words alone could burn the enemy down, but some suggested that away from the cauldron of war ice and not blood flowed in his veins.

Such things were spoken of in whispers, but Elysius heard much. He did nothing to persuade his brothers otherwise. Detachment was useful in the execution of his duties. Intimidation and reputation often went far

further than any chirurgeon-interrogator ever could.
Xavier had taught him that.

But that coldness he cultivated and encouraged
ebbed at the thought of Fugis's death. Elysius regretted
not being able to turn him from the desperate path he
had felt forced to take but respected his courage for
treading it nonetheless.

'Do you miss it, lord?' Ohm asked.

Elysius ceased kneading the stump of flesh that had
long since knitted and acquired a thick skein of scar
tissue.

'For a blind man, you see much.' The Chaplain
smiled rarely but allowed himself a moment of
humour then. Old memories of Fugis had blackened
his mood, though, and the levity soon fled. 'Not only
the arm,' he confessed, struck by the irony of him as
Chaplain unburdening his soul to a serf.

'You do not feel whole without it?'

'Do you feel whole without your eyes?'

'As you say, lord, I see much. I do not miss them. I
know my world. I *see* Nocturne in the tang of fire on
my tongue, the heat upon my face, the ash upon the
wind. It is vivid, lord.'

'There is beauty in that. Ohm. This here,' Elysius said,
running his hand reverently over the detached power
fist, 'is a thing of beauty, too. Master Argos fashioned
it for me. And it is potent, Ohm. With it I am stronger,
my enemies are felled easier. And yet… there is a sense
of *loss*, of disassociation with my own body.'

There was a pause. Ohm let it stand, knowing he had
no need to interject.

After a few seconds' introspection, Elysius clutched
the mag-clamps on the front of his battle-helm. Without a word, Ohm stepped in and disengaged the locks

around the back of the neck. The Chaplain had to stoop for the brander-priest to reach them.

Not since being ordained by Xavier had anyone ever seen Elysius's face. He often told himself it was the reason he still kept Ohm around, on account of the serf's blindness, but the bond went deeper than that. Rumours abounded concerning disfigurement or that the Chaplain's face and helm were one.

Elysius allowed himself a shallow chuckle.

The truth was far worse than any rumour or fiction invented by his battle-brothers.

Venting pressure signalled the locking clamps were disengaged. He lifted the helm off with Ohm's help, standing straight and then holding it with one hand.

It was a mercy to be free of the death-mask. At times, it weighed heavily. Breathing in the unfiltered air, relishing its acerbity, Elysius turned the battle-helm around so the rictus was staring at him. It was important to appreciate the visage that his enemies and allies saw. It reminded him of who he was and his sacred charge.

'Blindness must be a liberating disposition,' he muttered.

A votive-servitor, a brander-priest's constant companion in the field, clanked noisily into position from where it had been resting dormant at the back of the room. Ohm was intent on his work now. He thrust the dragon-headed iron into the deep brazier of white-hot coals pin-drilled to the servitor's back.

Elysius embraced the heat.

No, he thought. *Pain is liberating.*

As a veteran of many campaigns, hundreds of battles, the Chaplain's deeds of scarification were written across much of his body already. Ohm went to work on the neck, Elysius opening and splitting his gorget to remove it so the brander-priest could sear the flesh beneath.

The movements were slow and precise, a low hiss emanating from the super-heated rod as it dragged shallow furrows in the Salamander's flesh.

A few seconds and it was done, a muttered litany from Ohm and then echoed by Elysius completing the ritual.

'In Vulkan's name...' he breathed, closing his eyes and exhaling deeply.

Ohm didn't have chance to reply; another was standing at the threshold to the room.

'Brother-Chaplain...' the voice came from the doorway, an armoured warrior in green waiting there patiently with his head bowed.

Ordinarily it would be extremely disrespectful to interrupt another Fire-born's solitude. Isolationism, be it on the field or in the Chapter's solitoriums, was a sacred tenet of the Promethean Creed. Only brander-priests were permitted into that covenant. But Salamanders were also pragmatic – at times, covenants had to be broken. Judging by the warrior's demeanour, which Elysius read immediately, this was such an occasion.

'What is it, my son?' Elysius asked in an undertone, swallowed by darkness so only his silhouette was visible. Ohm, too, retreated into shadow.

It was Brother-Sergeant Ek'bar. He carried his battle-helm in the crook of his arm and his eyes blazed in the gloom but the fire there was dull and tempered by grief.

'I need you to perform the Rites of Immolation, Lord Chaplain' Ek'bar's voice was just above a whisper, 'Brother Drukaar is dead.'

Elysius paused, allowing the weight of purpose to return. 'Ignite the pyre,' he said, 'Brother Emek will be here soon. I will join you in the labour-yard shortly.'

Sergeant Ek'bar bowed and was about to take his leave when he spoke up.

'I served alongside him for ten years.'

'Death and rebirth, sergeant – they are part of the Nocturnean circle of fire. Drukaar will return to the mountain, as will we all in the end. Take solace in that…' a snarl crept onto the Chaplain's hidden face, '…and turn your grief to hate. Stoke that flame and unleash it upon our enemies.'

Ek'bar only nodded. As he walked away, his slow and steady footfalls resounded through the metal steps leading to the floor below.

Regarding the grinning rictus of the death mask, Elysius scowled. Staring into those hollow eye sockets, he didn't like what he saw.

BA'KEN MET IAGON in the labour-yard. Most of the Fireborn who had fought at Ironlandings were there. Brother Emek, the Company Apothecary, was inbound. Captain Agatone and the rest of the Inferno Guard would not be joining them.

The two sergeants were alone, standing apart from the others who mustered in small groups contemplating their fallen brother Drukaar whose body would soon be anointed by flame and whose ash would rejoin the earth.

Iagon's battle-plate was well chipped and scoured from his rearguard action a few hours earlier.

'You should have your serfs attend to that,' said Ba'ken, though it went against his every instinct to bandy idle words with the other Salamander.

Iagon scarcely glanced at the superficial damage, as if disinterested.

Not to be dissuaded, Ba'ken lumbered on. 'They are scars well earned, brother. You fought bravely with Sergeant Lok today.'

Now a wry, if slightly perplexed, smile curled Iagon's sneering lip. His eyes were cold as they regarded Ba'ken.

'There has never been much accord between us, Sol. May I used your given name? So, I have to ask myself: why do you seek to ingratiate yourself into my confidence now?'

'I merely offer camaraderie, Cerbius, as one Salamander to another.'

'Because I defended your back on the road to the Capitol? Is it guilt that drives this overture or ego that you have misjudged me as a brother?'

'Dak'ir was my sergeant and friend, you chose to ally–'

'With a hero of our noble Chapter, a *true* Fire-born whose deeds have seen him elevated to the 1st Company.' Iagon spat out the last part. Ba'ken mistook whom his anger was directed at.

'I merely wished–'

'To assuage your conscience, I know.' Iagon's eyes were cold like rubies, the sneer on his face lifeless. 'You have great strength, Sol, and an easy camaraderie that earns you many friends and scar-brothers. I am Salamander, yes, but not like you. Guile and intelligence, a survivor's determination – these are the traits I possess.'

'We are still brothers, Cerbius.'

'In name alone.' Iagon was about to turn away when he paused, showing his profile to the other

Salamander, 'but your words are noted, Sol. They are noted.'

He walked away, craving the solitude of the dark.

Ba'ken let him go.

The sound of a Thunderhawk's engines boomed overhead. In the labour-yard, a second pyre was lit. Its flickering light reflected off the armour of the Salamanders waiting to see Drukaar's final moments with the Chapter.

CHAPTER TWO

I
Gathering Strength

PAIN-REGRESSORS BIT INTO the flesh of his scar-ravaged face and Nihilan hissed. The barbs, administered by a grisly chirurgeon-servitor, went deep, right down to the nerves, but they eased the roaring fire there to a dull burning.

It had been that way since Moribar, since the flame... and Ushorak...

Hard images came back to him of that place often, of the grave world where he had changed from pupil to master, where he had been re-forged in crematoria fire. Sense memories pricked at his skin with hot needles for fingers, probing, burning. Then came the screaming, the last death shriek of a mentor who had become like a father he never knew.

If Nihilan had been capable of tears, he would have shed them then. Instead, he massaged his anger, honed it into a tight blade.

Soon… soon he would grip its haft and thrust it into the heart of his enemy, right to the hilt.

Darkness surrounded him, leavened only by the visceral glow of sunken lamps. Vents in the floor exuded scudding steam from the enginarium decks, like the breath of some fell creature of myth. Wrapped in the shadows, Nihilan relished the peace and solitude they offered.

Old habits, he thought with a bitter smile.

It wouldn't be dark and empty for long. Nihilan was expecting 'guests', hopeful supplicants and mercenaries who wanted to be party to his grand vengeance. As he dismissed the servitor-creatures, little more than a mesh of technology and bonded organs, an armoured figure emerged from the gloom.

'How long have you been standing there, Ramlek?' Nihilan made his displeasure at being spied upon clear, even if Ramlek had not the wit for spying, the dutiful killing hound that he was.

'I was waiting until your attendants had finished their rituals, my lord.' The armoured giant was clad in scaled ceramite the colour of fresh blood and spoke with the cadence of cracking magma. A sulphurous stench tainted the air with his every word and tiny flecks of cinder cascaded from the mouth-grille in his battle-helm. Oh yes, Ramlek was a killer through and through. His trappings attested to that.

He was also ferociously loyal and bowed low before his master, causing his scales to shift and grate.

'Arrivals?' asked Nihilan, shifting from the chair of dark iron which he had made his throne.

'Many. Several ships have already docked with the *Hell-stalker*.'

The strike cruiser was Nihilan's great pride. Wresting

the vessel from its original owners had been a bitter but glorious victory for his Dragon Warriors. They were little but raiders then, scrapping pirates snapping at the heels of larger war dogs. How the years had changed that. After Ushorak's death, oblivion stared them in the face and would have devoured them were it not for Nihilan and his obsessive belief.

'Where are they now?'

'The delegates wait beyond the chamber doors,' Ramlek replied, now standing straight and imposing. 'Shall I admit them on your order or destroy them, my lord?'

Nihilan smiled. The gesture pulled at the scar tissue marring most of his face.

'What would be the point of enticing them aboard ship if we were just going to slay them, brother?'

Ramlek waited pensively, as if the question still remained unanswered.

His smile broadened, even though it pained Nihilan to do it.

'You are an unsubtle creature, Ramlek, and your readiness to engage in carnage amuses me greatly. But execution isn't necessary at this point.'

A cloud of hot ash and cinder gusted from the Dragon Warrior's mouth in what might have been displeasure.

Nihilan laughed without mirth.

'You really are a brutal bastard,' he said. 'Disarm them and show them in.'

Nodding curtly, Ramlek turned and disappeared into the gloom like a wraith.

Ramlek's footfalls were still echoing heavily around the large room a few moments later when a crack opened in the dusky confines from the chamber door. Several figures filed through, ushered by a squad of

Nihilan's renegades clad in bloody red. Ramlek led the escort himself.

One by one, the figures fell into line before the throne. Some offered practised indifference, others outward belligerence. Many could not hide their fear of the superhuman renegades who had summoned them to this place, to this ship. Just under twenty ship's captains, warlords, pirate-kings, renegade generals and alien lordlings bent their knee to the Dragon Warrior upon his throne.

'Do you know who I am?' Nihilan asked, with the procession ended and his warriors in position at either flank of the delegates.

A giant, armed and armoured similarly to the renegades, although his apparel looked worn and patched as if it had seen more than its fair share of war, stepped forwards.

He looked about him, regarding their flanking escorts. Every one of the bloodstained warriors cradled a heavy-looking bolter in their clawed gauntlets.

'Dragon Warriors,' he said. 'You are all renegades.' His eyes, glowering behind a battered yellow battle-helm, came to rest on Nihilan. 'And you are their leader.'

Nihilan edged forwards on the throne. His crimson-lidded eyes flashed with power, evidence of the warp-craft flowing in his cursed veins. Like Ramlek, he too wore armour of incarnadine blood with a curved horn arcing from either shoulder pad. The force staff, just an arm's length away, lay dormant in its cradle. This was *his* ship, the *Hell-stalker*. Here, in this traitor's court, Nihilan was pre-eminent.

'Aren't you too a renegade now, *brother*?'

Though armoured in black and yellow of a slightly

more archaic design, the other warrior was in many respects the mirror of Nihilan. They had a similar caste, cut from once similar cloth. Ideologically, though, they couldn't have been further apart.

He bristled at the Dragon Warrior's usage of such a familiar term, but bit back his anger.

'Hard to accept at first, isn't it?' Nihilan goaded when met with silence. 'Your cause is just, your defection is not defection at all but merely following the hard path, the one your lords and masters do not have the courage to tread – is that about right, Astartes?'

'No. I am not motivated by any of those ideals,' the warrior replied in a grating whisper.

'Oh, really?' Nihilan sounded amused. 'What then?'

'Hate,' the warrior said simply. 'For the Salamanders.'

Nihilan's eyes narrowed.

'Now that, my dear brother, is something we *do* have in common. What is your name?'

The warrior slammed a fist against his breastplate. Given the circumstances, it seemed like an outmoded gesture now.

'Lorkar,' said the warrior, 'Sergeant Lorkar of the Marines Malevolent.'

Nihilan smirked cruelly.

The knuckles cracked in Lorkar's gauntlets at what he saw as an insult.

Ramlek shaped like he was about to react. The Marines Malevolent were little better than sanctioned, war-mongering psychopaths. Nihilan was amazed the Inquisition hadn't sectioned them *excommunicate traitoris* yet. Their reputation was certainly bloodthirsty and uncompromising. Lorkar's skin must be crawling surrounded by so many impure creatures around him.

Unhinged was the descriptor that sprung instantly to

mind when faced with a Marine Malevolent. Capricious, too. Nihilan wouldn't put it past them to infiltrate one of their brethren aboard his ship on some ill-conceived suicidal assassination mission. But, no, Lorkar was not here to murder – at least, that wasn't his intent.

Nihilan barely had to exercise his psychic will to discern that fact. Belligerent, yes, but not murderous.

A raised hand from the sorcerer put Ramlek back on his leash.

'I had heard a Malevolents ship had docked with the *Hell-stalker*. I didn't believe it until now.' Nihilan descended into partial monologue. 'Puritanical Astartes like the Marines Malevolent allying themselves with renegades…' he tutted, '…what must the sons of Vulkan have done to offend you so?'

'That's Malevolents business,' Lorkar growled.

'No longer, Sergeant Lorkar,' Nihilan corrected. 'Not any more. You are a Dragon Warrior now.' He spread his arms, 'One of us.'

Nihilan held Lorkar's fierce glare a moment longer–

His rage will be useful.

–before letting his gaze take in the rest of the assembly. He recognised kroot, avian mercenaries little better than half-trained beasts but valuable in a fight; half-naked Chaos cultists with graven sigils tattooed into their self-abused flesh; the sinuous dark eldar, lithe and deadly, wearing torturers' smiles; and other, stranger beasts and warriors. In truth, he cared little for any of them. The Astartes were a boon, and Nihilan would take great pleasure in their corruption. The dark eldar, too, had their part to play. But the rest were just fodder.

Recruiting scum was easy. Every system, every

sub-sector had them in abundance. Promises and offerings enticed such 'enterprising' individuals easily enough. Nihilan's own Dragon Warriors numbered in the hundreds. Together with this mercenary rabble, he would have enough bodies to execute his plan, his grand vengeance.

Nocturne was not Ultramar. A Space Marine Chapter's home world, yes, but it was not an empire.

One by one, the delegates came forwards at Nihilan's beckoning and made their pledges. The Dragon Warrior accepted them all, barring one. A hound-faced warrior, at least judging by the shape of his battle-helm, raved like a lunatic before the throne. He would spill blood in the name of his dark lord. He would visit flesh-reaping retribution on the sons of Vulkan. He would cast down their skulls in supplication to his god.

After this tirade, Nihilan had reached for his force staff and smote the barbarian down where he stood. It served two purposes, showing not only his considerable power but also the fact that he would not ally himself with mindless, uncontrollable killers.

The Red Rage he had called himself, another renegade Astartes no less, but a broken one. Even Lorkar's feral anger had focus and direction; this beast was little more than a frothing zealot. Such men, such creatures were not easy to control and Nihilan desired that above all else. He ordered the Red Rage's ship annihilated and its representatives slain immediately. A pool of slowly steaming bone and organs was all that remained of the fanatic now.

'Obedience is not a request,' said Nihilan to the others, who were trying to mask their shock. Even the flint-hearted Lorkar flinched. Only the dark eldar seemed unaffected, a male and female, the latter dressed in little more than strips of dark leather and pieces of plate armour. While the male looked vaguely amused, she was positively aroused by the warrior's agonising death and bit her lip, drawing blood, to suppress it.

The xenos delegates were an important element to Nihilan's plan, but he did not relish their presence and sadistic hedonism.

'And we are not madmen on a bloody quest to our own destruction,' he continued. 'There is but one agenda, my own. I have worked hard and sacrificed much in order to assure its fulfilment. Do your parts, you and your heinous kin, and you'll be rewarded.'

Nihilan leaned back in his throne, seemingly weary all of a sudden.

The sound of cracking bolter slides informed the delegates the audience was at an end. Ramlek and his warriors ushered them out just as they had ushered them in, only minus one body.

Of the Dragon Warriors who had entered the chamber, only Ramlek remained.

Nihilan closed his eyes. He rasped in a voice like cracking parchment, 'We are close, Ramlek.' He stroked a pair of scrolls alongside him on the throne. 'You have the decyphrex?'

Ramlek patted a cylinder mag-locked to the right thigh of his scaled power armour.

'I do, my lord. And I have summoned the others. They should be arriving soon.'

'Good, good,' Nihilan breathed. 'All is in readiness.'

The gloom split again and this time three more Dragon Warriors entered.

Before the throne, four dark runes had been cut into

its metal dais. Ramlek had taken the first already, to Nihilan's immediate right. A second renegade assumed the one next to him on the left. The other two stood upon the remaining runes.

'You are my *Glaive*, brothers,' Nihilan told them, 'My most trusted warriors and the ones who will gouge out the heart of the Salamanders for all their perfidy against us and our long departed lord.' He paused, regarding each of them in turn.

Ramlek's eyes burned with an unslakable rage; Nor'hak, the warrior to his left, was cold like iron; Ekrine, the only one without a helmet, licked vaguely reptilian lips as his eyelids flicked from side to side; Thark'n, the most recent addition to the Glaive, folded his thick arms and nodded with quiet determination.

'In the name of the slain do we do this,' said Nihilan. 'In the name of Ushorak.'

'Ushorak,' the Glaive intoned as one.

'And for Ghor'gan,' Nihilan added, paying particular attention to Thark'n. 'Who fell in his sacred duty, a warrior of the Glaive who we also mourn in this cabal.'

'Ghor'gan.'

'We may come from differing heritage, the Chapters that spurned us, that constricted and took our love and loyalty for granted. Storm Giant, Black Dragon, Iron Warrior, Marine Malevolent...' He paused before the last of the names, spitting it out as if it left a canker in his mouth. '...*Salamander*. These honorifics mean nothing to us. Now we are one. Dragon Warriors, all.'

Nor'hak couldn't suppress a snarl, baring his pointed fangs. Ekrine's bone-blades snapped forth as he fought his anger and emotions. Great gusts of cinder spilled from Ramlek's maw like dragon smoke, whilst Thark'n's knuckles cracked loudly in his gauntlets.

Nihilan smiled.

'On Moribar we unearthed the means to wreak our vengeance.' He pulled the scrolls to his side. 'On Scoria we enabled its realisation, whilst striking a stinging blow to our enemies.' This time he looked at Ramlek, who returned his lord's admiration without emotion. 'Old Kelock had no idea of the power he had chained. Scoria was nothing, a tenth of our strength. Now, we will harness all of it. Our Spear of Retribution is almost ready,' he announced to them all. 'And with it we shall tear out the heart of a world.'

Nihilan thrust out his clawed gauntlet in a fist.

'Death to Nocturne.'

The others followed suit, punching their knuckles together and forming a ring of red ceramite.

'Death to the Salamanders,' Nihilan concluded.

II
Devils' Bargains

ABOARD THE ETERNAL *Ecstasy* the air within the portal chamber rippled. It was as if an electric current had been passed through it. Slaves, shackled to its hot capacitors, wailed as their bodies were subjected to further tortures with the portal chamber's activation. Agonised shadows littered the barbed walls, hinted at in the ephemeral flare of power. Sunk into a deep recess, the two capacitors were like the metal horns of some unseen beast. Pallid faces, those still with eyes to see, stared piteously out of that hell-pit. None present who looked upon them saw them as anything but fuel.

Sacrificed to stave off She Who Thirsts, they were a means to an end – nothing more. The shriek of the capacitors lowered to a dull hum and darkness swallowed them again. A portal was opening.

It began as a crack of light, a jagged dagger thrust that tore through reality, exposing the myriad realm of the webway beyond it. Slowly the crack widened, ripples of electrical discharge raging at its edges. A dark void was revealed inside, a growing pool of blackness but not blackness, a strange *un*-reality that defied all laws of physics and matter. Flickering into existence like a bad pict-recording resolved into a coherent image, a figure stepped forth into the portal chamber onto a plateau of dark metal suspended above the hell-pit. He moved sinuously, abhorrently seductive, one foot overlapping the other in a perverted and suggestive mockery of grace. Eldritch wind whipped at the long dark hair that he let fall below the edge of his conical battle-helm. The strands writhed slowly like vipers, but there was only motion, no sense of air, no breeze as such, just its effects. Such was the mystery of the webway.

Another figure followed him, a female. Lithe and tall like the male but more muscular and near-naked, barring her leather and plate battle harness. Her gait was less affected, more warrior-like and purposeful, but she possessed a killer's poise. She wore no helm but preferred a sharply edged domino mask instead, she the player in her personal theatre of death. Her hair was white, long and bound in a tight scalp lock that fed the conjoined braids all the way down her bare back like a serpent.

'Extravagant, Malnakor,' a grating voice issued from the gloom of the chamber when the webway transference was complete and the portal had closed. 'The rest of your cohorts are still aboard ship and have yet to dock,' it added, its tone full of implication.

The sinuous male removed his helmet. It had a double horn on the left temple, two thin barbs of flat, dark metal. The front was engraved with a wickedly grinning face, reminiscent of a daemonic jester.

Malnakor cast his hair about, freeing up the long locks after their confinement beneath the battle-helm. 'I choose *better* company to travel with,' he replied. The lascivious glance he gave the female who had portalled with him was blatant.

The warrior-wych ignored him, bowing down before the voice and the silhouette framed by shadow in front of them instead.

'Wasteful and decadent, dracon,' said the voice. 'Slaves we can ill-afford to lose.' The silhouette figure stepped into the light.

It too was male. His xenos features were cold and stark, as if cut from marble. His face was blanched as if exsanguinated. The cheekbones protruded like blades. His nose was aquiline. Where Malnakor was arrogant and sneering, this one was impassive and unreadable. Only his tone betrayed his displeasure, and even then only because he chose for it to.

'An'scur…' the word issued from the wych's mouth like a seduction as she bowed lower still, careful to keep her cleavage visible for her lord.

'Helspereth,' said the archon, stepping forwards to caress her cheek with his right hand.

Dracon Malnakor arched his eyebrow when he saw the missing digit on An'scur's hand. His face was symmetrical, his complexion and physiognomy utterly unmarred and utterly unsettling. Every effort had been made by the dracon to become doll-like and perfect. It was as if his youth was cast in amber to endure for eternity, hinting at his surgical addiction. To behold such a deformity as a missing finger in his so-called lord and master only convinced Malnakor he had been right to try and kill him.

Fifteen separate assassination attempts had been made against Archon An'scur. All barring three had been thwarted and yet here he was, alive and imperious, if a little gaunter than before.

The disaffected dracon eyed Helspereth's naked affection jealously. He wanted her. Ever since he had witnessed her triumph in the Coliseum of Blades at Volgorrah, he had desired to taste her flesh, feel the warmth of her body next to his. That night, Malnakor had bedded and murdered thirty-one slaves and still his burning lust wasn't slaked. Only the wych queen could do that. He had heard rumours from those she had favoured. Most did not live long beyond the telling. He would gladly die at her torturer's fingers. Rapture beyond measure waited there – Malnakor could feel it, could see it smouldering like hell-fire in her predator's eyes.

And yet, she favoured the archon.

Unlike his minions, An'scur wore thin violet robes that suggested the wiry, muscular frame beneath. His hair, like his face, was white. His eyes were black like two almond-shaped pieces of jet with a pinprick of grey to indicate the pupils. Some within the cabal said his soul was promised to Kravex – that the haemonculus kept An'scur's missing digit under lock and key, and through the application of his torturer's science had resurrected the archon each time he was killed. Only a sample of biological matter was needed.

Gaining a haemonculus's favour was the difficult part.

But then Dracon Malnakor had studied the path to securing such a bargain diligently. Kravex was a sadist of a particular stripe and like all the haemonculi he was old, one of the First Fallen. His secrets were manifold. The way to unlock them lay in bartering. And in the many ports and lairs of Commorragh slaves were the only currency that had value for a haemonculus.

As Helspereth purred at his touch, Archon An'scur looked askance at Malnakor. The shadow of an amused smile passed like a wraith across his bloodless lips.

Whore-mongering bastard, thought the dracon with a twinge of jealous pride. *How I covet your power, sibling.*

An'scur seized the wych's jaw. His taloned fingers drew a little blood and she mewled with pleasure at his abusive touch. Then he released her and she retreated into the shadows.

As she slipped away, Malnakor watched her from the corner of his eye. He knew where she was headed and fought down his anger again. *What debaucheries will you commit for him, slave-whore?* He was almost salivating at the thought and had to drag his attention back to his lord.

'So, brother,' An'scur began, inspecting the droplets of Helspereth's blood on his nails, 'our pact with the Dragon Warriors is in place? They have made the slave pledges as previously agreed?'

Malnakor showed his perfect white teeth before ripping a dagger from its sheath and plunging it at An'scur.

The archon moved swiftly, as smooth as oil on water, and caught the flat of the blade between his palms. In the same motion, he twisted the weapon away from the dracon's grasp and drove it deep into Malnakor's thigh.

'Prosaic,' he said, laughing. 'I thought you were more creative than that, brother.'

'You're still fast,' the dracon rasped, pain and pleasure warring for dominance on his face.

'Faster than you.' The smile vanished. 'Now, tell me of the pact. It means much to the cabal that we *honour* it.' The word was hard to say. In his centuries of life, An'scur had not used it much.

Malnakor tugged the blood-wet blade from his thigh with a *schluck* of metal leaving flesh. A small hiss of ecstasy passed his lips.

'Why must we deal with the mon-keigh? They should be kneeling to us as their masters.'

'They are no ordinary mon-keigh, as well you know.'

'I do. I also know of Kravex's interest in them.'

A tremor of annoyance cracked An'scur's emotionless veneer. 'Oh yes? Tell me, brother, what you know of our haemonculus's predilections?'

'Only that he prefers the gene-bred ones. They last longer.'

An'scur was about to comment when he thought better of it. The emotionless mask was intact again. 'We *will* deal with the mon-keigh,' he asserted. 'In fact, you are pivotal to our plans in this regard.'

'Pivotal in what way?' Malnakor's suspicion was obvious.

'Kravex awaits you on Geviox,' said An'scur, the slightest flicker of amusement lifting his features, 'You are to leave immediately.'

'I SAID, LEAVE me!'

The throne room was empty, or so Nihilan thought.

He'd dismissed the Glaive after discussing their plans
for Nocturne and was scrutinising the scrolls with the
decyphrex. The device was a dodecahedral crystal fractured with strange geodesic lines. To the naked eye, to
the unschooled and the ignorant, it would appear a
valuable trinket, something to be parlayed for a greater
prize. The truth was much more esoteric and clandestine. It held the means of uncovering a devastating
power, a force the likes of which hadn't been seen
since before the Dark Age of Technology.

For though human, Kelock had been a genius. He
was also an opportunist. The extant scrolls in Nihilan's
possession had been created by the technocrat, reverse-
engineered by true science, providence or
daemonology from a device uncovered many years
ago.

The existence of the scrolls and the decyphrex was
the deed of another, a creature in Nihilan's temporary
thrall that made its presence felt now the chamber was
truly empty.

'I cannot, mortal. I am as indelibly bound to you as
the bone is bonded to your flesh.' The voice sounded
old and melancholic.

'I haven't…' Nihilan began, choosing his next words
carefully, '…*felt* you for some time.'

'The empyrean tides demand my attention, the ebbs
and flows of fate, the means by which you sit upon
your pre-eminence, oh *master*.' Now, it was cynical, sar-
castic. It shifted mood often, neither one thing nor the
next but a melange of emotion as difficult to predict as
the dimension that spawned it.

'There is news?' Nihilan ventured.

'None,' it replied emphatically. 'I come abroad to
remind you of our bargain.'

The voice emanated from everywhere and nowhere at once, first a grating whisper then a bellowing tumult. Other voices joined it, sibilant and non-sequitous.

Nihilan ignored them, girding himself with his psychic discipline.

The daemon was toying with him, caressing his defences with razored mental claws. One careless slip and his sanity would be shredded.

'You have no need to do that…' Nihilan said through gritted teeth, resisting the urge to glance around the room and pinpoint a sound that had no origin. 'I remember our pact. I will honour it.'

The presence was fading, retreating back into the tides.

'See that you do, sorcerer…' it whispered, like a dying breeze. 'Remember what you promised me…'

'Have no fear of that,' Nihilan muttered, slowly releasing the mental bulwarks he'd put in place to protect himself.

'A vessel,' the daemon rasped, its voice all but gone. 'A vessel…'

Nihilan's eyes burned with inner fire, a genetic echo of his forsaken heritage.

'I have the perfect candidate.'

CHAPTER THREE

I
Sigils and Portents

VULKAN HE'STAN OBSERVED the pict-captures with careful detachment.

The image on the viewscreen was rendered in grainy monochrome on account of the extreme weather wracking the surface of Nocturne far below. Auspex readers within Prometheus's superstructure gathered the data from picters arrayed in closeted bunkers within the threshold of the Sanctuary Cities. Even in the void of space high above, Nocturne's elite guardians could still keep watch over their fragile world.

Their fragile and volatile world.

The Time of Trial was ending and an arctic winter seized Nocturne in its icy fist. Where once there had been ash plains, now there was snowy tundra; where previously geysers of steam had vented across the rocky plateaus, now placid streams of vapour drifted wistfully on a chill breeze. In the mountain ranges the volcanoes were like vast beacons, illuminating the grey-white fog of drifts and ice flurries. Wreathed with smoky effusions, it was as if the calderas of the fire-peaks were dragons of myth slumbering beneath the snow and rock, their maws pointing to a smothered grey sky.

Even Mount Deathfire – the largest of all the volcanoes – was quiescent, content to wane in the wake of her explosive fury during the Time of Trial.

Across the surface of Nocturne, the Sanctuary Cities had closed their gates and engaged their void shields. Anyone beyond their walls now would be in the lap of Vulkan. Against the anvil they would be tested – reforged or broken. It was the way of the Promethean Cult.

A long trail of nomads, having trekked across the frozen floes of the Acerbian Sea, caught He'stan's attention as they closed on a gnorl-whale held fast in the ice. They carried barbed harpoons and encircled it with a hungry predator's disregard. Sustenance was scarce when Nocturne's fire ebbed. Many of the indigenous lizards and saurians were hibernating in the caves. The Ignean tribesfolk would already be fighting a bitter war against the restive ones for food and warmth.

Such was the planet's way of excising the weak and promoting the strong. It was a hard culture but one He'stan respected for its purity.

Such a fragile existence, he thought, feeling the plight of the people as his own. *I have been away from it for too long.*

'Harvest will begin soon in earnest. A few more months and the hillsides and mountains, the thawing lakes and the fringes of the lava flows will be full of Nocturneans.'

He'stan felt Tu'Shan's presence beside him, rather than saw him. The Chapter Master had a singular aura about him, a sense of the indomitable that He'stan had never felt in any other Salamander. He had been young when he'd assumed the mantle of Regent, but it was one he wore with great nobility and distinction. No two greater champions of the Chapter existed in the current decaying age of the universe. He'stan felt great pride but also profound sorrow at that revelation.

'The ice will recede, the mountains will weep, Death-fire shall speak her rumbling refrain once more,' He'stan said. He'd removed his battle-helm, a beautiful piece of his artificer armour rendered with saurian affectations and artistic flourishes. Underneath it, his face was sombre and grave. 'I am the bearer of Vulkan's Spear and I wear Kesare's Mantle,' he said. 'Upon my left fist is the Gauntlet of the Forge, but it is nothing matched against our mother's fiery heart. What is the will of a Forgefather or a Regent compared to that?'

It was at He'stan's request that they'd come to one of the viewing galleries in Prometheus space port. The long chamber was dark, illuminated by brazier coals. The flickering light revealed the icon of the Firedrakes as they pulled the shadows away, only for it to be swallowed as the darkness reasserted itself again a few moments later.

'Aye, we are humbled by her savage beauty, Lord He'stan.' Tu'Shan clapped a firm hand upon the Forgefather's shoulder.

For He'stan it was an odd sensation. He had been apart from his brothers for a long time. His quest for the lost artefacts of Vulkan had taken him to the edges of known space, to sights he would not describe and deeds he would never speak of. To them, his Fire-born kin, he was an enigma, a distant figure whose ways were inscrutable. It was no small thing to return. Something great and terrible had drawn him back. The signs as related in the Tome of Fire had led him to this point, to this temporal epoch.

He'stan turned his eyes away from the pict-viewer. The grainy feed had worsened on account of the weather on the planet far below, but he had seen well enough.

'You had best take me to it, brother,' he said at last.

'It's not far,' Tu'Shan replied. 'Follow me, brother.'

THE ARMOUR HAD been moved to a vault annexed to the Pantheon Chamber. So esoteric, so ancient and inscrutable were the sigils upon them that Tu'Shan needed the Tome of Fire close at hand to study them properly. That had been three years ago, ever since the 3rd had returned from Scoria.

They were standing in the sacred chamber now, the circular temple at the heart of Prometheus that contained the Tome of Fire. Volume upon volume of the mythic text lined its walls. It was supplemented by scrolls, charts, artistic renderings, well-crafted arcana and other, even stranger, objects. All wrought by the primarch's hand. Some had even been written in his deific blood.

Though shrouded in gloom, iconic representations of anvils, drake heads, great serpents and the eternal flame were still visible. Carved into vast menhirs of volcanic obsidian they shimmered wanly in the light from the low-burning torches that punctuated the room at precise intervals. Their glow also described the edge of eighteen granite thrones. Only vaunted members of the Pantheon Council were permitted to sit upon them. Seldom in the Salamander's long history had they ever been full. Deliberations of the utmost importance were conducted in this hallowed room, matters that affected the entire Chapter and, prior to that, the Legion.

The induction of the first Forgefather, the defection of the Warmaster, counting the cost of the aftermath at Isstvan, the disappearance of Vulkan – all had been weighed and measured by the Pantheon Council.

These seats, each bearing sigils that represented the role and position of its incumbent, followed the curve of the room. Each was positioned at the same height and no one was larger or more grandiose than another. Here, the Lords of the Salamanders were equals.

He'stan eyed his own seat, a place that had long remained empty amongst the council, and felt the longing for brotherhood return just as it had as when he'd docked at Prometheus.

'Forgefather…' said Tu'Shan, as if replying to his deepest thoughts.

A low grinding of gears and servos invaded the quietude as the Chapter Master unlocked and opened the vault appended to the chamber.

One of the menhirs, a lustrous chunk of hard obsidian, rolled away to reveal the vault door and behind that the inner sanctum itself.

Within, there stood the armour suits reclaimed from the bowels of Scoria, arrayed as they had been in Tu'Shan's throne room.

He'stan stepped into the room, drawn almost against his will to the artefacts before him. 'Ancient…' he breathed, reaching out to touch one of the archaic suits of power armour. It was gloomy in the chamber and the low red lume-light covered it with a bloody cast.

The armour was Salamander, no question – the iconography and design attested to that. But it was of a darker hue and crafted during a halcyon age.

'From the Great Crusade, brother,' said Tu'Shan, standing alongside him, 'and the Age of Darkness that followed.'

He'stan's voice barely reached above a whisper.

'Our darkest hour…'

'At Isstvan,' uttered Tu'Shan.

He'stan met the Chapter Master's fiery gaze, 'At Isstvan.'

Both knew and felt keenly the fell deeds of the Drop-site Massacre when the then-Legion had been all but destroyed by traitors in their midst. The violent ripples of it were still felt by the Chapter, almost ten thousand years later.

Allowing a moment of introspection to pass, He'stan asked, 'What have you learned?'

Tu'Shan frowned, scrutinising the symbols engraved onto the armour. Each individual suit carried a piece of a greater mystery. Alone, the marks were scratches, war-scars that held no intrinsic meaning; together, and when viewed from a certain angle with the eyes of one with sufficient wit to see it, they contained a piece of prophecy.

As of yet, Tu'Shan had been unable to decipher it.

'That the answer lies within the Tome of Fire. We were led to Scoria by the hand of Vulkan, Forgefather, of that I am sure.'

'And this was our father's intent, to furnish us with this shrouded wisdom?'

'I believe so, yes.'

'Was there anything else?' Now He'stan regarded the armour suits up close. Denuded of the bodies they once contained they were wraith-like and cold. Ghosts lived in those ceramite husks now, ghosts and dead memories.

'Only this…' Tu'Shan activated a rune-plate in the vault wall. A circular crack appeared in the metal floor of the chamber and the air filled with a dense pressure cloud around it. When it dispersed, a silver column with a force-fielded dome surmounting it had emerged from a compartment beneath the vault. In the crackling field there was a progenoid gland, held within an armourcrys vial and suspended in some kind of amniotic solution.

'The fluid within the vial keeps it from necrotising?'

'Apothecary Fugis manufactured it himself, before he took the Burning Walk.'

A raised eyebrow betrayed He'stan's interest in the taking of the spiritual path into the desert. He had often wondered if such a journey would reveal anything of his own destiny.

'Whose is it?' He'stan asked.

Tu'Shan stepped closer to regard it, as if drawing his answer from proximity to the vial. 'An ancient warrior of the Legio – Gravius was his name.'

He'stan turned sharply to regard his Chapter Master.

'He lived? After ten thousand years?'

'It would seem so, but his mind was shattered, crammed with the thoughts and memories of all of his brothers.' Tu'Shan encompassed the array of power armour in a single sweeping gesture of his arm.

'Incredible…' He'stan breathed. He scrutinised the suits. 'I recognise this passage,' he said. 'These sigils are familiar to me, Regent.'

Tu'Shan's pensive silence bade the Forgefather continue.

'Phrases and subtleties of meaning are lost to me, I suspect only the primarch could discern them, but there is reference to the *Ferro Ignis* here.'

'The "Fire Sword",' Tu'Shan translated. 'It is a doom prophecy. I've heard of it, but never seen it rendered in this form.'

He'stan ran his gauntleted finger reverently over one of the sigil fragments engraved on a vambrace. 'Sigil-dialect is old. The ancient Nocturnean earth shamans used it back when the world was young and our Sanctuary Cities were plains of rock and circles of stone. It was this language that led me to recover one of the Nine.' He'stan brandished the Gauntlet of the Forge.

'I see more…' He'stan added and read aloud, '"*A lowborn, one of the earth…*"'

'"*…Will pass through the gate of fire. He will be our doom or salvation,*"' Tu'Shan concluded.

He'stan met the Chapter Master's formidable gaze. 'You know who this warrior is, don't you?'

Tu'Shan nodded.

'His name is Dak'ir.'

He'stan turned back to the prophecy.

'And where is Brother Dak'ir now?'

'Vel'cona has him.'

That admission gave He'stan pause but he masked it expertly.

Tu'Shan continued.

'He's below Nocturne, training under the tutelage of the Librarius.'

'This Dak'ir, he was the one that led us to Scoria, wasn't he?'

'He was.'

'And he's powerful, too, isn't he?'

'Very. The Chief of Librarians has never seen such potency in a student.'

He'stan's voice dropped to a low murmur as his great mind turned over the permutations of everything he was learning, '*Doom* or *saviour*, indeed...'

II
Trial by Fire

DAK'IR'S WORLD WAS consumed by fire.

He knew there was rock at his feet because he could feel it, but he couldn't see it. Even through the retinal display of his battle-helm an impenetrable fog of smoke and drifting ash smothered the view. Flashes of fire tinged the grey pall a deep orange, and temperature spikes on the systems of his power armour that were still functioning relayed intolerable levels of heat and radiation.

Vaguely, he was aware he was crouched down. It was possible he'd passed out for a few moments. For a second, the gauntleted hand that he used to brace against a jagged spur of rock looked strange to him. Through the occluding smog he could just discern its outline and hue. Salamander green had changed to royal blue. Then he remembered. *I am no longer a sergeant...*

He was a Librarian. The colour of his armour signified that and his covenant with the order; the icons inscribed onto his battle-plate his lowly station within it.

Breathing came hard. Even through the helm's respirator, Dak'ir tasted cinder and raw daggers of heat. Pain-killing drugs flooded his body, damping the agony down his left side into a dull ache that only debilitated and no longer incapacitated.

Still, he needed a moment to marshal himself.

Rise, Lexicanum!

The voice was inside his head. Dak'ir wished he could take his force sword and cut it out of his cerebellum but even that wouldn't be an end to it.

Master the blade, the voice insisted. *Use it! Arise now!*

'I cannot!' Fire burned throughout his body; not the flames of the underworld cavern where Pyriel had left him to die, but fire from pain, from the grievous injuries the monster pursuing him had inflicted.

Dak'ir once believed only drakes prowled the humid deeps of Nocturne. Now, his eyes had been opened.

Endure it, Salamander. This is nothing. You are a son of Vulkan.

A series of low vibrations resonated through the earth releasing geysers of scalding steam, and spilling dust and debris from the cavern roof above. Like arteries veining a body, lava plumes erupted from the mountain's craggy flesh, filling Dak'ir's world with light and heat.

A world consumed by fire.

Shadows and smoke shrank and coiled in the magma flare. Pools of liquid fire bubbled and spat like cruel laughter nearby. A heavier percussion interrupted the steady *thump* of the golem's approach. With his senses compromised, it was hard to gauge just how close and from what direction it came.

The cavern itself was long, but also wide and tall. Stalactites jutted from a craggy ceiling, only just visible at the summit of the smoky cloud. Dak'ir couldn't remember how he had got here. He recalled his initial encounter with the golem had gone badly. He had been forced to retreat, down, deep into the earth. Respite was brief. The monster had found him and this time there would be no escape.

He was weak, in mind and body. Strength he thought he possessed, after he had mastered the burning, was mocked by the onyx-black giant intent on his destruction. He knew that now to his cost.

I will die in this place, Dak'ir thought grimly, making a fist as the tremors jarred his wounded frame.

Tentatively, he felt the cracks spoiling his fresh-forged ceramite. They were wide and deep. Blackened by soot, seared by fire, blue paint so reverently applied by the armour serfs chipped and worn, he would be broken by the time his body returned to the mountain.

Gripping the haft of his force sword, Dak'ir's fingers felt like spikes of unyielding stone. Tiny rivulets of lightning played across his knuckles as he tried to stir psychic energies into the blade.

Endure it! Pyriel's voice came again, hard and insistent across his head like a slap. *You are Salamander!*

Hard rain was falling onto Dak'ir's armour as the golem's footfalls loosened the rocks above. Fist-sized chunks of granite hitting his helmet forced him to stand. The drakescale cloak attached to his armour and falling beneath its power generator felt denser than before, like an iron anvil tethered to his neck.

Turning, Dak'ir closed his eyes and drew upon the burning. It had been over two years since he was first tested, since he had obliterated an ancient version of Nocturne in his dream-vision and nearly destroyed his mentor.

He harnessed the power, corralling it with a thought. The blade of the force sword ignited into conflagration. Beneath Dak'ir's feet, the ground shuddered.

It was close.

The heat, intense despite the arctic winter above, had masked the scent of anointing oils and sacred ash rubbed into his armour for a time, but it had cornered him now.

Dak'ir opened his eyes.

Standing under a hundred metres away, the golem was immense. The smoke and ash seemed to recoil from its presence, allowing Dak'ir to see the monstrous construct. It was over twice the Salamander's height and half again as broad. It was a man, or at least a simulacrum of one. Its skin was onyx-black from the volcanic basalt used like clay to fashion it. Carved psychically by Pyriel's mind, it was a creation of utter perfection and terrifying beauty. The enhanced musculature was exhaustingly defined. Its noble countenance was hard but eerily humanoid. Its bald pate shone like jet, the reflected fire light swathing it in an orange sheen. And the eyes… they burned like captured pools of flame.

Pyriel had given it no weapons. It needed none. Two massive fists were hard enough to pound rock and ceramite to dust. A mere glancing blow had cracked Dak'ir's armour so brutally.

Two red orbs blazed through the smoky haze. Tendrils of it clung to the golem's brawny body as it parted the grey miasma like a leviathan emerging from the Acerbian Sea. Hollow, pitiless eyes regarded prey.

Death has come, Fire-born…

For such a massive creature, the golem was fast. It ate up the distance between them in long, earth-pounding strides.

Dak'ir braced himself as it gathered speed. It broke the longer stalactites as they scraped across its unyielding shoulders and smashed the columns of rock in its path aside. A juggernaut of impervious obsidian, nothing could stop it.

With the golem scant metres away Dak'ir swung his force sword in a wide arc, fire trailing from the blade, before unleashing its fury. White fire thrashed against the golem's bulky torso arresting its momentum abruptly and violently. It staggered, sending granite cascading from above with the sudden jerking motion. Psychic flames engulfed it, wrapping its obsidian body.

Still it pushed, and Dak'ir took a back step. The golem thrust out its chin defiantly, though no discomfort or effort altered its blank face. It drove into the storm, matching its automaton's implacability against the fledgling Librarian's will.

Dak'ir fed more energy into the blade, marshalling his powers and attempting to master a weapon only more experienced Codiciers had any right to. He drew upon the burning, the well of nascent destructive potential within his core, and unleashed it.

Smoke, vapour and oxygen were devoured in an instant by the extreme heat. The backwash blistered Dak'ir's armour, sending warning icons flashing frantically over his retinal display. His arms ached with the effort of holding the blade aloft and directing its terrible fire against the golem.

Break. Damn. You, he willed.

But to no avail.

A massive fist loomed out of the blaze, wreathing in flickering bands. Flinging himself aside, Dak'ir narrowly avoided the blow. Behind him, the spur of rock he'd sheltered against was pulverised. Shards of it exploded against his armour. Several were embedded in the ceramite.

Beads of sweat were running down Dak'ir's face as he pulled himself up. Lances of agony skewered his side. He gritted his teeth. A chopping motion with the force sword sent an arc of fire into the golem, the beast turning when it realised its prey had eluded it.

Dak'ir might as well have used harsh words for all the damage he caused. He mustered two more psychic bolts, dragon-headed and surging on contrails of fire, before the monster swung again.

It came from the earth, moulded by fire… Pyriel's voice echoed inside his head.

Fighting just to breathe, Dak'ir didn't answer. He was moving again, dodging the overhead blow meant to shatter his spine and end his life. Sheathing his blade, he concentrated on running through the cavern. Lava pools, smoking streams of fire went by in a blur of motion. The golem's massive footfalls pounded behind him.

The hot veins feeding the heart of the mountain thickened as Dak'ir went deeper into its fuliginous depths. A vast magma river surged alongside him as the cavern opened out and the smoke thinned at last. The end of the subterranean chamber was revealed. A sheer drop gaped in front of Dak'ir, the river cascading over the edge into a syrupy morass below.

'Vulkan's mercy…'

Coming to an unsteady halt a few steps away from a fiery demise, Dak'ir suddenly found his battle-helm stifling. The hot metal seared his flesh, the smoke and ash clogging his respirator was choking him. He smashed at the mag-clamps urgently to disengage them.

What are you doing? Do not remove your armour, Salamander!

'Choking… can't breathe…'

The battle-helm came off with a jerk. Dak'ir let it fall from his fingers and land noisily at his feet. Without his auto-senses, even befouled as they were, his orientation worsened.

At least the smoke and drifting ash was clearing.

Something vast and powerful loomed from the thinning grey miasma…

Throwing up a barrier of flame, Dak'ir took one final step towards the chasm behind him. The golem was close.

'You have made a monster here, Pyriel…' Dak'ir muttered, collapsing a thick granite column into the monster's path.

It swept the obstruction aside, utterly heedless for its own safety, utterly committed to the destruction of the Librarian.

Such an implacable foe…

Sensing Deathfire's heartblood beating beneath the cavern wall, Dak'ir opened a fissure in the rock with his blade and unleashed a fountain of lava onto the golem. The creature was bathed in liquid magma and the Salamander dared to hope… until it emerged on the other side unscathed. Waves of scalding heat emanated off its body in a haze as it charged, determined to end the fight and take them both over the edge and to oblivion.

With all the incredible momentum of a battle tank, the golem couldn't have stopped even if it wanted to. Its rudimentary intelligence did not appreciate the danger it was in as Dak'ir levelled his force sword like a spear and raced towards it.

A tiny crack, the smallest of fractures was visible in its chest. Dak'ir had seen it when the monster parted his fire wall like it was air. The blast of white-hot fire had wounded it and the magma flow, expanding its igneous flesh, had exposed the weakness.

Seconds before impact, Dak'ir pulled the blade back the full length of fist to elbow and then thrust it forwards as the monster crushed him.

Dak'ir felt his rib-plate crack, the ceramite armouring it had already shattered exposing torn bodyglove and black Salamander skin beneath. Breathing was no longer possible; the air was punched from his lungs with all the force of a siege cannon shell. Blood filled his mouth, riming his teeth and releasing the heady stench of copper into his nose. The impact up his arm went all the way to his shoulder and fractured it, but the force sword had gone deep, splitting the golem's impenetrable skin.

Cracks webbed its onyx torso. Magma lines glowed inside them like the ichorous blood of the divine. Except the monster was not divine, it was a construct forged psychically from volcanic clay and fortified by Pyriel's warpcraft.

Consciousness fading, Dak'ir was vaguely aware of being carried along by the golem's massive momentum. A few more steps and they would descend into the abyss...

He fed a bolt of flame down the blade and the cracks widened. Lava gushed from the wound, corroding his armour where it splashed it. Dak'ir let his numbing fingers fall from the sword hilt, instead pressing his hand against superheated rock.

We are not only pyromancers... we are earth shamans too.

Pyriel's words from the first day they had come to the catacombs beneath the mountain returned to him even as the golem slowed, as if only now realising its folly. Channelling the last of his power, Dak'ir sent a huge seismic tremor through the cracking flesh and like a fault line exposed, the tectonic fury of its plates pulling apart, the golem separated.

Dak'ir fell backwards. His vision was fading. His last sight was of the golem breaking apart, devoured by its own heartblood into molten slurry… Beneath him, the chasm of fire beckoned.

CHAPTER FOUR

I
Unearthed

FEW AMONGST THE Chapter could navigate the Tome of
Fire as expertly as Vulkan He'stan. The Forgefather had
spent years studying the volumes, committed all of
their teachings, however obscure, however veiled, to
his mind.

He found the prophecy related in sigil-dialect upon
the armour quickly. Something as prosaic as a leather-
bound book contained an esoteric reference to it.
Within its pages, secrets were revealed.

'The icons are like a key,' he explained to Tu'Shan
who waited pensively as He'stan turned the parchment
pages reverently. 'Alone, the passages on these pages
are useless, without meaning.'

'The armour is a codifier of sorts,' the Chapter Master interjected.

'Yes…' He'stan was absorbing the writings in the
book, matching it against the sigil pattern he'd seen on

the armour and now committed to his memory. Such analysis would take a human lexicanum-savant weeks to complete; for the Forgefather it took only minutes.

'Vulkan's wisdom was indeed great,' he breathed. He'stan's eyes blazed with satisfaction.

'What other secrets did he conceal with it, I wonder?' Tu'Shan replied.

'Incredible things… terrible things, my liege,' He'stan closed the book.

Though almost empty, the Pantheon Chamber felt alive with nervous energy as if it might burst into flame at any moment.

'A revelation?' Tu'Shan asked.

He'stan nodded slowly.

'We must return to Nocturne and the catacombs below Mount Deathfire.'

A HOT WIND seared his face. He'd been lying on the ash-sand for some time. His skin burned as if on fire.

The pain of his injuries was gone. He felt his broken shoulder gingerly, but the bone was intact, strong. His ribs no longer hurt; they were fused again, as one. Then he noticed he wasn't wearing his armour any more, nor did he carry a weapon – the force sword was gone.

Dak'ir's last sensation was of falling, down into the chasm of fire to be engulfed by Deathfire's blood. The golem was dead but then so too was he, and yet here he was.

This was the Pyre Desert, or at least it looked like the Pyre Desert. But that was impossible. Nocturne was in the grip of arctic winter; this terrain should be snowy tundra and not scorched ash-sand. It didn't make any sense, but then so little of his Librarian training thus far had.

Propping himself up on his elbows, Dak'ir noticed he was wearing a nomad's garb. A long sand coat covered his body, with many-layered robes underneath it and voluminous pantaloons designed to keep out the heat. His sturdy boots were ingrained with sand and ash, affecting a smudged grey-ochre patina over the hard leather. Readjusting the scarves around his face and neck, he moved into a crouch so he could retrieve his wide-brimmed hat where it had fallen in the ash. Webbing around the back of the hat hung down in a veil designed to keep out the heat and the desert dust. Then he picked up his travelling cane, a black-wood staff with a dragon's head carved at the peak. This he used to lever himself into a standing position.

These were his trappings. He knew as he knew his own armour, and yet they should be foreign objects to him. The familiarity at their feel and heft was unsettling. It was like stepping into the flesh of another individual, like wearing their life as his own. But whose life was it?

Looking around, Dak'ir realised the ash-plain was deserted. At least, almost…

A tiny drygnirr regarded him from atop a small rock. It had coal-black scales with a blue streak down its back and spines. The lizard's eyes flashed blood red as it took in the hulking nomad in its midst. He had seen the totem-creature before. Pyriel used it, his familiar and psychic embodiment in saurian form so he could observe all that Dak'ir did.

'What now?' he asked it. 'Isolation in this false desert will not challenge me, Pyriel.'

The drygnirr turned its head away and looked to the horizon where a long line of fire blazed. The flames were rising with every passing moment. After they'd reached several metres, Dak'ir thought he could make out figures inside them.

He set off towards the horizon and the wall of fire.

This is the Totem Path, Pyriel's voice drifted on the hot breeze. *See those footsteps?*

Skirls and eddies of sand circled ahead of him, leaving shallow impressions in the desert plain. Dak'ir nodded slowly.

They are yours…

Dak'ir's eyes narrowed. Pyriel's meaning was lost to him for now. He only knew he must reach the wall of fire, treading his old steps to do it.

'Am I destined to relive my past, then?' he asked the rising wind. It grew fiercer by the second but no answer was forthcoming. Ash-sand, whipped up on the breeze, stung his exposed face. Dak'ir drew his scarves tighter and lowered the brim of his hat. Pulling a pair of goggles over his eyes, he walked on.

After almost an hour, he realised he had lost the path. The wall of fire blazed ahead, even further away than before. He cursed, his frustration palpable in the tension throughout his body. A monster, however implacable, he could destroy. This would require patience and subtlety.

The storms intensified, making it increasingly difficult to find the impressions in the ash-sand. Dak'ir wanted to remove the goggles. It was hard to see through the grimy plastek lenses. But without them he'd be truly blind.

For all his strength, the abilities he'd honed over the last three years, even mastering the burning, it counted for nothing in the endless desert. It was like stepping into a void without form, a null place bereft of markers or way points. This was a labyrinth of a kind, he realised, its walls erected by the disorientation of its traveller.

Discerning the path again was impossible. The maelstrom had engulfed him. Even the sun was consumed. It felt like a hammer blow as it struck, pitching Dak'ir to his knees. He had to dip his head or risk being choked alive. The roar of it was so loud it deafened him. But there was something on the wind, between the white noise of its fury… a susurrus of voices too faint and distant to really hear.

Displaced ash-sand was building around him, slowly burying him. With effort, he rose but was buffeted down again. Grimacing, Dak'ir got up a second time. His shoulders were heavy with grains and flakes from the desert floor. Keeping low, he was able to make slow progress through the dunes but had lost all sense of direction. Everywhere he looked there was an undulating barrier of ash-sand. Even the drygnirr was gone.

Pyriel… he cried out psychically.

Only the sibilant voices replied but their meaning was unfathomable.

Pyriel!

Mocking laughter resolved itself on the wind.

Dak'ir turned, trying to locate the source.

Ignean… the voice returned.

Dak'ir spun around slowly, first to his left then to his right, but there was nothing.

'Show yourself!'

He was struck in the back by a heavy blow like a battering ram and fell forwards. As he turned onto his back quickly, trying to rise, his attacker fell upon him and held him down.

The raging ash-sand made it difficult to see anything

other than a bulky silhouette, but Dak'ir's assailant was unmistakeable when it spoke.

Ignean, it spat.

'Tsu'g–' The choking hands around Dak'ir's throat cut him off.

His attacker's eyes blazed through the storm wind like tiny balefires of hate.

Dak'ir struggled against the figure's grip, seizing his assailant's wrists and trying to pull them away from his neck, but the fingers were locked fast like iron.

'Tsu–' he rasped again, his wide eyes accusing then slowly consumed by wrath.

Harder and harder his attacker pressed, gradually smothering Dak'ir beneath his hatred and the consumptive ash-sand. The Librarian thrashed, raging against the shadow figure, knowing whose avatar it was that had manifested to destroy him.

Anger fed the burning core within, stoked the inner psychic fires.

I will turn you into ash…

Dak'ir would immolate his would-be murderer. There would be nothing left but a charred mark on the plain.

Give in to it, brother, it mocked, further fuelling Dak'ir's ire until it was a blazing nexus of flame inside his mind.

We are no so different, you and I… it concluded and its burning gaze mirrored the image of fire cultivated in Dak'ir's witch-sight.

'No…' he gasped, and let go. His hands fell to his sides, the nexus of flame diminished until it was nothing but vapour and then even that was lost on the abstract wind of Dak'ir's psyche.

The figure evaporated at once as if made from a

pillar of sand, the grains breaking away on the desert zephyrs and carried off to rejoin the storm. Dak'ir heaved a breath into his lungs, coughing and spluttering as he fought to turn onto his hands and knees. His throat was sore, his windpipe almost crushed.

The maelstrom battered him still, paying no heed to his condition. Here, only the strong prevailed and the weak were swept away. Dak'ir looked up. Another figure loomed in his eye-line. This one stood just in front of him, seemingly untouched by the storm as if he existed in another piece of time and had broken through the temporal barrier separating parallel universes. Dak'ir could see him perfectly. His fists clenched.

Nihilan, sorcerer and warlord of the Dragon Warriors, impeded his path.

'You are the destroyer, Dak'ir,' he said. 'You will burn all of Nocturne until it is a blackened rock, bereft of all life.'

Dak'ir fell again, as if the weight of Nihilan's prophecy was physical.

'Fall now,' he continued, 'fall and save your planet from destruction. You are the one, you will devour it with your power. Fall and do not rise again.'

Perhaps he was right; perhaps it would be better if Dak'ir stopped now. He remembered with painful clarity the dream-vision he'd had during the burning. Nocturne was utterly enflamed – there was nothing left, its people were shadows on a dead breeze.

He had unleashed that holocaust. It had come from within him and he'd been powerless to stop it. Dak'ir already knew that Pyriel regarded him as dangerous, that his potential, if not properly harnessed, could outreach him and the dire consequences of that if it did.

It would be easy to fall…

Perhaps…

But these were not his words.

No. I am Salamander. I know my will and my mind. I shall endure. I shall overcome. It is the Promethean Creed.

'Stand aside, doubter…' he muttered, standing easily and passing through Nihilan as he evaporated like haze.

Revealed in the fading apparition's wake through the raging ash-sand was the outline of something large and blocky. It was only a few metres away. Dak'ir had almost missed it. The storm showed no sign of abating. He needed shelter.

Every step took several minutes, his momentary confidence at defying Nihilan having drained away like the final grains through the neck of an hourglass. Dak'ir slipped three more times before he reached out and touched what he hoped was salvation. Treading his old steps would have to wait…

Or am I on the path?

…Any longer in the storm and a bleached bone corpse would be the Salamander's only legacy.

Dak'ir moved slowly down the object, feeling with his hands and using its metal flank as a guide until he came to an opening. It was partially ajar, wedged fast with a build-up of ash-sand. With a grunt, he ripped it loose, just wide enough for him to enter.

His occulobe implant allowed his eyes to adjust in seconds from the glare of the desert to the gloom of an expansive troop hold. It was a vessel, or at least the gutted remains of one, and though its internal power was no more lamps strung over its exposed beams and struts provided luminance.

Dulled by the thick adamantium hull of the ship, the storm winds became an eerie howl. The metal bent and creaked as if shifting uncomfortably against it.

Dak'ir breathed deep, relieved to have found shelter, and sank down. After a few moments, he looked around.

'Stormbird…' he murmured, knowing the inside of the Astartes assault craft from the old versions he'd seen in the Promethean Hall of Remembrance. Few Chapters used them any more, preferring the faster and more manoeuvrable Thunderhawks to act as their gunships. This one was ancient. It had crashed a long time ago. Much of the hold had been reclaimed by the desert, the slow process of its digestion taking centuries.

Ship no longer, it was a haven now and not just for Dak'ir.

'Identify yourself!' he said when he saw the booted feet sticking out from around a corner. There was a promethium stove and a selection of excavating tools nearby.

'Speak now,' Dak'ir reached for a plasma pistol that was no longer there. Instead, he brandished his staff, adopting a fighting grip as taught to him by his trainer-sergeant when he was just a Scout.

Despite the implicit warning, the figure did not move.

Dak'ir lamented his lack of auspex or auto-senses, but his instincts told him either the stranger hadn't heard him or he was already dead. Rounding the corner, he found the latter to be true.

Slumped with its back against one of the hold's bulkheads, an emaciated skeletal figure regarded him with sunken eyes. Obviously another nomad, it was

similarly attired to Dak'ir, though its hat had fallen
from the head that lolled on one side in death.

Something about it was familiar and Dak'ir leaned
in close to get a better look.

The skin, which he had at first thought was decayed
or scorched by exposure to the sun, was black. It was
onyx-black, a Salamander's skin.

Realisation dawned and Dak'ir hung his head, muttering a name.

'Fugis...'

So the old Apothecary had not survived the Burning
Walk.

Real or imaginary, the sign wasn't good. Despite the
unreality of this place, Dak'ir felt it carried a certain
resonance with it into the actual world, as if what he
were seeing and experiencing were merely echoes of a
greater truth. On the Totem Path nothing could be
taken for granted.

A faint disturbance in the sand mounds that had
spilled through several of the Stormbird's hatches got
Dak'ir's attention. He trained his Lyman's ear on a
sound too sporadic, too loud to be merely subsidence.
As he got back to his feet, the first of the pyre-worms
breached the surface.

Chitinous armour lined their long backs, the segmented plates clicking as they moved. Each of the beasts
was over two metres long and as thick as Dak'ir's arm. A
round maw, filled with spine-like teeth, champed
eagerly as it tasted necrotic flesh on the humid air. Pyre-
worms were carrion creatures – they ate the dead.

Cast back into the fire, becoming one again with the
mountain and Nocturne – that was how a Salamander
should make his final journey. Not like this, devoured
by desert vermin.

Dak'ir willed a ball of flame into existence but found his hand empty.

His psychic core was drained. There was nothing left.

Turning on his heel, he hoisted the body of Fugis over his shoulder and ran through the hold.

'Come, brother,' he said, 'we'll return to the mountain together.'

Tiny spines lined the pyre-worms, long armoured bodies propelling them along the ground at speed. Such creatures were easy to slay alone. In packs they were deadly, even to an Astartes. And pyre-worms were never alone. Dak'ir knew it was a nest. A small colony chittered behind them, their mandibles clacking hungrily.

The end of the hold was looming, so too was the exit hatch leading out the side of the fuselage.

Enter the storm again and risked being buried alive or face the pyre-worms and allow Fugis to be devoured.

'No choice at all, brother,' a cracked voice told him. Old ceramite, blackened by fire, corroded by age and violence seized Dak'ir's forearm in a gauntleted fist.

Ko'tan Kadai, almost a cadaver himself and with a ragged melta burn cratering his torso until faint light showed through to the other side, looked on Dak'ir with dying eyes.

'My lord…' Dak'ir faltered, losing his momentum.

The pyre-worms were closing. He couldn't carry them both and get out of the Stormbird in time.

Dak'ir shook Kadai's hand loose. 'I cannot save you…' he uttered and barrelled through the exit hatch.

It gave with a resounding screech of tearing metal and flung open. They stumbled through to the other side, into the blazing sun and the utter silence of a barren desert plain. The storm had abated.

The Stormbird was gone too, as was Fugis's body. The wall of fire was closer than before. It burned and beckoned the Salamander onwards.

'What are you showing me, Pyriel? What manner of trial is this?'

There was no answer, no voice inside Dak'ir's head.

In the distance, sitting on a lonely rock, was the drygnirr.

The steps, *his* steps, were gone. The storm had erased them as surely as it had erased the crashed ship and the spectres of Dak'ir's subconscious mind. He focussed, imagining the impressions he had seen in the ash-sand. Banishing all doubt, all anger, even guilt, he drew deep of his psychic well. When he opened his eyes again, the footsteps had returned. Each one was filled with fire, ignited impossibly against the desert plain. They were beacons, leading him to his destination.

Good, the voice of Pyriel returned. *Only unshackled and unburdened can you reach the wall of fire.*

Dak'ir took his final steps confronting the eternal blaze bisecting the desert plain. Where it touched the ground, the ash became as dust and the sand as fractured glass. The heat of it was incredible and Dak'ir wondered if a Salamander in power armour could pass through it unharmed, let alone one wearing the trappings of a nomad.

Then he saw the figures within. They went the entire length of the wall, all the dead of Nocturne, all of those that had returned to the mountain, in rank upon endless rank stretching all the way to the end of the world itself.

They are Nocturne's heart, said Pyriel, *her lifeblood. It is the Circle of Fire, Dak'ir.*

'Resurrection,' he answered in a low and reverent voice. To be in the presence of such ancients, native Nocturneans and Salamanders, was humbling. They were speaking. Their lips were moving but the roar of the eternal flame that held them in its flickering grasp obscured the voices.

Dak'ir leaned in closer. His skin was burning.

The spirits were whispering.

Destroyer… some said.

Saviour… others hissed.

'Which am I?'

A pair of gauntleted hands thrust out of the blaze, seizing Dak'ir by the shoulders and dragging him into the wall of fire.

Incredible agony reached every nerve of his body, so strong he thought he would pass out.

Gravius would not allow it, though. He drew Dak'ir close, his ancient and withered face no different to how it had been on Scoria.

A low-born, one of the earth, shall pass through the gate of fire… The flames whirled around them, the other spirits coalescing into the blaze, becoming one with it. The heat grew. Dak'ir screamed as his clothes were burned off and his skin seared away in an instant until all that remained was bone.

He will be our doom or salvation.

II
Legends

A THUNDERHAWK BROUGHT them to the surface of the planet, touching down with flaps extended, landing thrusters melting the ice into a grey-black slush underneath. The gunship's green armour plating was soon dappled by snow after its clawed stanchions made purchase on the frozen plains of the Pyre Desert.

The vessel's hull was scaled like some mythical beast of the deep earth, its nose and glacis plate fashioned into the image of a mighty drake. Even the long, sweeping wings were clawed; the mouths of its cannons and incendiaries crafted into maws.

Primordian was Tu'Shan's personal carrier, though he seldom used it. The return of the Forgefather was a unique occasion, however. The gesture felt justified.

Regent and Forgefather stepped out into the white void, armed and armoured. A fierce arctic wind was tossing the drifts into frenzy and unsettled the heavy drake cloaks about their backs as if the beasts they'd been skinned from still lived.

He'stan was the first to alight, an icy veneer crunching under the weight of his ornate power armour as he stepped from *Primordian's* extended embarkation ramp.

Deathfire loomed distant on the horizon. Smoke exuded from its craggy mouth like a promise. A deepening glow burned in the nadir of its hellish cradle, waiting to be unleashed. Nocturne was a restless mother. She did not slumber long. Her volcanic heart would soon beat again.

++*To see it thus*++ said He'stan over the comm-feed – the weather was too hostile to speak openly without it, ++*it is truly beauteous*++

++*I prefer her savage face, brother*++ Tu'Shan replied standing alongside him.

He'stan laughed loudly. With a twinge of sadness, he realised he hadn't done that in a very long time.

++*These may be inauspicious times, Regent, but I am glad to be amongst my Chapter again*++

Tu'Shan clapped him on the shoulder. It was the only affirmation He'stan needed.

As they started off, two legends amidst a desolate arctic vista following the still bubbling veins of the mountain, the Thunderhawk took off behind them. Soon it was lost to the snowstorms, its turbine engines swallowed by the howling wind.

DEATHFIRE GLOWERED OVER Dak'ir like an unhappy mistress. Her craggy flanks were wreathed with lava, her maw slathered with magma as the Time of Trial neared. Earthquakes shook Nocturne's bedrock, its tectonic plates in turmoil as Prometheus's stronger gravity exerted its violent influence.

Halfway up the mountain, Dak'ir saw the mouth of a cave. Here, he knew, was the gate of fire and the place of destiny he was prophesied to pass through.

Slowly, he began to climb. His sandals did little to insulate his feet from the ash slurry and broken cinder burning beneath him. His bare flesh – arms, legs and much of the torso exposed in the metal-shaper's garb – tingled with the heat. Plumes of steam swathed him in a fever-sweat, though he was not sick. The forging hammer on his back was heavy, but it was a good burden, an honest burden at one with the earth.

He needed Pyriel's voice no more. Dak'ir knew his path. Even as the sky rained with fire and the earth below rumbled and moaned in agony, he was unperturbed.

By defeating the onyx-golem he had proven his strength. His successful passage across the endless desert and through the wall of fire had demonstrated his spirit. Here, climbing the rugged crags of Mount Deathfire, what could be left for him to prove?

Courage…

The word entered Dak'ir's mind as he reached the rocky plateau that led to the cave mouth. Inside it, the gate of fire was a flickering oval of intense heat. He only had to look upon the flames to know he would not endure them. But it was the beast outside, the gate's slumbering keeper that arrested the Librarian's attention.

Kessarghoth…

The drake's name was old. It was born when Nocturne was young, its people tribesmen and shaman, not giant warriors who waged war across the stars first in the name of a glorious father and then in the memory of His life-sustained corpse. Scaled plates looked as thick as Dreadnought armour as they shifted placidly with Kessarghoth's breathing. Its broad back was festooned with a ridge of spines twice as long as a Themian hunting spear. Their sharpness, Dak'ir did not doubt, was equal to any power blade in the Salamander's arsenal. The beast was immense, like a pair of Land Raider battle tanks stood end-to-end and twice as wide.

Yet it slept, and while it slept Dak'ir lived, for to awaken such a creature would surely be the end of him.

Dragging his body up over the lip of the plateau, Dak'ir crouched low to consider his options. A tremor ran up the side of the mountain and for a moment he feared Kessarghoth would wake, but the beast merely stirred briefly and continued to sleep.

It would take more than the shifting of the world to disturb it.

And also something much less, Dak'ir thought shrewdly. He eyed a length of chain that shackled Kessarghoth to the mountainside. The oval links were massive, far larger than a fully-grown Astartes. Though it blocked most of the cave mouth, there was room enough to squeeze through without touching the drake.

Unhitching the hammer from his back, though it seemed a moot gesture in the face of such a monster, Dak'ir edged slowly towards Kessarghoth and the gate.

As a boy, before his apotheosis to the ranks of the Salamanders, he had hunted in the depths of Ignea. The subterranean continent, like much of Nocturne, was a dangerous place. Saurian beasts, giant insectoid creatures and other horrors lurked in its darkness. Long ago, Dak'ir had learned to walk quietly and carefully whilst stalking prey and although Kessarghoth was no prize to be slain, he followed those lessons now.

He kept his steps short and light, the strides small so the resonance of his movements was kept to a minimum. Gaze never leaving the drake, focussed on its eyes and mouth for signs of disturbance, Dak'ir crossed the rocky plain and entered the threshold of the cave.

It was surprisingly cold inside. The gate of fire seemed to emanate no heat. Dak'ir's instincts told him the unreality of this place was trying to fool him. Bending down, with a half-glance at Kessarghoth to make sure the drake was still sleeping, he picked up a fist-sized rock and tossed it into the flames.

A short flash presaged its atomisation into a cloud of particulate ash.

Dak'ir thought about erecting a kine shield to

safeguard his passage through the gate, but something suggested to him that would not be enough. He wore the metal-shaper's garb for a reason.

Then he noticed the chain. Several of its links passed through the gate of fire. Whatever substance they were forged from appeared to be impervious to the flames. But they also held the creature in thrall, feeding several smaller chains that bound its mouth and claws. The angle of the larger chain suggested it was taut already, that Kessarghoth had reached the end of its limits and could come no further.

Like all Nocturneans and, by extension, all Salamanders, Dak'ir possessed a keen forgesmith's eye. As he appraised the links that made up the drake's mighty chain, he realised that one of them could be fashioned into a form of shield. With that braced against the infernal flames he could breach the gate and survive.

But to forge such a thing he would need to break the chain and release Kessarghoth. Dak'ir stepped towards the nearest of the links and raised his hammer.

The first blow rang out like a dull clarion, its report echoing around the mountain.

Still the drake slumbered.

A second and third had the same effect.

Kessarghoth did not stir.

Soon, Dak'ir found a steady rhythm and pounded at the joint in the link until it broke apart in two halves. The eldritch metal was hot, hot enough to reshape with his hammer. Finding a flat-headed rock, Dak'ir went to work levelling the link and then reforging its curved surface into a huge shield that would protect his entire body.

He had given up on Kessarghoth now. The ancient had slept for thousands of years. It would take more than the hammering of a lowly Nocturnean metal-shaper to rouse it.

Or so he thought.

Upon the last blow, his hammerhead still glowing red-hot, Dak'ir heard the drake stir at last.

Blinking back millennia of hibernation, the dust of ages veneering its body shaken free as it flexed old but strong muscles, Kessarghoth drew to its full height and bellowed.

The chains snaring the drake's mouth snapped like kindling, as if removing the one link in its bondage was enough to weaken the rest. As it shambled forwards, lashing the air with a leathery pink tongue, it shrugged off the other chains binding it. Kessarghoth's eyes narrowed to yellow slits as it regarded its prey. It hissed then roared at Dak'ir again, its ululating cry shaking the mountainside. The displaced earth cascaded in a miniature avalanche, as if fleeing from the beast's fury.

The cave was not far, but the drake now blocked it with its bulky body. Hefting the shield in one hand, the hammer in the other, Dak'ir advanced.

For they shall know no fear…

Except he was not a Space Marine in this place and the monster before him was not an enemy of mankind, it was a denizen of primordial myth, a fable told to Nocturnean children to ensure they obeyed their elders.

In Vulkan's name, Dak'ir could think of no strategy to defeat it.

Kessarghoth was fast. Its serpentine head shot out like a scaled dart and with the force of a seismic hammer. Dak'ir rolled, caught off guard but relying on his Astartes survival instincts to save him.

Jogging to its blind side, he tried to manoeuvre the beast away from the cave in the hope he could race by it and to salvation beyond. But the drake was wily with age and not to be fooled. It turned where it squatted, stout legs bunched as they crabbed in a half circle so it was facing its prey again.

It wasn't hard to see the tenacity of his Chapter in that beast. Ferocious intelligence flared in its eyes, the bestial echo of his battle-brothers.

One of you resides within all of us, he thought, backing off across the plateau again. Flames lighted Nocturne's sky. A chunk of fiery star-rock smashed into the mountain, tearing away a piece of Dak'ir's platform and preventing further retreat. The hell-storm in the red heavens was worsening. Time was against him.

Kessarghoth sucked in its breath. A sagging pouch in its gullet filled with volatile liquid before it unleashed it in a stream of fire. The blaze rolled off Dak'ir's shield, against which he had to brace his entire body lest the force of the blast pitch him off the mountain to his doom on the crags below.

It was over quickly, tendrils of smoke and steam evaporating off the metal as Dak'ir launched into a run directly at the drake.

A second meteor crashed into the plateau, obliterating where the Salamander had been standing. Chunks of the mountain fell away in slow motion to be sundered in the lava lakes below. Rocks cracked and grumbled as if the world was breaking and Dak'ir stood upon the last splinter of creation.

With the earth trembling beneath his feet, Dak'ir swept under Kessarghoth's bite. Flecks of acidic drool burned his skin as they splashed him but he ignored them. Stepping inside the reach of the drake's claws and dropping his hammer, Dak'ir used his forward momentum to scale Kessarghoth's grizzled hide. Its thorny carapace provided ready handholds, its spiny back the means to propel up and over the broad bank of muscle in its haunches.

The drake turned, snapping wildly, hissing and bellowing in frustration.

Dak'ir hung on with one hand, the other desperately gripping his shield. It was like riding a skiff on the Acerbian Sea during geyser-tide. Tail thrashing, Kessarghoth stomped back and forth hoping to dislodge the insect on its back.

Dropping to his knees, Dak'ir slid the shield over his head as the drake belched another stream of liquid flame. Though the plume wreathed its back, lighting tiny fires in the nooks of its ancient body, Kessarghoth didn't cry out.

It was mad.

This tenacious creature scratched at its hide but Dak'ir weaved away from its questing claws, refusing to furnish its hungering belly with flesh.

The cliff edge was looming. In its blind rage to throw Dak'ir off and devour him, the drake had moved away from the cave mouth and closer to the precipice's edge. A blow from Kessarghoth's flanged tail, harder than a power fist, almost unseated the Salamander. His shield arm rang painfully with the glancing blow but he hung on still.

With a deep, earthy basso the ragged fringe of the broken plateau finally gave way against the thrashing drake. At first, the beast didn't realise what was happening. Its bellowing stopped momentarily when one of its hind legs fell backwards into the growing void behind it. Then it lost footing in its other rear leg.

Now the drake panicked, releasing a high-pitched shriek, its eyes widening even as it knew its doom was inevitable.

Hate-filled eyes cursed Dak'ir as he let go at last and ran up Kessarghoth's neck before vaulting off its head onto solid ground below. He turned to watch it fall. Such a noble beast, so venerable and magnificent. Someone should witness its death. Though it was a manifestation of psychic unreality, the drake's death was a profound moment. Dak'ir vowed he would mark it, that the deed would not go unremembered. With scarification he would honour Kessarghoth.

But honour would have to wait. The gate of fire was before him.

He would have only once chance to pass through the flame. With Vulkan's name on his lips, Dak'ir raced at the burning oval. Less than a metre away, the strange cold of the cave chilling his bare skin, he lowered the shield and roared.

The moment of passage stretched into minutes then hours then years. A dark world loomed large in his vision. Tombs lined its ossuary roads. Sepulchres ringed its grey vales. Bones filled its endless catacombs. It was a dead world, a world he knew with harsh clarity. The scent of grave dust and old burning ravaged his olfactory senses. Cold, thin hands like talons seized his body. Parchment skin brushed his face. Gossamer strands of congealed dust bound his arm like rough silk. It called to him, this place of death and desolation. It had always called. For four decades it had dominated his thoughts until a moment of unique trauma had quashed it beneath a veil of guilt. But now that burden had been lifted. In the endless desert, he had met those fears and overcome them. The old wounds had resurfaced again, hard scar-tissue reopened with a ragged knife of remembrance. Its blade was cold; the sibilance as it sliced into Dak'ir's mind spoke a single word like a death rattle...

Moribar...

He thrust open his eyes, a feverish sweat chilling his skin, and saw Pyriel alone in a chamber beneath the labyrinthine depths of Mount Deathfire.

The Codicier wore his psychic hood without battle-helm. Spiral scarification edged over the lip of his blue gorget. A faint, almost imperceptible smile played at the corners of his mouth.

Pyriel had an unremarkable face. A thick shaven line of white hair divided his smooth shorn pate into two equal black hemispheres like an arrow that came to a sharp point between his eyes.

'Stand, brother,' he said, clasping his force staff like a badge of ceremony. In many ways, in this moment, it was.

Dak'ir had not realised he was kneeling. Penitence before his mentor seemed appropriate given the circumstances. He arose.

Pyriel nodded, a sagely wisdom Dak'ir could not yet grasp filling his eyes. They burned cerulean blue as he psychically augmented his voice to a deep, prophetic rumble. If nothing else, the Codicier possessed a flair for the dramatic.

'*Welcome, Lexicanum,*' he boomed, '*to the vaunted ranks of the Librarius!*'

In his outstretched hand, the naked blade laid reverently across his forearm, was Dak'ir's force sword. It was his, earned by right of fire trial.

The Lexicanum took the proffered hilt. The exquisite haft, cross-hatched by veins of emerald, felt warm to the touch. All of Dak'ir's fatigue and disorientation vanished in a pure instant of joining. This was *his* blade, tuned to his resonance and him to its. With clarity came remembrance and the irrefutable truth of what he'd witnessed passing through the gate of fire.

Dread, like a cold metal fist, slammed into Dak'ir's gut.

'Moribar,' he said, his voice cracked with sudden urgency.

A CRACK SPLIT the side of the mountain. Tiny rocks rolled down its rugged flank, shed snow broke apart and shuddered in their wake. Hot air escaped the gloom revealed inside the crack. A tempest of ice flurries was sent swirling with the sudden thermal updraft. Noises from concealed machines hummed and clanked, audible above the storm.

From a fissure it grew to a chasm, in fact a gate, the entrance to a hidden route to Deathfire's frost-shrouded heart.

He'stan withdrew the Spear of Vulkan from an invisible cleft in the rock. It was a magnificent weapon, a piece of artifice from a long dead age, the last of its kind. An artefact of the primarch, Tu'Shan was not surprised it was more than a mere weapon.

He entered the chamber ahead of the Forgefather, his drake cloak sweeping in his wake. A long passage led downwards. Ash and soot scented the warm breeze. It was good to be near the mountain again.

The gate ground shut with a thud that echoed loudly in the abrupt silence.

He'stan moved into step with his lord and the two Salamanders descended.

At the end of the tunnel the subterranean depths

branched off into several semi-naturally formed corridors and chambers.

'This way,' muttered He'stan, intent on his mission.

Tu'Shan followed without comment, stooping below a cluster of stalactites impeding his path. So deep were they that Nocturne's blood ran all around them, free flowing and vital. Above, the world shivered in the grip of arctic winter; below, its vigorous geology stirred.

So vast was the labyrinth below Mount Deathfire that two individuals could spend months abroad in its depths and never meet one another, never even witness a sign of another's passing. Much of its subterranean darkness was uncharted. Only Vulkan had ever known its every shrouded corner, its every tunnel and chamber. Beasts slumbered in the lowest deeps, old creatures jealous of men and his dominance of the surface. The unique acoustics of the rock, the veins of phonolite and other aurally conductive minerals within its composition, allowed the plaintive wailing of such creatures to be heard far from their dwelling places by human Nocturneans. Few natives ever braved the mountain depths for that reason. It was the province of the Salamanders alone and so the way was deserted as He'stan and Tu'Shan traversed the gloom to an ancient door wrought of carved adamantium.

'I have never seen this place before,' the Regent confessed, awed by the icon of Vulkan fashioned into the gate.

'Nor have I,' He'stan replied.

As one, the two legends of the Chapter sank to one knee and bowed.

'Vulkan's fire beats in my breast,' they intoned

together, 'he is my steel and I honour him with my loyalty and sacrifice.' It was a rare variation of the more common litany, used to express sentiments of utter devotion and duty.

They arose with perfect synchronicity, stalled before the immense gate.

Tu'Shan had to arch his neck to see its apex, whilst He'stan stepped forwards to lay his gauntleted hand upon the metal. Beneath his battle-helm, he closed his eyes.

'Fire surges through my veins, brother...' he breathed.

Tu'Shan pressed his own mighty palm against the metal. 'There is power here.' He didn't need to be a Librarian to realise it. 'And I can feel an indentation in the surface. I will summon Master Vel'cona. He will know how to breach it.'

He'stan opened his eyes and lowered his hand reluctantly. The Tome of Fire had guided him to this place. It had opened his eyes to the existence of the forgotten chamber. Vulkan's hand had been at work in this deed. The Forgefather took great comfort in that. It was as if the primarch were still with them, if only in spirit and not flesh.

'Vulkan's Sigil, who bears it now, my lord?'

'Chaplain Elysius is its custodian, but what relevance is that?'

He'stan faced him and removed his battle-helm. His war-aged face had never looked so serious. The many honour-scars there seemed to shimmer in the crystal-refracted lava light.

'It is the only thing that can open this gate. And make no mistake, Regent, we *must* open it.'

CHAPTER FIVE

I
Harbinger

I am Death.

Its shroud follows me like a shadow I cannot shrug off.

I feel the cold of it reaching around my twin hearts like a forging clamp even as the font of rage within me boils.

My father taught me to be thus. He taught with his blood and the genetic legacy of his mortal body.

Why then do my brothers, warriors all, not feel as I do?

Why does the guilt of my past deeds and lack of deeds haunt me like a spectre crouched on my shoulder?

I am invulnerable. I am war incarnate. I am the anvil upon which my enemies break.

But I am hollow, a shell filled with liquid fire.

How long before it overtakes my fragile form and burns me down to ash?

Tsu'gan opened his eyes. The branding rod had gone deep, a savage scoring in his right bicep that retraced his previous glories.

He found his teeth gritted with a rime of blood from when he'd bitten his lip. It wasn't pain that drove the Salamander to do this, but anger. Tsu'gan had hoped upon promotion to the 1st Company that he would re-find his purpose, quell the choler inside him. Induction to the Firedrakes, his isolation on Prometheus surrounded by relics of champions, fighting alongside the Chapter's mightiest heroes had only intensified the flame within.

It was as useful as it was debilitating. Unleashed on the battlefield, Tsu'gan's battle rage made him formidable if reckless. His *weakness* had been noticed, however. Before, when he was brother-sergeant of 3rd Company, it had been Fugis who got closest to discovering his destructive masochism; now it was Praetor, veteran sergeant of the Firedrakes and Tu'Shan's mailed fist in matters when the Regent was otherwise engaged, who watched him.

Mercifully, Praetor's duties were many and kept him busy. Tsu'gan had no reason to suspect the veteran sergeant's interest was anything more than mild concern.

The deaths of his battle-brothers bothered Tsu'gan greatly. Seeing heroes sundered, the other Firedrakes whom he regarded as invincible, shook his faith more deeply than he cared to admit. Only since Kadai had it been this way. He had idolised his former captain. His demise and the nature of it had left a crack of imperfection in Tsu'gan's psyche. Like any wound that is left untended, it had festered and grown.

He had accepted it; accepted death was part of his warrior calling, before that fateful moment. A strange divergence of destiny had begun after that mission. Tsu'gan was no psyker, but he felt the shifting of fate nonetheless. He had taken to reading scrolls of prophecy, absorbing the encrypted wisdom of his forebears. Admittance to the Pantheon Chamber and the Tome of Fire was not permitted but there was lore enough on Prometheus in its vault-chambers and reliquary-shrines to satisfy Tsu'gan's appetite. His path was his own. He would not allow another to dictate it to him.

Tsu'gan stood on a dais of burning coals. His bare feet smouldered, tendrils of smoke twisting through his toes, but he felt no discomfort. His body was inured to such things.

I feel nothing…

A drakescale loincloth preserved his dignity. This was the way of tribal Nocturne. Tradition was important to its peoples, so too to their superhuman guardians. Tsu'gan's arms were held loosely by his sides as Maikar, his brander-priest, went to work. Only the clanking of the nearby votive-servitor, its cumbersome brazier cradle crackling with heat, invaded the sepulchral silence.

There were no lights in the solitorium. He preferred the dark. It hid his thoughts, dampened them for a time. The flash of fire, glowing coals and the luminance of Maikar's cybernetic implants provided the only light.

Tsu'gan nodded and the brander-priest burned him again.

'Scour it all away, Maikar,' he said in a shallow voice. 'Burn it, until there is none left.'

I hope for nothing!

You fear everything…

Tsu'gan started. That was not the voice of his subconscious. It was a memory, one he hadn't recalled for three years.

'Nihilan…' he breathed, anger colouring his voice and filling it with strength. A snarl ruined the perfect Nocturnean heritage of his face. Besides the spike of red beard jutting from his chin, Tsu'gan was completely bald. Hesiod-born, his lineage was a noble one. But he chose to believe that meant being above man, to show them who their betters were. To associate too closely with humans, to adopt their traits, it brought the Salamanders low when it was they who should inspire and bring the humans up. Tsu'gan had never been able to see that was exactly what the Fire-born did. He was blind to it. His arrogance extended to one of his battle-brothers, a distant figure now. Tsu'gan hoped bitterly that Dak'ir had met his end underneath Mount Deathfire. Tsu'gan quailed momentarily at the idea that he hadn't and somehow managed to unlock the psychological fractures in his mind with his newly realised *gifts*.

'Enough!' he snapped, seizing the rod before Maikar could apply it again. This serf was more pliant than Zo'kar, his previous brander. The bond that existed between Salamander and brander-priest was meant to last eternally or as long as war called to the Astartes. All efforts were made to ensure that the servitor-like humans lived well beyond mortal thresholds. Zo'kar had died on the *Vulkan's Wrath* during a solar storm. His body was eventually found broken in one of the strike cruiser's devastated solitorium chambers. It looked like Zo'kar had suffered before he'd died.

Maikar recoiled from his master's wrath, finding solace in the shadows.

'Summon my armour serfs,' Tsu'gan muttered, stepping off the dais of coals and rubbing his arms. He winced – the pain was great, even for a Salamander. He focussed on it, pushing the darker thoughts down.

Four bowed serfs entered the solitorium in silence. Between them they carried Tsu'gan's power armour. It was his old suit, the one he had worn whilst part of the 3rd. Now its surface was rendered with the swirling iconography of drakes, serpents and flames. It had been meticulously artificed, re-forged and remade into a thing of pure beauty. Far superior to its former incarnation, it was armour worthy of 1st Company, of a Firedrake of Vulkan.

First came the black bodyglove, almost invisible against Tsu'gan's onyx skin. It was overlaid with an exoskeleton that interfaced with the systems of his power amour. Festooned with linking ports and conduit points, it would join him to his suit, enhancing his strength, speed and combat abilities exponentially.

Tsu'gan turned his wrists to face the ceiling just before his vambraces were locked in place. He saw the icon of Imaan, he who had died so that Tsu'gan could ascend the ranks. Imaan's power armour had been smelted down but he had bequeathed his Terminator armour to Tsu'gan after death. The marks upon the Firedrake's wrists were a reminder of that bond, and that when he wore the suit Imaan's spirit warred with him.

Last of all, after cuirass, greaves and pauldrons, was the long drake cloak that spilled down Tsu'gan's back around the suit's generator. So armoured, he felt a semblance of being whole once more.

With gauntlets locked about his clenched fists he took chainsword and combi-bolter before assuming his place on a throne of red-veined basalt. The sigil of the Firedrakes was carved into its rough surface.

'Vulkan's fire beats in my breast…' Tsu'gan intoned

as Maikar returned and traced a band of white ash
from the votive-servitor's basin on his face, '…with it I
shall smite the foes of the Emperor.'

Maikar bowed again and retreated. Tsu'gan took his
helmet, proffered from the darkness by an armour serf,
and slammed it down upon his head.

'Release the gates,' he commanded in a voice made
tinny and harsh through his helmet's vox-grille.

A sliver of light invaded the darkness, growing to a
wide rectangle of magnesium-white.

'War calls…' he said, rising from his throne and
striding from the solitorium.

'THE FIREDRAKES ANSWER,' Praetor's deep voice resonated around the docking pad. His warriors were
arrayed in a semi-circle, with the veteran sergeant at
the centre facing them. Armed and armoured for war
they were a forbidding sight, but the air around the
pad was one of ready camaraderie. Though they were
Salamanders, the epitome of the Fire-born in fact, the
1st Company had many rituals unfamiliar to their
other battle-brothers. On the field, they were formidable, disciplined and arch exponents of the Promethean
Creed; in their clandestine halls on Prometheus, they
were equals.

Overhead, the blackness of the void hung like a dark
canvas. A crackling force shield kept it from rushing in
and dragging the Firedrakes into cold space. Visible at
a distance through the shimmering field, one of
Captain Dac'tyr's vessels waited attached to one of
Prometheus's serpentine docking spines. The Master of
the Fleet had generously provided a frigate, *Firelord*, to
ferry the 1st Company warriors to their theatre of war.

The lume-lamps in the assembly area of the pad

were kept low. Their glow threw ruddy shadows into the deepest corners, hinting at a vast chamber beyond. A Thunderhawk sat in dock behind Praetor. A team of servitors and maintenance serfs worked tirelessly to prepare it for immediate launch. Tech-adepts and one of the Salamanders Techmarines, Brother M'karra, muttered litanies and invoked unguents over the vessel. Before the *Implacable* could soar into the stars on blazing contrails its machine-spirits had to be placated, their will and purpose defined. Brander-priests burned ritual scars into the adamantium plate for this very reason.

'On Gevion, a cluster of worlds in the Uhulis Sector, Segmentum Solar, contact has been lost with elements of 3rd Company,' Praetor continued the briefing. He was an impressive warrior, even clad only in his artificer armour. Despite the fact he eschewed his Terminator suit, he still carried his thunder hammer and storm shield. His drakescale mantle had been affixed to this lighter armour, too. Praetor's head was a black bolt sat between two hulking shoulders. Polished to a mirror sheen by his brander-priest, the armour reflected the light and gave a bloody cast to his features that only enhanced his stature.

'Initially, it was believed that raiders had targeted the worlds for the purposes of slavery. Uncharacteristically for the dark eldar, though, they entrenched their forces.'

Derisive muttering rippled around the semicircle of Firedrakes. No native of Nocturne had any love for the xenos. Victims of raiders in the ancient past themselves, they reserved a particular loathing for eldar pirates.

Tsu'gan longed to slake his chainblade's thirst against them. That such creatures had managed to silence elements of the Fire-born was unconscionable. He suspected xenos treachery and felt the fires of war stoked within him at even the thought of these baseless and unworthy aliens.

Lost briefly to the fog of Tsu'gan's rage, Praetor's voice came back into focus.

'…of paramount importance that Brother-Chaplain Elysius is extracted from the war zone and returned to Prometheus.'

'Who commands the Fire-born at Gevion?' It was Halknarr who spoke out. The brother-sergeant hung his helmet from a thick leather cord at his belt in the style of an old campaigner. His lined face and greying temples betrayed his age, but Tsu'gan knew this Firedrake was as unyielding as Nocturne iron.

'Adrax Agatone is captain of the 3rd,' said Vo'kar. The hard-faced warrior was a heavy weapon specialist. Tsu'gan had fought with him before on the wreck of the *Protean*. He'd been there alongside him when Hrydor, the one Vo'kar had replaced, was slain by the Night Lords.

'His forces and much of the 3rd are locked in battle along this area,' Praetor told them. He opened his clenched fist to reveal a small hexagonal device. It was a hololith projector. He clicked the activation rune and a slew of grainy continents came into focus rendered in blue monochrome light, 'The Ferron Straits.' A long tract of flatland, streaked with ferron ore deposits, came into view as the hololith increased magnification. The ridged landscape looked like a bank of grey dunes. Fat clouds of steam from the Geviox processor plants rolled across them in itinerant squalls of vapour. 'The territory suits the invader, but Agatone closes his mailed fist about them and will bring them to the anvil, of that I am certain. It is taking time, however. He cannot relent, a Salamander does not relent. So we will go to the aid of our beleaguered brothers.'

Vo'kar turned his attention to Tsu'gan.

'You served in the 3rd, did you not, Zek? What manner of Fire-born is Agatone?'

Amongst the other companies such enquiry would be regarded as impudent in the extreme, but in this half-circle Firedrakes spoke together as closely bonded brothers. Vo'kar meant no slight. His question was honestly intended.

Tsu'gan afforded him the same measure of respect.

'I left the 3rd soon after Agatone's appointment as captain, but I fought with him on Scoria. There are few in the Chapter better. If Agatone could have broken the enemy and reached our Brother-Chaplain, he would have.'

Praetor nodded in agreement, before he clicked another rune on the hololith and the image scrolled on to a different landmass. This one was much larger and heavily industrialised. 'This is Ironlandings, Chaplain Elysius's last known location. Geviox is the cluster's primary world, a processor-planet with several structures and strategic defence points. Ironlandings is, to all intents, its hub.'

'What about the native populace? Are there any labour-serfs holed up in this area?' asked Vo'kar.

'All dead, victims of the xenos,' Praetor replied.

Halknarr's face was grim when he asked, 'You believe we are entering enemy-held territory, brother-sergeant?'

Praetor's eyes were like hard, red-hot coals. 'Aye, I do.'

'Hence the smaller insertion force,' added Daedicus, a Badab War veteran who kept a black and yellow striped knee plate as part of his armour by way of com-memoration. 'And lack of Tactical Dreadnought Armour,' he concluded.

Praetor nodded at the nineteen warriors before him again. Two full squads, led by himself and Halknarr. The Forgefather was leader to them all, but would be unencumbered by command for the mission.

It is the worth of several armies, he thought proudly.

'The Night Devils, an Imperial Guard regiment, or elements of it at least, are also in the war zone but our mission is not to aid them,' Praetor went on, 'Elysius is our only concern.'

Halknarr folded his broad arms. 'May I ask why?'

'He is the bearer of Vulkan's Sigil,' said a calm voice from across the deck. He'stan's words seemed to resonate with power as he stepped out of the shadows and approached the Firedrakes. 'It is vital this artefact is returned to Nocturne. Alive or dead, we retrieve our Brother-Chaplain and the Sigil with him. Nothing else matters.'

All eyes turned from Praetor to the figure that came amongst them. Awesome as their veteran sergeant was, he could not command the same attention. Nor would he ever wish to.

Tsu'gan had never before met the Forgefather. He had never fought by his side. Vulkan He'stan bore the name of the primarch. He prosecuted their father's sacred duty. To be before such a legend was humbling. His deeds were almost as legendary as his trappings. Kesare was the name of the creature Vulkan had slain for his mantle. That magnificent cloak of scale hung proudly from the Forgefather's shoulders. In his mailed fist he carried Vulkan's Spear, a power blade of incredible potency from Nocturne's halcyon days. The other hand was encased in the Gauntlet of the Forge, an arcane weapon capable of summoning fire. But it was not these weapons, nor He'stan's superbly wrought armour, that empowered him. It was his *presence*. There was something about him – Tsu'gan felt it palpably – that resonated with mystery and unknowable wisdom. But there was distance, too, a separation necessitated by the isolation of his quest. In many ways, the Forgefather was the closest link the Chapter had to their long lost primarch. All who came within He'stan's aura felt it. The former captain of the 4th had come far and achieved much.

With purpose like that…

Tsu'gan wondered if his path could be changed.

Halknarr fell silent. He was the first to kneel and bow.

'My lord…' Profound emotion reduced his voice to a rasp.

The other Firedrakes kneeled too and lowered their heads. Even Praetor offered supplication.

'Grant us your wisdom, Forgefather, that we might harness it for our victory,' he said like a prayer.

Chin touching his chest, his eyes half on the deck, half on the hero standing alongside Praetor, Tsu'gan realised then what He'stan was. He was *myth*. But more than that, he was myth made flesh. It felt wrong to do anything but show fealty to him. Tu'Shan was their Regent and Chapter Master, he was their captain, but He'stan was something else.

The Forgefather's eyes narrowed. He was uncomfortable at the gesture but concealed it flawlessly. With Tu'Shan he had experienced a returning bond of brotherhood; now he felt as aloof and distant as he had ever been whilst exploring the galaxy for the Nine.

'I have stared into the pages of fate, witnessed the prophecies of Vulkan coming to fruition. An inauspicious time draws near. Nocturne stands on the brink of something momentous. We are, all of us, bound to this doom or salvation. But we must seize it and understand what our father would have us prepared to face. Only with his sigil can we do this.'

He paused, letting the import of his words sink in.

'Rise,' said He'stan, encouraging the Firedrakes with a hand gesture. 'I would have you treat me as a brother, not some untouchable figure of myth.'

Praetor rose first. His example emboldened the others.

'Forgive us, liege,' he said. 'But your coming here, it is a part of the prophecy, is it not?'

He'stan nodded.

'We see the primarch in you,' Praetor explained. 'It is hard not to offer genuflection when faced with such a legacy. But you *are* my brother,' he added, extending his gauntleted hand, 'and I bid you welcome.'

A smile slowly cracked He'stan's face, filled with the warmth of reflected camaraderie. 'It does me good to hear you say that, Herculon.' He shook the hand of the veteran sergeant, who nodded with brotherly approval. 'But Elysius needs our bonds of brotherhood extending to him now. Our Chaplain is in certain danger, I fear.'

When Tsu'gan dared to look up again, he noticed He'stan's eyes were upon him. From the gloomy confines of the assembly deck, they burned brightly. Tsu'gan imagined a fiery tempest in those eyes, waiting for the Forgefather to unleash it. They lingered for a time as if He'stan were seeing the turmoil inside the Firedrake's soul. Unlike the scrutiny of Pyriel, Tsu'gan didn't feel uncomfortable locked to the Forgefather. It was a sensation of calm that swept over him instead, a promise of redemption.

'Is he alone? Are any of our brothers with him?' Belatedly, as the attention of the group fell upon him, Tsu'gan realised the question had come from his mouth.

'Two squads are unaccounted for,' said Praetor. The veteran sergeant's expression was grave. 'Ba'ken and Iagon.'

A cold feeling grew in Tsu'gan's gut at the mention of their names.

Iagon had been his second-in-command. He had left him behind in the 3rd but had ensured he would become brother-sergeant in his stead.

Now it seemed he might have fallen to the xenos.

The rage inside Tsu'gan boiled, burning away the cold and threatening to overwhelm him.

'We must make all haste to Gevion,' he said, hoarse with repressed anger.

He'stan's glare was penetrating when he answered, the same fire igniting his kindred spirit, 'Oh, we shall, brother, and rain down furious vengeance upon our enemies.'

II
A Cold Wind

WITH A HISS of scalding skin, T'sek drew the brand across Dak'ir's shoulder and the icon of Kessarghoth was finished.

'A fitting tribute,' said Pyriel from the deep gloom of the solitorium.

Dak'ir examined the drake symbol embedded permanently into his flesh. It still shone with its fresh forging in the lambent glow of the votive-servitor's brazier coals.

'Even though the beast has not been seen on Nocturne for millennia, I felt its presence, master. Despite the unreality of the Totem Walk, I knew it was Kessarghoth's spirit I fought against.'

'And triumphed, Dak'ir,' Pyriel interjected. 'You vanquished it and survived. In so doing you became Lexicanum.'

'It's an uneasy rank to bear, still,' Dak'ir confessed.

'You miss your old command, the warriors of the 3rd.'

Dak'ir met the Librarian's fiery gaze and nodded once.

He is an unremarkable warrior in many ways, Pyriel thought as he regarded the Fire-born before him. An old wound afflicted him, a patch of off-white scarification on the left side of his face that marked Dak'ir as different to his brothers. It was more than that, Pyriel knew. He had suspected it for a while. Apothecary Fugis had spoken to him of it, of the dreams – the remembrances of his old life, his human life, with unusual clarity. Dak'ir was an empath of sorts. It was what made him such a naturally gifted Librarian.

Ever since the burning, though, when Pyriel had almost been destroyed by the nascent psyker's power, he had *known*. Dak'ir *was* different. More than that, he was significant. Vel'cona had confided in him the elements of the prophecy deciphered in the armour recovered from Scoria. Pyriel knew well enough of Dak'ir's involvement in it. What he, and no one else in the Chapter, knew was *how* and to what end he was involved.

A low-born of the Ignean caves, a unique battle-brother. He should never have survived the trials, he should not have reached the vaunted rank of brother-sergeant, he should have failed the rigours of the Librarius... and yet, here he was, donning the blue ceramite, becoming a Lexicanum before Pyriel's very eyes.

'This is your calling, Dak'ir. For good or ill,' he said at last.

Dak'ir looked up from securing his vambraces. The armour serfs had entered silently and worked swiftly. Mumbled intonation accompanied every affixed piece of battle-plate. Ash from the brazier cradle anointed every section in a veneer of white.

'*Good or ill?*'

Pyriel smiled, but there was no warmth to it. 'Only Vulkan can know all ends, Salamander. Who can tell where our purpose will lead us?'

'Mine leads me to Moribar,' Dak'ir replied, his tone betraying a hint of belligerence.

'Are you so keen to go back to that place?'

When he'd handed the force sword, *Draugen*, to Dak'ir he'd shared a mote of the vision the Lexicanum had witnessed upon breaching the gate of fire. Sense memory fooled the Codicier that he could still smell grave dust on the hot air in the solitorium. A grey world, full of shades and old stone lingered at the edge of his subconscious like a wraith. The creeping spectre of the sepulchre world shadowed all members of the 3rd and those warriors who fought with them.

'No,' said Dak'ir. 'I never wanted to go back, but it is my path nonetheless. It is at the heart of this somehow.'

'Even before he was captain, Ko'tan Kadai cast a long shadow.'

Dak'ir's gaze alighted on the ground as if seeking meaning out of the darkness.

'He led us into battle that day, to return with our wayward brothers…'

'Except Nihilan was too far from our captain's reach,' Pyriel interjected. He remembered the Dragon Warrior sorcerer from long before Moribar. The signs of his eventual defection were there to see, but it is hard to look at a brother as anything else but kin. Pyriel had learned the truth. He had learned it too late, before Vel'cona or Elysius could do anything about it. Nihilan had already fled to Ushorak and the Black Dragon's *new order*. His focus returned to Dak'ir.

'You couldn't have affected the outcome of what happened in the crematoria – you need to know that, brother.'

Dak'ir exhaled deeply, levelling his gaze. He was armoured again and accepted *Draugen* from his brander-priest, T'sek. All that remained was his battle-helm.

'It doesn't matter, Pyriel. It was what it was. All the lines of fate spin from that nodal point. At Moribar we'll find the core, where all the threads begin and maybe end.'

'Regardless, a return to Moribar will stir many memories and emotions. You are psychically awakened now, Dak'ir. But you must also be prepared for that. It will be an onslaught at first, more intense than you have ever experienced–'

'I am ready, master. And have progressed greatly since the burning.'

'Let us hope so,' Pyriel replied, before muttering, *'or all of Moribar will burn in the funerary fires.'*

'Lord…' Bowed before his master, lowly T'sek proffered Dak'ir's helm in both hands.

'Thank you, T'sek. You have the patience of Vulkan,' Dak'ir reciprocated the brander-priest's genuflection before taking his battle-helm.

According to the Lexicanum's request, it had been fashioned with a section of silver plate down the left side. It resembled a human face and Dak'ir had instructed it should echo his scarred visage as closely as possible.

Pyriel found it intriguing, but nothing more. If Dak'ir wanted a reminder of the battle in the Aura Hieron Temple, site of Kadai's death and his own maiming, then so be it. Salamanders bore their burdens stoically – this was no different.

The solitorium gate opened at Pyriel's order, spilling a red oval of light down upon them from above. The grinding of gears heralded the activation of a lifter-plate, which provided sure and steady egress from the oubliette. Their heads arched towards an imaginary crimson sky, Pyriel and Dak'ir closed their eyes and left the solitorium.

Beyond the gate the rest of the Chapter Bastion beckoned. This was Hesiod, one of the Sanctuary Cities of Nocturne. Here, in the dark halls of its Chapter Bastion, the Salamanders could gather and train. Many of the Fire-born lived outside of its coal-black walls amongst the people. Here, they would inspire with their example, learn humility and self-sacrifice from those who lived it every day of their lives. Some in the Chapter, those of vaunted rank or with closed minds, believed that to associate with the human populace was to encourage their weaknesses to grow in the Astartes; that by living amongst the native

Nocturneans they were somehow brought low when their purpose was to elevate. Tu'Shan, Regent and Chapter Master, did not hold that view.

Everything a Salamander needed was in the Chapter Bastion. Apothecarion and gymnasia provided for the body; solitoria and oratoriums for the spirit; lectorums and librariums for the mind. Armouriums contained weapons and battle-cages for training. The refectories offered repast and a place to convene. They were seldom used. Serfs and brander-priests trod these lonely corridors. The Salamanders were out in the Sanctuaries and beyond, on the plains and the deserts; plying the seas and ranging the mountains. Nomadic and solitary was how many of the Fire-born lived their lives away from the fires of battle, yearning again to return to the anvil of war and be tested. But they loved their people dearly. No other Chapter, Tu'Shan was sure, had such a close link to its charges as the sons of Vulkan. It was something the Regent took great pride in and reminded his warrior brothers of regularly.

Only the forges, the hot and smoke-shrouded catacombs below the rocky foundations of the Chapter Bastions, saw frequent use. Here, the Salamanders practised their art. Here, they expressed their craft and lore over anvils and the heat of burning coals. Not all fashioned weapons; some wrought artefacts of such beauty even the greatest artisans of Terra and Ultramar would weep at the thought of them being cloistered away beneath the earth, never to be seen or appreciated. It was the Promethean way. For a Salamander, even a native Nocturnean, it was the *act* that was most important. Adoration, acclaim and appreciation did not feature in such a pragmatic mindset.

The lifter-plate alighted in an alcove appended to a long corridor. The way was lit by dulcetly burning brazier pans that lent the air the redolence of smoke. Near deserted by all but the most diligent of serfs and servitors, the two Librarians walked together in silence. Their heavy footfalls echoed loudly through empty corridors, barren temples and relic halls. In short order they reached the Bastion's north gate, which led them out into Hesiod City itself.

The arctic winter that seized Nocturne threw a pall of frozen white through the shimmering void shield surrounding the towers, elevated roadways, hab-stacks, fabricated reservoirs, mining installations and all the many structures of the city.

Hesiod was thronged with people. Its lower highways, as seen from the lofty plateau of dark granite where Pyriel and Dak'ir were standing, were jammed with bustling citizens. These were the refugees of the outer regions, seeking solace within the city's high walls and the protection of its void shield generators until the Time of Trial had ended. The harvest would follow, when all the miners, prospectors, geologists and archaeologists would set out with crews of labour-serfs, servitors and pack-beasts to reap Nocturne's bounty. Fresh veins of ore, minerals and rare gemstones were often revealed in the wake of their mother planet's wrath. Such boons were a massive economical boost to Nocturne's fortunes. Without them, the planet would face ruination of an entirely different kind and one that could not be forestalled by stout walls and implacable void shields.

Without the Sanctuaries, though, Nocturne would not survive. Regions of tectonic stability were discovered millennia ago by the first settlers of the world.

These sacred sites were conquered by its tribal kings and mapped out by its earth shamans. They were as enduring now, the iron bastions and shielded metropolises, as they ever were when they'd been crude settlements of wood and stone.

Pyriel and Dak'ir stopped to survey the crowds. Rationing lines stretched far down a narrow road, the sanctum-guard doing their best to marshal it. Here and there, Salamanders appeared amongst the masses, their voices commanding authority and their presence assuring calm in all around them. On Nocturne, respect went both ways. It was not an easy time for anyone, but better that than enduring the cold and ice beyond the Sanctuary barrier.

Dak'ir wanted to descend to the lower levels and help them. He felt humanity's plight deeper than many of his brothers. His kinship to mortals was a subject of much debate amongst some quarters; in others, it was deemed an aberration.

'Despite our mother's wrath, they endure,' Pyriel's voice came from behind him.

Dak'ir gripped a dark balustrade as he stared out across the crowds. 'How many failed to make it, do you think? Reach the Sanctuary, I mean.'

'Thousands, ten of thousands,' offered Pyriel. 'How can we be certain? I'd suggest Master Argos could provide us with a more accurate calculation.' The Epistolary came to stand beside his brother, echoing Dak'ir's stance by holding onto the balustrade. 'But ask yourself this, how many survived by virtue of its aegis? How many more would have perished in Hesiod's absence?' He smoothed the stone beneath his armoured fingertips. 'Like the people, our city endures. Seven havens across the entire planet and still

Nocturneans endure. I find their humble spirit emboldening, Dak'ir. So should you. It's an example of our people's fortitude, self-reliance and determination to survive.'

'And yet all I see is their suffering, master.' Dak'ir turned away. 'So fragile, this world and its people. Why does it feel like a dactyl egg seized by a vice? The Time of Trial comes and the vice is cinched a little tighter, one half turn of the lever. I can see the force of its iron grip webbing the egg's surface, Pyriel. I fear for Nocturne's continued endurance.'

Pyriel faced him. 'What would you have us do? Uproot to another world? This is the beating heart of our people. Its blood, their blood, is the hot magma below its fragile crust. We could no sooner leave this place than excise a Fire-born's organs and expect him to live.' Overcome by passion for just a moment, the Librarian's eyes flashed cerulean blue. 'It is part of us, Dak'ir. One cannot exist without the other.'

Dak'ir's body language suggested his demeanour hadn't changed.

Clapping a hand upon his shoulder, Pyriel added, 'These dark omens, the vision of Moribar and all the half-buried memories there have unsettled you – that is all, brother.' He slapped the hard granite of the balustrade. 'Hesiod has never been breached. Despite our volatile mother's wrath, it continues to stand. None of the Sanctuaries have ever been sundered, Dak'ir. For millennia they have stood, in one form or another. I think they will endure still.'

Meeting his master's gaze, Dak'ir sounded grim, 'Then why do I dream about the breaking of the world? Why did I witness Nocturne's destruction in my vision? It feels like a strand of prophecy is slowly coming to pass and there is nothing we can do to avert it.'

Reminded of the deciphered words on the armour recovered from Scoria, Pyriel didn't answer at first. Dak'ir's insight, his awareness, his close communion with fate and his inevitable part in it alarmed the Epistolary more than he cared to admit.

'No one can know what will pass, Dak'ir. No one. If it is fate that Nocturne will face jeopardy the likes of which it has never known, the sort of peril that would see it destroyed, then we will confront that trial. It is Vulkan's way – the Promethean Creed tells us this. You know that.'

It was no use. A dark mood had stolen upon the Lexicanum. He wouldn't be swayed.

'Pragmatism won't save us, master,' said Dak'ir, turning and walking away.

Pyriel followed a moment later, crossing the rest of the way over the bridge and to the docking pad beyond. A gunship waited for them there, and a pilot to ferry them.

BROTHER LOC'TAR WAITED for them by the open embarkation ramp. He wasn't alone.

'Master Argos,' said Pyriel as he approached the gunship and the two warriors standing beside it.

Loc'tar was wearing his power armour, the icon of the 4th, Captain Dac'tyr's company, emblazoned on his left shoulder pad. He wasn't wearing his battle-helm. Instead he held it in the crook of his arm. Across his right eye an icon of a dactyl in flight was seared into the meat of his flesh. Only pilots were permitted facial scarification before the rest of their bodies bore the legacy of their deeds. Many of Dac'tyr's warriors carried the dactyl's sigil. The company captain himself carried it, only its tail was longer, its wingspan greater and more magnificent. Master of the Fleet, Lord of the Burning Sky, was the honorific it conveyed.

Argos was no pilot, though. He was Forgemaster, one of a triumvirate unique to the Salamanders Chapter. He too went unhooded, his facial augmetics there for all to see. A steel plate emblazoned with the icon of a snarling salamander sheathed half of the Techmarine's face. The other half was decorated with honour scars, all testaments to his veterancy and deeds in the name of the Chapter. A cold light filled the artificial iris of his bionic eye but somehow still possessed the burning fervour of his other human one.

A hulking servo-harness, replete with tools and other bionic appendages, sat upon his back. It gave the Forgemaster bulk and presence, not that he needed it. Like all of the Techmarines whose secret covenant with the Martian Priesthood was known only to them and the other servants of the Cog, Argos had a slightly aloof, unknowable aura.

'I am surprised to see you here, brother,' Pyriel added, as he and Dak'ir came to stand before him.

Argos's voice was cold and metallic. It possessed a machine-like resonance devoid of emotion. His meaning was clear, however.

'As am I to see you chartering a ship during the arctic tempest,' he said. 'An atmospheric breach in these conditions is inadvisable, Brother-Librarian, so I have to assume you have good reason.' His gaze rested briefly upon Dak'ir. 'Congratulations, brother.'

'What for, my lord?'

'For surviving.'

Argos's bluntness was the conversational equivalent

of a hammer, but Dak'ir respected the Forgemaster's frank and open candour. He nodded.

His attention returned to Pyriel. 'I assume this trip you're planning is not part of the test?'

'It is not.'

'And that you are not going to disclose its nature to me, either.'

There was, inevitably, a divide between brothers of the Technicarium and the Librarius. One dealt with the tangible, the tactile, what could be grasped and seized with one's own hands; the other dealt with the ethereal, the abstract and the amorphous. It was science versus superstition and the two did not always make easy bedfellows.

Master Vel'cona's vociferous posturing on the subject did not help relations, either. The Chief of Librarians was often famously quoted regarding his thoughts on the limitations of science.

I can pulp your flesh and snap your bones in less than a second, and without so much as lifting a finger. What is the power of technology compared to that?

All who had ever heard it, Tu'Shan included, knew the good-natured fire behind it but it was incendiary nonetheless, particularly to the likes of Argos and the other two Forgemasters.

'We follow the portents and tread the lines of fate where we can, brother. It is a journey that will take us off-world. Warpcraft is unpredictable, though,' Pyriel replied.

'As I thought,' said Argos, stepping aside – not that he had ever intended stopping them. He waited until the two Librarians, master and student, were walking up the embarkation ramp before he spoke again.

'To call it craft is a misnomer, brother. To call it craft

suggests creation, permanence. Whereas, anything arising from your *art* is ephemeral at best.'

Pyriel turned to object but the flare in the Forgemaster's human eye warned him against it. 'I have performed the machine rites on your gunship myself,' said Argos. 'The *Caldera* will get you to your destination, tempest or no.'

Pyriel nodded, entered the darkness of the troop hold and the ramp closed behind him with a hard *clang*.

'Why didn't you tell him where we were going, master?' asked Dak'ir as he strapped himself into his grav-harness. The Chamber Sanctuarine of the *Caldera* had room enough for thirty warriors so armed – with just two it felt positively desolate.

Pyriel's eyes glowed deep red in the gloom, the aftermath of his spat with Brother Argos.

'Because I am still uncertain as to the validity of taking this journey, brother. And if I question it then what would the Forgemaster's reaction be?'

Dak'ir closed his eyes as the shuddering of the gunship's imminent takeoff filled the hold with noise. In the darkness, he saw a vale of bones and a long ossuary road leading down into a heart of fire.

Moribar.

CHAPTER SIX

I

Remembrance

A THIN PATINA was forming on Nihilan's armour where his body faced the ash storm. Seconds after leaving the Stormbird's hold, he was almost as grey as the corpses buried beneath his feet.

Scads of fat flakes bustled across a desolate plain, obscuring the forbidding tombs and cryptoria. They looked like fell shadows in the grey dust, old silhouettes punctuating older memories. The wind that bore them was a choking death rattle that whispered… *Moribar*.

Heavy boots crunched into the bone of the ossuary road underfoot, interrupting Nihilan's thoughts. Ramlek alighted beside him, mouth-grille frothing cinder and smoke.

'Crematoria rain,' the Dragon Warrior sorcerer remarked to him, his cold eyes fixed on the bleached yellow plains ahead.

'Eh?' grunted Ramlek, checking the load on his bolter and surveying the landing zone.

Deserted, as planned.

'The ash,' said Nihilan, catching a few flakes on his outstretched claws. 'It's called *crematoria rain*.'

Ramlek stared back at his leader without discernible expression.

Nihilan smiled thinly behind his draconic-faced battle-helm. 'You really are a single-minded bastard, aren't you, Ramlek.'

The brute grunted and stalked off into the storm.

Moments later, Nihilan was joined by Ghor'gan and Nor'hak.

'He fails to appreciate the subtleties, lord,' offered Nor'hak, his scaled power armour festooned with weapons and blades.

'Ah,' said Nihilan, leading them off after Ramlek, 'but I have you for that, brother. Ramlek was ever a blunt object, but a true sadist in spite of that.'

Nor'hak hissed. The sound was tinny and resonant through his battle-helm's vox-grille. He had no affection for the mad dog. He saw only a killer disappearing into the ash-fog, and in that vocation there lay a challenge for the well-armed Dragon Warrior.

'This place,' said Ghor'gan, oblivious to what had just passed between the others. 'It feels strange to return.'

'How many years has it been?' asked Nor'hak, his distaste at the grave dust veneering his trappings obvious.

Nihilan rasped, 'It's hard to remember… I feel him here still, though. Ushorak is with us.' His tone darkened. 'And he craves vengeance.'

Behind them, thickening ash was slowly veiling their Stormbird. Soon it would be well camouflaged. The landing site was chosen with secrecy in mind. None must know they had come back. Not yet.

Ekrine, the vessel's pilot, came through on the comm-feed.

++*Make haste!*++ he snapped. ++*This muck is already infiltrating the engine vents. I have no desire to breath in air comprised of the long dead, either*++

'Our brother whines like a tortured slave,' said Nor'hak.

Ghor'gan spat a reply, 'It cannot be rushed. Respect must be observed for the fallen. Ushorak demands it.' He clenched his taloned fists and turned around abruptly. 'I will snap him in two for his insolence.'

'Stop.' Nihilan only needed to say it once. While Ramlek, who continued to roam ahead without comment, had the loyalty of a hound, Ghor'gan's obedience was earned with something far more iron-clad – *faith*. Ever since their first visit to Moribar, clad in the 'cloth of their former lives' as Ushorak would have had it, Ghor'gan had believed in Nihilan. It seemed like centuries ago now, since their erstwhile brothers had tracked them down. Even as Ushorak sought Kelock's tomb, Nihilan had vowed they would not go down easy. Outnumbered and outgunned, he had brought the renegades together, alloyed them with his master's borrowed rhetoric. Ghor'gan saw a sorcerer no longer; he beheld a prophet. And when Nihilan fell trying to save Ushorak from destruction, he had dragged him from the fire and seen a will so great it could defy death.

'Ekrine is right,' said the sorcerer. 'We cannot delay. Our presence won't go unnoticed forever.' In a lower voice he said, 'He deals with his grief differently to you, Ghor'gan. We all have our ways, since Ushorak was… *taken.*'

Ghor'gan swung his massive frame around, a cascade of shed skin seeping through his armour joints in a fine pall quickly lost to the ash storm. The bulky trooper hefted a multi-melta and checked the weapon's ammo count belligerently as they carried on in silence.

For Nor'hak it was too much.

'I hate this place,' he said after a few moments. 'It's already dead, with nothing left to kill.'

Nihilan pointed to the horizon, where one of the ossuary roads met a stepped barrow. Shadows moved through the billowing grey, heads bowed against the dust.

Ramlek's voice answered for him through the comm-feed.

++*I see cattle*++ His distant outline, hazed in the ash-fog, crouched down like a predator sniffing prey. ++*Permission to engage, my lord*++

'Denied.'

The resulting snarl over the feed betrayed Ramlek's anger, but like a dog commanded to heel he stayed still.

Nor'hak was already on the move, raking a long-bladed dagger with a serrated edge from its scabbard.

'Quietly, brother,' Nihilan called to the grey gloom.

Nor'hak had already blended into it. The Dragon Warrior was gone.

'As quiet as the grave,' Nihilan hissed, biting his lip until drawing blood. He hid his rage well, the grief that boiled within him like a tempest. Ushorak's murderers would pay. He would destroy them all in the end, but first there would be pain.

* * *

++WE SHOULD SLAY *them*...++ muttered Ramlek, a plume of cinder spilling from his fanged vox-grille.

He was crouched in an advanced position at the entrance to a catacomb-temple, a gateway that led deep into the vaults of the world. Beyond it there was a threshold of stone slabs and spiked mausoleums where a clutch of Ecclesiarchy serfs and notaries went about their business. Bizarre cherubim-like creatures buzzed in the high eaves of the temple like insistent insects. Cardinals and lesser priests waved censers of sacred incense silently over the many tombs and grave markers. A crew of servitors wielding promethium torches went from brazier to brazier lighting each and every one.

'I agree,' Nor'hak said to his brothers, who were several metres back, obscured behind one of the monolithic remembrance stones that led up to the gate.

A burning smell affected the breeze this far down from the surface. Above, the air had been cold, frigid with death. Here, Nihilan could detect the presence of the crematoria, the molten heart of the world. Despite the radiating warmth, his blood was chilled by old memories.

'No, we wait,' he said. ++*Hold*++ he added to Ramlek through the feed.

Nor'hak was insistent. 'We can take them!'

He was about to reach out for Nihilan's arm when Ghor'gan seized his wrist.

'Release me, cur!'

Ghor'gan leaned in and wished he could display his fangs through his battle-helm. 'I'll snap it,' he promised in a growl.

'Enough.' Nihilan gazed at the temple gateway, using

his warp-sight to penetrate stone and flesh. When the glow behind his helmet lenses had faded, he added, 'There is a way through without alerting the faithful lapdogs.'

++*I see it*++ said Ramlek, catching the psychic resonance of Nihilan's speech.

'Lead us, brother.'

It was a simple challenge. The cardinals and their charges were devoted servants for certain, but they did not expect to see enemies in their midst. Moribar was a sepulchre world. Here, the dead were supposed to rest. Theirs was a quiet duty. They were oblivious in their faithful ministrations, unaware that death stalked amongst them. In a few minutes, the Dragon Warriors were through the catacomb-temple's threshold and entered the bowels of Moribar itself.

Even in the darkness and the flickering crematoria shadows, bent-backed serfs toiled. They were gravediggers and corpse-men, the interrers of the dead, the burners of flesh and bone. Massive iron incinerators punctuated the lower tunnels like blockhouses. Lines of thin and sallow men, wheezing from the inhalation of too much tomb-dust, moved slowly towards the fiery gates of the incinerators. Upon their backs, or piled slovenly in carts and or on top of litters, were cadavers. Some were so emaciated they looked almost skeletal.

These were the labour tunnels and Nihilan was glad to avoid them. His destination and that of his warriors lay much deeper, far down into the basin of the catacomb world.

At its nadir they met the reaper.

Nihilan alone stood before it, unarmed and with arms wide in plaintive supplication.

'Why does he abase himself before that *thing*?' snapped Nor'hak from the shadows.

The others stayed out of sight as ordered but could still witness the exchange between the sorcerer and the grey giant clad in robes of stone. A heavy granite cowl concealed the reaper's features. It clutched a heavy bone-scythe in thin, long fingers. No sigils adorned it, no ornamentation or finery detracted from the purity of its form. It was like a hooded angel with its wings clipped, hewn from a tomb-maker's slab and given life. Only the whirring of servos, the click and churn of mechanical components gave truth to this lie.

'He shows allegiance to gain its trust,' Ghor'gan answered, rapt at the display.

Nor'hak whirled to face him. 'It is a machine. What trust can it possess?'

'The trust its makers have imbued it with.'

None shall pass.

The reaper's augmetic voice boomed like prophecy from the dark void of its hood.

Only the dead.

A loud *chunk* followed by a hiss of pneumatic pressure being released heralded movement. The stone cladding of its robes parted a fraction and it came forwards as if manoeuvring on a track-bed.

None shall pass.

Slowly, it raised the bone-scythe, its blade edge shimmering with electrical energy.

Nor'hak was on his feet before Ghor'gan thrust him down again.

'He'll be cut in two!'

Even Ramlek, though shackled by his master's orders, looked ready to break out his bolter. He turned to Ghor'gan, clenching and unclenching his fists, smoke and cinder spitting from his vox-grille in apoplectic fits.

'Wait…' Ghor'gan told them. 'Have faith.'

They watched the reaper's shadow fall over Nihilan who still had not moved. When it was close enough, the sorcerer uttered something too soft for them to hear. The effect, however, was all too obvious. The reaper froze as if cast in amber. Nihilan lowered his arms, beckoning the mechanised golem down with an outstretched finger. He leaned in when the reaper was at the height of his battle-helm and uttered something else, straight into the cerebral processor that passed for its brain.

Then he turned and walked away.

'What did you do?' asked Nor'hak when Nihilan had returned, one eye on his master, the other on the reaper as it returned to its post.

'Tell me something, Nor'hak,' he said. 'When we were preparing to face our end against the Salamanders, how do you think Ushorak infiltrated the catacomb vaults?'

'Past that thing, I have no idea.'

'Knowledge, brother,' Nihilan answered, tapping Nor'hak on the forehead through his battle-helm. 'I am no preacher,' he continued, 'but *words*, not just weapons, have power too.'

Nihilan laughed at the open belligerence in Nor'hak's posture. He enjoyed teasing the highly-strung assassin. Had he not been such a superlative killer, he might have disposed of him years ago.

'Once I had its attention, I left it with something. A *trigger*.'

'How can you be sure they'll come, master?' asked Ghor'gan as they stalked back up the tunnel.

'Oh they will come, brother. They will come, but they must not know what we took from here. After what we're about to do, they will hunt us, scour every battlefield they have ever fought us on. This, here on Moribar, is our birth site. Here is where they'll look hardest. One amongst them, his eyes will be opened. When they do, I will shut them again. Permanently.'

'And now?' asked Ramlek, his patience with cloak and dagger nearly spent.

Nihilan's eyes burned. 'Now we return to the ship, where Ekrine has a course ready-plotted.'

'To where?' snapped Nor'hak.

'A nothing world really,' Nihilan replied. 'But *they* will remember its name – Stratos.'

II
What Fate for Heroes…?

'Retreat, retreat in good order, by Throne!'

The vox-link went dead in General Slayte's grasp. Pressing his dry lips to the receiver cup, he was about to speak again but his only answer would've been cold static.

'Open a channel to Major Guivan,' he said to Sergeant Colmm, his aide and vox-man, in a breathless whisper. 'Tell him he has field command. Colonel Hadrian is dead.'

'And with him, the bulk of the 83rd battalion,' an insidious voice said from the shadows with more than a mere hint of accusation.

Wiping the sweat from his wrinkled brow, the general faced the speaker.

'If you have something *inspirational* to share with us, Krakvarr, I'd suggest now is the time.'

The commissar leaned forwards, a stick of tabac snared between his thin fingers drooling smoke.

'Only that we should advance, and crush this alien scum beneath our booted heels. Relent and it will only drive the jackals at us harder. They already have our scent.'

General Slayte scowled, showing his teeth before turning to his command staff. A clutch of aides, officers and tactical savants were huddled over a hololithic display plotting the movements of the Night Devils regiment and those of reported enemy sightings in relation to them.

The scene rendered in grainy amber, flickering with every percussive shell detonation felt through the bunker's ferrocrete walls, was an erratic mess. The xenos had pushed and pulled their forces in myriad directions, first dividing and then massacring. Small groups, isolated platoons or straggling squads, were despatched first. Weak before the strong, that was the way of it. Then the larger battle groups were hit with ambuscade or slowly withered away by lightning attacks when at camp or after dark. Fear like a contagion was running through the regiment with virulence and every man, even Krakvarr, bore symptoms.

General Amadeus Slayte was a proud man and an accomplished commander. His medals and laurels weighed heavy on his uniform, never more so than this moment. Reprimanded to the backlines by the Astartes, managing refugee columns and protecting assets already won, Slayte was secretly overjoyed at Commander Agatone's order for him to return to the front. Joy turned to dismay when he learned of Chaplain Elysius's disappearance.

Locked in battle at the Ferron Straits, the

Salamanders could not intervene. Not yet. The Night Devils answered the call. A slow but determined march to the edge of Ironlandings followed a rapid muster, the men eager to fight and die for the Emperor. And die they did, all too readily.

Slayte believed that with the troops and armour at his disposal, making inroads to the Capitol would have been relatively straightforward. After all, these xenos, dusk-wraiths as the Astartes called them, were scavengers.

He remembered the quiet before the screaming. It was a dark lullaby that sent him to nightmarish places when he'd managed snatches of sleep in the intervening weeks. The advanced elements were hit first, seemingly from all directions.

An insect drone presaged an attack from gliders, skiffs and hover-bikes. Half-naked warrior-wyches plunged down from on high, reaping heads with their barbs and glaives. Creatures with gelid skin the colour of alabaster, strange even amongst the xenos, materialised out of the air and set about butchering with sharp, flashing knives. What passed for troops of the line, their segmented armour edged and bloody, shot whickering bursts of flechette fire into the Imperial ranks. A side glance at his carapace armour, and Slayte saw the remnants of splinter fire still embedded in the torso section and shoulder guard. His first adjutant, Nokk, had been shredded in the general's place. He was not alone.

The road to Ironlandings had run red with blood, its rugged ore fields soaked in gore.

Dusk-wraiths, the Salamanders had called them, foes from a bygone age. Slayte knew them as the dark eldar. He knew them as nightmares made flesh.

In his command bunker, a prefabricated structure of ferrocrete and leather tarpaulins, his command staff pored over battle plans whilst he tried to contact his commanders in the field. So far, the only tactic that had worked a damn was a retreat by degrees to the Ironlandings border. At least, it had worked at first. Now the xenos had blood in their nostrils and a hunger that had to be slaked.

'They have us outmanoeuvred,' offered Major Schaeffen, somewhat redundantly. He chewed on an unlit pipe, an affectation he'd acquired since he'd run out of tabac.

'We are slowly being encircled, major...' Slayte replied ominously, giving up on the vox cup and picking up his battered armour. He thought again about trying to remove the splinters but they were hideously sharp. Colmm had tried with a pair of pliers but ended up just wrecking his tools.

'What are you doing, general?' asked Krakvarr from the shadows.

Slayte shrugged on the carapace body armour, fastening the straps while Colmm fixed the shoulder guards. 'Stepping out. I'll not cower in this bunker waiting for them to come to us. They are on their way. Let's meet them.'

Krakvarr nodded, taking up his bolt pistol and cap. 'This is the Emperor's work we do, Amadeus.'

'No, they're the deeds of mad men, but what other choice is there?'

'*Only in Death does duty end,*' the commissar quoted from the Tactica Imperium.

'Guns and boots, men,' Slayte told the command staff. 'Leave the maps. We won't be needing them any more.'

A strange fatalistic resolve had settled over the command bunker even as the familiar drone started up in the distance. It would be much louder outside the ferrocrete walls.

In the assembly yard beyond, Slayte's storm-trooper platoon awaited him. Three armoured Chimera tanks, pintle gunners sat idly at their posts, would convey the general and his staff.

'Sergeant Colmm,' said Slayte as he strode from the bunker to see a sky as visceral as freshly shed blood. Jagged silhouettes, like unsheathed blades, were moving towards them across it. 'Contact the other commanders. Converge on our position, full assault.'

'Suicide or glory, general?' Schaeffen posited, the unlit pipe bobbing up and down between his grinning lips.

'I think suicide, major,' Slayte replied, 'We have grossly underestimated our enemy. Even the Emperor's angels cannot contain them. They are not scavenging or raiding at all.'

'Then what?' asked Krakvarr just before mounting the embarkation ramp to the second Chimera.

'I wish I knew, commissar. I wish I knew.' Slayte disappeared into the troop hold, followed by his command staff. The ramp slammed shut and the last of the Night Devils platoons headed towards certain death.

IT WAS APPROXIMATELY three hundred and fifty-six metres past the Ironlandings border that they met their end.

Krakvarr's Chimera was the first to be hit. The commissar was ensconced in the hatch, using it like a pulpit, spitting dogma and phlegmatic rhetoric to the

men. He was halfway through a sermon evincing the
weakness of the alien when something inhumanly
fast, and so sharp it made a scything noise through
the air, flashed by the tank. Krakvarr was arrested
mid-speech, his idiot mouth lolling before his head
fell from his shoulders. A half-second later a long
range salvo from a distant skiff ripped into the front
of the tank. The armoured glacis parted like
parchment before a dark beam that skewered three
crew and four storm-troopers riding in the troop hold
before passing out the other side. Fuel tanks cooked
in a micro-second. The carrier exploded with a loud
crack, fire, smoke and shrapnel filling the air around
it.

Slayte, standing proud in the hatch of his own
Chimera, Sergeant Colmm alongside him acting as
gunner, gave the order to adopt defensive formations
and repel attackers.

The dark eldar fell upon them like scythed rain. One
moment the threat was distant, the next it was
amongst them cutting and cleaving.

They manoeuvred in packs, held aloft on anti-
gravitic boards and bikes or borne along by their
hovering, bladed skiffs. Long-nosed cannons set at the
skiffs' prows spat dark lances of energy that tore apart
metal and roasted flesh. The warriors aboard, gripping
long chains and strips of leather as they bent over the
long platforms running along the spine of the skiffs,
cackled and wailed with perverse glee as they dis-
charged their rifles.

On one skiff was a horde of semi-naked warrior-
wyches, males and females both, though such was the
androgynous nature of the race it was hard to tell the
difference. They wielded barbs and tridents, nets and

glaives, smiling maliciously at the thought of imminent carnage. Together, the raiders moved in low,
sweeping arcs. It was obvious they were trying to encir-
cle the Imperial battle group.

Slayte sighted down his pistol at a trio of xenos
mounted on anti-gravitic boards. His shot missed, the
shrieking hellions able to change course in an eye-
blink. Then Colmm was choking, dropping the heavy
stubber before he'd had chance to yoke the triggers.
His hands went to his neck where Slayte just made out
a long, silver thread. The aide was ripped from the
hatch, gurgling blood, and lofted into the air, lost in
the hellish Geviox sunlight.

Around him the sharp crack of hellguns met the
whickering report of eldar splinter fire. Men were
screaming, spun about, their faces embedded with
shards and streaming blood. From his vantage point,
Slayte could see lithe figures moving through the carnage, splitting bodies with their blades. One
somersaulted acrobatically onto the front of the other
Chimera. Major Schaeffen had drawn his laspistol and
was firing off bursts from the hatch. But it was as if
time had slowed around the wych and she ducked and
weaved around every blast. Each step took her closer
until she was face-to-face with the Night Devils major
who brought his sidearm around for one last desperate shot. With serpentine speed she sent the flat of her
hand into Schaeffen's mouth, propelling the unlit pipe
into his throat for him to choke on. As he spluttered
his last breaths, turning as grey as his uniform, the
wych woman opened him up with her blades and
spilled the major's innards all over the front of his
tank. It took seconds, and after she was gone before
Slayte could draw a bead.

'Pull together!' he cried through the loud hailer attached to the hatch. 'Hold the line!'

It was insane. *He* was insane. They never should have left the bunker. Damn Geviox to the Night-Hells and damn the bastard eldar. He seized the heavy stubber, ripping it from its pintle mount as a cadre of jet-bikers hove into view, the general in their sights. Bracing the weapon against the lip of the hatch, he backed against the opposite side of the rim and hauled on the triggers.

The recoil was so fierce it reminded him of his first Valkyrie air-drop. He'd been a member of the elite storm-troopers back then. So many years ago. They were less complicated times and Slayte found himself longing for them again as the stubber spat hot metal from its mouth. A long line of tracer fire tore into the bikers, winging one machine and exploding another.

'Feggers,' spat Slayte, employing an old oath from the Night Devils' home world. The grin on his face was born of fatalistic abandon, for one of the bikers survived the salvo and was coming for him. She didn't wear a helmet and her eyes were alight with perverse malice as she swung a long, serrated blade around.

Slayte yanked on the triggers again. His heart sank when the hard *chank* of a jam came back at him. She'd ducked, the alien bitch, anticipating the move. When she returned, her expression was etched with sadistic glee.

You're mine, said the eyes. *You'll suffer*, said lips pursed in the shape of a kiss.

A storm-trooper, looked like Sergeant Donnsk, popped up in the hatch next to Slayte, hefting a hell-gun. A burst of splinter fire from the biker's front-mounted cannons ripped up half of his face and tore his shoulder to hot, red ribbons of meat. Donnsk dropped without a whimper.

Slayte had his pistol out again. If this was to be the end then he'd die with a weapon in his hand, by Throne.

The Night Devils were being massacred. Encircled and out-positioned, they were like cattle being led to slaughter. All barring Slayte's Chimera had been gutted, though now the general came to think of it, there were strange, gurgling noises emanating from below him. Small pockets of resistance made a brave fist of it. These men were some of the Imperial Guard's finest – even faced with such odds they didn't flinch or retreat. But the xenos bodies that peppered the almost wholesale slaughter of the humans weren't enough, not nearly enough.

This, Slayte perceived as time condensed into a single moment, his last moment upon this iron-soaked, rusting rock.

The hammer fell on his bolt pistol and the round boomed from the chamber with all the slow purpose of an avalanche. The cone of fire projected from the muzzle flared incandescently for what seemed like minutes, extending and retracting like a flicking tongue.

She weaved around the burst on her jet bike, as if moving in some different, more advantageous, temporal sphere and Slayte accepted the inevitability of her reaching blade. He expected painful death. He didn't expect a green comet to come from on high and smite her where she hovered.

A heavy weight slammed into the Chimera, denting the armoured glacis. It bore the jet-bike down with it, the whirr of chainblades cutting the rider's screams to an inchoate half-shriek.

Time resumed its normal rate and Slayte beheld the form of a giant standing in front of him. More comets were thundering down around him, across the entire battlefield. The warrior half-turned, showing one side of a battle-helm fashioned into the snarling form of a lizard. At his back, a scaled hide fluttered.

'To your men,' said the warrior, his voice deep and rumbling. 'The Salamanders are here for your salvation.'

CHAPTER SEVEN

I
Dragonfall

FROM THE OPEN side-hatch of the gunship's troop hold, Praetor beheld a slaughter. The dusk-wraiths were running rings around the Guard's defensive cordon, pulling their fire hither and thither until it was almost totally ineffective. He marvelled at their discipline, to sustain such grievous casualties but still maintain formation. But discipline would not save them.

Even now, leather-clad harridans were moving through the Guardsman ranks cutting and shrieking. They used the smoke and processor haze to conceal their assaults, leaping down into the abyssal steam and emerging only to kill before disappearing again. Around the edges of the slowly fragmenting formations, the warriors ranging on the skiffs, hover-boards and jet-bikes tightened the noose. From within, their firing lines were undermined by the semi-garbed assassins.

Through his retinal display, Praetor saw it all. The steam and smoke was no barrier. It angered him to see such wanton massacre. He also saw the larger blade-prowed vessel, kin to the other, smaller skiffs. A command transport, Praetor had no doubt. He knew the dark eldar menace well – the Salamanders Chapter was well-versed in lessons of their depravity. He also knew of their secrets, some of them at least, of the curse they harboured and the malady that had plagued them since the dawning of time itself. Few in the Chapter knew much about it; Praetor was one of them. He'stan's knowledge of the dusk-wraiths was unrivalled, even by that of the Chapter Master himself.

Standing alongside him, the Forgefather's body language was unreadable.

Behind them, nineteen more Firedrakes had released grav-harnesses and were mag-locked to the deck ready for deployment. The assault pattern was called *dragonfall*. It had been a while since they'd attempted it.

Praetor spoke into the comm-feed of his gorget, linked to the *Implacable's* pilot.

'Bring us in close, brother.'

A clipped affirmative returned from the cockpit. They'd attracted some attention already. A lance of dark energy stabbed passed the hull sending heat warnings across Praetor's retinal display. He ignored them, intent on the battlefield below.

'Closer,' he repeated, and the gunship dropped another five metres.

The wind was ripping into the hold with the speed of their descent but the Firedrakes didn't move. They remained still, only their glowing eyes providing any clue that their power armour was even populated.

'You must attack swiftly, break the links in the chain

and release those men from its bondage,' uttered He'stan.

Praetor smiled. Only the Forgefather would ever speak like that. It felt old, full of gravitas and import. Even his words and manner were impressive.

'And you, my lord?' the veteran sergeant returned.

He'stan didn't turn; his gaze was fixed on the battle unfolding beneath. Already, he was reading, predicting, strategising.

'I will seek the serpent's head,' he answered, 'and cut it off.'

Praetor felt He'stan tense next to him, the slightest bend in his knees.

++*You have your mission protocols*++ the veteran sergeant said quickly over the comm-feed. ++*Shatter that cordon, brothers. Rescue those men*++

Seventeen metres from the ground, he turned to the others.

'In Vulkan's name,' he roared.

Beside him, He'stan leapt from the hold and into the blood-red light.

A few seconds later, Praetor followed.

THE AIR THUNDERED past him in a blur, collision warnings flashing amber across Praetor's tactical display. A few metres below, He'stan had angled his body like an arrow. His spear was held out in front of him, the Gauntlet of the Forge clasped to his chest so he was as aerodynamic as possible. He hit the ground less than five seconds before Praetor but the veteran sergeant marvelled at the carnage he wrought in that short space of time. A blow from the Spear of Vulkan severed a skiff in half, its bifurcated ends pulling away from each other like a sinking ship with its back broken. Fire and shrapnel from the engine explosion tossed ragged eldar corpses into the air. He'stan was engulfed but merely moved through the storm, plumes of fire rolling off his armour in waves. The Gauntlet of the Forge was unleashed and the survivors of the blast burned.

Praetor lost sight of the Forgefather when he hit the ground feet first, thunder hammer aloft like that of a descending god.

'We are the hammer!' he bellowed, smashing the weapon's head down as he landed. A brutal shockwave rippled across the ground centred at the point of impact that threw dark eldar warriors off their feet. Leading with his shoulder, Praetor kept up the momentum. A screaming wych-woman aimed a barbed trident at his face that he deflected with his storm shield. He missed with his thunder hammer, but dented her face in with the drake boss on his shield. Another he crushed with the backswing. A third he broke with a blow from the hammer's haft. Even without Terminator armour, he was brutal. Lead by example – that was the Promethean way. Praetor was as merciless as a volcano, as unyielding as an avalanche.

Sustained bolter fire raked air already fraught with screaming. Shells streaked past the veteran sergeant as he led the charge, exploding the frail xenos in gory eruptions. Blood and viscera spoiled his power armour in a fine spray but Praetor was undaunted, intent on reaching the edge of the circle and breaking it.

According to the battle plan, the two squads of Firedrakes had split into four, five warriors each tackling an aspect of the dark eldar's cordon of death. Upon landfall, Praetor broke off with his squad, the

Forgefather ahead of them and fighting where he chose. Halknarr and four of his warriors went northward, designated *Assault Point Spear*. Praetor was headed east on *Assault Point Hammer*.

Daedicus and another Firedrake called Mek'tar, both acting as de-facto squad leaders, came a few seconds later when the *Implacable* had repositioned, at the opposite arc of the circle. They took *Anvil* and *Flame* respectively.

Used to fighting forces that were outmanoeuvred and outmatched, the dark eldar reeled against the shock and awe tactics employed by the Firedrakes. In moments they'd struck the toughest elements of the xenos force and managed to break the barbed ring around the Night Devils. Slowly they dismantled the raiders.

'Break them on the anvil, brothers!' Some of Praetor's old bombast was returning. He crushed the skull of a hellion, who was struggling to rise from the wreckage of his hover-board. With a stomp of his armoured boot, he mulched its fragile ribcage. A squeal of perverse pleasure slipped from the wretch's lips before it died. Praetor scowled behind the snarling visage of his battle-helm.

++*These creatures disgust me*++

It was Halknarr who replied.

++*Then let's crush them swiftly, brother, and find our Chaplain*++

As he killed, Praetor reviewed the data streaming across his retinal display. Ironlandings' Capitol was nearby. Elements of the Night Devils were locked in battle around it, having abandoned more advanced positions when the xenos had forced a retreat.

Galvanise the Guard, cohere them, marshal them

forward – once the Firedrakes had achieved that they could penetrate the Capitol and discover Elysius's fate and that of the Sigil.

All that mattered was the Sigil.

In the distance, Mek'tar's combat squad made land-fall. Praetor pressed on. Already, the Forgefather was getting ahead of them. One of their squad seemed to be keeping pace, however.

Tsu'gan revelled in the act of war. He had fought battles before, many of them. The blood he'd shed in the Emperor's name and the name of the primarch would turn the Pyre Desert red, or so he'd always imagined. Death had haunted his dreams, now it plagued his waking hours too – only by enacting it upon his enemies did he feel any peace. This was different, though. Firedrakes made war like avatars of death. Though stoic and implacable as any Salamander, they fought with such… fire. Stripped of their Terminator armour for this mission, they moved with a dynamism and intent that belied their Nocturnean heritage.

A spit of flame surged across Tsu'gan's flank. His snarl turned to a feral grin as he watched the xenos who were caught in its blaze burn.

Brother Vo'kar offered no apology as he ran on, twisting around to send another burst of super-heated promethium into the dark eldar ranks.

Increasing his pace, Tsu'gan overtook him. The Forgefather was just ahead in the thick of it. He was determined to stay on the great warrior's heels. Something about him, his spirit or his unknowable presence quieted the darkness in Tsu'gan's soul. He saw more than a hero before him, rending and burning the xenos scum; he saw the possibility of salvation.

Thick squalls of factorum-steam from the ore pro-cessing plants were swathing the battlefield now. Blood-mist from exsanguinated Guardsmen merged with heavy metal dust, filling the air with a coppery stink. Filtering out the interference through his retinal display, Tsu'gan found He'stan.

He had a dark eldar impaled on his spear, hoisting it into the air before turning it to ash with his gauntlet. Even as the corpse was flaking away on the breeze, He'stan swept the haft around and decapitated a screeching wych-warrior with the blade.

Coming up alongside him, Tsu'gan hacked the head-less corpse down with his chainsword before gunning another apart with his bolter.

More dark eldar were coming. They pressed in from the sides, slipping through the ragged Night Devils ranks with ease and closing on the real threat, the Space Marines in their midst. Tsu'gan missed the clash by the smallest of margins as Praetor and the others were swept up in a tide of mutated beasts and dark eldar cult warriors now running rampant across the field.

++*Stay with him!*++ urged Praetor through the comm-feed.

Tsu'gan released a burst from his combi-bolter, shredding a wych, before switching to the flamer attachment and burning down a horde of gibbering mutants. He had no intention of letting He'stan fight alone.

'This rabble are nothing,' he cried.

'Hone your anger, Tsu'gan,' said He'stan, allowing the Firedrake to come up alongside his left flank. 'Use it.'

Another Firedrake had once said something similar

to him. Gathimu. But that warrior was long dead. Tsu'gan used his rage to quash the sudden grief welling inside him.

'They already flee, though, my lord.'

Tsu'gan was right. Jet-bikers and board-riding hellions were pulling out of the fight, letting the fodder take the strain. A distant, but closing, figure railed at them to return from the back of his skiff but the xenos only laughed and jeered.

'Honourless dogs,' muttered He'stan. His gaze was locked on something ahead, something through the mists that Tsu'gan couldn't see.

They pressed on through a sudden surge of dark eldar warriors diverted from slaughtering the Night Devils, presumably at the distant commander's bidding. He'stan cut a bloody path through them, intent on the skiff and the leader of the raiders. Two warrior wyches closed in on either flank, their blades flashing like lightning on the sun. The Forgefather caught one in his armoured fist and snapped the other with a blow from his spear.

Together, they cut through the warriors. The brief engagement ended when Tsu'gan gunned down the startled wyches with a pair of bolter bursts.

++*Close the dragon's jaws*++ said He'stan over the comm-feed. ++*I have the serpent in my sights*++

Three command runes winked on Tsu'gan's retinal display, confirmation from the squad leaders. The icons representing his brothers' positions in the field started to close in.

The two Salamanders were in the thick of it now. Isolated pockets of Guardsmen still held out, retreating into circle formations, hellguns held out and spitting las. Where he could, He'stan dragged the humans out of harm's way or interceded where a splinter blast would've killed one. All the while he advanced, and Tsu'gan marvelled at how he balanced the taking and preserving of life so expertly.

Gliding swiftly through the hot miasma of steam, knifing through the air with its bladed prow, the command skiff was soon upon them. It hovered a few metres away, the leader's cohorts poised to leap from its barbed flanks and attack. Tsu'gan estimated around twenty warriors aboard, mostly clan troops but with a single, tall wych-woman wearing a strange, domino mask. She carried a pair of bloodstained daggers, held at rest against her thighs.

Three long-nosed cannons of dark, ridged metal made up the command skiff's frontal arc. With a shriek of xenos dialect, the leader-caste ordered them aimed at He'stan.

The Forgefather didn't wait for the salvo. He launched his spear with all the poise and grace of a supreme athlete and tore a hole through the skiff's engine rig. Smoke and fire plumed from the vehicle that was losing loft by the second, upsetting the aim of the gunners who clung to the railings of their stations desperately.

An explosion followed swiftly, rippling up the long insectoid body of the skiff, tearing its mounting platforms into twisted metal and throwing its passengers skyward. The vehicle ditched, flames now wreathing its fragile hull, and went down bladed nose first into the ruddy dirt as a secondary explosion ripped what was left of it into scrap.

Tsu'gan tracked a silhouette as it leapt from the skiff's broken back. For a moment he lost it in the scudding steam banks but then it landed a few metres from the wreckage on one knee with its head bowed.

The dark eldar leader had avoided the blast. So too had his female concubine, though Tsu'gan had not even seen her escape and yet here she was, standing alongside him.

Two against two. Xenos versus Astartes.

Tsu'gan revved his chainblade. It was about to get messy.

He'stan was already running towards them, focussed on the leader, ready to pummel the creature with his gauntlet.

The leader rose fluidly, like a silken shadow, and raced to meet him. A two-handed glaive, crackling with dark energies, appeared in its grasp where before it had seemingly been unarmed. The long mane of hair flowing from beneath its wildly grinning battle-helm caught in the breeze and snapped like irate vipers.

He'stan's first swing missed.

The xenos dodged aside, almost impossibly, and caught the Forgefather a glancing blow against his forearm. Without the spear he was at a disadvantage, one the dark eldar exploited with sharp thrusts of his pole-arm.

Tsu'gan reached the duellists and weighed in against the wych with a swipe of his chainblade. Clad in strips of leather and metal plates, much of her body was on display. She was more muscular than the male but moved with a dancer's grace. She avoided the attack with audacious ease before flipping away from Tsu'gan's return blow. Then something very strange happened. She gave the leader a lascivious glance, pursed her lips in a mocking kiss and fled.

Suddenly two against two had become two against one.

The leader evidently didn't like his odds and backed off, but couldn't escape. Like desert nomads herding a recalcitrant sauroch, Tsu'gan and He'stan encircled the dark eldar and drew in close. Despite his supreme acrobatics, the xenos was breathing hard from his exertions.

'You are doomed, alien,' He'stan told him, edging towards him with caution. 'Submit now and I will make it clean.'

Glancing at his retinal display, Tsu'gan saw his brothers were still engaged battling the rest of the horde. He alone fought with the Forgefather. His pride soared and he longed to strike the killing blow with He'stan.

The Salamanders were less than three metres away when the dark eldar bowed and a strange sensation stole over Tsu'gan. It was akin to all of the air being sucked slowly from his body, except it wasn't air he was losing.

When the xenos stood up straight again, he had a speculum held between the thumb and forefinger of his left hand. The other still grasped the glaive, though upright and planted into the ground like a banner.

When he made to move forwards, Tsu'gan's footing faltered. He was weak, his vision spinning. He felt thin, thinner with each passing moment in front of that mirror. His armoured face was reflected in it, the burning light in his eyes reduced to dying embers.

'Wha...' was all could manage to say as his chain-blade and bolter fell from his grasp and he collapsed to one knee clutching his chest.

'Steel yourself,' snarled He'stan, though the effort in his voice was all too clear.

Was it warp sorcery? The xenos didn't have the bearing

of a psyker... Tsu'gan's mind reeled as he tried to cling on to something as incorporeal as smoke leaking from his body.

He'stan took a step forwards then he, too, fell to one knee. He raised the Gauntlet of the Forge, fingers grasping.

Laughter, shrill and cruel, emanated from beneath the dark eldar's helmet.

'Overconfidence,' growled He'stan through ragged breaths, 'will prove your undoing. I promised you a clean death if you gave in. Now you'll suffer.'

A bright plume of flame gushed from his gauntlet. The cackling xenos saw the danger too late and was unable to skip away as the conflagration engulfed him. The speculum shattered in the heat. Tsu'gan felt his vitality return in a rush. As he was rising, He'stan was already fully recovered and on his feet. He wrenched his spear from where it had embedded in the ground and rammed it through the flailing dark eldar's burning torso. With a grunt, he tore it free and the xenos slumped down, blood oozing from his charred remains.

'What was that... *artefact*?' asked Tsu'gan, still rubbing his chest but virtually recovered. 'It felt like a piece of me was bleeding into the glass.'

'It was,' He'stan answered simply. 'Much longer and you would be a shell standing next to me, not a Fireborn at all.'

'Was it the warp?'

Around them the battle was slowly winding down. With the death or flight of their leaders, the dark eldar were finished. Their circle was broken, the majority of their warriors fled, the rest dead or soon to be put down by jubilant Night Devil troopers.

'Not the warp, brother,' He'stan told him. He grasped Tsu'gan by the shoulder and looked into the lenses of his battle-helm where his eyes blazed once more.

He held him like that for several seconds – all the while Tsu'gan felt his resolve and purpose returning – before letting him go.

'You are whole,' He'stan added. 'It was a webway mirror the fiend used against us, ancient science, not sorcery of any kind. It was your soul it was draining, Tsu'gan.'

Tsu'gan knew the dark eldar, like all of the xenos races, had infernal technologies they used to prosecute their wars and bring man beneath their yoke, but this? To strip another's soul? A shudder of the closest thing the Salamander could feel to fear ran down the back of his neck.

There was no time for further discussion. Praetor and the others had joined them.

The veteran sergeant carried a heavy gash to the right temple of his battle-helm but appeared none the worse for wear. As expected, they'd sustained no casualties.

'The chain is broken and the xenos flee into the mists,' declared Halknarr somewhat unnecessarily. The presence of the Forgefather was affecting his demeanour.

'Aye, but they'll return,' said Praetor. 'We should make all haste to the Capitol. Vulkan knows what Elysius's fate might be by now.'

'And the fate of our battle-brothers,' whispered Tsu'gan in a hollow voice. His thoughts were of Iagon. He remembered the pain in his brother's eyes when he'd told him of his ascension, that he would not be joining him. He regretted leaving Iagon behind, but what choice did he have? Iagon had not taken it well.

His manner was calm and curbed, but Tsu'gan could read the Salamander's humours. Iagon had felt betrayed.

Through the slowly clearing mist, a small party of men approached the Salamanders. They looked in awe of the massive warriors, who turned as one to look upon the Night Devil command group. The Space Marines' posture and bearing was unintentionally, but unavoidably, intimidating.

Only one of the men, a gruff-looking general who wore the black and grey of his uniform as proudly as the Fire-born wore their power amour, seemed undaunted.

'General Slayte,' said the man, introducing himself and sketching a crisp salute. His fatigues were battle-worn, his officer's jacket and cap splattered with dark patches of blood. Some of it was his. The bolt pistol in his holster was an heirloom but well-used. This was a man of war that stood before them, not some toy soldier more concerned with polishing his medals than fighting on campaign.

Praetor liked him instantly.

'Brother-Sergeant Praetor,' he said in return, extending his gauntleted hand.

The general took it, though it dwarfed his own, and removed his cap once his had had been released again.

'We are in your debt, Astartes,' he said, wiping his brow with a bloodstained sleeve. He shifted his gaze to Halknarr, 'and I to you personally, my lord.'

Halknarr merely nodded, affecting an air of aloof disdain in the presence of the human commander.

'What is the status of your force, general?' asked Praetor, making a rudimentary visual assessment of the troopers that were slowly gathering back into formation at the bellowed orders of their sergeants.

Slayte's attention returned to Praetor.

'My commissar is dead. I have lost a major and two corporals. I survive by dint of the Emperor's intervention and I'd posit just over two hundred and fifty of my five-hundred-strong battle group still live. And of those, close to another hundred are wounded. In short, my lord, we are in ragged shape.'

Praetor exchanged a glance with Halknarr. The other sergeant had removed his battle-helm to better taste the heat on the air. His eyes were hooded but stern. They told Praetor they could ill-afford stragglers. Without the Firedrake escort, though, Slayte and his men might fall foul of another ambush. And in their current condition, they'd likely be massacred. That couldn't happen.

'You'll accompany us until you can be rejoined with the rest of your forces,' Praetor decided. He sought He'stan in the throng for his silent approval but the Forgefather was gone. So was Tsu'gan. 'But we are moving swiftly. Stay with us or fall behind. We are not here as liberators, general,' he added. 'Ironlandings will have to look to its own protection.'

General Slayte smiled, exposing his bloodied teeth.

'Just get me to the rest of my men, and I'll take care of that. You've broken their backs, we can do the rest.'

Tsu'gan met He'stan a few metres away from where their brothers had gathered. His gaze was in the distance, at the looming spectre of the bastion; so too was his mind.

'What is it, my lord?' Tsu'gan asked.

'Something is wrong here,' He'stan replied, the

Geviox sunlight bathing his armour an ugly, visceral red, 'something is very wrong.'

'Is it Chaplain Elysius?'

'It is more than that, Tsu'gan.'

'Is he... he's not *dead*?'

It was an impossible question. There was no way He'stan could have known Elysius's fate, yet Tsu'gan asked it all the same. Something powerful was at work with the Forgefather, a wisdom and insight that wasn't prescience but was also stronger than merely instinct.

'I don't know,' He'stan replied, facing him, 'but I do not think he is even here.'

II
Loss and Lamentation

A CRACK OF lightning threw the grooves in Elysius's armour into sharp relief. An eldritch wind pricked at his long white hair that hung low, obscuring his naked face. His back was arched, the heavy weight fastened to his neck forcing him to learn forwards. He braced his hand against the hard metal of the deck where he kneeled. The other one, his power fist, had been removed and a tangle of ragged wires sagged from the socket like intestines. There were furrows in his battle-plate where the barbs and lashes had stung him. He'd forgotten what had happened to his battle-helm. It was lost. They were all lost. Silently, surrounded by darkness and the perpetual lightning storm, he beseeched the Emperor for aid. His lips moved soundlessly as he performed a benediction over his brothers and the others not of the Chapter shackled alongside him.

'Look, Helspereth,' cried one of the dark eldar whelp-masters aboard the great slave skiff, 'the mon-keigh babbles to the night. Madness has claimed him so soon.' He laughed. The sound was shrill and sharp, like a blade drawn across a wire.

Elysius knew the dark eldar loathed using the speech of 'lesser races' but realised this remark was fashioned as a barb. It was nearly a successful one. He had to grit his teeth to stop from rising up and tossing the alien filth into the hot darkness surrounding them. But that was what the wretch wanted, an excuse to inflict further agonies. These parasites, the skulking pallid-faced creatures manning the skiff, fed on torture and pain. It was sustenance to them. Elysius resolved he would not give them another morsel.

Starve. I'll give you nothing but indifference, scum.

Others aboard the vessel, those without the stoicism of the Fire-born, were not so resilient.

Some of the men, the remnants of the Night Devils who had arrived to secure the bastion at Ironlandings, shivered uncontrollably against a pervasive cold that surrounded the vessel.

'Hold firm,' the Chaplain muttered to a man beside him, a sergeant judging by his rank pins, 'the Emperor has not forsaken us.'

At Elysius's words, the man ceased quavering. Faith had not abandoned them yet.

'Idiot,' Helspereth snarled at the whelpmaster. The wych was reclining across the skiff's fuselage but detached herself from it to stalk with feline grace up to the Chaplain. When she was close enough, she leaned into Elysius's ear and whispered, 'He prays to his god. He prays for deliverance.' She stood up, maintaining her balance easily as the skiff bucked and jerked against the aetheric storm. 'This one will try to defy us,' she promised. 'Won't you,' she hissed, raking a nail over the Chaplain's cheek and drawing a ruby of blood.

She tasted it and hissed with pleasure.

'Oh, but you *are* strong, aren't you...'

'Choke on it, you bitch,' Elysius replied through clenched teeth.

'And full of fire, too,' purred Helspereth. 'I will enjoy your fire, *super-man*. How long before I can expend it, I wonder? How your death-throes will nourish me...'

The harsh scrape of metal could be heard above the wind and the skiff's engine as Elysius dragged a groove through the decking with his fingers.

'Plenty of time for that later, my prey,' whispered the wych before returning to her languor draped across the fuselage.

For the first time in what felt like hours, though time held little meaning in this place, Elysius raised his eyes. Through the flickering strands of his white hair he made out jagged spires in the distant dark. Boiling clouds, travelling against the wind, masked them. The mists clung to the long, razor-edged structures that were dotted with evil pinpricks of light, as if reluctant to detach themselves and surrender to the whim of this place. A cascade of lightning illuminated the spires briefly and Elysius realised there were further structures upon them and even vessels attached to the spikes protruding from their surfaces. It was a port or city of some sort. The spires were districts and quarters, but it was like no city the Chaplain had ever seen. It also meant there were people down there, more slaves like them. And perhaps other things too...

'What is this place?' asked Ba'ken in a low murmur.

The sergeant had also lost his battle-helm and his armour was cracked in several places. Like the Chaplain, he too was weighed down by a heavy spiked gorget and shackled to the deck.

'I know not, brother,' Elysius replied, 'but wherever it is, it is not of the mortal world.' Above them, a spur of fire lit the darkness from a stolen sun. It threw a strange cast upon the scene. The Chaplain watched the solar flare fade and then looked at Ba'ken. 'How is Iagon?'

'I will live.' A choked rasp came from the other side of the deck. Three Night Devil troopers sat between him and the other two Salamanders. A fourth Salamander, Brother G'heb, kneeled on Iagon's left.

Elysius knew, on the far side of the long, bladed skiff, there were more. He recalled the attack on the Capitol vaguely. His memory was fogged by his injuries and what had followed after he'd been taken with the others through the portal. The dark eldar had attacked swiftly and without warning. Instantly, he had realised they'd been drawn into a trap. Somehow, the xenos had bypassed their sentries and alarms. They had penetrated the inner quarters of the bastion using webway technology and arrived in the Salamanders' midst en masse.

No defence, however meticulously planned, could have prepared them for that. They'd been fortified by units from from the Night Devils, the holding force designed to occupy the bastion and allow Elysius and Brother-Sergeants Ba'ken and Iagon to redeploy at the Ferron Straits. With the rest of their battle group already en route, they were weakened, but it was clear to the Chaplain from the outset that the intention of the xenos wasn't merely to slay them, though several

Fire-born had lost their lives in the assault, it was to *capture* them. Perhaps it was to capture *him*, though Elysius knew not for what purpose.

The ways of the alien were anathema to him. He did not wish to understand them, only to crush them beneath his armoured heel. The fact of his incarceration meant he was impotent to do that and this chafed at the Chaplain greatly.

'Hold to your oaths as Salamanders,' he said, returning to gaze upon the rapidly closing spires. Through the lightning it seemed to Elysius that they were rising *above* the city. 'Remember your purpose. Remember the words of–'

Elysius screamed. A lash wreathed in hot, sparking energy wrapped itself around the Chaplain's torso and burned. This was not a pure heat, like the fires of a forge or the touch of the brander's iron – at that thought, a twinge of regret pricked him concerning Ohm – it was tainted, alien, an invasive and dirty pain Elysius reacted to.

'Silence!' hissed another one of the whelpmasters, a female judging by the cadence of her voice.

There were several of these sadists aboard, each armed with long energy whips that coiled and lashed with viperous energy. Even power armour was no proof against its painful effects. The whelpmasters were joined by a cohort of clan warriors in dark, segmented armour and carrying long, alien rifles. The one called Helspereth had joined them later, alighting from a seemingly isolated spur of rock floating in the darkness. Elysius had seen her step aboard but had no idea how she had come to be upon the rock spur. It was clear, though, that she held rank above the rest. Even the skiff's captain, sat smugly upon his command throne, deferred to her in the most obsequious fashion.

The female whelpmaster released the lash and Elysius sagged before forcing himself upright again.

'Remember the words of Vulkan,' he continued, 'and the teachings of Lord Tu'Shan.'

The power whip spat and sparked as another blow was about to be delivered when Helspereth spoke up.

'Leave him,' she ordered coldly. 'I like this one. He is defiant. I will relish breaking him. It will be exquisite. Krone,' she added, arching her neck and body seductively to regard the skiff's captain, 'take us higher, my love.'

Krone did as he was bid, smiling like a kept dog all the while.

The skiff rose higher into the growing maelstrom.

'Tell me something, mon-keigh preacher,' Helspereth said. She hefted something in her delicate but deadly hands. It was cumbersome and bulky, and looked utterly incongruous in her grasp. She held a broken crozius arcanum. The mace and symbol of office had belonged to Elysius. 'Does this crude stick you wield contain the strength of your god?'

'It is a sacred tool,' Elysius countered, trying to hide the agony in his voice, 'used to smite the unclean and the heathen. You will be acquainted with it soon enough, hell spawn.'

Helspereth laughed. It was an unpleasant, mirthless sound.

She leaned forwards on the fuselage, drawing back her leg and showing Krone a little more flesh than he could really handle without wanting to act on it.

'I look forward to you *smiting* me, then,' she said, and tossed the crozius onto the deck next to where the

Chaplain was kneeling. It skidded, scraping against the metal, and came to rest against his armoured leg. 'But first,' she added, 'you have to learn how to fly.'

The skiff was poised directly above the spire port-city now.

Elysius looked down over the edge and saw an abyss of razor-barbs and lightning.

At a command from Krone the chains shackling the prisoners to the skiff were released. Without orders, the whelpmasters came forwards.

'Faith in Vulkan and the Emperor,' said Elysius to his charges, snatching up the crozius in his hand before diving off the side of the skiff and into the darkness below.

'Slain, my lord,' said Daedicus. He gave a solemn shake of his head.

The dead Salamander had been pinioned to a vertical strut supporting the warehouse roof of the Capitol building. The warrior's armour was badly rent, the left lens of his helmet a shattered and bloody ruin. Most disturbing of all though were the gaping crevice in his chest and its smaller twin in his gorget.

Moving up alongside Daedicus, Halknarr could scarcely believe what he was seeing. 'His progenoids have been removed.'

'Ripped out,' added Daedicus.

'No,' offered Mek'tar, kneeling by another of their fallen brothers on the other side of the floor, 'the cuts here are almost surgical, analytical.'

'Dusk-wraiths are debased creatures,' said Praetor, caring little for the disparities in how his kin had been mutilated. He ranged ahead of the others and surveyed the carnage around them with a wary gaze. Something about the scene bothered him – it was evident in his body language – and he interrogated every patch of shadow, every benighted nook and darkened vault in the high ceiling of the warehouse space. 'Our ancestors, the first Nocturnean settlers, knew the evil of that race. Some enmities are built to last millennia, especially when forged in innocent blood.'

Low mutters of agreement greeted the veteran sergeant's statement. Every Firedrake in the room was affected by the debauchery committed by the dark eldar but they kept their anger in check under a mantle of stoic resolve. All, except one.

Tsu'gan was in a dispersed formation called *claw* with the rest of his combat squad fanned around him. Each of the other three squad-leaders did the same, taking a separate quarter of the broad warehouse floor. His rage was like a font close to bubbling over. Only the presence of the Forgefather kept him still. He wanted to find the dark eldar responsible and slay them. Nothing short of a river of alien blood would account for these crimes. He revved his chainsword, his agitation echoed in its mechanised growling.

++*Calm yourself, Tsu'gan*++ said Praetor through a closed comm-link channel. The veteran sergeant was looking at him. ++*Have Gathimu's teachings had no effect on you whatsoever?*++

++*Brother Gathimu is dead, my lord*++

Slain by a daemon-engine unleashed by a Khornate cult called the Red Rage, Gathimu had been Praetor's intended mentor for Tsu'gan. He was supposed to have been a guide to temper his anger and hone it into something useful and less self-destructive. After Gathimu's death, Praetor had yet to find a replacement.

++*But not his words and deeds. They live on*++

Praetor turned away and closed the link.

Tsu'gan's black mood remained unleavened.

'I am death,' he thought. 'Its shroud follows me like a shadow I cannot shrug off.'

The Firedrakes had moved into the building through the open bastion gate. That, in itself, was unsettling. This place had once teemed with labourers and, latterly, Imperial troops. Now it was empty and dead. With their bolters trained on the dark, the Fire-born had been met with the grisly remains of sentries in the outer corridors and then came the warehouse where the real carnage had begun.

The slaughtered bodies of Night Devil troopers lay strewn about like refuse, sundered and cleaved. Some were even beyond human recognition such were the tortures the dark eldar had visited upon them. Shell impacts pockmarked the walls, and loose casings littered the ground together with the spent power packs from lasguns.

'They fought hard,' said Halknarr, his armoured boot disturbing a welter of scattered ammunition spilled from an improvised heavy weapon nest.

'But their efforts were ultimately for nothing,' snarled Tsu'gan, stalking around the perimeter. Stabs of light from his battle-helm's halo-lamp array cut into the deepening shadows revealing further atrocities. Men hung like ragged cloth on a line, their skin flensed open, innards sagging to the floor in wet piles. Others dangled by their ankles, throats cut and having bled out a slow death. Some were dismembered; the collection of body parts so numerous that attributing them to any individual was impossible. Decapitations, exsanguinations, eviscerations and bifurcations: the cruel and grisly handiwork of the dark eldar was prevalent throughout the vast room. The air reeked of blood, the tiny drifting molecules of the slain clogging the rebreathers in the Salamanders' battle-helms.

'Here,' shouted Mek'tar. He was standing in front of one of the roof's support columns. An elderly serf was staked to it, arms splayed and legs together in cruciform. Thick nails pinned his hands and feet. A branding rod impaled his thin chest through a ragged mess of robes that hung on his thin frame like scraps of skin.

Mek'tar's halo-lamp lit the victim's face. A mask of pain was frozen upon it. The cheeks and forehead were swollen and purple. Dead hollows for eyes returned the Salamander's stern gaze.

'He was a serf, no warrior, just an old man. And they took his sight, the hell-kites.'

Praetor sighed lamentingly when he recognised the wretched figure.

'He was already blind, brother. That is Ohm, Chaplain Elysius's brander-priest.'

Mek'tar turned, the quickness of the move betraying his concern.

'Then...?'

'Our Chaplain's fate is still unknown, and should be treated as such,' Praetor returned quickly.

'How many of our kin?' asked He'stan, his voice breaking through the sudden tension. His eyes blazed with a fierce flame lighting the shadows around him. It was the first time the Forgefather had spoken since their cautious ingress into the Capitol, this but the bastion's threshold.

'I count four,' said Daedicus, surveying the high rafters where two more of their brethren had been bolted and crucified. His combat squad flanked across the right.

'Five,' Praetor corrected. The veteran sergeant had moved towards the large doors at the far end of the warehouse where another Fire-born was slumped against the wall, bolter hanging limply in his dead hands. The warrior's head had been removed and placed in his lap. The mouth was arranged in a savage grin.

Praetor found a piece of cloth nearby and covered up the warrior's face.

'These are bad deaths,' he muttered, reminded briefly of the Firedrakes he had lost most recently on the missions aboard the *Protean* and on Sepulchre IV. They were regrettable enough but at least they had been clean, warriors' deaths.

Tsu'gan strafed the blackness with his helm-lamp, picking out a spastic silhouette locked in its final act of agony before expiring.

So much blood and human wreckage – it was like a charnel house, a butcher's block. Sundered flesh lay all about him. Tsu'gan believed humans to be weak, both physically and mentally. He was not surprised the dark eldar had slain them so easily. Doubtless his Fire-born brothers had given their own lives protecting them, or so he discerned from the positions of the dead. But to be degraded so, to be subjected to such heinous and sadistic mutilation... his combi-bolter quivered with channelled wrath in his clenched fist.

'They feed on pain and suffering,' said a dulcet voice behind him.

Tsu'gan half-turned. He hadn't even heard Vulkan He'stan approach. The Forgefather appeared melancholic, a strange distemper affecting him. It obviously grieved him to see such wanton destruction inflicted by the old enemy.

'Feed?' asked Tsu'gan in a half whisper, regarding the

scene with fresh eyes. Was their some method to this insanity? He had taken it for alien savagery, nothing more.

'Their souls, Tsu'gan,' said He'stan, 'are dying.' He made a fist and slowly started to unclench it. 'Imagine a ball of sand here in my gauntlet. Their souls are the sand and my fist is too loose to hold them. Slowly, as the grains would trickle free and into oblivion, so too would the souls of the dusk-wraiths dissipate and fade. Only by yoking the suffering of others can they forestall their destruction, being devoured by ruinous powers.'

Tsu'gan was rapt. He knew the Salamanders possessed lore about the dark eldar, that as their ancestral enemies the primitive Nocturnean earth shamans had learned much about them. Upon his arrival on the world, the Primarch Vulkan had devoted copious amounts of study to fathom the nature of dusk-wraiths, but this was the first time Tsu'gan had ever heard it related so candidly and with such authority.

'You mean the warp?'

He'stan nodded. 'Look around you, brother, and tell me this is not the act of Chaos or at least in reaction to the threat of it.'

'Life signs, further into the bastion,' the voice of Daedicus interrupted them. He was reading an auspex in his left hand. 'Distant but numerous,' he added.

Praetor looked again at the position of the now shrouded Fire-born. The head was removed as an afterthought, he realised. This was where the body had landed when his brother was felled.

'They attempted to make a last stand in this room,' he began.

'But when that failed, they retreated,' He'stan finished for him, moving towards Praetor.

All the Firedrakes now converged on their veteran sergeant.

'There were twenty Astartes in that force,' added Tsu'gan, his agitated manner making his anger obvious. 'Fifteen of our brothers, our Lord Chaplain included, could not be so easily overcome.'

Halknarr's eyes flashed behind his battle-helm.

'They fight still.'

'What is wrong, brother-sergeant?' asked He'stan. He was looking directly at Praetor.

'Why do I feel like a sauroch drawn to the hunter's eye?'

Halknarr stepped forwards to emphasise his purpose. 'Whatever is beyond those doors, we will be ready for it, Herculon.'

Praetor regarded the doors now. They were thick and layered with plasteel rebars. A mechanism, operated by a servitor or labourer and located in a small control booth above, was required to open them.

Such things were not impediments to Astartes, certainly not those with the determination and strength of Herculon Praetor. The veteran sergeant was as pragmatic as any Salamander. Misgivings or not, they would not discover what had befallen Elysius until they had delved further into the bastion. Hefting his thunder hammer he smashed open the massive doors open with a single blow.

'My lord?' he asked, turning to He'stan. Before them, the gloom of the inner bastion loomed.

'Lead on,' said the Forgefather, a fresh flare of fire lighting his eyes. Gone was anger; now vengeance roared within his red orbs. 'Find our brothers and the xenos who took them.'

CHAPTER EIGHT

I
The Dead Speak

THICK CLOUDS OF ash rolled across the grey plains, whispering with dead voices.

The grave dust was clogging the lenses of Pyriel's battle-helm as he and Dak'ir moved through the crematoria fog. Flakes smeared swathes of grey over the Librarius blue of their power armour. Pyriel had used his gauntlet to clear his vision on more than one occasion, despite the fact he could see well enough with his psyker's sight.

They'd left the *Caldera* several kilometres behind them with Brother Loc'tar. Lost to the storm, the Thunderhawk was a distant memory now. As soon as Lexicanum and Epistolary had stepped onto the ossuary road and beheld the soaring bone-tombs and barrow-monoliths of Moribar, all other thoughts had vanished. This place held a special significance for the Fire-born of the 3rd. Especially for Dak'ir, it represented a dark episode over forty years in his past.

189

As soon as he'd left the gunship's Chamber Sanctuarine, images had flashed into his mind demanding his attention. They spoke of fire and of dragons and of the betrayal of brothers. A twinge of guilt and accusation warred within him for dominance. It was just the psychic resonance of the place trying to assert itself. Dak'ir was stronger now. Unlike in the Aura Hieron Temple, where such visions had crippled him, he had now endured the burning. His training at the hands of his master beneath Mount Deathfire had girded him. He marshalled the images in his stride, compartmentalising them for later use.

He knew that Pyriel had felt the mental echo of the deed and silently lauded him for his control.

'Sleeping dragons lie beneath these plains,' Dak'ir said, drawing ahead of his master. Instinct guided him. With the shifting of the ash, the ravages of the decades and the ever accumulating monuments to the dead, the way to the crematoria had changed. It remained at the heart of the world but then the world itself had been altered and reshaped around it. Like he knew every contour of the plasma pistol holstered at his hip, though, he knew how to get to the crematoria.

So much had happened there. It seemed perversely fitting that they return and confront whatever spectres might lurk in the depths of Moribar.

'Just memory echoes, Dak'ir,' counselled Pyriel. He drew his salamander mantle around him to ward off the raging dust and ash. 'An inauspicious time for a visit, though,' he added ruefully.

'When is there a good time to visit such a place? It reeks of the dead, of old and forgotten things.'

'Except they are not forgotten, are they? Not by us and not by them.'

'Kadai's fate was sealed beneath these grey vales, in its hollow catacombs.'

Pyriel seized Dak'ir's shoulder and turned him around. 'Kadai's fate was his own, Lexicanum. Never lose sight of that. Whatever he did to try and bring Ushorak back was right and just.'

Dak'ir shrugged him away. 'But you were not there, Pyriel. I saw what happened. I was part of it.'

Pyriel looked about to retaliate but relented. Instead, he sighed and the sound joined the deathless chorus of the wind rising around them. 'No, that's true. But I knew well enough of Nihilan and his twisted ambition.'

'He blames you for his fate, doesn't he?'

They were walking again, wading through the grey fog, ash up to the rims of their leg greaves.

'He blames all of us, and he blames himself and Ushorak. Nihilan is insane, Dak'ir. That's what makes him so dangerous. We are still pawns in his plan, make no mistake of that. There is a higher power guiding his hand, I can feel it.'

'So what can we do, master?'

Ahead, the shadow of a barrow-monolith loomed. Framed with a sepulchral archway depicting effigies of the Emperor's cardinals and saints, it was a magnificent entrance that led into the lower domains of the world. It was one of several ways down to the crematoria. Its ossuary path was well-trodden. A low wall on either side was punctuated with skulls inscribed with holy sigils. Scripture nailed to the vertical columns of the arch fluttered violently in the wind.

'Nothing but what we are doing. We must trust that we are guided here by Vulkan's will, that the primarch is watching over us in this. Nocturne's darkest hour approaches, Dak'ir. It is so close at hand I can almost taste the blood on the air.'

Beyond its ash-swept threshold, the sepulchral archway was lined with tombs and crypts but only the dead inhabited its halls. The two Librarians were alone.

'If Nihilan is truly the arch-manipulator of all that has transpired so far then he will have anticipated our return to Moribar, too,' said Dak'ir.

Pyriel nodded, drawing his force staff once they were far enough inside the barrow-monolith and out of the ash storm.

'There may be more than the dead waiting for us in the darkness.' Dak'ir drew *Draugen*, his force sword. His empathy with the blade was still naked and untempered but the bond would be forged soon enough.

An army of graves and mausoleums stretched into the shadows ahead of them. The way was lit by flickering brazier-lanterns but they did little to lift the gloom.

'We stand beneath a shroud, Dak'ir,' said Pyriel, leading them down the aisle between the tombs. 'It occludes the truth.'

'Then let us draw it back and expose what lies beneath.' Dak'ir paused, regarding the darkness for a moment. He was listening. 'They are calling to me,' he said.

'Who?'

'The dead.'

The wind became a shriek in the Chaplain's ears as he plummeted from the deckplate and into the beckoning void. So fast was his descent, it tugged at the corners of his grimacing mouth. The tendrils of his long, white hair flared.

Beside and above him, the other slaves fell too.

A shock of lightning ripped out of the dark, striking a screaming Night Devil trooper and turning him to ash. Another Guardsman hit one of the higher spires and was ripped apart like offal. A third was lost from view, his body and his flight arrested when he struck a thin spike of metal and was impaled.

It was like descending into a forest of blades; a forest of blades wreathed with lightning. Darkness came and went, illuminated by the fury of the storm. Plateaus and what appeared to be docking platforms passed in a blur of hard edges. Deeper and deeper they fell, navigating the jutting spires and artificial razor crags of this hell-place.

Elysius felt a jagged spark of heat flash by his face. He winced against the flare of light but sped on, somehow spared from immolation.

'The Emperor is my shield,' he began, closing his eyes as he recited the benediction. He spied a potential landing point below him, through a web of blades, and made a mental note of the distance to it. He had, as of yet, no idea how he would arrest his descent so he didn't break every bone in his body upon landfall. 'He will protect my soul from harm. I am His watchful lantern, seeking out the darkness and bringing it to the light. With His sword I will smite the foes of mankind, bring justice to the weak and retribution to the perfidious.'

Another lightning flash, penetrating his eyelids despite the fact he had closed them. They were descending into the heart of the maelstrom. Close now, he could almost feel the pressing spires drawing nearer and the cutting promise of their razor-edges.

'Vulkan's will is righteous. He is the anvil. We are his

hammer. The forge is my bastion and by its fires are my enemies sundered.'

The chill that had entered Elysius's bones began to ebb as the heat from the spires, from venting plumes of steam and tall furnace fires warmed him. It wasn't a pleasant heat; it was a prickling, stabbing sensation at once familiar and horribly alien.

The Chaplain opened his eyes.

The hard flank of a razor-spire loomed in his sight. Desiccated corpses and bleached bone skeletons clung to its spiky protrusions in deathless desperation. Angling his body into the shape of an arrow, Elysius dived headlong towards it. A distant shout above, a curt cry of anguish, signalled the death of another Guardsman.

He knew his brothers would be behind him, perhaps not through this selfsame vent, but navigating the deadly sea of barbs and chained lighting all the same.

As close as he dared, Elysius brought his body up, angling his feet downwards and his body towards the flat face of the spire. He struck the hard metal and bounced, plates scattering free into the void like shed skin with the force of impact. He struck again, this time snagging a length of chain that screeched as it burned through his clenched and gauntleted fist.

Slower. That was good. The hard flank of the spire was long. Where the edge of the spire terminated, a relatively short drop beckoned and then came a jutting platform. The chain snapped and Elysius found the momentum of his fall returning. He thrust his fingers into the metal and the plates began to shed again like scale.

Half-glanced out the corner of his eye, he saw his brothers doing the same.

Ba'ken had taken the opposite spire, the two so close they almost touched at the base but wide enough for the Salamanders to slip through the small vent between them to the waiting plateau. He held onto one of the Night Devils with his spare hand, cradling the veteran warrior like a child in his mighty grasp.

Iagon seized the same side as Elysius with two hands, a Guardsmen clinging to the power generator on his back in desperation.

It was the same with the others. Where they could, the Salamanders taken by the dark eldar protected the more vulnerable humans and tried to ferry them to the plateau.

Elysius saw two Guardsmen attempt to scale the sides of the spires with grapnels. One man was bounced off into oblivion, his screams soon lost to the dark; the other crumpled against the hard metal before getting caught in a length of chain and joining the ranks of corpses spitted against the spire's hard face.

Elysius lamented all of their deaths. He had time for a final benediction of the dead men's souls before the vent between the two spires loomed and he plunged over the edge.

II
Hunters and Hunted

THE CREAKING REPORT of the doors receded into the gloom of the corridor beyond the warehouse floor. In its wake there came a new sound, a gibbering, shrieking refrain that set Tsu'gan's gritted teeth on edge.

'Something is moving in the shadows.' Halknarr brought his bolter up to his shoulder. The other

Firedrakes took this as their cue to ready their weapons too.

'Form two firing lines,' ordered Praetor. The warriors around him slipped effortlessly into two ten-man ranks, flamers at the front. The electrical discharge from his ignited thunder hammer lit the snarl on his face. The fires of battle within him stirred. 'Daedicus...'

The squad leader looked up from his auspex. 'Over a hundred bio-signatures, brother-sergeant.'

The chittering, gibbering noise increased in volume.

Tsu'gan's narrowed eyes made out figures in the void-like gloom, misshapen and grotesque figures. He wanted desperately to engage them now, to vent the fury building inside him in a single, glorious tempest of violence. Abruptly, he was aware of He'stan's presence beside him. The Forgefather's influence was dramatic, even though he spoke no words and gave no gestures. Tsu'gan felt immediately focussed. The reckless anger pulling at his leash ebbed and he found order to his emotions.

'Rear rank,' He'stan's calm voice rose over the shrieking throng, 'turn and raise bolters skyward.'

The Firedrakes obeyed without question, as a second force of dark eldar came screaming from their hiding places in the vaulted warehouse ceiling. They tore from the lofty rafters riding bladed sky-boards and barbed jet-bikes, hooting and jeering. Half-naked wyches descended on lines of gossamer-thin cord, their eyes wild with lustful and violent excitement. Descending like birds of prey from their eyries, heavily armed warriors plummeted towards the Salamanders on wings of serrated steel. Fouled by some manner of arcane science, the auspex had failed to detect these ambushers. Vulkan He'stan needed no device to see the truth of the trap that awaited his brothers. He had known it since they'd entered the room. His eyes searched the deeper shadows in the vaults above and found what they were looking for.

A shrivelled and emaciated figure hovered on a sky-board. He did not join the attack, but merely watched from the darkness. Though his mouth seemed stitched, his ancient eyes were alight with glee. Parchment-skinned, the colour of stained alabaster, this thing was almost a walking corpse.

'I see you now,' He'stan hissed. 'I have drawn you out, cadaver... *haemonculus*.'

At a clipped and sibilant command from the withered haemonculus, a coterie of warriors emerged on the high gantries girdling the room and proceeded to unleash splinter-like fire into the Firedrakes' ranks.

The Salamanders took the first salvo on their power armour before unleashing a bolt storm.

'Unto the anvil!' roared He'stan to the sound of tearing gantries and the ecstatic screaming of dying xenos.

A macabre rain of dark eldar warriors fell from the shadowed heavens in half-exploded chunks. In their wake came the hellions on their sky-boards and the jet-bikers.

Tsu'gan lit up one rider with a burst from his combi-bolter, burning down a second with a spurt of promethium from the weapon's flamer attachment. A third he locked fast with his chainblade, the teeth spitting sparks as they met the hellion's trident. The creature cackled madly before disengaging and flying off for another pass.

Instinctively, the Firedrakes changed their formation into an outward-facing circle. It was how they were born to fight, it was Vulkan's way.

Form the anvil, break our enemies upon it.

'We are the hammer,' he heard Praetor cry. The veteran sergeant echoed all their thoughts. From the shadowed gallery beyond the warehouse the mutated beasts were shambling into a run.

Tsu'gan had no time to witness it. The winged warriors and the wyches had begun their assault.

'Slay them,' he bellowed, feeling the swell of battle lust overtaking him, 'slay them all!'

He'stan thrust Vulkan's Spear into a winged scourge, tearing out the heart. With the Gauntlet of the Forge, he put a wych coven to the torch. The lithe forms of the warrior women twisted in pleasure as they died.

'In Vulkan's name!' he cried.

Tsu'gan's heart soared.

As THE GROTESQUES charged, the lume-lanterns flanking the gallery erupted into sudden brightness. At once, the full extent of the creatures' deformities was revealed. They were lumpen, mutilated things. Some waddled on stumps for legs, others cantered on long reverse-jointed limbs. Claws and bone-spears, barbed tails and flesh-fused mace fists served as weapons. They were abominations, mewling and frothing through fanged mouths.

Praetor recognised the forms of human men and women, some conjoined into one body. They had once been the populace of Ironlandings, the labourers of the bastion.

Smiting them would be a mercy.

As they spread out, the slower lumbering beasts giving way to the lighter and more agile, a circle of warriors appeared through the parting throng.

'Our brothers!' cried Halknarr. The anguish in his

voice touched them all. An urgent tremor ran up the line. The sense of imminent motion filled the air around Praetor.

Lashed together with hooked chains; battered and pinioned by spikes, the bloodied remnants of the Salamanders who had been garrisoning Ironlandings were revealed. Most hung their heads, too weary to raise them. For some, their eyes were filled with a bitter rancour and still blazed in the darkness. The dark eldar had humiliated them.

'Hold positions,' said Praetor, his voice like a rock his brothers could fasten their resolve to. He was the bulwark against reckless abandon. He stemmed the tide of the Firedrakes' anger and honed it into a single cohesive blow.

'We are the hammer. Unleash it!'

Bolters screamed as the flamers spewed into the first wave of grotesques.

They howled as they fell, curling into blackened shapes that hazed with the heat. Expressions of pain and relief warred for dominance in their altered mouths.

The first to break through the web of explosive shells lunged at Praetor. It was a brute, with strong malformed legs, broad upper back and muscle-packed shoulders fraught with bulbous growths.

Praetor crushed the grotesque's skull with a single blow, before uppercutting a second creature that came in the brute's wake with his storm shield. Hot blood struck the metal in a dense spray. A line of it streaked his face like a dagger slash. Praetor ignored it. There were more to kill.

They were in it now. This was where it became thick and dirty. Bolters hammering around him, the flare of promethium throwing a ruddy glow on the scene, Praetor did what he was born to do – he killed in the Emperor's name and for the glory of his primarch.

THE MESH OF the flung net screeched as Tsu'gan cut through it, parting the fanged snare in two with his chainblade. The wyches were upon them, dancing and weaving around the Firedrakes' rapid bolter bursts to close with hook and blade.

Pain receptors slaved from his body to his battle-helm lit up in Tsu'gan's retinal display. Grunting, he took the haft of the spear that impaled his shoulder and snapped it. Aiming a downward swipe with his chainblade that the leather-clad wych dodged with ease, he then brought up his bolter like a club and smashed her across the chest and face. Daedicus brought his weapon around and finished her with a desultory burst of fire.

Tsu'gan snarled behind his battle-helm. She was his to kill. He would speak to his over-zealous brother later, once the aliens were dead. No time now. The dark eldar were swarming them.

Outnumbered at least three to one, the slaughter perpetrated by the Firedrakes was prodigious. As he severed a hellion's torso, Tsu'gan wondered if this was how his brothers had fought. Perhaps not. They had been dispersed around the warehouse floor when the Firedrakes had found them. Distracted out of a desire to protect the humans, they had compromised their own lives into the bargain. No such concern existed for Tsu'gan and his company brothers. And they had He'stan.

The Forgefather brought down a pair of wyches,

several score marks in his armour attesting to their futile efforts to kill him, and began to move.

At first Tsu'gan wasn't sure what was happening, only that something in the dynamic of their defence was changing. Then he realised.

He's breaking formation.

He followed He'stan's gaze to where it alighted on the graven corpse loitering above the battle mounted on a sky-board. The wretched creature's thin lips were drawn into a tight line like a slit throat but he rubbed his emaciated, talon-like hands together. The death and carnage was fortifying him. Tsu'gan remembered what He'stan had told him earlier, of the dark eldar's need to forestall soul death by feeding on the suffering of others, even their own kin.

Without thinking, Tsu'gan broke formation too.

Through his chosen pilgrim, Vulkan had shown them the way. It felt almost like divine purpose was guiding him as Tsu'gan cried to his battle-brothers.

'Fire-born, with me. To the Forgefather!'

A pair of jet-bikes screeched out of the lofty warehouse roof, ducking beams and broken struts with calculated ease. They homed in on He'stan. His pace and urgency was such that he was caught in the open. Tsu'gan sent a burst of bolter fire into one, but the rider jinked and rolled, cackling derisively at the Salamander's pathetic attempts to hit him. Vo'kar brought up his flamer and the promethium burst burned the rider down, turning his derision into screams of agony. Tsu'gan had corralled the xenos into the other Fire-born's path. The last laugh was his.

He'stan destroyed the second bike himself, driving the blade of his spear through the fuselage and splitting the rider in two. A third, buzzing in the wake of the others, fell to a blast of fire from his gauntlet. Flames ran down the vehicle's nose in a bright bloom, igniting the rider and cooking off its fuel tank in an incendiary burst. It spiralled away from its intended trajectory, the dark eldar's control lost to agony, and the growing fireball around the bike engulfed a pair of hellions, consuming them too.

The haemonculus's guardians were gathering to his defence. The xenos could see the purpose in the Forge-father's eyes, what he intended for their depraved master.

Tsu'gan saw it too.

'Take them!' he roared, arriving at He'stan's side with Vo'kar, Oknar and Lorrde. The others were not far behind. They fought in small packs, twos and threes; sometimes back-to-back, at other times rushing headlong into the enemy. It was fluid, dynamic. It was not the Fire-born way of war at all, but then He'stan was not a typical Salamander and Tsu'gan an all-too-willing student of his art. It was a fact that Herculon Praetor had not failed to notice.

PRAETOR CURSED UNDER his breath. 'Hold, Kesare damn you,' he muttered. A half glance behind him revealed Brother Lorrde struck in the neck by a flung trident. He buckled, going down on one knee, before a wych skipped in past his defences and slammed a hooked blade into his shoulder and back. The injured Fire-drake crumpled. The icon on Praetor's retinal display went from green to amber.

A second warrior, Brother Tho'ran, juddered as a whickering burst of dark-light skewered him. He fell, smoke spuming from the cauterised wound in his chest.

Praetor snarled, returning to the fight at his front, as Tho'ran's icon ran through green to amber to red. Their backs were exposed. Though the Firedrakes running with He'stan had torn a hole through the dark eldar throng, they had left the veteran sergeant and his rank in an indefensible position. They were already giving ground, the edges of the line bending back to form a half circle.

Cursing Tsu'gan's recklessness a final time, he embraced the pragmatic side of his Nocturnean heritage and gave the only order he could.

'Firedrakes, forward on my lead. Bring the fight to the enemy! Bring them flame and fury!'

Praetor surged out of the front rank, bludgeoning grotesques with his thunder hammer like he was an automaton.

Haft thrust. Hammer blow. Shield smash.

He performed the manoeuvres by rote as if in the training pits on Prometheus.

A staccato chorus of hard bolter bangs and the aggressive *whoosh* and *crack* of spewing flamers resonated around him as his brothers followed his lead.

'Defensive formation. I am the rock,' he ordered. The Firedrakes responded as one, closing around their veteran sergeant and moving with him as he advanced. The mutant beasts couldn't get close. Between sustained bolter fire and up-close chainblade attacks, the grotesques were kept at bay. It wasn't long before a sea of bloody, dismembered body parts littered the gallery floor.

It wasn't merely fury that drove Praetor, though; he was too experienced a warrior and a leader for that. He had a plan. They were outnumbered and the dark eldar had them engaged on two fronts. The conclusion was simple. They needed reinforcements.

The circle of chained Salamanders, the survivors of Squads Ba'ken and Iagon, were just ahead. None held their heads low now. They saw Herculon Praetor coming for them, calling them to the fires of battle.

A DENSE THRONG of dark eldar stood between He'stan and his quarry. The haemonculus was marshalling his forces to him. The tremble of fear affecting his skeletal frame seemed to invigorate him. The carnage only fascinated and engrossed him further. Slowly, he was drawn from the vaults and down into the melee.

No wych or hellion could stand before the wrath of He'stan's entourage; no scourge or jet-biker could deter them. This was fury untempered. It was anger unleashed with all thoughts of stoicism abandoned. Fire reigned and in it the violent potential of the Firedrakes was laid bare.

Dark eldar were spun away from the juggernaut of green ceramite, their bodies broken and sundered. It was as if a rolling flamestorm had been let slip in their midst. It was moving inexorably towards the haemonculus. Nothing could stop this fire-tempest. It would blaze until its rage was burned out.

The cadaver creature appeared to sense the inevitability of his fate.

Tsu'gan thought he saw the haemonculus clip a finger end from his left hand. The severed digit went into a small iron box that disappeared beneath the creature's tattered robes. The foul rite was lost on the Salamander but then the mores of aliens were not a thing to be understood, rather to be abhorred.

A second artefact replaced the first in the

haemonculus's bloodstained claw. This one was pentagrammic, flat but also fashioned from dark metal. It spun wildly in the flat of the dark eldar's palm, tiny ripples of lightning playing over its sharp edges.

Behind the haemonculus, reality itself seemed to *change*.

It began as a pinprick of darkness, an insignificant blot against the canvas of the actual world. It grew steadily, from something the size of a coin, to then a tank hatch and finally a sprawling, circular void.

'He is opening a portal to the webway,' said He'stan urgently. The Forgefather quickened again, incredibly outstripping the others for pace.

The gateway shimmered like watery night. The ripples of its rapid creation ebbed, and it became a quiescent pool of still, utter black. Electricity crackled around its perimeter. The fabric of reality had been wholly torn and this gaping, unholy firmament was the thing that lingered between its skeins. Faces seemed to dwell in the darkening pool, too – tortured, hellish faces.

Even as the battle to reach the portal raged, something was emerging from within it. A bladed prow cut through the blackness first, followed by a ridged nose of angled plates. The long fuselage was that of a dark eldar skimmer-machine, the insectoid engines they used during their slave raids. It was much larger than the vehicles the Salamanders had encountered so far. Three long-nosed cannons, their dark metal glinting in the half-light, bristled in their armoured gun-ports.

The fighting was too dense to unleash the cannonade. The skimmer-machine had come for the haemonculus.

Realisation crept upon Tsu'gan like a silent thief,

even as he killed the creature's kabal warriors, even as he witnessed He'stan arch his back and pull his arm for a spear throw.

This was how the dark eldar had surprised their brothers. It was obvious. The portal had allowed the xenos to infiltrate Elysius's defences. And now the cadaver creature was trying to escape by the same means.

The dark eldar got as far as turning his foul body towards the portal, the skimmer hovering close before the Spear of Vulkan sheared through his torso and pinned him squealing to the warehouse wall.

He'stan's reaction was exultant.

'Rally to me, brothers,' he cried, 'and turn this xenos scum to ash!' The Gauntlet of the Forge spoke next and its words were fire and death. He strafed the skimmer, bathing its crew in liquid promethium. The machine sank quickly after that, hitting the ground hard. Smoke exuded off the hull and some of the deck plating was bent, but it was otherwise operational.

There would be no escape for the haemonculus now. He'stan had declared his wrath upon him. For the justice demanded by the dead, it would be meted out in full.

THE HAMMER BLOW shattered the dark iron chains and they fell away from the captured Salamanders under their own weight.

'To arms, brothers,' said Praetor, tossing one warrior his storm shield, 'Unto the anvil of war.'

Honorious took the weapon eagerly and surged forwards to smash down a grotesque. He used the shield like a bludgeon at first, before decapitating the creature with its hard edge. Spitting on the corpse, he searched for another enemy.

The surviving Salamanders of Squads Ba'ken and Iagon roared as one. Handed spare weapons by their 1st Company kin, they laid into what was left of the grotesques with relentless violence.

Let them vent, thought Praetor, taking a moment to watch his freed brothers unleash hell. Like the terrible anger of Mount Deathfire, their fury had been laid dormant by the xenos. Now, he had unfettered it and it was erupting amongst the mutants in a tide of blood.

'Back to the door,' he ordered, voice booming. The carnage in the gallery was nearly over. The grotesques were almost slain to a beast.

He felt the fires within ebbing. The battle was all but done. It was well met. Only two Firedrakes down, one maybe permanently, though. But a thought niggled at the forefront of Praetor's mind as he followed the others. Chaplain Elysius had not been amongst the survivors. Neither had he been one of the dead. Several of their battle-brothers were unaccounted for, Sergeants Ba'ken and Iagon amongst them.

So where are you, brothers? What have the xenos done with you?

CHAPTER NINE

I
The Razored Vale

There was no way back. Elysius's grenade belt had seen to that. The dust from the explosion was only just settling. Tiny motes and fragments of debris drifted from the ceiling of the sewer in a dark pall. The warriors penetrated the veil easily with their enhanced vision. Elysius revelled in his newfound strength and abilities. Upon his apotheosis to Scout, he felt empowered, invincible.

'We have the creature now,' he said to the darkness around him. Elysius marvelled at the Lyman's ear implant. He could pick out the exact positions of his two other squad brothers with ease.

'Aye, and Master Zen'de will laud us when it takes us to its lair,' offered M'kett. Elysius heard the chunk-chank of his heavy bolter as G'ord panned it across the corridor. It was tight in the sewer but there was enough room for the weapon to make a pass.

'The blood trail leads this way,' said Elysius. He'd snapped

209

on a luminator attached to his bolter and used an ultraviolet spectrum to illuminate a ragged line on the sewer floor. At least it was just dank and they weren't knee deep in effluence. Xenos hunting would be markedly more difficult in those conditions.

'We should exercise caution, brother,' said another voice, the rearguard.

Elysius turned. It had been his idea to trap the creature in the first place.

'You concern yourself too much, Argos. It is but one genestealer.'

'They are pack creatures,' Argos returned, 'seldom alone. How can we be sure this one is isolated? We should be careful, that's all.'

Elysius had not deigned to reply. Argos overthought everything. Ever since they had met on the training fields of the Cindara Plateau he had always calculated, and exercised caution and logic to all of his dealings. To Elysius, he was more of a machine than a man.

He led them onwards, strafing the way ahead with his bolter lamp and checking on the blood trail.

After a few more minutes, Elysius broke into a run.

'Increase pace,' he said, 'the trail is thinning. We are losing it!'

The dense footfalls of G'ord echoed behind them as he struggled to match Elysius's strides with the encumbrance of the heavy bolter slung across his body.

'Stay together!' snapped Argos, moving ahead of G'ord in an attempt to try and rein Elysius in.

'I can tag the beast alone,' Elysius muttered, slipping the tracker bolt into his weapon's breech. The explosive tip had been removed by the Chapter's Techmarines and replaced with a tiny beacon that would transmit to the rest of the Salamander battle group. It would hurt, but it wouldn't kill.

The plan was for the 'stealer to reveal the site of the nest when it returned to it. Find the nest, they could burn it and end the infestation.

'Brother!' urged Argos.

Elysius snarled as he turned. 'Wha–' he began and stopped short when he saw the creature descend from the tunnel ceiling where it had been hiding and shadowing them to fall upon G'ord.

The heavy-weapon Scout died when the genestealer tore out his throat and much of his face. The carapace armour he wore did little to protect his body either, which the beast gored with its fangs. A desultory burst from his heavy bolter lit the tunnel briefly but managed only to frame G'ord's death in stark monochrome and send his brothers darting for cover.

A bark of bolter fire, triggered prematurely, saw the tracker bolt miss its target. Elysius cursed as he rolled. He came up ready to empty a clip into the 'stealer, in spite of the mission. What he saw froze his blood. It had moved, so quickly and silently that it was in front of him before his targeting instincts could kick in.

A flash of claw, and a deep red line of hot pain opened up along Elysius's arm. He dropped the bolter and could only watch as the acid-sacs in the genestealer's maw bulged and its venting glands expanded.

He was about to lose his face.

'Elysius!' Argos cried, and slammed into him...

HE AWOKE TO pain. It was a sharp burning sensation in his right leg, fuddled by the dull ache resonating along his temple.

The echoes of the nightmare faded in his consciousness like smoke tendrils carried on a faint wind. It had been a long time ago. He still bore the scar, its place on his body one of remembered shame amongst the other honour markings on his remaining arm.

Elysius looked up through blurred eyes and saw the gaping hole he'd made in the structure's roof. The memories dwindled to ether and he became Elysius the Chaplain again; Elysius the Scout no longer. He'd been aiming for the flat ground but had been diverted when his body had struck the vent made by the two spires, and had crashed through the roof of some graven temple instead.

Dizziness subsiding, it was hard for Elysius to tell just what kind of structure it was he now found himself in. So much of this place was alien and incomprehensible. It was a ruin; that much he was sure of. His rough landing had only added to the destruction. Flakes of metal and glass slivers cascaded from above like black dust motes where the domed ceiling was open to the sky. They *tinkled* against the Chaplain's power armour discordantly.

His leg was impaled by a dark iron spike. One of the structure's spires had collapsed inwards with the Chaplain and its barbed tip was pinning him. Grimacing, Elysius ripped the spike out and tried to stand. He faltered at first, but found his strength quickly. Standing straight, the Chaplain went to his weapons belt out of instinct. He'd dropped the broken crozius.

Elysius cast about in the debris and the ruins but couldn't see it anywhere. He suspected he'd lost it in the fall, or perhaps it had been dislodged when he'd crashed through the roof. The chemicals in his body, advanced combat drugs, were working hard to stultify the pain in his leg and heal the wound. At least now he could walk. Glass shards and a patina of grit fell off his armour as he moved. Elysius brushed off the worst of it with his hand. The absence of the other, even as a simulacrum in the form of the power fist, was... *disconcerting*. He thought briefly of Ohm, felt a pang of guilt and regret then quashed the remembrance under a hammer of pragmatism.

The dark eldar had not killed them for a reason. This was their arena, Elysius was certain of that. They meant to play with them before they died, draw all the agony and psychic sustenance they could from the Fire-born. But there was something more, something he could not fathom. His fingers traced the edge of another item shackled to his armour. It was old, having existed for many millennia. Even the merest touch of it brought hope him and inner strength. It was a sigil, Vulkan's Sigil, and with it came the blessings of a primarch. In the darkness of the ruins, Elysius was drawn to the hammer-shaped icon. He did not know why, but believed that all would become clear.

I have been sent here, he thought. *I am not as my Chapter needs me to be. This is my crucible of fire and within it I shall be reborn. My flesh, my purpose, as metal in the forge – remade strong, remade anew.*

The crack of broken glass intruded on his benediction, and the Chaplain dropped into a crouch. He took up position behind the fallen spire, using its bulk to shield him from view. Lit by the ephemeral flare of the lightning strikes above, Elysius became aware of two shadows closing in on him and he edged around to the split end of the shattered spire. Instinctively, he reached for the crozius. Only when his hand grasped air did he remember it was gone. The sigil was a relic, despite its hammer-like form. Elysius would not sully it in combat. He made a fist instead, bringing to mind all of the unarmed combat drills of Master Prebian.

With only one arm, he'd need to adjust his tactics. Elysius made the mental and physical adjustments in an eyeblink.

'Vulkan, hone my fury to the dagger's point,' he hissed.

One of the shadows shifted suddenly.

They have heard me...

The other one paused then followed the first who was heading in the direction of the spire, heavy-footed and cautious. They were searching for him.

Come to me then...

The pair advanced another few metres, sniffing around in the dark. They were close enough to strike.

Legs pumping like piston-hammers, Elysius exploded from his hiding place. He brought his fist around, intending to shatter the first assailant's jaw. A headbutt into the bridge of the nose would incapacitate the second.

'Lord Chap–!' G'heb managed to blurt before the blow to the side of his head felled him.

Seeing a friend not a foe, Elysius pulled the punch at the last moment, diverting the force away and glancing the side of G'heb's face instead. Even still, the blow was powerful enough to put him down.

Ba'ken smiled ruefully. The big warrior was a head and a half taller than Elysius but still looked small compared to the formidable Chaplain. The sergeant's bald head was like a piece of squared granite, hewn from the raw material of Nocturne itself. The smile, like a fissure in the rock of his countenance, softened it.

'I see you're in no need of rescue, my lord.'

Elysius kept to the shadows. Ever since he'd taken the black power armour, none amongst the Chapter save Tu'Shan and the other members of the Chaplaincy had ever seen his face. Unhooded, he was reminded of that fact starkly as Ba'ken watched him.

G'heb was picking himself up, rubbing his jaw painfully, as Elysius answered.

'We are all in need of rescue, brother-sergeant,' he said. 'This place is both prison and execution chamber.'

Ba'ken fell silent, having forgotten the Chaplain's sense of humour had been removed along with his fear. Elysius had heard it whispered often when they thought he wasn't listening – the fact amused him greatly.

His thoughts were abandoned when the temple started to move. It began as a slow trickle of dust shards dislodged from the roof and standing columns, building to a cascade of larger debris. Underfoot, the ground trembled as if an armoured column was rolling past nearby.

'In Vulkan's na–'

The words were punched from Ba'ken's chest in a blast of air as Elysius tackled him and bore him to the ground.

'Move!'

A vast chunk of spire wrenched loose by the quake split off and smashed down into the temple. Upon impact it shattered like a fragmentation grenade, showering the three Salamanders with razor-edge slivers.

G'heb hissed as a shard cut his face.

Elysius and Ba'ken missed being crushed by the spire itself by an arm's length.

A low bass rumble resonated through the temple structure, a raucous announcement from some alien instrument. The sound reminded Elysius of a dying sauroch herd left to bake in the Nocturnean sun, only deeper and more plaintive. Beneath the long mewling note, he also detected something else – a shifting of servos and gears, the scrape and whine of metal.

'What in Deathfire's blood is that?' asked Ba'ken above the growing din.

The entire temple was shaking now. The ground shuddered violently as if in seizure. Chunks of cracked columns tumbled into the middle of the chamber, adding to its ruination. Great slabs of stone and dark iron sheared away, sliding off their foundations with slow finality, only to strike the ground and break into pieces.

'Stay back,' Elysius told his brothers. They'd scattered after narrowly avoiding being crushed by the fallen spire. All three were braced against the walls, backs pressed against it as they rode out the quake, but Elysius was estranged from the others, shrouded by the darkness a few metres away. 'Hold here,' the Chaplain added, showing his outstretched palm in case he hadn't been heard.

Like the passing of a sudden storm, the tremors ebbed into extinction as quickly as they'd arrived and silence resumed.

As soon as it was over, Ba'ken activated the comm-stud on his gorget.

++*Fire-born, report*++

A spate of crackling voices returned a few moments later. The brother-sergeant nodded to G'heb. All was well.

'What just happened?' he asked, turning to Elysius.

From across the other side of the temple, the

Chaplain looked to the ceiling where the lightning-wreathed sky seemed to twist in torment. 'I'm not sure,' he admitted. 'But I suspect we felt an aftershock of it. Whatever just occurred didn't originate here.'

'Is it over? asked G'heb, reluctant to venture too far from the walls.

'For now. We are as safe here as anywhere, brother.' Elysius shifted his attention to Ba'ken. 'How do we stand? Who lives?'

The Chaplain kept to the shadows, unwilling to reveal his face. To his credit, Ba'ken didn't try see it. His expression darkened.

'Adar is dead. He fell into the abyss trying to help the humans, may Vulkan preserve his flame.'

Elysius bowed his head, muttering a prayer for Brother Adar, and made the sign of the circle of fire against his plastron. It represented the great cycle of life, death and rebirth as taught by the Promethean Creed. The grief at how the Salamander died was strong – his body was lost. It couldn't be returned to the mountain, its ash could not rejoin the earth. The circle of fire was broken.

After a moment of reflection, Ba'ken continued.

'There are six Fire-born left. Iagon and Koto are searching for you on the opposite side of the plateau. I kept the radius small, believing you could not have deviated that far.' He paused. 'In truth, I hoped you had not succumbed to the same fate as Adar. L'sen and Ionnes are with the humans at the landing site.'

'How many of them survived?'

'Eight Night Devils still live, my lord. G'heb and I are what are left of our forces.'

'What *forces* do you think we possess, Sergeant Ba'ken?' Elysius replied a little caustically.

Ba'ken was about to respond when the Chaplain showed his palm in apology.

'Sorry, brother. I'm weary, that's all.'

'I don't wish to presume, my lord, but Kadai and N'keln's deaths still weigh heavily on us all.'

Elysius narrowed his eyes. They were just slits of fiery red to Ba'ken, without a face and only darkness to frame them. 'You are shrewd, sergeant. I can see why Dak'ir chose you as his replacement.'

Ba'ken bowed his head, uncomfortable at the compliment. He had never wanted command but accepted it with the stoic belief that he would do his very best to live up to the honour his friend had given him.

'We cannot dwell on the past,' Elysius decided, 'in the same way we cannot be shackled by concern for the future. There is only now and the time of the moment.'

'Zen'de?' Ba'ken ventured.

'A philosopher, too?'

'Not really, my lord. An old friend taught it to me.'

Elysius paused, discerning the subtext of Ba'ken's remark.

'The 3rd has been through much change,' he said. 'It is like the broken blade going back to the forge to be renewed. Transition is never easy. Sometimes the metal must be melted back down to what lies at its core before it can be solid again. Vulkan tempers us all, brother. The forge is where he measures us. The 3rd will be reborn, Agatone will see to that. Right now, though,' he added, 'we have more pressing matters.'

Ba'ken looked to the shattered dome and the lightning-split sky above.

'What is this place? Where are we?'

'A hell-place of sorts, a nether realm over which the

dark eldar have dominion. Our enemies hold the ter-ritorial advantage here. It's only a matter of time before they come for us.'

'So we *are* to be hunted, then?'

Elysius stooped to retrieve something from amongst the debris underfoot.

'Make no mistake, sergeant. In this realm, we are *prey*.'

A lightning flash revealed the Astartes battle-helm Elysius had retrieved. It was black and well-worn.

'Allies?' Ba'ken asked.

'Loyalists, but this helmet is old. They are likely long dead,' said Elysius, donning the battle-helm.

'I found this, my lord.' Ba'ken held out the broken crozius. 'It must have come loose when you fell.'

Elysius nodded, stepping forwards to take it.

'I have found several blades and other weapons amongst the ruins,' said Ba'ken.

'This will do just fine.'

'Its power is broken, though,' Ba'ken replied before he checked himself and added, 'I'm sorry, my lord. I meant no disrespect.'

The Chaplain waved Ba'ken's contrition away. 'Is it, though? Is it broken?' He struck the crozius hard against the fallen spire, splitting the metal but bending the mace back into a shape where it could at least be used to bludgeon.

Ba'ken was nonplussed. G'heb, too, looked on with a furrowed expression. 'It is dead, my lord. Its power cell is depleted.'

'A crozius is more than an energy mace, brother-sergeant. It is a symbol. The power it represents comes from belief.'

'But you cannot ignite it. The metal is just that, metal.'

'And yet I can still draw strength from its presence. There is fire within it still. I can feel it.'

Ba'ken's frown deepened. 'I don't understand.'

'You don't have to understand, brother. You just have to *believe*.'

A distant baying echoed through the hollow ruins, cutting off any reply. The sound was deep and distinctly canine but with a resonance not entirely earthly.

'We are not alone in this place, not nearly alone,' said Elysius. 'Gather the others. The hunters have come.'

II
Paths Unknown...

THOSE DARK ELDAR whose bodies didn't litter the warehouse floor had fled. Some had sped through the portal that still shimmered like a lidless, black eye bridging reality and the other world beyond. With their ambush beaten and the return of Praetor and the Salamander survivors, the xenos's will was broken. The defeat and capture of the haemonculus was the final act that routed them.

'They took them,' said Brother Honorious. 'Chaplain Elysius and the others. They took them into *that*.' He was pointing at the portal.

He and the rest of the survivors were in the warehouse with He'stan and the other Firedrakes. It grieved them to see their slain battle-brothers. Some of the 3rd Company had already started to bring them down.

He'stan shared a dark glance with Praetor. The two of them stood with Honorious as he delivered his report. 'It's as I feared, brother.'

The veteran sergeant wasn't wearing his battle-helm. His face was hard as stone.

'What happened?' he asked Honorious.

'There was no warning. All of our sentries and alarms were bypassed. They bled out of the very shadows themselves.' He looked as if he wanted to say more but stopped himself.

'Go on, brother,' Praetor told him. 'You are amongst friends here. There'll be no judgement, save that of the primarch.'

Honorious licked his lips, as if deciding how he should proceed. Like Praetor, he went unhooded. There was a large gash down the right side of his face where a dagger had struck him. It left a jagged line of gummed blood. The dents and rents in his armour were everywhere. He'd fought hard before he'd been taken. To be subdued whilst his brothers suffered, it would not have been easy for a warrior like Honorious to bear. He was loyal to the Chapter, as loyal as any. It made what he said next even harder to countenance.

'Despite the surprise attack, the xenos could not have bypassed our defences without help.'

Praetor's eyes widened in disbelief.

'You are saying you were betrayed?'

Honorious nodded.

'By whom?'

'I don't know, sergeant. But I set those flares and posted sentries myself. We could not have been taken unawares without them being tripped, without someone raising the alarm.'

Praetor looked to He'stan for an answer, but the Forgefather had none to give.

'Make a pyre for the dead,' he ordered instead. 'Night Devils and Fire-born will share the same flame. They fought and died together, so too shall they return to the earth the same way.' He looked Honorious in the eye. The battle-brother found it hard to meet He'stan's gaze, but held it to his credit.

'Gather your fallen and prepare the Rites of Immolation. Do you know how to?'

'I have seen the Chaplains do it before. I know enough.'

He'stan clapped him on the shoulder. The gesture seemed to give Honorious immediate strength. 'Go then, brother. We will take it from here.'

Honorious bowed his head before going to join the others reclaiming the dead.

'They are wounded,' said Praetor when he was gone.

'Aye,' He'stan agreed, 'the 3rd have been through much these past years.' He looked to Tsu'gan who was standing nearby guarding the haemonculus.

The wretch was still pinned by the Spear of Vulkan, drawing slivers of pleasure from his own agony as he squirmed. As Tsu'gan glared, a hiss escaped the haemonculus's lips. The creature's limbs shook as if with palsy but it managed to reach into its robes and pull something out.

'Forgefather...' Tsu'gan cried, reaching for the haemonculus.

He'stan was quicker. He seized the creature's withered limb in a tight fist of ceramite. He turned the wrist, exposing the alien's palm to the half-light and forcing its fingers open.

'What have we here?' He'stan's voice was low, laced with threat.

The haemonculus showed a row of blackened nubs for teeth, the stitch-mouth parting like a wound in old cloth.

In a blink the portal vanished, leaving a stench and a strange sense of dislocation where it had manifested.

'No!'

'It's gone,' said Praetor.

'And with it the only way to reach the Chaplain.' He'stan's eyes flared bright with anger. 'Open it, cadaver,' he snarled at the haemonculus.

Tsu'gan took the shaft of Vulkan's Spear that still impaled the creature. As he touched the revered metal, the strength of eons flooded through him. The sensation was fleeting but in it he glimpsed the possibility of another path.

Ever since Aura Hieron and the death of Captain Kadai he had felt drawn towards a certain doom. The anger that drove him, that gave him strength was also consumptive. Only a matter of time before it ate away his purpose and his honour. But the spear, and by association the presence of its wielder, had shown him there was another way, that salvation was possible.

He let the anger back in, but this time he was its master.

'Do it now, wretch!' Tsu'gan turned the blade, churning the desiccated remains of the haemonculus's internal organs. It only drove the thing to greater frenzy. Something old and racking escaped from its dry lipless mouth. It took the Salamanders a few seconds to realise it was laughter.

'Let me crush its skull,' said Tsu'gan.

Praetor gripped his brother's forearm. 'Hold.'

The laughter ebbed, concluded by a death-like rattle but still the haemonculus lived.

'What kind of *thing* is this?' asked Halknarr, having approached from where the other Firedrakes were standing sentry.

He'stan released the dark eldar's wrist. His voice took on a sinister tone. 'Torturer, murderer, techno-sorcerer – the haemonculi are all of these things and worse. No weapons we possess hold any fear for him. The cadaver is an ancient one, amongst the first of his kind.'

As the Forgefather spoke, the creature's eyes glittered with malicious amusement. He knew there was nothing the Salamanders could do.

A susurrus of language spilled from between its lips, delivered through an evil grin.

Though he couldn't discern its meaning, Tsu'gan knew the creature was mocking them. He turned to Praetor. 'I'll snap it in two.'

'No,' said He'stan, 'release it.'

Tsu'gan wrenched the spear from the wall. He needed both hands and most of his strength to do it. He'stan's throw had been incredible. He gave the weapon back to the Forgefather.

Without the spear to support him, the haemonculus collapsed. Praetor grabbed him and hoisted him up. 'On your feet, stain.'

'Lift its chin to face me,' said He'stan, drawing in close. He was eye-to-eye with the creature now.

What happened next surprised them all.

The Forgefather spoke in the alien's language. It was an old, rasping tongue that sliced and cut the air as if even its syllables were razor-sharp.

The haemonculus replied, making He'stan repeat his previous words only more vehemently.

This time, the dark eldar paused. The pentagram in its palm began spinning again and the portal resolved itself anew, its black canvas fresh and unsullied.

He'stan eyed the gate to the webway. The air was foul and unnatural around it.

'Tsu'gan,' he said. His gaze settled on the haemonculus. 'Your bolter.'

Tsu'gan handed it over without hesitation.

'A deal is a deal…' He'stan murmured.

A thunderous report echoed around the warehouse as the bolt shell destroyed the creature's skull. Congealed blood splattered the Salamanders around him, before the body crumpled and dried away to ash in moments.

He'stan returned the bolter. 'Thank you, brother.'

A shocked cadre of Firedrakes watched as the Forgefather stalked to where the dark eldar skimmer-machine had ditched and currently rested on the warehouse floor.

'My lord?' asked Praetor.

'Organise the Fire-born, brother-sergeant,' he replied. 'Ten of us, you, I and Brother Tsu'gan included, will venture to the shadow realm. The rest must fortify Ironlandings and rejoin Captain Agatone. He will need to know all that has transpired here.'

'We are entering the webway then?'

He'stan reached the skimmer and mounted its deckplate. 'If we want to find Chaplain Elysius, then yes.'

Praetor had followed him and came close. Tsu'gan was in earshot.

'It is a myriad realm, my lord. How will we navigate it?'

Looking up from the skimmer's control column, He'stan replied, 'With the Sigil of Vulkan. Its resonance can be felt by all the Forgefathers that had have ever been or will be. It is more than a relic, Praetor. It is a beacon. I hear its call, even through the skin of the portal, even here in the mortal realm. The sigil was the primarch's. The spear, the gauntlet and cloak I carry, all belonged to him. They will guide us. We need only to find a way.'

After a few second's pause, the skimmer-machine thrummed to life and rose a half metre off the ground. He'stan looked to Praetor again. His mood was optimistic.

'*This* is our way, brother. Gather the rest of the ten. We leave immediately.'

Praetor was aghast, but saluted crisply. He went to the others to make his selections.

Tsu'gan nodded to him before leaping onto the skimmer. It felt strange to be buoyed aloft by xenos technology. He would tear the graven machine to scrap metal when they were done with it.

'How?' was all Tsu'gan could think to ask.

'I have searched the galaxy for the Nine. I have learned many things during that time. I have fought many foes, and made unlikely allies. But the dusk-wraiths and their ways are of a special interest. They were the original oppressors of Nocturne. Our bond with them is old. Do you understand?'

Tsu'gan nodded slowly, surprised that he actually did. He looked at the pile of dust that was all that remained of the haemonculus. 'What did you say to it to make it reopen the portal?'

He'stan stopped what he was doing. 'Death and pain hold no terror for the dark eldar, certainly not for one as old and venerable as a haemonculus. Do you know what the dark eldar dread?'

Tsu'gan stayed silent.

'Ennui. Boredom, brother. They are sustained by sensation. Without it they would soon dissipate, become as ash like that cadaver I slew with your bolter. That one was ancient and he is far from deceased.'

'The finger,' Tsu'gan realised, 'and the box it was put in, they were not with the body.'

'Science is merely sorcery to those without the wit or knowledge to see it. What we don't understand we regard as mythical, impossible. The box was a portal. The finger resides in some gene-lab now, awaiting the resurrection of its owner.'

'Diabolical,' Tsu'gan breathed. Did the depravity of the xenos have no end or limit?

Praetor was returning with the rest of the expedition that would brave the webway.

'And to answer your question, I told the cadaver if he did not reopen the gate I would lock him in a chamber without light, without stimulation, devoid of windows or doors. I would simply *forget* about him. Resurrection or not, the creature could not face such a fate.'

'My lord,' Praetor announced, 'we are ready.' The veteran sergeant eyed the skimmer-machine with suspicion. 'Master Argos would not approve.'

He'stan was pragmatic. 'Perhaps not. But to penetrate the lava-wasp's nest we must ride upon its back.'

'Then let us hope,' Praetor replied, heaving himself up onto the deckplate, 'that we are not stung into the bargain.'

'It's a risk I'm willing to take.'

Vo'kar, Oknar, Persephion, Eb'ak and Invictese – Tsu'gan had fought with Invictese before on the wreck of the *Protean* where they'd lost so much. It brought back painful memories of his battle-brother, Hrydor. Five other Firedrakes, Sergeant Nu'mean amongst them, had died in that mission. They had almost lost Apothecary Emek too.

He beseeched Vulkan for better favour as they neared

the edge of the webway portal and reality as they knew it.

Halknarr and Daedicus were the last to board the skimmer-machine. Behind them, the pyre flames were rising. They all wanted to stay behind to observe the ceremony. Honorious would conduct it. But there was no time to waste, and no way of knowing how long it would take them to track Elysius down and secure the Sigil of Vulkan. So much rested on it, perhaps the future of Nocturne itself.

Mek'tar was left in command. He watched the Rites of Immolation silently. The lenses of his battle-helm captured the reflected flame.

'Brothers,' He'stan addressed the late comers. Halknarr had one foot on the deckplating. The old veteran was clearly uncomfortable with riding the xenos machine, let alone entering their lair. Daedicus merely stood by and waited.

'There is one more thing we need,' He'stan said, then told them both what he wanted them to do.

CHAPTER TEN

I
Beneath the Veil

DAK'IR WAS LISTENING. Brazier-lamps, set into the alcoves of the bare rock walls, sent flickering tongues of light across his armour. The crown of his psychic hood threw deep shadows over his battle-helm. The lenses were cold and empty. Dak'ir's eyes were firmly shut.

In the background the low grind of industry invaded the silence. Labour-serfs – the grave-diggers, the corpse-masters and bone-gatherers – toiled nearby in legion-strong numbers. On Moribar, the dead outnumbered the living by many billions. The work for the armies of tomb-keepers was never done. While the cardinals and the priests and the preachers scribed in their ancient books, made the dead-lists and inked parchment with the details of Imperial bureaucracy that saw to the running of this world, the bodies grew and the grave pits deepened underneath them.

'Nihilan's psychic spoor is everywhere,' breathed Dak'ir. 'It thrums in the very air.'

Pyriel's reply came from the shadows behind him. 'He seeks to baffle us. By saturating the atmosphere with his warp-shadow, Nihilan knows we will find it harder to pinpoint the path he took.'

'His last visit was more recent than decades, though. It's obvious.'

'Obvious?' asked Pyriel. He kept his voice low, out of respect for the dead. The hollow sockets of the skulls pockmarking the walls seemed to stare in approval. 'Not to me, Dak'ir.'

A note of uncertainly crept into the Lexicanum's voice. 'You think I am wrong, master?'

'No, I think you are right. But you are just a novice and I, allegedly, the master. You discerned the truth of Nihilan's psychic resonance much faster than I did.'

Dak'ir opened his eyes.

He saw again the subterranean world of Moribar's catacombs. Here the dead were venerated. A tunnel stretched before him, cast in amber light from the lanterns lining the walls. Monolithic effigies of robed guardians supported its vaulted ceiling. They were called reapers, the massive servitor-statues that guarded these lower chambers. Though merely machines, the reapers were potent servants for the dead that ensured eternal rest was just that. The main channel leading deeper into the catacombs was ribbed by sepulchral arches and branched into several tributaries. Tomb-gates barred access to mausoleum chambers and the lesser crypts of the minor veins. The main artery was wider than a strike cruiser's hangar and twice as tall. In the highest echelons, though in reality several kilometres below the surface, fluttering cyb-organic cherubim and darting servo-skulls could be seen weaving between the chains of hanging censer cauldrons. Great gusts of dark smoke exuded from the censers, wreathing the ceiling in a dense and unnatural fog.

The lower deeps were filled with funerary pits and immolation cradles. The iron crucibles were stacked with burning coals to ignite the hordes of corpses fed to them by the labour army toiling below. They were pale shadows of the crematoria, though, the fiery heart of Moribar raging at the planet's core.

A bridge, cut from the same rock as the catacombs themselves, spanned a deep chasm filled with bones and ash. Iron gantries arced across a vast grate. Beneath it were row upon row of incinerators. Only pallid-skinned servitors could work the nadir of the chasm and even they were fitted with rebreathers and gas masks. The hot vapours from the incinerators formed as beads of sweat on the drone-like men and women some several hundred metres above. Nothing slowed them. Their barrows reached the funnels at the edge of the gantries that would take the dumped bodies to the incinerator floor. Shovelled into the fiery cages by the servitors, the dead would become bone then ash until finally joining the vast Moribar deserts.

Dak'ir saw a perverted version of the Promethean Creed in what was being done on Moribar, but he didn't voice his thoughts. This was cold, mechanical and bereft of ritual. It signified nothing more than the efficient disposal of waste and the rendering down of life into matter. It was not the way of earth, but the way of industry.

Having seen enough in a few short seconds, he faced Pyriel.

'What does it mean?' he asked, 'that I recognised the truth of Nihilan's passing faster than you, master?'

Pyriel opened his eyes too. He kept his tone neutral. 'Your power is growing.'

'I can feel it,' Dak'ir confessed. It unnerved him, but he chose to keep that part to himself. During the burning, he'd been close to losing control. Even now, he sensed something within him, a nascent flame slowly being coaxed into a conflagration. Let it slip, even for a moment, and the whole world would burn.

Pyriel's gaze narrowed. 'What else can you feel, Dak'ir?'

Dak'ir focussed, trying to push the desperate toiling of the labour-serfs out of his mind. It was less about psychic resonance and more about tapping into his instincts.

'If we find out why Ushorak and Nihilan came to Moribar, we will discover why my vision sent us here and perhaps what fate awaits Nocturne.'

'We will see what lurks beneath the veil.'

'Yes.'

A flash of cerulean blue lit Pyriel's eyes through his helmet lenses. 'I sense reluctance in you, brother.'

'Don't do that,' Dak'ir snapped.

'Then hide your thoughts, Lexicanum! I can read them like they're writ upon your face.'

A tremor of disquiet went through Dak'ir's body as he realised Pyriel might have also seen his concerns about what happened during the burning and the doubts about his power that still plagued him. If his master did, he chose not to say anything.

Dak'ir unclenched his fist and exhaled. 'I am sorry, master. It's been over four decades since I was here. I know this place is significant. I'm not sure I want to find out why.'

'Go on.'

'I am afraid, not in the sense of feeling fear. I am Astartes and have long since come to deny that emotion. Rather, it is… *unwillingness* to accept whatever destiny is before me.'

Now Pyriel regarded him shrewdly and Dak'ir knew he had discerned the truth about the Lexicanum's doubts and reservations.

'We make our own fates, Dak'ir. I've told you this. You, me, Kadai, ultimately we must *choose*. Even Nihilan had that luxury once.'

'And what if I don't like the options before me?'

'Then make another, but sometimes we have to face impossible decisions.'

'And if I make the wrong one?'

Pyriel laughed. It was a clipped and mirthless sound. 'The only wrong decision is to do nothing and not act. There is more to courage than wielding a bolter and blade, Dak'ir.'

'If only Tsu'gan realised that,' he muttered.

'What does it matter what your brother does and does not realise? Zek Tsu'gan is Firedrake, now. He's amongst the Lords of Prometheus. He *chose*.'

'I saw him in the desert.'

'The Pyre Desert, the Arridian Plain? What do you mean, Dak'ir?'

'Below Mount Deathfire, during the Totem Walk and the final part of my training, I saw Tsu'gan. He tried to kill me.'

'And you think this was prophetic, that your brother will turn and attempt to slay you?'

'No. I think it might mean he has cause to do it, that I will be the one who turns.'

Pyriel was growing angry. 'You are one of the

Emperor's Angels, a First Founding Salamander. *We* do not turn.'

Dak'ir's voice was barely a murmur. 'Then how do you explain Nihilan?'

Pyriel looked away. His ire was obvious from the energies roiling over his force staff.

'An aberration. Ushorak's doing.'

Stepping forwards, Dak'ir asked, 'But how? Was Ushorak *so* convincing?'

'There is much you don't know about Vai'tan Ushorak. I was there when Nihilan took his first steps on the path. Like you and Tsu'gan, we were brothers once. I never thought it possible that…' Pyriel's voice trailed away, lost to remembered sorrow. His shoulders had sagged but now he straightened his posture.

'It is history long dead,' he said, facing Dak'ir again, 'and matters not. Can you discern the path Nihilan took?'

Dak'ir's eyes flared cerulean blue. He nodded.

'A few years or four decades ago – both paths lead to same destination.'

'Where?'

The Lexicanum paused, as if unsure of his own psychic instincts. He shook his head slowly. 'Not the crematoria, not at first anyway…'

'You fought them there, though,' said Pyriel.

'At the end, yes. But that wasn't where they were going.'

'Where then?'

Dak'ir looked along the dark tunnel. It sloped downwards, deeper into the earth. The crematoria was nearby, but another branch in the catacomb network would take them to a different place, one the Salamanders had overlooked.

'The cryptoria – a voice there speaks louder than the others.'

Menials, peons, the masses of the insignificant dead all resided in the catacombs. It was the right of more vaunted Imperial servants, the ecclesiarchs, the lord-commanders, the aristocrats and the pious rich to be interred within the mausoleums of the cryptoria. Much like the world of the living, even the realm of the dead had a hierarchy.

Dak'ir pointed. 'We take the bridge across the incinerators.'

Pyriel nodded, approving. 'Lead us.'

II
Reapers

THE REAPER'S CHAMBER lay not far past the labour tunnels beyond the bridge. Both Librarians sensed the ending of their journey and brandished their psychic weapons in readiness for whatever challenge might still await them.

Nihilan had come here after the death of Ushorak. He had come recently, in the last few years. To what end, Pyriel did not know. But he was certain it could not be good.

'The cryptoria entrance is beyond that statue,' he said, pointing to the giant form of the reaper.

It stood still before a massive arch. An underground field of mausoleums, tombs and crypts was hinted at in the shadows beyond. Hooded and robed, the reaper had the aspect of a priest. Its skeletal hands, resting on the blade of a giant scythe, betrayed that notion utterly.

This was the *lair*, a massive plaza of stone-clad earth.

Bones had been fashioned into the walls, turning it into a macabre ossuary temple. Headless skeletons held aloft their own skulls. Fused femurs became columns. Vaulted arches, fashioned from spinal cords and fragments of rib, framed a bleached yellow ceiling. The chamber's periphery, shrouded by flickering shadow, was littered with coffins and sarcophagi. The vessels were made from marble, dark granite, even more bone and were sunk into the soft soil like the broken teeth of some half-buried giant.

It was a grim place that reeked of death and eked away vitality. Neither Salamander had any wish to linger.

'Do you hear that?' asked Dak'ir. He slowed, stalling a few metres from the reaper.

A low scratching sound was just audible above the sound of the labour-serfs toiling in the distant tunnels behind the Salamanders.

'Could be tomb rats or perhaps a skull-scribe?' suggested Pyriel.

'It's coming from this room.'

Louder now, the scratching became more distinct, until both Librarians could detect the source.

Pyriel sent a flare of psychic fire up the haft of his force staff. 'Get your back to me, brother.'

Dak'ir's eyes were already aglow with warpcraft. He ignited the blade of *Draugen* in a heartbeat and took up a defensive posture with his master.

Several of the coffin lids were rattling. The motion became increasingly violent as the seconds passed. One of the lids slid off and cracked when it struck an adjacent sarcophagus. Something within was moving, framed in silhouette.

'We have descended into a trap,' snarled Pyriel as

three more coffins shuddered loose on his side of the chamber.

'I have at least six on my flank,' said Dak'ir.

'There must be hundreds in here...'

A great clamour filled the chamber as all of the half-sunken tombs and crypt-vessels joined the chorus. All the while, the reaper looked on, his shadow eclipsing the two Salamanders standing back-to-back in the centre of the room.

As the first of the wretches dragged its rotting carcass into the light, Dak'ir was reminded of the servitors aboard the Mechanicus vessel *Archimedes Rex*. True, they did not possess any weapons, save their filth-encrusted talons or the implements used to bury them with, but their movements were syncopated in the same fashion and their hollow eyes gleamed with an evil fervour.

'Nihilan has raised the undead to slay us!' Dak'ir crafted a ball of fire in his palm. He was about to unleash it into the growing throng of corpses advancing on him when Pyriel stopped him.

'Wait until they get close, until enough are beyond the protection of their vessels.' Dak'ir held onto the flame, nurtured it within him, shaped it within his mind. He closed his eyes, and heard Pyriel's voice.

'Master Vel'cona, your teachings guide my fury, let the fire become a conflagration and render my enemies to ash.'

The grave-stink was filling Dak'ir's nose and mouth, even through his battle-helm. The scrape of the undead's limbs as they dragged across the chamber floor was loud in his ears. He imagined their lopsided gait, the awkward shambling of limbs and muscles long atrophied forced into motion again. He could feel their collective animus, a pale echo of Nihilan's own. The Dragon Warrior had invigorated these creatures. He had kept them quiescent until his enemies had come to this place. He *knew*.

'They are close, master,' Dak'ir muttered, concentrating on his craft. This was to be its first real test since his training.

Pyriel left a few seconds pause. The talons of the dead could only be a hand's width away...

'Purify them!'

Dak'ir opened his eyes. As he unleashed the flame, he viewed the world through a fiery veil. It was a roiling wave, snapping serpents at its crest, and it rolled over the walking corpses with such intensity that skin and flesh flaked to ash in seconds. Echoes, soot-silhouettes, were all that remained of the foremost undead. The ones that followed crumpled against the heat, their desiccated bodies quickly collapsing. Others, those who had only just surfaced, carried on, their bodies ablaze.

'Break formation, brother,' cried Pyriel. 'Take them down!' A stream of bolter fire stitched a rank of flaming bodies, filling the chamber with the dense thunder of explosions.

Dak'ir waded in hand-to-hand, seeing an opportunity to anoint *Draugen* in true battle. The corpses provided little challenge. Limbs and heads cascaded onto the ground, only to be stomped underfoot or forgotten as the next enemy came on. They were fearless, relentless creatures. For what did the dead have to fear? He thrust his sword into the chest of one creature and ignited its entire body with psychic fire. The ashen remains were still flaking off the blade when Dak'ir took the head from another. A third scrabbled at his shoulder pad, trying to drag him down. The Librarian drew his plasma pistol and put a bolt through its torso, ending it. The next shot vaporised the skull of a second.

'We are breaking the sanctity of this place,' he snarled to Pyriel, splitting a creature's torso.

Facing the opposite side of the chamber, the Epistolary was possessed by a similar fury.

'It's too late for that. Nihilan defiled it when he cast his warp-sorcery.'

The two Salamanders fought in one half-circle each, defending an arc and leaving a void of open ground between them in the centre. That way no creature could get behind them. One relied on the other for his protection. Trust was paramount.

Despite the carnage, more and more undead were shambling into the fray. Whereas before they'd attacked individually, now they struck in a mob. Dak'ir counted over thirty on his flank alone. More were coming.

'In Vulkan's name, they're endless!'

'Burn them, Dak'ir,' said Pyriel, a surge of fire channelled through his force staff interrupting him. 'Unleash the deathfire.'

His combat doctrines came by rote – the blade of *Draugen* dimmed and became just a sword, his pistol thundered at precise intervals. The undead were kept at bay whilst Dak'ir's focus travelled inwards, seeking the fiery core within and the catalyst with which he could release it. The name passed his lips without him realising it had been spoken.

'*Kessarghoth...*'

Dak'ir's eyes went from cold, cerulean blue to ardent flame red. He roared with the ancient voice of a long-dead drake, and the terrifying din drowned out all others in the chamber. Molten death spewed from his mouth, through the grille in his battle-helm, and bathed the deathless horde.

'Pyriel, down!' The voice did not sound like Dak'ir's, but the other Librarian crouched as the lava flow scorched overhead, engulfing the other side of the chamber. The walking corpses, hundreds strong, were swept up in a terrible maelstrom and melted away in moments. The coffins and sarcophagi proved more resilient but lasted only seconds more before they too had sloughed to insignificant wisps of smoke on a hot and undulating magma sea.

It was over in moments. The lava cooled rapidly into rock, the two Librarians standing on a circular plateau surrounded by a ringed crater. Of the dead, of their vessels, there was no sign. Dak'ir had obliterated them utterly. Hundreds of them.

'Wisdom of Zen'de...' breathed Pyriel. He straightened up to face his saviour.

Fire wreathed Dak'ir's body, incandescent and alive. Just being near him seared the other Librarian's armour and sent radiation warnings spiking across his retinal display.

'Lexicanum...'

The heat was still growing. Dak'ir slumped to one knee, using *Draugen* for support. Tongues of flame lashed out from his aura of conflagration. Pyriel reached out to shake him, but recoiled as his fingers were burned even through his gauntlet. He had scarcely brushed the other Librarian's shoulder guard.

'Dak'ir!' he cried more urgently, stepping back and throwing up a psychic shield. Blackened cracks were already forming in its surface when the Lexicanum met Pyriel's pained gaze.

'Dak'ir...' he repeated, less forcibly now his strength was fading, and retreated from the terrible fire, '...marshal it.' Pyriel's mind returned to the burning again, to the moment when his apprentice had almost killed him in an uncontrollable flamestorm. Master Vel'cona had stepped in then and between them they'd averted disaster. Now, Pyriel was alone. He knew he didn't possess the power to stop the Lexicanum's tide of fire.

Slowly, Dak'ir's fiery aura ebbed as he corralled the violent energies that threatened to engulf them both. The heat faded to a flickering haze around his body that eventually dissipated into nothing. Tendrils of smoke exuded from his armour, becoming grey translucent mists carried away on a shallow breeze.

'I... I am...' he stammered, his voice deep and thick with effort, 'in control.'

Pyriel's battle-plate was badly blistered. As he stood up, the ceramite lurched and cracked. 'You have nearly destroyed my armour,' he breathed. The words with Vel'cona, spoken years ago when Dak'ir had first lost his grip on the flame during the burning, returned to the Epistolary.

'And if he loses control again?'

'Do what you must... destroy him.'

Except Pyriel didn't think he could do that. He didn't know if he was capable. Dak'ir's psychic potential was simply frightening. It was a weapon. If fettered, a potent and useful one. If left unchecked, one that could bring about a cataclysm.

Much of the battle-helm was scorched from the fire. The lenses were cracked and smeared black with soot, so Pyriel cast it aside. He breathed deeply. Until that point, the air had been stifling.

'Never have I witnessed such power,' he said with something close to awe, but closer to fear.

Dak'ir removed his battle-helm too, and mag-locked it to his belt. The scar Ghor'gan's melta had left him glared starkly against his onyx-black skin. The flesh was near-white down one side of his face, a product of cellular regression caused by intense radiation of the beam.

'You are more human than any of us,' Pyriel continued, 'and yet, at the same time, something else entirely beyond it.'

'It stirred within me, master. It was a pyre-flame and the legacy of Kessarghoth.'

'Your empathy has a psychic application I did not expect.' Pyriel looked around at the crater and the blackened carnage Dak'ir had left in the wake of his power. 'You almost killed us both.'

Dak'ir nodded solemnly. 'I am not ready. It's too soon after my training. I–'

'Stop,' Pyriel warned, gesturing to the force sword in the Lexicanum's hand. *Draugen* was blazing with the psychic resonance of Dak'ir's emotions. 'Calm your humours, brother, and sheathe the blade now.'

As if scalded by the hilt, Dak'ir returned *Draugen* to its scabbard.

'Your psychic hood,' Pyriel added, not deigning to step any closer but content to point at the metallic collar that arced around the back of Dak'ir's neck, 'advance it to maximum capacity. Do it immediately.'

Dak'ir obeyed. The psychic hood was, in part, a nullifying device. It aided with the concentration of psychic force, whilst at the same time reducing the risk of its wielder succumbing to the predations of the warp. Here, Pyriel intended for it to staunch the roiling fire within his apprentice from a roar to a whisper. Gauged to maximum, the hood would prevent almost all psychic conductivity and leave Dak'ir effectively *nulled*.

The Epistolary hoped they had already endured all the snares left by Nihilan. His own strength was sapped and returning slowly; the Lexicanum's could not be employed beyond seeking the Dragon Warriors' trail. Anything more was simply too dangerous to even comprehend using. As soon as they were back on Nocturne, Pyriel avowed he would seek Vel'cona's counsel.

Satisfied he had shackled Dak'ir sufficiently, he turned to regard the statue of the reaper.

'Stand aside,' he ordered.

It was standing atop a granite plinth. Only the lowest of the plinth's stairs had sustained any lava damage.

None shall pass.

'We are servants of the Imperium. Stand aside.'

Only the dead.

'What's wrong?' Dak'ir hissed, eyeing the statue warily.

'I don't know,' Pyriel replied. 'It should yield.'

None shall pass, the reaper boomed again, and began to shift. Stone and metal creaking in protest, its massive limbs slowly extended. Its fingers gripped the haft of its power-scythe. Energy being fed down the blade filled the false creases of its robes with shadow. Its cowled face was a featureless, black void.

Only the dead.

It came forwards to descend the first step.

'In the name of Vulkan and the Fire-born of Nocturne, I demand you step aside, automaton!' Pyriel clenched his fist. The reaper was a formidable guardian. Fighting in his condition and with Dak'ir effectively neutered was unthinkable.

The decision was swiftly taken out of the Epistolary's hands.

Fire-born... uttered the reaper, the timbre of its voice changing, becoming more deep and resonant. Pyriel knew at once the sound was beyond the range of its vocal-enhancers. He started to retreat, only now realising the danger they were in.

'Mercy of Vulkan...'

The reaper dwarfed the two Salamanders, its shadow engulfed them. It raised its power-scythe, sharp enough to cleave ceramite with ease.

Nihilan had left one final surprise for them. Pyriel had just triggered it unwittingly.

As the Librarians backed away from the effigy of death, Pyriel knew there would be no escape.

Death to the Salamanders!

The scythe came down on them in a glittering arc.

CHAPTER ELEVEN

I
There be Monsters...

MONSTERS. THAT WAS how he would describe them. The things pursuing them through the haunted alleyways of the dark city were unlike any hounds Corporal Tonnhauser had ever seen. What was more, they were not entirely in this place. Through snatched glances, he'd seen their forms shimmering, the edges of their obscene musculature blurring. It was as if the hounds were not entirely synchronised with whatever plane of existence the survivors found themselves upon.

'Hurry, human,' snapped one of the giants. His green armour plate was badly battered. A gash along one side was gummed with blood. A thin line of onyx-black skin was revealed beneath an inner mesh.

Tonnhauser was no artificer or enginseer – he knew almost nothing about power armour. It was the aegis of the Space Marines. It was supposed to be almost impregnable. Surrounded by seven of these legendary warriors, ushering him and what remained of his troops through a nightmare of bladed streets and spiked structures, Varhane Tonnhauser should have felt safe. He did not.

Two of the Salamanders ranged ahead, trying to find a route through the alien byways and keep them ahead of the chasing pack. Two more roamed on either flank, the Night Devils between them. Another three served as rearguard behind. Most of Tonnhauser's men had their heads down, some even ran with their eyes shut, clinging desperately to the belts of their fellow Guardsmen. These men were lost, just like the ones whose screaming had devolved into a piteous mewling. He didn't blame them.

Tonnhauser's head hurt from the shrieking of the beasts and the calls of their whelpmasters. The dark eldar were travelling behind the pack on a spiked skiff that hovered above the ground through Emperor-knew-what infernal technologies. His mind was reeling. This place was hell, Tonnhauser decided. It bent reality and twisted what he accepted as possible.

As the dark city passed by in a blur, even the sight of its barbed edges making him sicken, Tonnhauser thought of his father. He was back on Stratos and fought as part of the Air Corps. He'd wanted the same for his son, but Varhane had left as part of a planetary tithe of men and materiel to the Imperial Guard. He'd wanted to see the galaxy. If he was to die then he'd do it under a foreign sky and in the Emperor's name.

Hunted down in the desolated streets of some alien city between realities had not been a part of his glorious vision. He didn't know what had happened to his father. Varhane hadn't seen or spoken to the man he knew as Colonel Abel Tonnhauser, or just 'The

Colonel', in years, ever since he'd shipped out on the
heavy lander. At that moment he hoped he'd see him
again.

Tonnhauser slipped, losing his footing on a jagged
spur jutting from the ground. It gashed his leg, even
though it only struck a glancing blow.

'Be mindful,' said the giant beside him, hauling
Tonnhauser along so he didn't break stride. This one
was massive, even bigger than the others. His head was
squared like a block of black granite and his eyes were
sunken like molten pits of fire. 'The way ahead is
sharp,' he warned. 'Stay with me and watch your footing. We can evade the creatures.'

At the mention of the hounds, Tonnhauser glanced
over his shoulder. He wanted to believe the Salamander but their pursuers would not be shaken. Even now,
they were gaining. The acid-burned hides of the beasts,
shaggy with clumps of blood-flecked hair, came into
greater detail as they closed. Their sulphur-yellow eyes
glared hungrily. Where the skin was bare, it shimmered
like oil on water. It was neither one hue nor another,
but an iridescent melange of many. Faces were trapped
behind that flesh, the half-devoured victims of the
hounds beckoning others to join them in eternal torment.

It was no fate for a soldier, no fate for any man of
flesh and blood.

When Tonnhauser started to hear their plaintive
voices he turned away.

'They're herding us,' said the massive Salamander.
One in black, the leader and some kind of preacher,
answered.

'We have to keep moving. Be ready.'

Tonnhauser didn't like the sound of that. A loud cry

made him look behind again to see a Salamander hurl a spear into one of the beasts as it pounced.

The barbed tip of the flung missile tore into the hound's unnatural flesh, spilling ichorous fluid akin to blood. But the beast had momentum and the warrior was borne down under its massive weight. Though impaled, the hound rent his armour plate and flesh. A welter of blood marred the green as another Salamander whacked a flat-bladed sword into the beast's flank. This one was just a vanguard. More were coming. A third warrior, the last of the rearguard, took the creature's head with an axe. Together the two uninjured Salamanders dragged the carcass off their fallen brother and hauled the spear-hurler back to his feet. Tonnhauser thought he must be dead. Incredibly, he managed to run.

'Here,' shouted another from up front. He was slighter of frame, though still bulky in his armour. He wore a perpetual snarl from some kind of burn. He beckoned towards a narrow cleft in the razor-edged avenue ahead.

Darkness within. It didn't look like salvation to Tonnhauser. It looked like a dead end. Perhaps the Salamanders thought that too. Perhaps they'd elected to make a last stand. War could be glorious when you were engineered for it, when you were superhuman. Tonnhauser was just a man, with a man's desires and dreams. He didn't want to die here but if that was to be his fate then he'd meet it with the same resolve as the giants around him.

'Give me a weapon,' he said before realising he'd spoken.

They had almost reached the cleft. Just a few more metres...

'Forge the armour strong,' said the other outrider opposite the massive warrior. His voice was grating. The bloody gash in his neck – looked like it was from a garrotte – forced a rasp. 'No weak links.'

The big warrior regarded Tonnhauser. 'No weak links,' he repeated, and tossed him a dagger that in the human's hands was more like a sword.

'Once on the other side, form up in a defensive phalanx,' the preacher – Tonnhauser had heard them call him 'Chaplain' – was swift to add.

'Make a wedge behind me,' said the big warrior. He too carried a spear. To Tonnhauser it was massive, far too large for a man to wield, yet the giant hefted it like it was nothing. There was something old in his movements, as if he'd learned his war craft somewhere other than the place that had trained his brothers.

Tonnhauser had no more time to think on it. The Night Devils were being ushered through the gap and into the darkness within.

Seconds felt like hours as they waited. The hounds were coming. Their slavering voices presaged doom. Tonnhauser thought they were in some kind of amphitheatre. Rows of broken seats delineated a wide elliptical expanse that was strewn with debris from the upper floor. Several columns, razor-edged and sculpted with obscene and daemonic faces, had collapsed in the centre too.

Dust, disturbed upon their arrival, swelled in fat clouds. Several men coughed. It was like breathing in powdered glass. It stung Tonnhauser's eyes enough so that when he looked up to the highest echelons and thought he saw a bulky figure flitter into view and out again, he passed it off as vision blur.

'They are coming!' said the big warrior. His spear was

levelled and his footing braced. His brothers made an arrow behind him, two at either shoulder, two more at the shoulder of the next. The last two formed a rear-guard, ready to step in should any warrior fall. Tonnhauser and the Night Devils were in the middle. The distance to the opening was barely a metre. The fighting wedge filled it. Close quarters and bloody was the how the fight was going to play out.

Tonnhauser gripped the haft of his sword and prayed to the Emperor.

'Show Vulkan your mettle this day, Salamanders!' Elysius was brandishing his crozius, his spitting fervour coming through his borrowed battle-helm in a roar. 'Break them on the anvil, Fire-born.'

Ba'ken's twin hearts were pumping hard. His Brother-Chaplain had stirred his warrior spirit. Three hounds were coming for them. The cleft was narrow, though. Unless they were breached, only one beast could get at the Salamanders at a time. Iagon had chosen well. The other sergeant was on Ba'ken's right shoulder, wielding a serrated sword. The weapons could have come from any wielder. This hell-place was like a battlefield in parts. Ba'ken shuddered at the thought of the lives taken by it, at the sport made of the captives by its hunter packs. Simple blades and spears, large enough for Astartes to wield, had been easy to procure. They would only do so much. He wished he had his heavy flamer. But as the lead hound closed on Ba'ken, a spear would have to do.

Feels like home, he thought with a sad spike of nostalgia, *back in Themis*.

The Sanctuary City was another world away; more than just galactic distance separated it from the

Salamander. Sentiment had no place in war. The battlefield respected only blood and sweat.

The hound reared up and Ba'ken stabbed it in the chest.

It struggled on the barbed tip of the spear, thrashing, exerting all its strength to free itself. Ba'ken stepped into its killing arc, ducking a swiping claw that would've taken his head had it connected. He came close, getting under the beast. The hound's efforts only impaled it further.

'Shoulder-to-shoulder!' Ba'ken cried, taking a firmer grip on the spear and lunging hard. Iagon and G'heb obeyed, *thunking* sword and axe blade into the beast's flank.

It howled – an unnatural and reverberant sound. Ba'ken smiled. It was hurt. He pushed harder and grunted when the barbed tip punched through the hound's back, spraying gore.

He let go of the spear, bracing its haft diagonally against the ground. Muscles straining, Ba'ken seized the stricken beast's forelegs and heaved. Iagon and G'heb rammed their shoulders in, lending weight.

The beast tipped over, spine cracking as it twisted awkwardly, and the spear was wrenched back through its chest.

At last it fell, oozing ichor, and rolled into a ragged heap.

'Wedge forward,' said Ba'ken, taking up his spear again.

Two more were coming. They appeared reluctant.

'They recognise a hunter of the Arridian Plain before them, a man of Themis,' Ba'ken revelled. He brandished his weapon in triumph, eager for another kill. Too late, he realised the beasts were being held back. A skiff hovered into view. A dark beam spat from the cannon on its prow.

It took Ba'ken in the shoulder, shredding the armoured pad and spinning him hard into Iagon. The two sergeants rolled and collapsed. One side of the wedge crumpled. In the same instant, the hounds were let slip. G'heb was still trying to fill the gap, L'sen and Ionnes coming from the rear to support him, when the beast smashed into him. It glowered over the Salamander, who was still flailing for his axe when the hound snapped its jaws and G'heb lost his head.

A fountain of blood spewed up from the dead warrior's neck cavity, bathing human and Salamander alike. Some of the Night Devils were screaming in terror. Barging into the amphitheatre, the hound made room for its kin.

Elysius met the second beast with Ionnes and L'sen.

The first hound sprang off. A savage blow raked along Iagon's flank and sent him sprawling off into the darkness. His scavenged sword scraped away along the ground, useless. Ba'ken was still coming to his senses when the loping beast came for him. On his back, he crabbed away and felt for his spear. The hound knew what its prey was attempting and trapped the haft with its paw. Hot saliva that smelled like oil and copper dribbled from its distended mouth. Up close there was something distinctly alien about these monsters. This one was partly scaled, with a long saurian maw. Its eyes were yellow pinpricks, beady and evil.

Ba'ken was about to leave the spear when the hound yelped and released the weapon as it turned about.

The human he'd given the dagger to was standing his ground in front of the beast.

A surge of pride turned to horror in Ba'ken as his

saviour was struck a glancing blow by the beam weapon on the skiff. He lost the human from sight, but snatched his spear and got up. Ba'ken drove a heavy blow that skewered the hound from shoulder blade through to the gullet and out the other side. It was a vital wound and lathered the ground in viscous fluids. A death rattle sounded before the beast gave out and slumped dead.

'Fall back!' he heard Elysius cry, 'Deeper into the ruins, fall back!'

The Chaplain's crozius was drenched in blood and matter from where he'd bludgeoned the third hound to death. But more were coming, the skiff and the hunters too. The dark eldar had but one cannon. Judging by the blackened scar and the shorn ceramite of Ba'ken's shoulder pad, it was a deadly one. He barely registered the pain. Suppressors in his bloodstream filtered it out, nulled it, but kept him alert. He left G'heb, mouthing a silent prayer to the primarch as he did so. The Sala-mander was dead. With no Apothecary in their ranks, G'heb's legacy to the Chapter was sadly ended.

'Brother-sergeant, move now!'

Elysius was calling him. Ba'ken was the last of them. He stooped as he made to retreat, finding the fallen human who had come to his aid, and hoisting him up onto his back.

'Tonnhauser,' he said, reading the boy's ident-tag on his uniform. 'I fought with another man who shared your name. He was brave too.'

Tonnhauser's eyes widened in realisation before he passed out.

Elysius had arranged them into a circle, chunks of cracked stone from the upper tiers forming makeshift barricades in its arc.

They'd lost more of the humans when the hounds had broken through. Ba'ken counted four left, not including Tonnhauser. Dead or lost to the dark, he didn't know. They were no use now, anyway. Those who remained cowered like children, unmanned by the nightmare they were living.

'Hell has come, hell has come,' one was saying, before L'sen cuffed him into unconsciousness.

'Weak links,' he reminded Ba'ken, as he joined them in the circle.

'No so weak, brother,' he replied, setting Tonnhauser down within the protective circle.

L'sen grunted, though it came out as a rasp. His eyes narrowed and Ba'ken followed their gaze.

Four more hounds entered the amphitheatre. They moved with a slow yet perverse grace, like the muscled leo'nid of the T'harken Delta and ash-adders from the Themian ridges in one. Ba'ken had hunted both of these creatures. Their pelts adorned his cave in the mountains. It was a place of peace and solitude. Like many Salamanders, when on Nocturne, Ba'ken was a loner. Only through isolation could a warrior learn self-reliance and endurance. The cave seemed very far away now but the lessons learned in its confines gave him strength.

Like the inexorable tightening of the executioner's noose, the hounds began to circle them. Ba'ken lost sight of one when it loped up a ruined stairway to the higher levels. Suddenly, the protective cordon didn't feel quite as impregnable.

Weak links… The words of L'sen came back to him. Except now, the chain was flawed because it no longer defended all angles of attack.

'In the higher echelons,' he said.

'Eyes on the enemy around our perimeter,' Elysius replied, holding back on another sermon for now. They would have need of them when battle was joined.

Ba'ken nodded then looked sidelong at Iagon. The other sergeant was cut up badly but had managed to retrieve his sword.

'Don't concern yourself with me,' he snapped, reading his brother's expression. 'Look to your own protection.' The snarl quickly faded, despite Iagon's facial injury, and he nodded back.

'A shame we understand each other now, only to die in a last stand,' Ba'ken remarked.

'It's not over yet.'

The hounds closed again, still circling. Three of the beasts rotated between the cardinal points of the Salamanders cordon, a fourth unseen and waiting to pounce.

Instinctively, the Fire-born moved back a step and tightened the wall.

ELYSIUS WAS STANDING on a chunk of fallen column in the middle of the circle. His vantage point gave him a commanding view. He could watch for cracks in the line. He tracked the beasts as they moved into his eyeline but never once shifted position. Instead, he used his other senses to stay aware of their stalking pattern and trusted in his brother Salamanders to remain vigilant where he could not. They all did.

Again, he thought of Vulkan's teachings, of the crucible of fire and the need for his will to be tested. He resolved not to fail and felt a palpable hum of approval emanate from the Sigil. It was unexpected. Had he imagined it?

When the narrow cleft they'd used to enter the amphitheatre was torn apart by cannon fire, the Chaplain abandoned all thoughts but one: *Fight or die.*

Through a miasma of dust and crumbling stone, the skiff emerged. Long and jagged, it reminded Elysius of a blade. Much like the raider which had dumped them here, this one was festooned with skulls and other trophies. It hovered low to the ground and agonisingly slowly, all to the whistles and crowing of its alien riders.

Elysius counted six, hanging off the skimmer's fuselage or languishing on its deckplates, males and females both – though the inherent androgyny of the dark eldar race made it difficult to tell – armed with tridents, barbed nets and whips. Sadism dripped from their every pore, from the bonded leather surplices, the leering hell-masks and spiked collars.

'Why don't they attack?' asked a dazed-looking Night Devil officer.

Elysius glared down at him.

'Because of you, human,' he said simply. 'Look around at your men. They are huddled in fear. The xenos are feeding on that. They are feeding on you.'

The officer grimaced but then looked up as a gargled yelp of pain resounded from the upper tier.

Elysius followed his gaze. 'Wha–' The carcass of one of the hounds came plummeting from on high and smashing into the skiff interrupted him. The heavy weight of vat-grown muscle and otherworldly sinew snapped the skimmer's fuselage in two. Its occupants were sent sprawling. A moment later and something long and fast tore through the gloom, pinning one of the unseated riders before he could reach for his weapon. A thickly hafted spear transfixed him. A second rider collapsed, several hard black quarrels protruding from her neck and chest. The survivors screeched and wailed. Retaliatory fire whickered into the darkness above as they pulled out splinter rifles. Someone grunted and fell. Others were moving down to ground level. Elysius discerned maybe five ambushers, small-framed, humanoid. One in particular caught his interest, larger than the rest and using a familiar combat style. He caught a few slashes of movement then the figure was gone.

Who are you? the Chaplain wondered, but more importantly, why are you helping us?

'BREAK RANKS!' BA'KEN gave the order. In the last few seconds, the hounds had faltered. He didn't know who their allies were or what their plan was. He didn't care. Kill the hounds, interrogate their newfound allies later. Bitter experience aboard the *Archimedes Rex* and the Chapter's dealings with the Marines Malevolent had taught Ba'ken the importance of mistrust when confronted with unannounced 'friends'.

The circle broke apart, Ba'ken and Iagon fanning warriors left and right into a dispersed attack formation. All thoughts of a last stand were forgotten in the face of the tactical alternative provided by the unseen ambushers. For that, at least, the brother-sergeant was grateful.

The hounds adapted and charged at the warriors coming for them. Without their handlers, who were still intent on punishing those who'd attacked them directly, they were savage but unfocussed. The Fireborn paired up swiftly. With G'heb slain, though, that left Ba'ken on his own until Tonnhauser and another Night Devil he didn't know arrived at his side. Elysius, too, fought solo but then the Chaplain needed no assistance. Even with only one arm, he was a prodigious fighter.

'Stay behind me,' Ba'ken told both his charges. 'I'll draw it out. When it comes for me, attack its blind side.'

Tonnhauser and the other trooper nodded, their faces etched with determination. Both paled when the beast rushed them. Barrelling out of the darkness, clouds of grit and glass displaced in its wake, the hound was phantasmal. Horror piled on horror as its slitted eyes blazed and three fleshy flaps opened wide to reveal a grotesque tri-pronged maw. Lashing the air, its puckered tongue slavered at the approach of the kill.

Slowed by his earlier injury, Ba'ken failed to move quick enough and the hound raked his side as he tried to dodge it.

'Hnnng!'

Three deep grooves tore up the right flank of his ceramite. The inner mesh hung ragged and open like skin. Ba'ken staggered but kept his body between the beast and the humans.

The Night Devils managed to stay clear, hurrying behind the Salamander as he angled to face the hound for another pass. It turned swiftly for such a brute and was on them again moments later. Ba'ken jabbed, using the spear haft's full length, and caught it in the shoulder. The hound snarled in pain but the blow was weak and glanced off its muscled body, leaving an ichorous gash but nothing more. It swatted the Salamander, putting a fresh crack in his armour's plastron and punching him onto his back. He held onto the spear and jabbed again. The beast evaded Ba'ken's thrusts, pausing to rend the unknown Night Devil who'd rushed it with his bladed staff. The human died gurgling blood, his throat ripped out. Tonnhauser jumped over the trooper's slowly crumpling form to hack at the beast with his sword. He got in close, taking a piece of ear, but was butted in the chest for his bravura. Ba'ken heard the crack of broken ribs. A strange wheeze escaped Tonnhauser's lips as he sagged and fell, clutching his chest.

The distraction was enough for the Salamander to regain his feet.

'Come on, you ugly spawn,' he spat with a gobbet of his own blood.

His mind went back to Themis. Just a boy then, he had faced a wounded leo'nid on the Arridian Plain. Ba'ken, or Sol as he was known when he was a child, had tracked the beast for days. His snare had injured it, slowed the creature so he could finally confront it. Sol had come from a large family – the memories of them were indistinct and hazy now, subjugated by his Astartes conditioning – the leo'nid had slain nearly half of them when it came upon their camp four nights previously. A mean, scarred brute, its scaled haunches were leathery with age and its tendril-mane ropey and thick. Sharp, yellow eyes spoke of cunning but they also contained malice. It was a killer. Ba'ken had faced death on the plain that day and triumphed. The leo'nid's pelt was a trophy of special significance. In the xenos hound he fought a similar beast. The old instincts returned.

As he rolled the spear in his grasp, Ba'ken became dimly aware of the other battles unfolding around him. The rest of the hounds were going down hard, too. He saw L'sen in his peripheral vision, unmoving on the ground. Somewhere, Elysius was raging with litanies of hate. The whelp creatures were fast, but so were his brothers. Several skirmishes played out at once with incredible pace and intensity.

Ba'ken lunged as the hound charged again and tore into its chest this time. Momentum kept the beast going. Warp-fuelled muscle met genetically enhanced physique and one broke. For Ba'ken, it was like being hit by a Land Raider. Super-hardened bones broke with an audible *crack* as the big warrior was boosted off his feet and hoisted into the air.

For a moment, the hot sun of the Arridian Plain bathed his face and the scent of the leo'nid filled his nostrils... Like smoke banished before the breeze, the sensations disintegrated and he was in the dusty amphitheatre again. He clutched his spear, twisting and yanking it to increase the damage, hoping to find a vital organ. Ba'ken landed hard. Searing agony crippled his wrist, and not from the fall. The beast's jaws were clamped tight around it. The sheer strength of the hound lifted Ba'ken ferociously into the air again, his wrist the fulcrum about which he was being thrashed.

Dark spots blossomed in front of his eyes and his pumping blood thundered in his ears. If he'd still worn his helmet the damage readouts on his retinal display would be flashing amber. Even the leo'nid hadn't taken him this close. He was dying.

Elysius caved in the monster's skull with his crozius. An ignited mace would've made the task easier, but the weapon killed well enough. Breathing rapidly despite his superhuman physiology, he tried to get some bearing on the battle. His Fire-born were still engaged with the beasts, well dispersed around the amphitheatre but fighting hard. L'sen was dead – the Chaplain didn't need a red rune in his absent retinal display to know that much. The anvil had broken many – Elysius mourned them all.

Then he saw Ba'ken.

Tossed into the air, his wrist a bloody ruin, the giant Salamander would not live out the fight. Elysius was running, shouting something he couldn't make out even though it came from his own lips. Too many were dead, lost to this hell-place and so far from the mountain. He couldn't lose another.

Ba'ken hit the ground and rolled. He came up on his elbows, spitting blood. The beast landed on top of him before he could drag himself clear. A savage blow ripped a chunk out of his generator. The latent hum in Ba'ken's power armour ebbed.

Even *with* the aegis of his battle-plate intact, there was no way he could survive another attack.

The Chaplain was still several metres away.

He'll be slain before I can reach him.

One more sundered against the anvil.

At least Elysius would have vengeance.

A black shadow surging from the hound's blind side denied both. It moved with power and purpose, slamming into the beast to dislodge it. Fists clenched, Ba'ken's saviour punched the hound's flank. Like a freight sentinel hauling a heavy load, the figure kept on moving. Legs driving like pistons, the black-armoured warrior upended the beast. With a shallow cry, he leapt on its back, fists stabbing though he had no visible weapons.

Elysius closed and he saw the bone-blades. Now he knew what manner of Space Marine it was who'd saved Ba'ken's life.

He beheld a monster before him. This was a savage, feral thing. Fangs filled the beast's mouth, a calcified crest bifurcated his forehead. Swathed in gore, blood streaking his armour, he was an apparition, a nightmare made flesh. But then what else but nightmares and monsters could survive in a place such as this?

The beast was long dead before the warrior stopped stabbing. He looked up, the efforts of his grisly labours sprayed across a snarling visage. Wild eyes regarded Elysius, and for a moment the Chaplain assumed a battle posture. Slowly, reluctantly, the fervour dulled and the battle ended.

The hounds were dead. They were all dead.

A circlet of Salamanders surrounded Ba'ken, the slain beast and his strange protector.

'Brother...' said the big warrior, offering his hand.

'Stand down!' The bone-blade was at Ba'ken's throat in an eye-blink. Several of the Fire-born moved, but Elysius stayed them with a glance. The feral warrior was indeed a Space Marine, one who wore black armour. His Chapter signifier was so degraded as to be all but lost. Elysius knew his origins, though. It was why he made the others hold. A rash move here and Ba'ken's life-blood would be washing the ground.

The black-armoured warrior cast around him like an animal cornered by its hunters. He kept the bone-blade, protruding from his very flesh, at Ba'ken's neck. An inching step forwards by Iagon made him press the edge closer and draw a bead of blood.

'No closer,' he warned, his voice a deep-throated snarl with an almost saurian cadence. His yellow eyes glared at Ba'ken. 'Name thyself! Do it now or suffer the same fate.' He gestured to the butchered hound.

With the bone-blade pressing on Ba'ken's gullet it

was hard to speak without rasping. 'Brother Ba'ken,' he said, 'Of the Salamanders 3rd Company.'

The feral warrior's breath was like spoiled meat as he leaned in close. Chunks of gristle were wedged between his ruddy fangs.

'You are far from home, sons of Vulkan. What are you doing here on the Volgorrah Reef? Answer swiftly!'

'Not before you answer a question for me, brother,' Elysius interrupted. In his urgency to reach Ba'ken, he was closer than any of the other Fire-born. 'Who are you?' His tone was stern, unyielding. He would show this Astartes iron, and he would respect him for it.

Feral eyes narrowed. The bone-blade was kept close. Trust was evidently not one of the warrior's virtues.

'Zartath,' he said, 'of the Black Dragons.'

A tremor of unease ran around the Fire-born at the mention of the Chapter. To some amongst the Astartes ranks, the name 'Black Dragons' was a byword for 'cursed' or 'aberrant'. Certainly, with their onyx skin and eyes of fire, the Salamanders had their fair share of detractors. It was part of the reason why honour and humanity were such important tenets of their belief structure. But this black-armoured warrior before them, his face a mask of blood, barely restrained murder in his eyes, was... a *mutant*.

'Zartath,' Elysius didn't move and kept his tone level, 'we are brothers here. Let him go.'

The Chaplain knew something of the 21st Founding. It occurred before the Age of Apostasy, during the 36th millennium, and was the largest single tithe of Astartes since the glorious 2nd Founding so many years before. A 'Cursed Founding', some had said. Something was *wrong* with the Chapters created during its genesis. The reasons why were not known to him. He did know, however, that the Black Dragons were amongst those charged as aberrant. Their deviancies were obvious. Bony growths from the elbows, fists and forehead were monstrous and abhorred. If rumours were to be believed then the Apothecarion of the Black Dragons encouraged such mutancy, nurtured it. Correlation between the bone-growths and increased aggression and feral temperament amongst the Chapter's battle-brothers had never been established. As a survivor in an alien dimension, doubtless having been hunted and tortured, Zartath was hardly a fitting subject for study to prove or disprove that theory.

Elysius had fought with the Black Dragons before. He had known one of their number well. Ushorak had betrayed them. He had orchestrated the betrayal of others. It was long ago, but the wound was still fresh.

Zartath hadn't moved. His breathing was elevated, his plastron heaving up and down with nervous regularity.

'Release him, brother. *Right now.*' Elysius gestured to the Salamanders around them.

The Black Dragon didn't relent. Instead, he smiled, showing off the bloodied ranks of his spine-like teeth. 'Did you think I survived this place for so long *alone*?'

The staccato snap of racking weapon slides filled the amphitheatre.

Elysius and the others looked up and saw twenty ragged human warriors emerge from their hiding places amongst the higher echelons. Almost half were armed with automatic weapons, stubbers, shotguns and heavy-bore rifles. Some carried heavy crossbows or bows. One other Astartes, also a Black Dragon, aimed a bolter.

Too many were dead already; Elysius wanted no

further blood to mar his hand, especially if it could be avoided.

'I am not alone,' Zartath muttered darkly.

Mag-locking his crozius to his armour, Elysius then removed his battle-helm. It was the first time he had openly showed his face in over a century.

His eyes were penetrating. 'You see me now for what I am – an ally. So, tell me Black Dragon, will you slay him and force me to end your life and the lives of your men or will you accept me as your brother?'

Still the bone-blade didn't move.

Elysius ignored the shocked glances of his kin, offering his hand.

'Decide quickly. Friend or foe?'

II
Fire and Stone

FLIGHT WENT AGAINST a Salamander's every instincts. Astartes were bred to ignore fear, to compartmentalise it and lock it away.

And they shall know no fear.

It was amongst the oldest edicts, since the time of the Great Crusade, when the Space Marines were young and they could still dream of untainted glory. Salamanders were stoic like no other. They would stand and fight when many had long left the field of battle. No cause was ever lost. No Chapter ever fought as tenaciously. It was Vulkan's legacy and it had stood for millennia.

As the power-scythe came down between them, splitting the ravaged earth in two, Pyriel and Dak'ir fell back. A torrent of shells from Pyriel's bolt pistol traced

an explosive line that stitched the reaper's flank. Barely
a scratch registered after the fire and smoke had died.
A half-aimed shot from Dak'ir's plasma pistol had similar effect. The reaper was unscathed.

'It's tougher than Dreadnought armour,' the Lexicanum gasped, snapping off another ineffectual shot.
Streams of plasma ran off its granite-grey skin like
water on oil. The golem-creature was advancing
swiftly, its servos warmed up and impelling it to
increase motion.

'Try to hold it off,' Pyriel replied, his pistol's muzzle
flare lighting up his battle-helm. He'd stowed his force
staff. He was too exhausted to wield it.

They backed away further as the reaper came on, its
power-scythe poised.

With the physical weapons the two Librarians possessed, the reaper was unkillable.

But Dak'ir had something more in his arsenal. It
lapped at the mental bulwarks of his mind like a turbulent sea.

Unleash it. Let it all burn...

'I can destroy it.' Dak'ir went to the psychic hood's
dampener. One twist and the power, eager for release,
would return.

Pyriel flashed a furious glance at him. 'No! You'll kill
us both. Maybe even level the catacombs and the cryptoria beyond.'

'I can vanquish it with a thought, master. Let me save
us.' It craved release. The power within him wanted to
be let slip.

Feed me with your will.

He was taken back to the subterranean depths of
Mount Deathfire where'd fought the giant of onyx. On
the precipice's edges, the lake of fire churning below,

the monster had nearly ended his life. He was stronger now. A ripple of power jolted through him like a miniature shock wave, threatening to overload the psychic hood and throw open the mental flood gates.

'Harness it, brother,' Pyriel was imploring. He couldn't *make* Dak'ir stop, all he had left was reason. 'Don't become like Nihilan.'

Like ice down his spine, Pyriel's words chilled him.

Nihilan... The sorcerer had trod a similar path. Pyriel had trained with him. Pyriel had betrayed him. There was no choice.

The universal truth of it resonated in Dak'ir's mind like a bolter shot and brought with it a startling revelation. The flame within him was a monster, something he couldn't exert his influence over. It had to be shackled. His hand fell away from the dampener. The reaper was upon them.

Dak'ir flung himself aside, the scythe parting rock where his head had been a moment before. Debris shorn off by the blow cascaded onto his armour. A burst of gunfire from Pyriel dragged the golem-creature's attention away. The Epistolary was more than a mere Librarian, he was a warrior with warrior instincts and took up a position on the reaper's blind side.

Despite its size and strength, the golem-creature was still just an automaton, little more than a servitor. Even the psychic impel left behind by Nihilan couldn't change that. It could be manipulated, goaded like any mindless, unthinking monster. Oil flowed in its veins instead of blood, machine parts not muscles drove it, but it was still just a thing.

Pyriel drew it on, all the while his psychic strength returning.

++We make for the doorway++ he said through the comm-feed.

In the brief respite his master had provided, Dak'ir replaced his battle-helm. *++We are to escape? What about the cryptoria? We must gain access–++*

Another line of bolter shells strafed the pseudo-stone hide of the reaper, stalling but not stopping it. Pyriel was already moving again before the last round had detonated.

++Trust me, Dak'ir. Make for the doorway. I will not be far behind you++

Though he didn't like it, Dak'ir ran for the doorway to the lair. He closed the distance in a few seconds, not even looking back as he burst through a short corridor and into the labour tunnels. The hot glow of the incinerators bathed his armour as he stood upon the bridge. Bent wholly on their work, the army of toiling serfs didn't even acknowledge his sudden arrival let alone cease what they were doing.

Halfway across the bridge, Dak'ir waited for Pyriel.

Beneath him, a caged sea of fire raged and spat. A sense of realisation awakened within him. Nothing could withstand those flames…

++Master?++ It was taking too long, Pyriel should have appeared by now. Dak'ir was about to go back when the Epistolary rushed from the gloom. His bolt pistol was holstered and he was clutching his force staff when he reached the apprentice.

'Stand firm,' Pyriel told him. His breathing was laboured and there were energy-seared chips in his armour.

'Master…'

Pyriel's red eyes flashed angrily. 'Stand firm,' he repeated in a stern voice.

A second later and the forbidding effigy of the reaper emerged from the darkness, death incarnate.

It had to bend to get through the archway into the labour tunnels, servos protesting in an automated squeal. The reaper was supposed to be confined to its lair; it was not meant for the labour tunnels. Warp-sorcery had corrupted its central programming. The doctrina wafers slotted into its cerebral cortex were just blackened fragments of overridden data impulses. A slave to Nihilan's psychic command, the reaper stepped out onto the bridge.

It swung its power-scythe, leaving a trail of latent energy humming on the air.

Dak'ir's body tensed. His instincts screamed to attack or take a tactically superior position. Pyriel refuted both.

'Hold,' he said.

The bridge was narrow, at least for the reaper. Compelled it might be, but it still couldn't throw its machine-life away recklessly, so advanced with slow purpose.

'Hold,' Pyriel continued, aware of the hypno-conditioned battle responses flooding Dak'ir's brain – they were flooding his own, too.

A crackle of energy went up the haft of the force staff, a primer for what was to come.

The reaper was a few short metres away; the death arc of its scythe even less than that.

'Lexicanum…' Pyriel's eyes were ablaze with cerulean blue fire.

The psychic echo of his thoughts resonated in Dak'ir's mind, a command unspoken but understood all the same. He gripped the force staff with his master and channelled the small tributary of his psychic strength into the weapon where Pyriel could mould it.

It was called *conclave*, when two or more Librarians shared their mind-strength and unleashed it together.

Dak'ir could not control his powers, not at their apex, not yet, but he could siphon a portion of it into the staff for Pyriel to focus and direct.

Within striking distance, the reaper uttered its last.

Death to the Salamanders.

'Death to traitors,' snarled Pyriel, 'and all who serve them!' A bolt of fire surged from the end of the staff, slamming into the reaper to send it staggering. There was enough force to push it to the end of the bridge, where it teetered, swinging its scythe in impotent rage.

Rushing forwards, Pyriel fired the last of his bolt pistol's rounds. 'Finish it!'

Following his master's mark, Dak'ir put a trio of plasma bolts into the reaper's scorched torso.

Like a slab of mountain surrendering itself to the elements as it collapsed into oblivion, the reaper held on for a moment and then fell. Heavy like a gunship, the golem-creature smashed straight through the cage, killing a swathe of serfs on its way, before crashing into the incinerator. Hot flames lapped around its body, which was suspended for a few seconds on a bubbling lava bed before it finally sank and was gone.

Together, the Librarians watched it die. Klaxons were sounding below. Servitors and maintenance crews emerged from bulkhead-sealed hatches. The incinerator's work must not be interrupted. The dead would not wait. The corpses were endless and the machine would go on. It was paramount the cage be repaired and the labour-serfs replaced. It took just minutes.

'Another Imperial servant turned to Chaos,' Pyriel muttered. He sounded bitter.

'What did you mean,' asked Dak'ir, 'when you said "don't become like Nihilan"?'

Bowing his head, Pyriel sighed. It was like he'd been burdened by a sudden invisible weight.

'It was long ago,' he answered in a quiet voice, 'Before Moribar. I was a Lexicanum then with aspirations of becoming a Codicier. Nihilan, too.'

'You were battle-brothers?' Dak'ir tried to keep the disbelief from his voice. He hadn't known the strength of connection of between his master and his nemesis.

'Yes, but that was before...' Pyriel tailed off, uncomfortable at unearthing the old bones of his life.

'What happened?'

The Epistolary faced his apprentice. The flame glow in his eyes dimmed with regret.

'He fell.'

A memory, dredged from Dak'ir's mind, came out in his reply.

'We were only supposed to bring them back.'

'What?'

'Back here,' Dak'ir gestured to the fiery chasm below and the hard rock around them, 'more than four decades ago, I dreamed of it. Nihilan led a minor rebellion. He and the others weren't meant to be our enemies. They were wayward sons, polluted by a stronger mind.'

'Ushorak had a gift.' The praise was given through clenched teeth.

'Like the traitorous scions of Lorgar.'

'It wasn't a rebellion, though,' Pyriel corrected his apprentice. 'It was him and one other. They weren't the Dragon Warriors then. That came much later, though when exactly we do not know. It was a travesty, wrought by Ushorak's hand – all of it.'

'Some do not *want* to be brought back, some can't. An old friend told me that.'

'Who?'

'Fugis. It was one of the last things he said to me before Stratos. Cirrion came soon after that. And the Aura Hieron…'

'We've lost much.' Pyriel didn't need to be psychic to read Dak'ir's thoughts.

'Fugis isn't dead, master. Our Apothecary will return from the Burning Walk.'

Pyriel's tone verged on paternal. 'Such hope… I always liked that about you, Dak'ir.'

The image of Fugis's corpse, putrefying in the ship's hold in Dak'ir's vision came back to the Lexicanum unbidden.

'He *will* return.'

'Alive or dead, lost or returned, it matters not. I won't stand by and let further destruction be waged upon us.' Pyriel gestured towards the doorway at the end of the bridge. It was cracked, the stone splintered where the reaper had forced itself through. 'The way is open. We make for the cryptoria,' he added, trudging back across the causeway. It wasn't fatigue making him weary – any Astartes could overcome that as easily as they could wield a bolter or chainsword – it was sorrow.

Dak'ir followed him in silence.

IF THE CATACOMBS of Moribar represented the lowest level of squalor for the dead then here, further below, was the very peak of opulence.

Gilded mausoleums, silver-chased crypts, tombs of cut marble and crystal obelisks lined a concourse of pristine alabaster that ran throughout the entire cryptoria. It was a vast space, the equal of any starship's footprint, and teemed with the interred dead. Heady incense flooded the air, overwhelming the grave-dust stink and ash-soaked reek of the pauper levels. The entranceway was immense, like the triumphal arch of some great cathedra or palace. Effigies of saints and ecclesiarchs were carved into its columns. Vines of onyx rose, strangle-ivy and helsbane wreathed the arch from base to apex. This great gate was open but shielded by a force-field that sparked and cracked as the minute specks of dust collided with it.

Passing through it required disabling the field long enough to walk the connecting chamber. The reaper was its intended guardian and with it destroyed, getting into the cryptoria was a matter of lowering the shield via a control port. Even still, the hermetically sealed environment beyond the force-field had to be preserved. Before Pyriel and Dak'ir had reached the other side of the conduit, air-scrubbing servo-skulls were sanitising the atmosphere.

Ranks of servitors tended expansive grounds, which were lush with manicured lawns and topiaried flora. A damp patina of vapour swathed the Librarians' armour. The air was heavy with oxygen and hydrogen to maintain the health of the cryptoria's gardens.

Pyriel paused on the road, absorbing the view. There were skulls embedded beneath him, their eye sockets glistening with jewels, bleached white and inscribed with litanies for the deceased.

'Hard to believe that utopia exists amongst all this death.'

A fluttering of censer-bearing cherubim drew his eye up to a false firmament of starry glass. They were internal lume-globes, their polished silver as bright as a solar flare. Through the flocks of cyb-organic creatures above, it bathed the world in microcosm below with a refulgent aura.

Dak'ir was unmoved. All he saw was ash, and the rendering of what the cryptoria *could* be if the flame inside him was unleashed.

'It's as grey as the rest of Moribar.'

'Perhaps…' They were walking again, following the concourse.

The air was cold, sanitised. It ghosted through Dak'ir's mouth-grille.

'I can feel it.'

'The voice?' asked Pyriel.

'Yes, it speaks still. Our enemies came this way.'

'Can you discern the speaker?'

'It's in thrall, in a limbo between realities. The agony gives it resonance. Up ahead… here.'

A crypt of black obsidian stood out amongst the throng of tombs. It was grand, imposing. Whoever this monument was meant to commemorate had been wealthy. Incredibly so.

'Do you recognise that mark?' Pyriel pointed out a simple icon steam-carved into the glassy rock.

Dak'ir shook his head.

'It is a dynastic sigil, one associated with a house of rogue traders. This one was a technocrat.'

Crouching down, Dak'ir traced an armoured finger across the sigil. It was the icon of a man, split in two and with his legs and arms splayed in a star shape. One half was flesh, the other metal.

'How can you know, master?'

'Because I've seen it before, emblazoned on one of the dynasty's vessels.'

Dak'ir turned.

'When Nihilan and I were neophytes, we fought a

campaign with the Black Dragons,' said Pyriel, by way of explanation. 'Ushorak commanded our allies. Captain Kadai led the Fire-born, as he always did.'

Dak'ir stood. 'None of this is in the Chapter records.'

Pyriel gave a sniff of amusement. 'I daresay Elysius could unearth something. It was buried deep, much of it proscribed except to the higher ranks, and the darkest accounts to the Reclusiam only.'

'Ushorak's damnation,' Dak'ir guessed.

'The inception of it, yes.'

The Lexicanum regarded the crypt. It was, after all, the reason they had come to the grey world.

'Do you know who is buried here, who Ushorak coerced into serving him?'

Pyriel shook his head. 'No. But whatever knowledge is held by them, once in life and now in death, must be terrible indeed for Nihilan to have followed his master's intended path as far as he has.'

The Epistolary held out his hand, palm flat to the crypt.

'Stay very still,' he warned.

Dak'ir watched and waited.

After a few seconds a dull, red glow suffused Pyriel's hand. The air grew heavy with heat, the vapour-laden atmosphere boiling off into clouds of steam against it.

The voice came first, no longer just in Dak'ir's psychic consciousness but aloud for anyone to hear. It was screaming, intermittent and as if from a great distance. The pitch rose and fell as an image, struggling to resolve itself, stretched and yawned.

Slowly, the outline of a figure shimmered into existence. It was a shade of sorts, a warp echo. Dak'ir was reminded of the apparitions they'd fought at Aphium and the Imperial bastion of Mercy Rock. A dark canker had infected that place, filled with disquiet energy that had manifested in the tortured revenants of the dead. The thing before him, twisting in its ethereal agonies, was uncomfortably familiar.

Pyriel's hand was shaking and he'd twisted it into a claw. His fingers flexed as if pulling on the invisible skeins between the mortal world and the *other*.

'He struggles...' said the Epistolary in a strained voice. He still hadn't fully recovered from the ordeal against the reaper, 'but I have him. Ask of it.'

Dak'ir could feel the emanations of the warp echo tugging at the edges of his mind. It sent a spike of empathic pain through his fingertips as he reached out like his master to mentally brush against the void.

'Who are you?' asked the Lexicanum.

The baleful eyes of the revenant were like cold blue lampfires, the body itself incorporeal and transparent. As it lifted its chin, Pyriel seizing the invisible string that bound it, it smiled and then opened its mouth.

At first, its utterances were out of synch with its lolling jaw movements. The voice came out in a deep rasping timbre, slowed to the point of incomprehension. Like muscles that had atrophied with the weight of years, so too had the revenant's ability to speak been degenerated.

'Again,' Pyriel urged. 'It will remember how.'

Dak'ir refocussed, using what little psychic power the dampener afforded to impel the revenant.

'Your name, creature, speak it to me now.'

'*Caaaaaaalllllleeeeebbbbbbb...*'

It came out as a moan, drawn out and abyssal deep.

'*Caaaallleebbb...*'

Clearer this time, the resonance was fading.

'Caleb,' Dak'ir repeated to the shade, understanding.

'*Caleb Kelock,*' it uttered.

Like a partially recorded pict, fraught with static, the image of a man flickered in front of the Lexicanum. The spiritual personification of Kelock wore a fine suit in the manner of the rogue traders with a brocaded jacket and attached cape. A thin strip of beard ran the length of his chin, ending in an arrow at the very tip. He wore gloves and his knee-length boots shone with an ethereal echo of what they must've been like when Kelock was still living.

Dak'ir realised it was the man's funerary attire, that if they wrenched open the crypt they would find a decayed and eroded version of these clothes attached like strips of flesh to a skeleton.

'Who did this to you, who trapped your essence between worlds?' Dak'ir asked. Back on Aphium the warp echoes malingered because they had unfinished business. They craved peace that could only be brought about by blood-retribution. The Salamanders had granted them their vengeance and so lifted their curse on Mercy Rock.

Kelock was no unquiet spirit, he was a prisoner.

His incorporeal face twisted with anger and the lampfires in his eyes blazed.

'*Your kind,*' he accused.

'Ushorak,' Dak'ir muttered, feeling the chill of the technocrat's ire as it formed ice on his battle plate. 'Black armour,' he said to the shade, indicating his partly frozen suit.

Kelock nodded, forming an angry scowl.

'Dak'ir...' It was Pyriel. His voice sounded strained. 'Hurry up. I can't hold it... indefinitely.'

The Lexicanum was about to go on when the solar glare bathing them from above suddenly died. A grey pall settled quickly over the massive cemetery. The lawns lost their lustre, the glory of its monuments seemed faded and dull. Hope and warmth bled away. It was the ashen wasteland Dak'ir had first imagined. How different the cryptoria appeared with the absence of light.

Shadows were moving through its benighted depths. They flashed like balefires in Dak'ir's retinal display. Minimal heat traces. He remembered the hordes of servitors tending the funerary gardens. Picks and shears could easily be turned into weapons. He suspected these creatures served a dual purpose – groundsmen and guardians, both.

Rain was falling. Only it wasn't really rain. It was the vapour in the atmosphere, condensed into heavy droplets in order to simulate rain. In seconds it turned from a light shower into a downpour.

'Something is coming...' Heavy rain hammered on Dak'ir's battle plate, turning the ingrained ash into black slurry. The glowing embers of mechanical optics were closing on the Librarians.

'Then our time here is ended,' Pyriel had to snarl through clenched teeth. He was hanging on to Kelock's apparition, but only just.

The shade flickered briefly out of existence before resolving again.

'What secrets did the Traitor glean from you, technocrat? Answer me and your torment will be ended.'

Kelock beckoned him with an emaciated finger. Without time to wait, Dak'ir came forwards.

'Sto–'

Pyriel's warning arrived too late, the substance of it lost to a chorus of screams in Dak'ir's head as the apparition clenched his fingers around the Salamander's battle helm.

Images flooded the Lexicanum's mind in hypno-conditioned flashes as Kelock divulged all that he knew and had seen in a single, cathartic release. For a brief moment, apparition and Astartes became one. Their disparate chronologies, both living and dead, fused. Threads of fate bound them together. One entity, one shared history. Awareness was like a lightning strike and Dak'ir was its grounding rod.

Dak'ir staggered, falling to one knee. He shuddered once then again. Etheric smoke was rising from his armour. Ripples of energy coursed ephemerally over the ceramite, turning the blue edges black.

'Release him…' he breathed when it was over, acutely aware of the servitors tramping closer. He had everything they needed. The truth of it made him feel hollow.

'I cannot,' Pyriel admitted, and an anguished Kelock blinked out of existence.

Dak'ir managed to stand. The servitors were still coming, just a few metres away. Their bladed implements shone in the half-light. 'I made a vow.'

'Which I broke. Only Ushorak or Nihilan can free the shade.'

Dak'ir glared at his master. 'Show me how to bring him back and I'll do it myself.' He unsheathed *Draugen*, ready for the servitors, but kept the blade dulled.

Pyriel turned to face their attackers. They were close enough to strike. 'No time,' he said, unlocking his force staff. The Epistolary whirled it around his body, severing a mechanised spine with the first arc, punching through a servitor's stomach with a heavy thrust at the end of the move.

Dak'ir cut down a third, cleaving it from shoulder to groin. Oil spewed to the ground in thick gouts, wires dangling like intestine. He sliced the head from a fourth, the automaton collapsing first to its knees and then falling face-forwards. The earth was churned beneath their feet, becoming mired.

They were all dead, not traitors or possessed machines, just loyal Imperial servants doing their duty. It left a bitter taste, but more were coming. These first few were just a proximal vanguard.

'What happened?' Pyriel couldn't wait to ask. 'What did the technocrat show you?'

Dak'ir's eyes narrowed, the slits of fire in them turning into blades. He wrenched out his plasma pistol.

He declined to answer.

'We have defiled this place. Our sacrilege is no better than that of Ushorak.' A sizzling bolt tore a chunk from the base of a tall obelisk and sent it crashing like a felled tree into the path of more servitors. Those that escaped being crushed were suddenly impeded.

There was a note of desperation in Pyriel's voice as he reached for Dak'ir. 'Lexicanum, I must know.'

They were advancing along an oblique line, moving away from their attackers but keeping them in sight as they did. The few that reached the Salamanders Pyriel destroyed with efficient but deadly blows from his force staff. He was a master in more senses than merely the psychic. Dak'ir had heard about the Epistolary's staff-fighting rotas. He followed the tribal katas of Heliosa, his Sanctuary City, blended with the pole-arm drills of Master Prebian.

'Dak'ir!'

The Lexicanum ripped off his battle helm. Rivulets

of fake rain teemed down his face. There was pain and disbelief in his eyes.

'I saw the end,' he said. 'I saw Nocturne's doom.'

With the mangled wreckage of the servitors around them, Pyriel and Dak'ir ran.

Master glanced at apprentice as they sped through the tombs, their pursuers dogged behind them. A few had swelled to almost fifty. More were gathering, consolidating with the pack.

Nocturne's doom.

It was just as the armour suits from Scoria had predicted.

CHAPTER TWELVE

I
Allies and Traitors

Elysius was stunned. He'd hit his head in the fall. No, that wasn't right. He hadn't fallen. Argos had pushed him.

G'ord was dead. His blood washed the walls in long, grisly trails. Elysius's enhanced olfactory senses rankled with the stink of copper.

The screaming cut through the fog of dizziness. He recognised the voice. It was Argos. As the blurring went away, Elysius saw his brother Scout collapse with his hands to his face. His smoking, steaming face. Where the acid burned it. The acid meant for Elysius.

He still had a partial clip of shells. The auto-readout glowed ugly red. Enough. His aim was off. Elysius could barely see. Argos, now with one hand on his ravaged face, tried to fend the xenos off with his combat blade. Once it closed, Argos would meet the same fate as G'ord.

Elysius yanked on the trigger and filled the tunnel with

the bolt pistol's noise and fire. The first shell struck the 'stealer in the torso, pitched it back so it slammed into the wall. The second and third punched into vital organs. The resulting explosion from the mass-reactive rounds bathed the immediate area around the creature with xenos viscera.

There'd be no tracking it now. Mission fail.

Holding his wounded arm to his chest, Elysius managed to stumble to his fallen battle-brother.

'You saved my–' The sight of Argos's acid-maimed visage made him stop. One hand could barely cover such a horrific injury. Angry red flesh, bubbling and burn-twisted, glared from between trembling fingers. He was going into shock.

'Get up,' Elysius heaved Argos's free arm over his shoulder and supported him. The wounded Scout's footing was unsteady but he could walk.

'Why did you do that?'

The voice that replied was a grating parody of the battle-brother Elysius used to know. 'You would've too... What about G'ord?'

'He's dead, and no Apothecary will revive him or his gene-seed.'

They struggled forwards, the two of them. Elysius managed to raise the comm-feed in his armoured collar.

'Command echelon, this is Squad Kabe requesting assistance.'

++Speak, brother. This is Captain Kadai++

'My lord, our mission has failed. We are trapped in the sewer tunnels, Argent Quadrant East, and require extraction. Threats proximate and numerous.'

Elysius was guiding them away from the caved-in entrance and deeper into the sewer network. It meant drawing closer to the nest.

++Engage your emergency beacon. We will be with you soon, brother. Fortitude of Vulkan. Faith in the Anvil++'

'In his name, my lord.'

The comm-feed returned to static as the link was severed. Elysius shut it off. It could be hours before they were found. He clicked the emergency beacon in his collar, part of the mission failsafe should the tracker be misdeployed.

'I can walk unaided,' said Argos. *That throaty rasp, robbed of its humanity, so unlike him.*

'You've suffered a massive trauma. You are in no fit condition to do much of anything unaided.'

'I can walk alone.'

Elysius let him go, surprised to see that Argos could do just as he'd said he could. He lowered his hand and the view made Elysius grimace.

'It's bad, isn't it? The pain is lessening. My body compensates.'

'I am so sorry, brother. My hubris brought this upon you, upon G'ord.' *The cooling corpse of the dead Scout was behind them now, but the copper stink remained like an accusation in Elysius's nostrils.*

'You were prosecuting the mission. How's your arm? Can you fight with it?'

Elysius tested it. Stiff, but the blood had clotted. He was healing. The marvels of Astartes physiology, even that of a lowly Scout, continued to amaze him.

'Bolter and blade,' *he replied, brandishing both.*

'That beacon will transmit all the way to the surface?' *said Argos, pointing at his brother's flashing collar.*

'Brother-Captain Kadai is tracking us as we speak, leading an extraction team. Why do you ask?'

Argos checked the load on his bolt pistol and the two spare clips mag-locked to his belt. 'Secondaries?' *he asked.*

Elysius showed him the two extra clips attached to his own belt.

Argos nodded. 'A beacon in the hands of two Astartes Scouts is better than any tracker bolt.'

'You want us to find the nest?' Elysius couldn't hide his incredulity.

'We must be close.'

Elysius laughed. It would be one of the last times he ever did, and his mirth was tainted with fatalism.

'Into the fires of battle then, brother,' he said.

Argos racked the slide of his bolt pistol. The auto-readout snapped to 'MAX'.

'Unto the anvil of war, and may death take us should we be found lacking.'

ALL THE RUMOURS and speculation, the grim beliefs passed from neophyte to neophyte, from battle-brother to battle-brother – unfounded. All of them.

Ravaged by bio-acid, twisted by xenos-toxin, emaciated by the taint of warp sorcery, a bleached bone skull to match his battle-helm, Chaplain Elysius suffered from none of these. He never had. His face, his perfect, handsome face was his greatest shame, so he hid it behind a mask of death and bone.

Ba'ken saw, but he did not quite believe. He always thought seeing the Chaplain's visage would somehow lessen him, that his mystique and power would fade. The man was greater than the myth. He had given up the secret covenant he had made with himself and used it to make an ally of a warrior he didn't even know.

'Brother Zartath,' Elysius pressed. 'I think there has been enough loyal blood spilled here already. We are kin, you and I. All of us are.'

Zartath retracted the bone-blade with a *snikt!* as it raked against ceramite and finally into flesh.

'You have my battle-helm,' he said, rising.

Elysius looked down to where he'd mag-locked the helmet to his armour and smiled. He detached it with a faint *chank* of metal.

'Now,' he said, handing the battle-helm over, 'how do we escape?'

'This is the Port of Anguish,' Zartath replied, extending his finger and twirling it around in a circle – his henchmen reacted by staying their weapons and disappearing from view as they made for the lower floor, 'the gateway to Volgorrah,' he added, fitting his battle-helm. 'There is no escape.'

'There must be a way–' Ba'ken winced, still feeling his injuries acutely as he got up. The mark on his neck inflicted by the Black Dragon's bone-blade was a sting to his pride more than his body, and he rubbed at it ruefully. Slowly his body's reparatory systems were healing him, but he was still weak.

Iagon was close by and came to support his fellow sergeant.

'Concerned for my wellbeing, brother?' asked Ba'ken.

'I would feel safer with your bulk between me and the dark eldar, is all,' came the taut reply, but there was some warmth in it.

Zartath was already walking away, signalling he had no intention of answering Ba'ken.

'No way of escape at all?' asked Elysius, standing aside.

'Six years I have existed in this place,' snarled the Black Dragon, pausing as he went past the Chaplain, 'and have found none. We are trapped here. All we can do is survive. Kill when we can, run when we cannot. That is all there is left.' He stalked away. 'Follow if you wish,' he said, voice diminishing with the distance, 'or not. It doesn't matter to me.'

'This one has fallen far,' remarked Koto. His voice was accusing as he watched the Black Dragons and his cohorts disappearing into the shadows of the amphitheatre.

'Something that could be levelled against the Chapter,' added Ba'ken.

'I agree,' said Iagon. 'Can we trust this castaway and his followers?'

Elysius looked on thoughtfully. 'We have no other choice. Our survival in this place depends on us staying together. Brother Zartath has achieved that feat for six years–'

'If he is to be believed,' remarked Iagon, butting in.

The Chaplain glared at him, the perfect contours of his face like cut jet even when expressing displeasure. 'Trust is in short supply in this benighted place already – let us not add to it, brothers.'

A shout from Brother Koto interrupted Iagon's apology.

The Fire-born turned as one to see a gaggle of emaciated creatures lingering in the penumbral shadows.

'Shall I engage, my lord?' asked Koto, a barbed trident in hand. Elysius had seen him in the battle cages. With a single throw he'd punched a training spear through the body of an armoured servitor. Reinforced carapace with a ceramite plating meant the servitors were tough. Not tough enough for Brother Koto. The Fire-born originally hailed from Epimethus, the only one of the Sanctuary Cities surrounded by the Acerbian Sea. Koto was a weapon specialist second and a spear-fisherman first. The gnorl-whales that inhabited the Nocturnean oceans had volcanic rock for their hides. Breaching them was no easy task, even for an Astartes. Any action taken by Koto would be bloody and final.

'Negative.' Now he saw them, Elysius realised these things were wretches, little more than shrivelled ghouls, voyeurs to the recent carnage.

Zartath's harsh voice rang out across the amphitheatre. He was barely visible, half-swallowed by the darkness and well-camouflaged in his armour. A crack of light behind him framed the warrior from a hidden passageway leading further into the city.

'Leave them,' he bellowed, 'and come with me. I have something to show you.'

The Fire-born looked to their Chaplain. Elysius eyed the Black Dragon and then the wretched creatures, creeping closer by the minute. He regarded the dead dark eldar slavers and could guess what the ghouls were waiting for.

'Leave them,' he said at last, echoing Zartath. He led the Salamanders and what remained of the Night Devils off after their new allies. The emaciated wretches gathered closer in their wake, eyes hungry and dirty talons eager.

Not all of the slavers had been dead. Some were critically injured but alive.

Elysius consoled himself with that thought as they left the amphitheatre, and the ghouls to their feast.

It was an iron box, roughly a metre in length and a half-metre wide. It was steam-bolted with iron rivets. Rust collecting around the rivets reminded Elysius of blood.

Zartath had led them a fair distance from the amphitheatre, but the strange geography of the place made it difficult to gauge exactly how far they'd travelled. He'd learned it was called the 'Razored Vale' by the human survivors and was a bridging point into the webway proper. The Vale was merely part of a much larger settlement called the Port of Anguish, and situated in an area of the webway known as the Volgorrah Reef.

When Elysius had asked how he came to know all of this, Zartath had smiled and beckoned them onwards. Standing before the iron box in the wrecked shell of a temple with Ba'ken and Iagon, Elysius was still no wiser as to the Black Dragon's meaning.

'Kor'be,' Zartath called to his second-in-command, the only other Astartes, another Black Dragon, in his ragged warband. The others were difficult to pin down: ex-Guard perhaps, mercenaries, rogue traders – the xenos were indiscriminate in the acquisition of slaves. Zartath had alloyed them, however. They were lean and wire-taut, ready for anything. But sometimes even that wasn't enough; sometimes nothing could stop you from getting killed. They'd seen death and lost everything. It had made the ragged company hard.

The hulking warrior called Kor'be came forwards. He was missing his right shoulder pad and arm greave. His bare flesh was tanned like leather and just as rough. There were marks in the skin that indicated where several bone-blades had been removed surgically. Kor'be also carried the electoo of his Chapter, a white dragon head, imprinted on his shoulder.

'He is mute,' said Zartath, unnecessarily, 'dark eldar took his tongue long ago. Took his blades too. At least he cannot question my orders,' he added. His curt laughter quickly fell away into serious introspection.

Ba'ken and Iagon shared a furtive glance with one another.

He is mad, then, Elysius thought to himself, watching as Kor'be rammed a spear into the side of the iron box and, with an impressive feat of strength, prised open the lid.

It hit the ground with a heavy *clang*.

All eyes were drawn to its contents.

'They are named the "Parched",' Zartath explained.

Within the iron box was one of the ghoul creatures, a particularly thin and wretched specimen. The thing was partly desiccated and its eyes were swollen shut. As the half-light of the Razored Vale touched it, the creature squirmed, sticking out its needle-like tongue to lash the air.

Naked but for a small cloth to preserve its dignity – what precious little it had left – the Parched was covered in tiny wheals and lesions. The contusions and internal haemorrhaging didn't appear to be the work of Zartath or his men. Rather, it looked to be synonymous with some kind of invasive illness. From his conversations with Fugis, Elysius had learned of such diseases that affected humans, of how a body could turn on and destroy itself. The Apothecary had been vivid and detailed in descriptions of these maladies. The Chaplain knew enough that he could recognise them or something similar when he saw it.

Zartath grinned, displaying his saurian incisors, as if reading Elysius's thoughts.

'Shut inside, no light, no stimulation,' he said, 'it's like torture to them. Slowly they waste away to nothing.'

'Degeneration through sensory deprivation,' the Chaplain clarified. 'It is the soul hunger.'

The Black Dragon punched the Parched savagely in the ribs, making it squeal in pleasure-pain. 'I keep it fed on scraps,' he said, showing the dried blood on his gauntlet from where he'd just struck it. 'You can keep them alive for weeks like this. After a few days they reveal their secrets.'

Elysius kept his disapproval to himself, but saw it written on the other Salamanders' faces.

Zartath noticed it too.

'How else do you think we survived this long?' he snapped, seizing the Parched by the throat and shaking it. 'Eyes and ears, *brothers*!' he sneered, letting the creature go when it mewled for more.

The Black Dragon turned on Elysius. By now, the rest of the group, having been occupied sharpening blades and checking ammunition, were watching.

'You are of particular interest to them, Chaplain.'

Elysius fought the urge to crush Zartath's pointing finger. Kor'be was nearby, bolter in hand. He couldn't have many rounds. During the fight, the Chaplain couldn't remember it being fired once. It might be on empty already. Still, he wasn't about to test a theory.

'Helspereth is looking for *you*,' the Black Dragon concluded. 'You've piqued her interest.'

'How fortunate.'

'No, it isn't. She is An'scur's hell-bitch, his rabid dog,' Zartath spat, 'and she wants to sate her fangs on your flesh.'

'We've met already.' The Chaplain gestured to his missing limb. 'She already took a trophy.'

The Black Dragon laughed. It was an ugly, hollow sound. 'She'll want more.'

'Who is An'scur?' asked Ba'ken, growing tired of Zartath's histrionics, 'The overlord of this place?'

Zartath nodded. 'Aye, he rules the Reef. When we,' – he slammed his plastron and pointed at Kor'be – 'had numbers, before the reapings, I tried to kill him.'

Iagon smirked, finding accord with Ba'ken. 'Needless to say, you failed.'

The Black Dragon bared his teeth and snarled.

'And lost over a dozen warriors,' he concluded bitterly. 'Now you're here, you think it will be different?'

'Our brothers are coming for us,' Elysius assured him.

'You must've hit your head, preacher,' Zartath replied. 'There is no one coming for us. *We* are all we have.'

'You're wrong.' The Chaplain brandished Vulkan's Sigil. 'They are coming for this.'

IAGON'S EXPRESSION TOLD Ba'ken his fellow sergeant knew nothing of that fact, either. Ever since Ironlandings and the fight to breach the bastion, a bond had been forming between them. Ba'ken had always thought of Iagon as a serpent dressed in ceramite, a poisonous creature unworthy of the title 'Fire-born'. Polar opposites, like their feuding sergeants had been, Ba'ken and Iagon had never liked each other. Like Dak'ir and Tsu'gan before them, it bordered on enmity. They fought together – they were still battle-brothers after all – but it was far from a ready camaraderie. Yet, in the last few hours held prisoner on the Reef, something had changed. They had changed. Perhaps without the legacy of their old commanders overshadowing them they had broken free of the shackles that stopped

Dak'ir and Tsu'gan seeing eye-to-eye? As he broke eye contact, Ba'ken hoped that was the case. His gaze went to the Sigil.

Ba'ken knew it was a relic, a piece of the primarch's armour, his trappings. It was recovered from the shattered ruins of Isstvan and venerated in the then-Legion's reliquary halls. During the breaking of the Legions the Salamanders had become a Chapter, though in truth there was little left to break. Ba'ken knew less of the Sigil's fate during that time than he did during the Heresy, but it wasn't long before it was brought into battle as a holy relic. Xavier had once been its custodian. Upon his death that honour fell to Elysius. And here, now, the Chaplain was suggesting some additional significance to it, some purpose none of those present knew or understood.

'I can feel it,' Elysius concluded with the sort of conviction that suggested he was certain.

More than a relic then, thought Ba'ken, *even more than an anachronism from the Great Crusade...*

Zartath smirked, his eyes drawn to a sharp rise they'd descended to reach the temple confines.

'Then they'd best be quick, for she is already here.'

All eyes followed the Black Dragon's gaze. There, upon a steep precipice of rubble, of broken columns and the sediment of shattered structures, stood a lithe figure. She was tall and carried a long barbed trident in one hand. Two blades were cinched to her waist and a long mane of braided white hair flowed to the peak of her thighs like a clutch of venomous adders.

Helspereth.

* * *

II
Follow the Beacon

VARKETH NARLN LET the flensing knife slip from his fingers and sighed. It was a deep, frustrating sound. The slave, a grey-skinned *inferior*, had not lasted long and yielded little sustenance. Varketh *craved*. The soul hunger was upon him. She Who Thirsts was ever present. He needed more slaves, and in order to get them he needed to enhance his standing in the Reef. Too many petty dracons, and with An'scur lording it over the rest of the cabal, how could he, a humble watchman, hope to prosper?

Skimming slaves from the bounties coming in off the pirate raiders was a way, he mused. Exorbitant flesh-taxes were easy to impose but hard to refute. Only those in Volgorrah with the right pull and hierarchical clout could deny an overseer. Without an overseer's seal, there was no way into the Reef. The Port of Anguish would close its gates. No access, no slaves. All became forfeit to the cabal, with a small percentage taken for Varketh's pleasure of course.

But then that was Varketh's problem. Appetite. So easy to succumb to; so hard to sate. *I need more slaves.* So when the crackling 'korder came to life in his oubliette he smiled. Another raider. A big one by the sound of Keerl's enthusiasm.

Just a taste for you, underling, Varketh thought. *For you and the rest of the peons.*

An'scur might be lord of the Reef but here, at the Spike, Varketh Narln was master.

He dressed quickly, donning his red, segmented armour and slipping on his open-faced helmet before scaling the egress pipe and emerging into the way station's basement. It was dark below, but Varketh heard the approach of a heavy grav-engine thrumming through the walls. His latent excitement heightened.

Many slaves on a rig that large.

The overseer was still performing the calculations in his head for the flesh-currency when he hoisted back the trapdoor that led into the station lobby. Narrowed eyes met him as he ascended. His crew, his minions – all murdered him with a glance. At least, they would if they could. Keerl was loyal. The splinter cannon cradled in the large warrior's grasp – he had the build and sheer strength of an incubus – ensured the others stayed loyal as well.

'What have we got?' Varketh asked. He peered down the wide slit in the lobby floor through which the bladed dark eldar ships could dock and disgorge their cargo for inspection.

The mechanism was churning already, a slow grind as the slit widened to accommodate the larger raider's bulk. Spiked pins either side of the growing chasm snapped into place, ready for insertion into the vessel's hull.

'Heavy Ravager, my lord,' remarked Tullar, spitting poison with his words, particularly the last two.

'Just one ship?' Varketh glared into the lightning-void. The vessel was coming in slow. Perhaps the grav-engines had been damaged in the raid. He hoped they wouldn't need repairs. It was unrewarding work. Maybe he could demand more flesh-currency if they did?

'Weapons ready.'

Twenty splinter rifles and Keerl's cannon came to life. It wasn't unknown for particularly 'enterprising' pirates to try and overcome a way station by force.

They often carried slave caches and the flesh-cattle records they also possessed were invaluable to certain haemonculi and cult-dracons. After all, this was the Reef, a wild and unruly extension of Commorragh. If the heart of the dark eldar empire was its urban sprawl then this, the Port of Anguish and its many way stations, was its untamed frontier.

As the Ravager came in, gliding almost silently now, its crew like statues, Varketh's grip on his splinter pistol tightened.

'My lord…' a gaunt-faced warrior addressed the watchman.

The Ravager was just entering the outer boundary of the Spike. It would be with them in seconds. The docking slit yawned like a fanged metal maw.

Varketh turned on the warrior, who was at the lobby's instrument panel. Data streamed over a dark screen in hazy emerald flashes. Sigils ran vertically and horizontally, detailing the vessel's schemata and slave-bearing capacity. 'What is it, Lilithar?' he snapped.

'The Ravager bears Kravex's mark.'

As he turned to see the vessel sliding into the docking slit, Varketh's pale skin bled to alabaster white.

The haemonculus!

'Stow weapons!' he said, 'Do it now, whelps!'

Kravex, here, attending the Spike? Much influence and affluence could be derived from associating with the flesh-surgeons of the Reef. Word was that Kravex had the ear of An'scur, and more literally, his finger. The archon had many enemies. Rumours permeated to the outer frontiers that he'd been assassinated more than once already. Kravex's patronage ensured that death didn't stick.

Oh yes, Varketh desired very much to be in the good graces of the haemonculus.

But as the Ravager glided in, he couldn't see his would-be patron aboard. It was dark in the lobby, though. The crew, their weapons held stiffly across their armoured chests, still hadn't moved.

'Boarding lamps,' Varketh ordered and felt the faintest tremor of unease ripple through his lithe body.

Light, stark and flaring, described the Ravager. It lit the corpses of the crew as well. It illuminated their wounds, rapidly concealed but enough to fool an overseer and his entourage in the webway darkness.

'Hells of Commorragh...' breathed Varketh as the first of the dead crewmen fell forwards to reveal a looming giant in green armour.

He was reaching for his splinter pistol, half-tugged from its holster, when the lobby filled with fire. Varketh's world exploded, his dark machinations with it.

THE AMBUSH LASTED seconds. Bolter smoke and echoing thunder were all that was left in its wake. That, and the twenty-something corpses broken all over the lobby by the Firedrakes' percussive gunfire.

Halknarr was examining a groove in his armour left by a splinter round.

'I'll add it to the collection,' said the old campaigner, whose battle-plate was riddled with almost as many scars as his honour-scathed body. He'd left his helmet on the leather thong, looped around his belt, and smiled viciously at Praetor.

'I think you enjoy this too much at times, brother,' the veteran sergeant replied, a small smirk betraying his composure.

He'stan was first to disembark. His booted feet rang

heavily against the metal lobby floor. He was headed for the instrument panel. The rest of the expanse was sparse. It was a dock with that as its sole function. A trapdoor led to a basement where Daedicus and Vo'kar found hanging chains and other instruments of incarceration and torture. Lower still was an oubliette that Daedicus reached first and shone his lume-lamp into.

'Tortured xenos,' he remarked impassively. The two of them vacated the basement, Vo'kar using his boot to close the lid.

Tsu'gan followed He'stan, grimacing as the dark eldar blood touched his boots. He longed to burn this place, to burn it all.

'Forgefather?'

He'stan turned and his eyes narrowed through the lenses of his fanged battle-helm.

'Brother,' Tsu'gan corrected himself, still finding the familiarity that the Forgefather desired uncomfortable.

'I can feel the Sigil,' He'stan explained, returning to the instrument panel. 'But our search will be much faster if we can narrow down what part of the Reef the Chaplain is on.'

'How?' Tsu'gan asked, leaning in and immediately feeling revolted by the barbed xenos script crawling all over the screen. 'What is this... *scratching*?'

'Dusk-wraiths have language, too,' Praetor told him, joining them at the screen. 'Although, it has no purity and is a baseless tongue.'

'You can read it, brother-sergeant?' Tsu'gan's tone was incredulous. He wanted to tear the machine from its housings, demolish it with his chainsword. No good could come of such devices.

'No, but I can,' said He'stan, manipulating the unfathomable controls like an expert. More scything sigils cut across the display, spooling quickly now. It stopped on what appeared to be some kind of list.

'The Reef keeps logs of all its slaves,' He'stan told them.

Tsu'gan shared a concerned glance with Praetor, but the veteran sergeant nodded for him to keep listening. Again, Tsu'gan marvelled at just how different the Forgefather was to the rest of them. He was Fire-born, no doubt of that. He practically bled Deathfire's molten ichor. But he was a warrior apart. The quest for the Nine had changed him in ways none of them could comprehend. Tsu'gan found his devotion for the Forgefather increase.

Nearby, the rest of the Firedrakes adopted defensive positions. At Halknarr's command, they watched the dark and turbulent skies. In enemy territory, it wouldn't go well to be caught unawares. All it took was another returning skiff or heavy skimmer and their presence would be exposed to every band of hellion, scourge and sky-riding jet-biker dwelling in the Reef. Slaying a cadre of unprepared and gullible overseers was one thing; taking on the mercenaries of this benighted place was quite another.

He'stan turned. 'Flesh is currency on the Reef. Its scales are kept ever-busy with its bloody acquisition, but they are scales nonetheless and so must balance.'

Tsu'gan frowned. 'I don't understand.'

'To us, the dusk-wraiths are savages, hedonistic pleasure-seekers and torturers who adhere to no rule or structure. Not so. There is a society at work, a highly complex and hierarchical regime. He or she who holds slaves, holds power. Pacts and deals are not uncommon. They too are currency. It is fundamental, it is how they *exist*. So, therefore, careful records are kept. How many? What nature? Owning cabal? Disposition on the Reef? Everything is noted. Everything is logged. Here.' He'stan tapped the screen with his gauntleted finger, making a shallow *plinking* sound.

'Elysius is not alone,' He'stan revealed.

How he knew that, Tsu'gan could still not discern but he accepted it.

'He was left at one of the northern spires. Its name translates as the "Razored Vale".' Without warning, He'stan swung a fist and shattered the screen. Smoke, and wires palsied by venting electrical discharge, spewed forth like innards from the instrument panel. He was angry.

'What is it?' asked Praetor. 'What's wrong?'

The Forgefather's body was stiff with fury.

'The Razored Vale is not a lord's dominion,' he said. 'It is a hunting ground.'

'They mean to throw our Chaplain to the wolves,' muttered Tsu'gan.

'I suspect they already have,' He'stan replied. To Praetor, he added, 'Assemble the Firedrakes. We are already running out of time.'

CHAPTER THIRTEEN

I
Wych Hunt

BEFORE ELYSIUS COULD signal for the Fire-born to adopt defensive tactics, Zartath was sprinting up the rise. His brother, Kor'be, was not far behind him. Even the ragged mercenary militia he had bonded together took up the charge.

Helspereth hadn't moved. She watched, her serpentine hair tossed about by a sudden breeze. The wind was quickly whipping hard, driving down the incline, kicking up grit and splinter shards as sharp as daggers.

Ba'ken looked to his Chaplain, caught by indecision.

Zartath was almost halfway up the rise. His bone-blades *shucked* free, ready to gore. He'd missed the chance to avenge his brethren on An'scur. It looked like he'd settle for the archon's 'hell-bitch' instead.

Elysius cursed under his breath. Four Fire-born were left, one of those wounded, and a trio of injured humans. The Chaplain didn't like his options, and they were narrowing with every metre the Black Dragon gained up the rise.

'Ionnes, watch them,' he said. 'The rest, engage and destroy.'

Hefting the borrowed blades of dead warriors, three Salamanders led by their Chaplain sped up the ridge.

Survival should be the primary mission. Honour was secondary to the safety and sanctity of the Sigil. But Elysius could not abandon his brothers, not even those feral kin from a cursed and aberrant Chapter. Do that and all the Sigil stood for would count for nothing. Vulkan had made them warriors and so they would die as such. Elysius gave voice, as the hot wind scorched his face and the splinter shards cut him.

'Surrounded by shadows, we are as rock. Bonded like the slopes of Mount Deathfire, our purpose is solid and unyielding...'

He increased his pace, eating into Zartath's lead, impelling the others to match him.

'...Our righteous fury shall burn the enslaver and the arch-potentate. Our will shall break down any fortress of oppression...'

Zartath was only moments away from attack. Helspereth let him come. She was smiling. Elysius finished the litany.

'None shall stay our blades. We are Salamander and in Vulkan's fire are we forged!'

They reached her at the same time, bone-blade and crozius slicing through air as the wych sprang into the sky and flipped acrobatically out of harm's way.

Zartath snarled, about to give chase, when he saw what waited on the other side of the ridge in a valley walled by ruins.

Helspereth had company. She had brought her hell-maidens with her. Hungry-eyed, licking their blood-red lips, the wyches rushed the ridge in a flood of barbs and blades.

Elysius counted thirty warriors, not including their grinning matriarch. He seized Zartath by the arm.

'We cannot win this.'

The Black Dragon flashed the Chaplain a savage glance. 'Not the Salamander pragmatism I have seen before.'

'Vengeance is the province of the damned, brother. She'll let her cohorts bleed us first and then devour us both, flesh and soul. I don't fear death, but there are higher stakes here than you know.'

Zartath bared his fangs. 'You had best be right about your relic, son of Vulkan,' he said and bolted back down the ridge the way they had come.

It was a fighting retreat. No way could they hold the ridge against such numbers and with the weakened state of their forces, but they couldn't hope to outpace the dark eldar either.

Elysius was falling back when he blocked a falchion intended to cut his throat. He headbutted the shrieking wych and sent her tumbling. Out the corner of his eye he saw one of Zartath's mercenaries fall to a spear in the chest. Another became tangled by a net of razor-wire and swiftly bled to death. The Astartes were holding their own.

Ba'ken and Iagon had made it back to the base of the ridge. Koto was engaged in running battle still. Zartath and Kor'be were reluctant to give ground and fought savagely.

'Fall back to defensive positions!' Ba'ken cried. The strain in his voice betrayed the severity of the wounds he'd sustained fighting the hound-creatures in the amphitheatre.

It wouldn't be enough. A last stand here would be just that. The Sigil. Something had triggered a desire to preserve it in the Chaplain's mind. He needed to keep it safe. Help was coming. With the dead scattered across the ridge, the human mercenaries all but wiped out, Ionnes farthest back with the surviving Night Devils, Elysius countered his brother-sergeant's order.

'Retreat! Keep moving!' Through the melee, breaking another wych against his crozius, Elysius found a way to Ba'ken's side. 'Stand now and we'll be overrun.'

The brother-sergeant nodded, before making a laboured parry against a wych's serrated blade. He swung himself, trying a get a blow in, before she sprang away to engage a different enemy.

Ba'ken was panting hard – his wounds, the battle, were taking a toll on the big warrior. 'Why doesn't she attack?'

Helspereth had regained the summit of the ridge but had yet to commit herself to battle. She held a third of her coven back with her, too.

Even the wyches that had engaged them were taking bites at the Astartes but then feinting away before they could be drawn into a deadly combat. All the while the Salamanders and Black Dragons were giving ground.

Elysius's gaze narrowed. Both groups of Astartes were bunching. Barring the Night Devils, the humans were almost all dead. 'They're herding us. Culling the chaff first and then priming us for the kill. It's sport to them. And it extends the sensation, the soul reaping.'

Pegged back like cattle surrounded by a ring of patient predators, the Astartes came shoulder to shoulder and the fighting stopped.

'What now?' snapped Iagon, wearing a fresh gash across his cheek.

The wyches were closing. Twelve of the twenty Helspereth had unleashed remained, their blades blood-slick but far from sated. Hell-red flared in their cruel eyes.

'Here is where you tell us you have a way out of this place,' Elysius hissed to Zartath.

A deep rumbling, the distant sound of churning machinery buried far beneath the earth, answered for him. Gripped by sudden superstitious paralysis, the wyches ground to a halt. Rivulets of dust and dislodged pieces of debris were cascading from the structures around them.

It was the same as before, when they'd originally landed in the broken temple. Elysius realised the city was moving. Some infernal engine, its science lost to myth or intellectual decay, compelled it. Avenues and corridors shifted, bridges and platforms rose and fell, dead ends became conduits, towers plummeted and new levels rose out of the darkness. Capricious will manoeuvred it without discernible scheme or design. The way behind the Salamanders and their allies opened, a vast crack splitting the platform they were on. The endless city became an ever-widening chasm behind them, the level they were on a precipice.

Zartath had his back to the Chaplain. The Black Dragon was laughing. Out beyond the edge of the precipice, hot winds squalled and twisted. Splinter dust abraded the Astartes' armour and made their skin itch. A lightning flash from higher up threw their shadows in front of them. The wraith-like silhouettes were there and gone in an instant, like the echo of their lives.

'We were already dead when we came to this place,' growled Iagon, before Elysius's glare silenced him.

Ba'ken couldn't say much of anything. He was holding his chest, a recently revived Tonnhauser and the other two Night Devils supporting him.

'Well?' Elysius pressed the Black Dragon.

Helspereth and the rest of her coven were descending the ridge. The wych queen's shrieking commands overrode their fear at the sudden dysjunction.

'You're not going to like it,' Zartath replied, legs braced as the tremors slowly started to abate. He turned to Kor'be. The big Black Dragon nodded as he recognised some previously held agreement between the two of them.

'Make 'em count,' Zartath whispered. There was a flash of acknowledgement in Kor'be's eyes.

'On the shores of Cable, a small iron world in a sector I've long forgotten,' Zartath began, slowly backing away, 'my brothers and I fought the warband of the Incarnadine Supplicants to the edge of a fire-blasted cliff. It was called Doomfel on account that no living thing could survive the drop. An alkali ocean had existed there centuries ago but had drained, and left a deep trench in its wake.'

Iagon interrupted. 'Is this really the time for war stories?'

Zartath ignored him. They were less than a metre from the precipice now. A dark chasm yawned beyond it, getting ever wider, filled with lightning and blades. 'Face death at our hands or take Doomfel. Do you know what those traitors did?'

Elysius shook his head but could see where this was going. Helspereth had almost reached her kin. When she did, she'd signal the attack.

Zartath grinned and mouthed, *Farewell, brother*, to Kor'be. 'They jumped.' Turning on his heel, Zartath sprinted off the edge of the precipice and leapt into the gloom.

II
Apocalypse Near

A STORM WAS rising. Out in the ash wastes of Moribar the winds were picking up. Grey squalls, congealed bone dust and stone, grew in intensity with each passing minute. A world was suddenly out of balance. Watching his ward with wary eyes, Pyriel couldn't be sure that Dak'ir wasn't the cause.

'Not far now, master,' he said, just audible above the growing storm.

'Move swiftly, Dak'ir. We don't want to be caught in whatever is coming on the horizon.'

At his master's word, Dak'ir looked there and saw the cloud of dust slowly obliterating dunes and monuments. Grey death was approaching, fast and pitiless on a howling wind. Warning klaxons, blaring all across Moribar, announced it. None save the Salamanders heard them – them and the dead, of course. The pilgrims and missionaries had fled to underground bunkers; the servitors were dormant inside their subterranean cribs. The land above was bereft of life and yet in utter turmoil.

'It's as if Moribar itself is in upheaval.'

'You can feel it?' asked Pyriel, trudging through the thickening ash a few paces behind.

'I feel something,' Dak'ir confessed. His gaze tracked east. He recognised the rocky overhang where they'd left the *Caldera* several hours before. Hopefully, Brother Loc'tar would be there too, waiting for them.

Already the paint was being eroded from their armour, the glossy blue reduced by slashes of gun-metal grey.

'This wind will shear us to pieces. It's harsh enough to cut ceramite,' muttered Pyriel, his displeasure at the vandalism done to his armour obvious. Even in the face of a growing hell-storm, the Epistolary was fastidious about his appearance.

A pregnant pause passed between master and apprentice before Pyriel spoke again. He used the time to catch up to Dak'ir and was walking alongside him.

'You said you witnessed the end, the doom of Nocturne,' he said tentatively. 'What *exactly* did Kelock show you?'

Dak'ir stopped and faced him. 'I'm not sure the apparition showed me anything. What I saw, I saw because–' A wave of heat, rising from the east, interrupted him. 'I saw–' Dak'ir began before his body was wracked with seizure. His arm was flung out and he gripped his master's vambrace. In that moment Pyriel saw everything too.

A wall of fire, so high it reached the heavens, surged from the earth. Nocturne's surface had become a web of fissures, the planet's lifeblood seeping out of them in rivulets of lava. The sky was ablaze. In the blood red firmament a star was falling. Prometheus burned, the metallic orb wreathed in re-entry flare as it cascaded like a doomed comet towards the planet below. Its gravity had failed. Death was certain.

From the hellish night above an incandescent beam speared down to strike Nocturne's heart, impaling it. From the lowest depths of the world, a death cry sounded. It came from the ancient drakes who had lived in the bowels of the

*earth for millennia. Their spirits were dying. Nocturne was
dying. Their mournful sound was a lamentation for a
doomed world.*

The rest came in flashes, each a jolt of lightning
through Dak'ir and Pyriel, their consciousnesses
linked in brief symbiosis.

*The Acerbian Sea boiled into a great pall of steam, burn-
ing away the skiffs, eradicating the gnorl-whales and
scalding Epimethus from existence.*

*On the Arridian Plain, Themis – City of Warrior-Kings
– was dragged under the sands, lost to the wailing dunes.*

*Mount Deathfire belched fire and fury, the haemorrhag-
ing of a vital artery bared open by a mortal wound. She
spluttered, like a body with its lungs ruptured, her breaths
the last from a life almost ended. The Dragonspire ridge collapsed, the craggy rises falling one by one into smoke and
ruin. It was followed by the chain of the Serpent's Fang.
Forests of granite shattered, broken by the atomic blast wave
coursing through them. Then came the Cindara Plateau,
that most holy of monuments, swallowed beneath the frac-
turing earth.*

*Chapter Bastions, tribal settlements that had stood upon
inviolable bedrock since the dawn of ages cracked and
crumbled against the cataclysmic forces unleashed in the
planet's death throes.*

'Tempus Infernus' – the words burned into the
Librarians' minds as indelible as a blacksmith's signature on a blade, but still it wasn't over.

*Ignea, an entire region of subterranean caves, was sun-
dered in a single, devastating instant. The only legacy of its
existence, a deathly cloud of displaced ash.*

*Hot winds came from the east, transforming the Gey'sarr
Ocean into a blanket of fire and scorching the white walls
of Heliosa, the Beacon City, black.*

*Aethonian, the Fire Spike, ruptured and split, lava oozing
down its once proud flanks like blood.*

*Hesiod, Clymene, as far as the Themian Ash Ridges, as
deep as the T'harken Delta where the leo'nid preyed and the
sauroch herds gathered – all of Nocturne became as dust.
Its cities were shadows; its peoples not even a memory.
Burned from the galactic sky, it was a warning, a caution-
ary tale. An entire civilisation was gone, rendered into
atmospheric dust.*

The fires grew and grew until they eclipsed the
Librarians too. They had seen it before, during the
burning. Except now the reality of it was closer than
ever. Prophecy and destiny were coming together, closing in towards an apex of inevitability. The course of
fate was locked; there would be no turning from it.

'Tempus Infernus' – Time of Fire. And all would burn
before the last of its sands had run out.

Pyriel collapsed, his body seizing in the psychic
aftermath.

Dak'ir shook his head free of the visions and found
the solidity of the Moribar ash deserts beneath him
again. His heart was racing, his eyes firmly shut. It took
an effort of will to open them again. It took him a
moment to realise he was on his knees, the vision
felling him as surely as a hammerblow. The storm had
engulfed them and the rocky overhang where the
Caldera waited was slowly becoming obscured. Delay
much longer and they would never find it, the senses
in Dak'ir's armour baffled by atmospheric interference.

Rise, he willed, *rise up and overcome.*

It was the Promethean Creed, to endure what others
could not, to fight when the body rebelled.

Rise now. Vulkan's strength is in my veins.

Dak'ir got to his feet.

Save for the nerve-tremors, his master wasn't moving. His armour was turning grey as the thrashing whorls of spinning sand abraded it. When a small chip appeared in the shoulder guard of his own armour, Dak'ir knew it was time to go.

Hefting an unconscious Pyriel onto his back, he quickly activated the comm-link in his battle-helm.

++*Fifty metres from your position, Brother Loc'tar*++ he said ++*Lift her now and come for us, or we're not getting off this grey rock*++

A grainy affirmative returned from the Thunderhawk pilot and after a few minutes the sound of blazing engines intruded on the storm winds. Dak'ir had trudged a few metres when a dense black shape resolved itself in the grey fog surrounding it. He stood beneath it and engaged the link again.

++*Master Pyriel requires recovery. Unconscious but stable*++

Through the gloom a winch hook glinted, attached to a strong line. It was less than half a metre away before Dak'ir saw it, tossed about in the breeze. He managed to grab it when it was close enough and cinched it around Pyriel's waist. Two hard tugs on the line and the automated mechanism kicked in and retracted it.

Within seconds, a rapidly ascending Pyriel was lost from view. Once the Librarian was safely aboard, the *Caldera* risked a further descent. When it was low enough for Dak'ir to jump, he boosted the final few metres and hauled himself onto the embarkation ramp.

++*Go now!*++ he cried as the tumult smashed into them.

Engines whining, Loc'tar punched the *Caldera* into a

savage ascent. Dak'ir clung on, fingers denting the metal of the ramp, until they were clear of the worst of it. When he'd dragged himself into the Chamber Sanctuarine, he rolled onto his back. His hearts were hammering, his breath ragged in his heaving chest.

'Tempus Infernus...' he rasped, and shut his eyes.

CHAPTER FOURTEEN

I
Sigil Fires

IT WAS AS if the world had split and been remoulded by savage hands.

A jagged wound ran through what might have once been an amphitheatre or temple. Its bifurcated hemispheres now sat at uneven levels, where once they might have been joined. Between them there rose a bridge of stone, wide enough for a trio of Land Raiders abreast. Smaller spans bled off from this grey artery. They were fringed by spikes and razored balustrades. Columns punctuated the main span – skeletal remains, human and xenos, hung from them by chains and steel cords. In the distance, there was a spire. Several figures were impaled upon it like graven offerings.

'It's called *dysjunction*,' said He'stan, who'd halted the Firedrakes at the threshold to the temple, where the bridge began. There they waited together, in two lines of five. They'd heard and felt the capricious motions of the twisting city as they closed in their borrowed raider. It was junked now, rendered inoperable by Tsu'gan's hand. He'd taken great pleasure in its destruction and bemoaned the curtness of the task. Deep in the avenues and conduits of the dark eldar's frontier settlement, the Firedrakes had no further use for it. Besides, it could be tracked and at this point covertness was paramount. The rest of the way would be conveyed on foot.

Halknarr, for one, was glad of it.

'Even their cities are twisted aberrations.' He hawked and spat in the tradition of old campaigners.

'It is the dusk-wraiths' way,' counselled He'stan. 'Their borders are ephemeral, their pacts and allegiances likewise. It bodes well.'

'How so, my lord?' Halknarr asked. 'Bad enough we must navigate this labyrinth without it changing on us constantly.'

'The city's denizens will require time to adjust, redraw their tiny empires and claw fresh lines of dominion in the sand. We can exploit this distraction, use it to get closer to the Sigil undetected.'

'You mean closer to Elysius, my lord,' ventured Daedicus.

'No, brother, I meant what I said. The Sigil is all. I fear for Elysius.'

Daedicus's silence betrayed his shock.

'If there is a way, he will survive,' Tsu'gan noted grimly. 'The Chaplain is a tough and unyielding bastard.'

Praetor let the remark go. It was true enough.

'Look!' It was Halknarr, pointing towards the bridge. All eyes followed to alight on a body caught in the balustrade, snagged on the spikes; a body that wore green power armour.

'Brother,' cried Daedicus, starting to move before He'stan's raised hand stopped him.

'He's dead,' announced the Forgefather grimly, noting the absence of life readings through his retinal display.

The sound of a clenching fist signalled Tsu'gan's anger. 'But they are not...' he said and nodded in the direction of the bridge.

A cluster of emaciated, grey-skinned, ghoulish figures was thronged around pieces of a broken dark eldar skiff. From this distance they had blended in with the debris at first and it was hard to tell what the undulating mass was doing. After a few moments, though, it became apparent.

They were gnawing... on *flesh*.

The distaste in Halknarr's voice rang out, 'Carrion-eaters.'

'More of our brothers could be amongst them,' said Daedicus.

'Depraved bastards...' Tsu'gan brandished his combi-bolter only for Praetor to push his aim downwards.

'No, brother,' said the veteran sergeant. His mouth was set in a tight line. 'We go hand-to-hand this time.'

Tsu'gan grinned beneath his battle-helm. The hard red flash in his eyes mirrored He'stan's own. The Forgefather's decree was emphatic.

'Slay them all,' he said, and was running at the creatures.

Like the hive of a lava-ant, as soon as the ghouls were disturbed they broke apart and attacked en masse. There were at least a hundred of the wretches,

shrieking and clawing, so pumped up on their canni-
balistic activities as to eschew all sense of
self-preservation.

Halfway across the bridge, the Firedrakes met them.
Tsu'gan was reminded of the zombified servitors
aboard the *Archimedes Rex* as he killed. These creatures
had no deadly tools or cutting saws, just tooth and
claw, but fought with the same automaton-like abandon. He felt invulnerable, hacking off limbs, hauling
dozens over the edge into the dark abyss below the
bridge, taking out his anger one cut at a time.

Fighting back-to-back with Halknarr, Tsu'gan marvelled at the glimpses of the old campaigner's prowess.
The wretches barely laid a claw on him. He'd drawn
combat blade and chainsword, cutting and thrusting
with the poise of a fencer but the bullishness of a
pugilist.

Where Tsu'gan was wrath and fury, Halknarr was the
careful execution of force and aggression. There was
much he could learn from his more veteran brothers.

Vo'kar, denied use of his flamer, fought with fist and
combat blade. His years as a weapon specialist had not
dulled his close quarter instincts. Invictese, his comrade aboard the *Protean* and fellow survivor of that
ill-fated mission, stood beside Vo'kar carving lumps
out of the creatures with his chainblade. Oknar,
Persephion, Eb'ak – they all battled like heroes, crushing the wretches. Their blades and hammers slashed
and bludgeoned with almost regimented discipline,
each a masterpiece weapon forged by its owner's hand.

No one however, not even Praetor, could keep up
with He'stan.

These foes were beneath the Firedrakes, little better
than xenos fodder, but they needed to be slain all the

same. The Forgefather did that with efficient lethality. No blow was wasted, every strike was a kill. He ground a circle of death around him so thick that the bodies piled up into a barricade of flesh.

Praetor barged and smashed them, using his bulk and strength like a human battering ram. His thunder hammer rose and fell in electric arcs like a pendulum. The creatures were pitched off the bridge in a shower of corpses, their heady screams lost to the void below.

It was pure. It was a massacre.

To Tsu'gan, it was beautiful.

The fight lasted only a few minutes. By the end, the creatures were dead, cut down by hammer and blade. Many fell to their dooms far below. The Firedrakes were drenched in gore, but relieved to discover no Salamander was being devoured by the frenzied pack.

'The Parched,' said He'stan, rolling one of the half-chewed corpses onto its back to reveal a female dark eldar, 'are like their kin but starved of sensation. They are dregs,' he explained, 'cowards and wretches, but like their entire race they are vicious and bitter.'

'I once fought against the Plague of Unbelief,' said Halknarr, regarding the masticated bodies. 'They too ate the living, but their minds were lost to Chaos. They were little better than walking corpses, driven by their base instincts. This,' he added, a sweep of his arm encompassing the grisly scene, 'this I cannot explain.'

'They are damned,' said Tsu'gan, tearing a chunk of flesh from the teeth of his chainsword.

'That is precisely what they are, brother,' replied He'stan.

'Another here, my lord,' called Daedicus from the far end of the bridge. With the battle over, the Firedrakes had spread out to search the area for further casualties.

He'stan was determined if they could not bring their slain brothers peace, they would at least burn them. He muttered a litany for the one caught in the balustrade. The Salamander's head had been removed. Doubtless it was mounted on some trophy rack or spike. The Forgefather had to marshal his anger at the thought.

Others were not so temperate.

'It's G'heb,' snarled Tsu'gan, his rage impotent without anything to pummel. He settled for the bridge instead and demolished a chunk of stone from the balustrade. 'He was 3rd Company. I recognise his armour markings.'

'We will avenge him, brother,' said Praetor, arriving at Tsu'gan's side. He had Persephion in tow.

'Any sign of Chaplain Elysius?' asked the veteran sergeant.

'It seems unlikely, my lord,' Persephion replied.

Praetor seized him by the arm. His voice was stern. 'Be certain. Search everywhere.'

Persephion nodded and went about his business.

He'stan was already heading for the end of the bridge where Daedicus knelt by the fallen Salamander.

'L'sen,' Tsu'gan told them. He and Praetor had followed the Forgefather, who was now kneeling by the body too. It had been left in repose, but without an Apothecary to harvest L'sen's progenoids his legacy was ended.

'Obviously Elysius came this way,' said Praetor, searching the lightning-wracked horizon for some fresh sign of their brothers' passing.

'He lives then,' said Tsu'gan in a quiet voice.

'The Chaplain would've done what he could, I am sure,' said He'stan. 'Stay silent for a moment, brothers,' he added, closing his eyes.

Tsu'gan shared a wary glance with Praetor but soon became enrapt by the Forgefather's ritual.

In a kneeling position, he bowed his head and pressed the haft of his spear against it. He clutched the weapon in both hands, holding it upright like a banner or lightning rod.

He was muttering something, some benediction or invocation. It didn't feel like warp sorcery, but there was something unknown and intangible about it. Tsu'gan had heard of the clandestine rituals conducted at the heart of Prometheus. Even as a Firedrake himself, he was not privy to all of their secrets. In fact, he knew very little of the inner workings of the 1st Company. Barely three years had he been one of them, it was a flickering flame compared to the blazing braziers nurtured over the decades by his warrior-kin. But then again, Praetor was pre-eminent amongst the Drakes and even he looked nonplussed.

After a few minutes, He'stan stood.

'There is a signal, faint, but the trail of fire is there. They are not far,' he announced to no one in particular.

Behind him, the Firedrakes had gathered, awaiting his pronouncement in respectful silence.

'The Sigil is within our grasp,' he concluded.

'What trail? I see nothing,' Halknarr hissed beneath his breath.

As the Forgefather led them off, Praetor leaned over to Tsu'gan.

'Truly, the mysteries surrounding our Lord He'stan are incredible,' he said.

Tsu'gan could only nod in agreement. His voice was choked with reverence. 'Truly,' he whispered.

* * *

II
Despair and Faith

TONNHAUSER WAS GLAD Leiter and Fulhart were helping. The giant was heavy. His weight pressed on the trio of Night Devils with greater intensity every step they took. Tonnhauser could feel the shallowness of the warrior's breathing through his armour, and smell the thready scent of blood every time he exhaled. The giant Salamander was dying. Tonnhauser didn't need to be a field medic to know that, even a layman trooper could see it. During the few harrowing hours they'd spent in the Razored Vale, Tonnhauser had come to believe that angels could die. He'd seen one with his head removed, the explosion of gore no different to when Trooper Kolt had been decapitated. Another had fallen to multiple wounds, his tenacity incredible but no less futile than a common man's.

Space Marines could die. It was a startling, terrifying revelation.

He'd caught the battle in snatches. The wych-warriors were so fast, like blade flashes against the sun. He'd heard the action on the plain with General Slayte over the vox, though he had no idea where the Night Devil commander was now. Dead, presumably. Everyone was dead. How could they be anything other, fighting against these *things*? He tried not to give in to despair but it was all too easy in the wake of his wounded faith. When they had defeated the monstrous hounds, Tonnhauser had dared to believe they could survive. Now the truth was glaring him in the face, truth that carried serrated blades and spiked tridents.

Shuffling towards the edge of the precipice, Tonnhauser shook his head to banish his fatalism. They'd endured this long, this far.

'Tempered against the anvil,' one of the Salamanders had said. Tonnhauser didn't know what that meant but there was strength in it and the words brought him comfort. He owed it to the memory of his father to keep trying. But the wych-warriors were close and their formerly-indestructible guardians were beaten and seemed more vulnerable than ever.

The feral one in the black armour was relating some story to the rest. Tonnhauser found it hard to make out the words, such was his grating cadence. He caught fresh glimpses of the wych-warriors through the wall of armour in front of him – they were prowling nearer. He did not think death would be swift beneath their blades and barbs. He'd tried to look away several times but kept coming back – for all their ferocity, the strange androgynous creatures were alluring.

When he was done, the black-armoured warrior broke from the group and ran. Tonnhauser blinked twice as he leapt off the edge.

'Did he just…' Leiter began.

'I didn't think Space Marines were capable of suicide,' added a breathless Fulhart.

'Not suicide…' rasped the giant. He staggered and almost took the three Guardsmen with him before he righted himself.

'He is failing, Lord Chaplain,' said another Salamander, the one with the narrow face and the scar that turned his mouth into a perpetual sneer.

Their leader, the black-armoured preacher, answered.

'We have no choice–'

The giant Salamander shrugged off Tonnhauser and his other wardens. 'I can stand.' His voice was firm but his legs were not. He sagged and the narrow-faced warrior caught him.

'You are wounded, brother,' he hissed in his ear, loud enough for Tonnhauser to hear him. 'And can do no further good here.'

Behind them, Tonnhauser saw the other black-armoured feral warrior racing up the ridge. His massive bolter flared intermittently.

'Iagon, I can fight,' the giant asserted.

'I'm sorry Ba'ken, you cannot. Now, brace yourself.'

They were less than half a metre from the edge when the one called Iagon pushed the giant off. He fell, his face a mask of anger before he was lost from sight completely.

'Take the humans,' Iagon added, taking in Tonnhauser and the others in a glance. 'Kor'be won't prevail alone.'

'Nor will you,' said a third Salamander, this one brandishing a long spear.

The black-armoured preacher seemed to pause in indecision before he nodded.

'May Vulkan take you to his fires, your souls eternally in the warmth of his flame.' He touched a clenched fist to his breast, before turning to the last of the Salamanders.

'Ionnes…'

The Salamander came forwards and Tonnhauser felt himself being lifted off the ground. 'Long way down, little human,' said the warrior, not without benevolence. 'Be sure to hang on tight.'

Then Tonnhauser's world became a rush of darkness

and lightning flashes as he was taken over the edge of the precipice.

'HOLD THEM AS long as you can, brothers,' said Elysius, picking up the other two humans and following on Ionnes's heels.

'Our sacrifice shall not be in vain,' Iagon replied to the shadows. He was alone at the edge. Below, the world was shadowed and barbed – not unlike his own existence, ever since Tsu'gan had forsaken him, ever since his *betrayal*.

He had fought against it, fought against *the plan*. But some things cannot be fought, they are inevitable. Ba'ken's brief friendship had masqueraded as fresh purpose, but Iagon saw the fleeting truth of it now. You can't fight fate. To deny nature was akin to refuting something as inexorable as time.

Koto was already running to Kor'be's reinforcement, his spear held at his waist as he charged.

'In Vulkan's name!' he roared.

'Aye,' whispered Iagon, 'for the primarch…' and flung his sword. It pierced Koto's back, just below the heart, punching through his plastron at the front in an explosion of bloody grue.

Koto managed to turn before he toppled, a look of anguished disbelief on his face. He tried to form words but the meaning was lost on Iagon. Then he was gone, shredded by a whirlwind of blades as the wyches descended on him.

Oblivious to Iagon's betrayal, Kor'be didn't last much longer. His spent clip *chanked* in his empty bolter for a few rounds before he turned the weapon around, using it like a club. He battered one wych, crushed the skull of another. Helspereth was not to be denied, however. She weaved around his next blow, clumsy and child-like compared to her supreme prowess, and impaled Kor'be on her trident. With a feat of incredible strength, belied by her supple frame, she lifted the thrashing Black Dragon into the air and then drove the trident into a column of stone, pinning him. Fluidly, she drew her twin blades and severed his neck with a flick of silver.

Iagon was unarmed and went to his knees as the wyches approached, his hands in the air signalling surrender.

'A traitor in the midst.' Helspereth sounded amused. She fended off her charges with a daggered glance. The wyches parted before her so she could be relatively alone with her supplicating pet.

Iagon bowed his head.

'And subservient too,' she added with a soft, lilting laugh that contained only malice, 'you are a twisted little thing, aren't you, mon-keigh…'

She slashed Iagon hard across the cheek with her talons, opening a deep wound, forcing him to look at her.

'Answer me then, whelp!' she snapped, her mockery engulfed by a mask of hatred.

'Nihilan,' was all Iagon said. 'I wish to speak to Nihilan.'

Helspereth's eyes narrowed before the feigned amusement returned to her cold features. She had sheathed her swords after killing Kor'be and instead drew forth a metal glove. There were spiked links and tiny pins that fed down her fingers like spines. A translucent mesh crackled as it was stretched over her pallid skin.

She tensed her hand and long needles unsheathed

themselves from her fingertips. With a snarl she rammed the needles into Iagon's chest, easily penetrating the ceramite of his power armour. Electrical shocks wracked his body, cutting right to the bone. He jolted, once, twice then again. His racing hearts conveyed the trauma he was experiencing. Iagon's nerve endings felt as if they were on fire.

Helspereth leaned in close to sample his agony. Licking the blood streaming from his ruptured cheek, she cooed, 'Delicious…'

'Take me… to Nihilan,' Iagon demanded, spitting blood. 'I am his ally.'

Helspereth wasn't done. 'Oh you're mine, now. Your little priest can wait. I'll whet my appetite with you.' Her perfumed breath was oddly soporific. She dug around in Iagon's chest again. He could feel his guts churning. The Larraman cells in his blood attempted to clot the multiple wounds Helspereth was opening in his chest, but even a Space Marine's enhanced physiology had its limits. She'd eviscerate him there and then. Only Iagon's rage at being denied his revenge kept him going.

'Hell-bitch…' he snarled, half-gasping, half-gurgling, '…take me to Nihilan.'

'Such resilient little men,' Helspereth said, slowly becoming lost to rapture. Around her the wyches crowded as close as they dared, taking up the psychic scraps from her butcher's table.

'I sabotaged the sentry points…' Iagon confessed, 'I… let you in…'

Helspereth ignored him. She was enjoying herself far too much, her desire threatening to overcome her malice. 'I can see why that corpse, Kravex, finds such entertainment with you. Is your priest as hardy? I bet he is. I cannot wait to sample his pain. I might even let him hurt me a little first.' One of her swords wavered into view. Iagon found his vision fogging. Kor'be's blood still shimmered dully on the blade. 'This dance is over for you, now, mon-keigh.' She smiled, a serpent's smile, a presage to death. 'It has been fun, though.' Her eyes were empty pits of ennui as she raised the blade to Iagon's neck.

'Nihilan…' he rasped.

A voice from out of the ether stayed Helspereth's hand. It spoke in a language Iagon didn't understand. He was blacking out, but clung on to consciousness. After all, his life depended on it.

Helspereth answered the disembodied voice in the same sharp dialect. Her words were clipped and angry.

Iagon was to be granted a reprieve. She was angered because her kill had been denied to her. Another, one who held sway over the wych queen, perhaps the lord and potentate Zartath had spoken of, had decreed Iagon's survival.

He knew the Dragon Warriors had a hand in this. He could detect Nihilan's treachery from leagues away; it was not so dissimilar from Iagon's own.

After a few more words of debate, Helspereth withdrew the electro-talons from Iagon's chest and lowered her sword.

'You have friends in high places,' she spat at him in Low Gothic, before turning her back.

'Not my… friends,' Iagon rasped before darkness claimed him and he passed out.

CHAPTER FIFTEEN

I
Blind Horizon

THE CALDERA'S TROOP hold shook violently, buffeted by the ash storm.

The gunship's pilot, Loc'tar, was engaged in a battle of wills with the vessel, struggling to keep it steady in the tumult rising from Moribar's surface. As the gunship was being tossed about, Dak'ir could hear his brother-pilot's litanies through the internal vox. All efforts to appease the Thunderhawk's machine-spirits appeared to be in vain, however – they were going down, unable to breach even the upper atmosphere of the planet.

The shuddering Chamber Sanctuarine jolted Pyriel awake where he lay prone on the deck. Dak'ir was still recovering from his leap onto the embarkation ramp and hadn't had time to secure him. Pyriel was sliding back and forth, the back-mounted generator he wore grinding loudly against the metal floor as he moved.

The Epistolary was still groggy. In his delirium, he'd been muttering.

'Tempus… infernus… tempus… infernus… tempus… infernus…'

'Time of Fire,' Dak'ir translated into Gothic-Latinum, a reassuring hand on his master's shoulder guard. 'I don't know what precisely it portends.'

A crackle indicating damage to his battle-helm's internal systems came from Pyriel's mouth grille. 'I saw… destruction.' He was still weak, even the effort of speaking was hard for him. 'A spear of light…'

Before Dak'ir could answer the Thunderhawk bucked violently, slamming them both against an interior wall. Pyriel cried out, his head rebounding off a metal bulkhead. The noise inside the hold was incredible, protesting engine sounds mangled with those of the howling storm. Hard ash flakes, compacted into solid grains of matter, struck the outer hull. Through the protective armour of the gunship, they sounded like flak.

'I've seen it before,' Dak'ir told him, 'On Scoria. It's a weapon.'

Pyriel hadn't fought on the barren world, though he had heard of the massive defence cannon being wrought in a workshop-bastion by the Iron Warriors.

'The seismic cannon,' he breathed.

Dak'ir nodded, and the *Caldera* pitched hard against the rising squall outside. They were thrown towards the ship's stern. Warning icons flashed amber on Dak'ir's retinal display as a detailed schematic of his power armour relayed a damage report.

'A relic of the Dark Age of Technology,' said Dak'ir. 'Kelock discovered its existence, found a way to construct it.'

'A weapon capable of annihilating a small moon…' The implication in Pyriel's words trailed off.

'The one on Scoria was just a test. They wanted to see if it would work.'

'They?'

'The Dragon Warriors, who else? The beam I saw in the vision was much greater, mounted on a starship. Nihilan means to destroy us, master.'

'His bitterness runs deep, poisoning him.' Pyriel looked like he might say more, but another abrupt turn thrust them across the opposite side of the hold again.

'What's happening?' Pyriel attempted to stand but collapsed almost as soon as he tried. 'My mind… Like pieces of a shattered kaleidoscope.' Everything was broken, out of place. Pyriel's lucidity was coming and going, his focus divided.

'It's just the psychic aftermath. It'll fade. Be steady, master,' said Dak'ir, clinging to a handrail overhead as Loc'tar's frantic reports came through the vox riddled with static. 'We left it too late. We're caught in the storm.'

Pyriel gripped Dak'ir's arm. 'Master Vel'cona,' he said. 'He told me to kill you if your power became too great.'

'I know, master.'

A tremor of movement up Pyriel's arm hinted at his surprise. 'How?'

Dak'ir's reply was reluctant. 'I read your thoughts.'

'Not possible, I…'

'They appeared in my mind, unbidden. I'm sorry, master.'

Pyriel veiled his shock with a mirthless laugh. It sounded like there was blood in it.

'Even if I wanted to I couldn't stop you, Dak'ir. I'm not sure even Vel'cona could do that now.'

'Ever since Aura Hieron I have resisted it. Even below Moribar, I couldn't let go. Something burns within, almost sentient. I'm afraid if I unleash it, I won't be able to call it back. What am I, Pyriel? What does it mean?'

'Choose for yourself, Dak'ir. Salvation or destruction, what do you think?'

The hold lurched again, the *Caldera's* armour plating protesting loudly against the strain.

'I think it won't matter if we ditch and burn in the Moribar sand.' Dak'ir went to the vox. 'Loc'tar! Can you bring us out of this?'

A long pause followed while the brother-pilot wrestled the gunship's controls.

'The *Caldera* is one of Captain Dac'tyr's best vessels but its spirit is in turmoil. I expect the worst, Librarian.'

Dak'ir's voice was grim. 'Vulkan preserve us.'

Pyriel locked his gaze. 'You can save us.'

'I can what?'

'Use your power, Dak'ir. Lift the ship, burn away the storm.'

'In the chamber, you said–'

'I know what I said, but your abilities are growing stronger with every moment that passes. Burn away the storm, take control of your power.'

'What if I can't?'

'A Salamander does not forgo action because of doubt. If you fail, we are all dead anyway.'

'But to unleash it…'

'Is our only chance.' The *Caldera* was shaking incessantly now. Much longer and the gunship would tear itself apart, scattering them all to the funerary winds. 'I only regret not having more time to train you properly. But that doesn't matter now. Learn by *doing*, Dak'ir. This is Vulkan's way – it is the anvil against which all we Fire-born are tested with bolter, blade or psychic fire. Do it now!' he urged.

Dak'ir reduced the nulling effect of his psychic hood and the dull insistent throb he had felt since activating it became a roar. He staggered at first, acclimatising to the rush but found his composure.

Just before he began, Pyriel seized Dak'ir's wrist.

'I cannot rein you in this time. I might not even be able to get through to you. Lexicanum, you're alone in this.'

Dak'ir nodded. His eyes flared cerulean blue and the fire came.

'Mass… heat signature… outside… ship!' Loc'tar's anxious report came through the vox in fragments.

Flames were bleeding off Dak'ir's body. They fed through the rivets and the micro-fissures between the deckplates, through the smallest gaps in the embarkation ramp and out in the storm. The *Caldera* became a beacon in his mind's eye, wreathed in fire. Waves of heat peeled off the hull in a pulse. The ash became as nothing, the air devoured by the hungry conflagration surrounding the gunship until the wind was reduced to a vacuum.

A roiling fire-ocean stretched out in front of Dak'ir, his self-awareness a skiff tossed about on its psychic waves. He needed an anchor, a place to tether his mind or he risked it unravelling. Inside the hold of a gunship, the effects of that happening would be catastrophic. Philosophies of Zen'de, the earthy wisdom of Master Prebian, Dak'ir recalled their words to his mind in an effort to find equilibrium. When that

failed, he thought of Ba'ken, his closest friend in the
Chapter – how long it had been since he'd seen the
giant warrior. Pyriel's teachings, the stony voice of
Amadeus, Ko'tan Kadai's temperate demeanour –
nothing calmed the fiery waters where Dak'ir was
adrift. He felt himself slipping, lost to the flames until
something eased his consciousness to a place of inno-
cence. He was below the surface of Nocturne, in the
caves of Ignea. The cavern walls felt cool to his touch,
shielded from the oppressive sun by layers of rock.
Glacial meltwaters ran in rivulets down the stone, cre-
ating strange patternation. Penetrating further, Dak'ir
found where the rivulets became a cataract. He
allowed it to wash over his hand and then his body,
soothing the prickling heat on his skin. The seas
calmed, the fire ebbed. Anchored to the memory,
Dak'ir found his equilibrium and opened his eyes.

The *Caldera* slowly stopped bucking and steadied
into a smooth rise.

'Controls returning...' Loc'tar announced, 'We are
gaining altitude, praise Vulkan,' he added, not bothering to mask the relief in his voice.

'Praise Vulkan,' echoed Pyriel, watching the fiery
aura around Dak'ir dwindle into a haze and finally
nothing.

The Lexicanum sagged where he was kneeling. He
had to prise his grip from *Draugen's* hilt. Dak'ir yanked
off his battle-helm, gasping. He smiled at his master,
but Pyriel had fallen unconscious again from the
strain. Despite what he'd said, Pyriel had urged Dak'ir
towards his psychic anchor.

He believed in him, perhaps. Dak'ir was not even
sure he believed in himself. Pyriel had sanctioned his
use of psychics to rescue the *Caldera* from certain

destruction. It was a pragmatic decision but, if what the Epistolary said was true and none, not even Lord Vel'cona, could stop him, then it might have been one out of Pyriel's hands.

All those years ago, back on the Cindara Plateau, had Tsu'gan been right? Was Dak'ir an aberration? Or was he something more, something transcendent sent by the primarch to deliver the Salamanders and Nocturne from annihilation? During the Librarian trials, there had been solace under the earth. It was easy to know what must be done, survival and the execution of the next trial Dak'ir's only concern.

Now, he didn't know what fate held for him, or if his destiny was even his to shape. He rode upon a storm, a symbolic one, towards a blind horizon. The doom-laden prophecies weighed heavy around Dak'ir's neck. It was an unhappy burden but only he could bear it. If that made him aberrant then so be it, he would carry that too.

Resolved, Dak'ir raised Loc'tar on the vox. 'Soon as we're clear of Moribar's gravity well, take us to Nocturne, brother,' he said. 'Take us home.'

II
Tender Mercy

IAGON AWOKE TO find himself suspended several metres off the ground. Awareness came slowly but he realised he was attached to some kind of machine. Its design was hard to fathom, much of the device beyond his field of vision behind him. His arms were above him, each shackled by three rings whose inner surfaces protruded with needles that were embedded into his deep tissue. Iagon's fists were clenched, not in anger, not yet, but because they were encased in a lozenge of gleaming metal. His legs and feet were similarly restrained. He no longer wore his armour. A cold breeze coming from above cooled his feverish skin. It was dark, but not completely. As the pain-blur behind his eyes faded, he looked down as far as his neck would allow and saw the terrible wounds Helspereth had inflicted. He saw also the honour-scars drawn by his brander-priest. How hollow and inconsequential those deeds seemed now.

A deep voice, sharp and edged like a blade, made Iagon look up.

Cold, alien eyes regarded him from the gloom. Their owner wore a surplice of black and violet over lamellar armour plates, vaguely insectoid in nature. It carried a long, barbed helm in the crook of its arm. There was a falchion-like blade attached to its slender hip in a jet-black scabbard. Iagon also thought he saw the silhouette of a long rifle strapped to the creature's back.

As it came further into the light – the source of which the Salamander couldn't pinpoint – Iagon saw it was dark eldar and male. The face was rigid, almost like porcelain. The cheekbones cut outwards, like blades carved out of the skull bone. A long mane of white hair unfurled down his back – it matched the hue of his marblesque skin. He was old, if such a thing was possible to discern with this race, his eyes telling the wisdom of millennia. There was malice too, just an undercurrent, well hidden beneath an impassive veil. A long black cloak of some shimmering material Iagon couldn't place trailed behind this lord, its undulating fluidity giving it the appearance of oil. This then was

An'scur, the one Zartath had been trying to kill, lord and master of the Volgorrah Reef.

A cadre of warriors waited patiently behind the archon, heavier-armoured and taller than the others the Fire-born had encountered so far. Iagon assumed they were the lord's bodyguards and retainers. There was no sign of Helspereth. He was also no longer in the Razored Vale. His surroundings resolving slowly, Iagon realised he was aboard a ship. He could hear the low thrum of its engines, either impelling it through space or anchoring it to one spot. Another figure lingered in the background, bulkier than the rest, but its identity was lost to shadow. For now, it seemed content to watch.

An'scur smiled in a sickle shape, exposing teeth that ended in sharp metal-tipped points, and a surge of pain raced up Iagon's spine. The Salamander convulsed, his chest wanting to thrust him forwards away from the source of the agony but his body bound hand and foot to the machine. He cried out, despite trying to stifle it.

More strange words from An'scur cut the air. Unlike his henchwoman, he was unwilling to sully his tongue with the language of lesser races.

Another jolt from the machine sent fresh agonies through Iagon and the sheen of sweat veneering his body came off him in a spray of bloody perspiration. His head sagged for a moment, chest heaving against the lingering pain, before Iagon raised it again and glared.

'That all you've got?' He caught An'scur's surplice with a thin line of crimson-veined spittle.

Iagon blinked and the dark eldar's falchion was at his neck, a bead of blood running down the flat of its blade where the edge had bitten into flesh.

'Stop.' The command came from the shadows, at the back of the chamber.

Iagon recognised the voice and at once knew who was watching his torture.

'Nihilan…'

There was the acrid stench of cinder in the air, too, though Nihilan's lapdog, Ramlek, was nowhere to be seen.

The figure didn't respond to his name, though An'scur acquiesced and withdrew his blade.

Exhausted to the point of near-death, Iagon sagged again. The pain-engine wouldn't let him rest, though. A cocktail of agony-inducing chemicals was pumped into his system ensuring his lucidity. Iagon snapped to with a muted yelp, drawing a sliver of pleasure from An'scur, though the archon hid it well.

Nihilan spoke again, this time in the scything dark eldar tongue. An'scur's pleasure turned to annoyance.

Again, Iagon couldn't understand the response but caught the word 'mon-keigh' and several others that had the ring of caustic invective.

An'scur debated a while longer before he was eventually browbeaten into obeisance. Incredible that Nihilan had power over these pirates and raiders. Iagon had always believed the dark eldar served only themselves. Even the tenure of their own lords and masters was fleeting, governed by the politics of murder and assassination.

'You are fortunate,' he said, the words spat from his tongue like a bitter tonic, 'that my chief torturer is in regeneration. Kravex would have performed such wonders on you, spawn. The machine you're strapped to is his design.'

'What's it supposed to do?' Iagon slurred through a drool of blood.

An'scur swore in his native tongue, before remembering his place. With a viperous smile, he regained his composure.

'Oh, there will be more time made for you,' he promised. 'You will be wailing for me to end it before I am finished.'

'You can't threaten me...' said Iagon, expecting another burst of pain from the machine.

None came.

'Oh?'

'I have nothing to lose. I am betrayed, xenos-filth. My own kind has betrayed me, a beloved brother forsook me and looked to his own ascension. My ties are cut. The blood on my hands turns my world red. Your hatred is nothing compared to my own. *Nothing!*'

The pain came this time, though for An'scur's idle amusement rather than the brief satiation of his anger.

'Enough,' said Nihilan. 'I have need of him, An'scur. His rage will be useful.'

An'scur replied in his own language and Nihilan answered in the same.

Iagon was only semi-conscious from the pain but he caught one word, repeated by both.

Ushab-kai.

He mumbled it, his inflection interpretable as a question.

Nihilan moved in slowly from the shadows, revealing the crimson scale of his horned power armour and hideous visage. Despite the horrific scarring, Iagon could still see a trace of the Salamander Nihilan had once been in the sorcerer's puckered skin. The burns, inflicted by the heat of Moribar's vast crematoria, would never heal.

'*Ushab-kai?*' Iagon said again.

As Nihilan pursed his lips, a faint glow of power flared behind his eyes. 'It means "vessel".'

CHAPTER SIXTEEN

I
Thinning the Herd

IONNES WAS DEAD. The spike of metal had punched right through his back, opening up his chest and destroying his primary and secondary hearts. Even if an Apothecary had been present, there was nothing they could've done for him. Before the end, Ionnes had possessed the presence of mind to throw Tonnhauser clear. The Night Devil was on the ground, dazed and prone, nearby.

Elysius was standing over Ionnes's body. His eyes were closed as he muttered a benediction. When he was done, he didn't open them immediately.

Am I to be tested? he asked of himself. *So much death and loss. The circle of fire is broken. My faith teeters on the brink. This black cauldron sends my soul into turmoil. Oh Vulkan, steel my purpose beneath the hammer, shore up my resolve in the forge's fires. I shall endure. I shall protect your Sigil. In your name, so do I swear it.*

The Guardsman was stirring, the one Ba'ken had called Tonnhauser. His mumbling interrupted the Chaplain's thoughts. The other two Night Devils had also lived, and went over to their comrade.

Of the Salamanders, Elysius and Ba'ken were the last. The giant warrior had survived the fall. He was slumped against a slab of rock holding his chest. He was breathing hard and the fire in his eyes had dimmed. Elysius was no Apothecary, but he knew Ba'ken's wounds were severe.

Was it Elysius's fate to be the sole survivor of this trial? The dark eldar could not crack his body, so had they chosen to attack his spirit instead? Kadai, N'keln – two captains had fallen during his tenure as Chaplain. It was his duty to minister to the faith and belief of his charges within the company. How, then, could he do that when his own beliefs were in upheaval? His thoughts went to Ba'ken.

You will have need of it too before the end, brother.

'He's weak,' said Tonnhauser. The Guardsman was back on his feet. The other two had gone to sit down on whatever debris was lying around while he'd approached the Chaplain. He was referring to Ba'ken. 'And by the look of him, labouring with a punctured lung.'

Evidently, Tonnhauser had some medical training. The Night Devils' uniforms were so ragged and dirty it was hard to tell man from man, let alone rank or position.

'It's likely two,' said Elysius, 'with a cracked rib-plate.'

'Rib-plate?'

'It's fused, medic. Like all Astartes. Takes a lot to crack it.'

Tonnhauser tried to hide his surprise. Human and

Astartes physiology were a lot different to one another, despite their homogenous origins.

'I suspect he has several internal injuries, too.' Tonnhauser paused to lick his lips. Elysius glowered, waiting. When they'd leapt into the darkness, the dysjunction had closed the chasm behind them as a new level slid over it. It prevented direct pursuit, but only for a while. Soon they would have to move again. Zartath was already gone. For now, they would let Ba'ken rest.

'I know little of your biology, my lord,' ventured Tonnhauser, 'but I understand it is capable of regeneration. Why isn't he... healing?'

'The trauma is too great.' He looked at Ionnes. 'Even we have our limits.' Elysius was not just talking about the physical as he regarded Ba'ken. The sergeant's jaw was clenched. 'In fact, his sus-an membrane should've activated by now and put him into a regenerative coma. The stubborn sauroch is blocking it.'

'I can walk...' Ba'ken protested, 'and *hear.*'

'You can barely stand.' Elysius turned when Zartath appeared in his peripheral vision. 'Thought you'd abandoned us.'

The Black Dragon snarled. 'We must hasten, Vulkan-priest,' he snapped. He gave Ba'ken a half-glance. 'Leave him. He will only slow us down.'

'No one is left behind, aberrant!' For a moment Elysius let his anger get the better of him. His eyes flared red.

Zartath bared his fangs. The bone-blades just peeked from their sheaths in his forearms. Thinking better of it, he turned away and started to walk. 'A safe route is near. Be quick,' he called.

A strange sense of warmth radiating from the Sigil

caught the Chaplain's attention. 'Do what you can for Ba'ken,' he said to Tonnhauser, his eyes still on the Sigil. 'He must be ready to move.'

'What will you do, my lord?'

'I will lay my dead brother to rest, though there is little time for it.' Elysius unclamped the holy relic to get a better look at it. The icon of Vulkan engraved upon its surface gleamed softly in the light. Elysius dared to hope.

THE WAY AHEAD was slow and Elysius had no idea where they were going. He had to trust Zartath to lead them to safe haven and hope that their rescuers found them before Helspereth did. He staggered, the weight of Ba'ken on his back a heavy burden. The Salamander was barely conscious now. Tonnhauser had patched him up as best he could but he was no Chapter artificer who could repair power armour, nor was he an Apothecary who could mend the stricken Space Marine's wounds. Ba'ken couldn't walk and had to be carried.

Together, after Elysius had lifted Ionnes off the spike and laid him in repose, they'd removed most of Ba'ken's armour. The power generator was barely functioning anyway, at less than ten per cent effectiveness. The breastplate remained. It was bound in cloth, the scraps of Imperial Guard uniform jackets, and was about the only thing keeping Ba'ken's intestines inside his body. Much of the remaining armour was discarded. Many Astartes Chapters would balk at such an idea, reticent to leave such relics behind. Salamanders were possessed of Vulkan's pragmatic spirit. Armour could be remade, fashioned anew even – warriors of the Fire-born could not.

Zartath was waving them on. Tonnhauser and the

other Night Devils had become Elysius's outriders. Inwardly, the Chaplain applauded their courage but doubted they'd be much more than a distraction if an attack came. The Black Dragon had found a tunnel and was urging them inside.

A flicker of movement made Elysius look up. He saw a spire, towering over the other ruins, overshadowing the wide avenue they were traversing. It appeared to be armour plated at its tip, like overlapping pieces of chitin on an insect's back. It was the plates that were shifting; settling and resettling as a bird adjusts its wings on a lofty perch. They *were* wings, but it was no flock of birds clinging to the spike.

Elysius was shouting a warning when the scourges broke away from their eyrie, powerful legs boosting them into the open air where they extended their metal wings and descended on the survivors in a screeching flock.

The dark eldar arrowed down, sacrificing loft for speed, their wings angled close together and behind them like blades. The stutter of rifle fire split the air, a hard refrain to the shrieking chorus of the scourges, and one of the Night Devils staggered and fell. A black beam, coursing from a heavy cannon cradled by another of the flying devils, speared a second Guardsman. He didn't even get time to scream as the dark lance skewered his throat and took off his head.

Tonnhauser was scrambling, Elysius bellowing at him to move. A third scourge, the last of the flying pack, took aim with its rifle. A thrown spear shredded its left wing and sent it spiralling downwards, its shot going wild. Tonnhauser reached the safety of the tunnel, while Zartath was pumping his fist into the sky and swearing thickly at their attackers.

Slowed by Ba'ken's bulk, Elysius still had a few metres to go. He stumbled, but regained his footing just in time to see the remaining pair of scourges circling above him. Zartath hurled rocks at them but a raft of splinter fire kept him at bay inside the tunnel.

Elysius was staring down the barrel of the lance cannon. A litany of hate and the rejection of all xenos was on his lips when the scourge raised its cannon. It was laughing. They both were. Such arrogance and assuredness – even for dark eldar, the scourge were imperious.

Elysius had not stopped running. As he broke the threshold to the tunnel, the winged warriors flew off into the darkness.

Once the Chaplain was inside, Zartath sealed the tunnel shut.

'A lucky escape,' he said, a hint of mania in his voice. Elysius wondered how much longer the Black Dragon could hold it together.

Tonnhauser was slumped against the tunnel wall, his eyes on the ground.

The scourges had had more than enough time to kill the Chaplain. Elysius knew they had him cold, and yet...

'Yes, very lucky,' he answered, his suspicions lost to the dark as Zartath led them on.

II
Endure the Anvil

STANDING ON THE ridge, Tsu'gan stared down at a battlefield.

As well as the wych corpses, strewn about but

stripped of plunder, there were humans and Salamanders.

The humans appeared to be mercenaries of one stripe or another. Their uniforms and attire were eclectic, customised. He discerned Guard insignia but also the apparel of rogue traders, pirates and freebooters. Tsu'gan also noticed another body, that of an Astartes, but it was no Fire-born.

'Have you heard of the Black Dragons, Tsu'gan?' asked Praetor. The Firedrakes were descending the ridge, moving towards the basin of the blood-soaked valley. They were arrayed in a dispersed line, He'stan a few metres in front at their lead.

Tsu'gan shook his head. 'Only rumours.'

'Probably just as well. You wouldn't like them.' Judging by his expression, Praetor wasn't being even slightly facetious.

Tsu'gan returned his attention to the Forgefather. 'What is he doing, brother-sergeant?'

'Seeking a trace of the Sigil, I think. The ways of Vulkan's namesake are one of the Chapter's deepest mysteries. Only Lord He'stan can claim to know of them.'

The Firedrakes were moving slowly, tracking their bolters across the shadows, laying down overlapping fire arcs in case of attack. Covert operation was still the key. If the dark eldar knew of an insertion force in the Reef, they would send troops to stop it. Elysius's survival, the recovery of Vulkan's Sigil, depended on that not happening.

'We must save him,' said Tsu'gan. 'I know it's not our mission, but it's not enough to just bring back the Sigil.'

Praetor replied in a low voice. 'I know, brother. I know.'

He'stan had stopped by the body of the Black Dragon. Tsu'gan and Praetor broke from formation to join him. Before they did, Praetor had a quick word with Halknarr and sent the old campaigner ahead to scout for tracks. Following the Sigil was one thing, and Praetor had every faith in the Forgefather's esoteric methodology, but he would still prefer some solid evidence of their quarry too.

'Torn apart,' said He'stan, without looking up from the dead warrior.

The Black Dragon's armour was a mess of rents and tears. He'd been stabbed so many times it was impossible without detailed medical analysis to tell where one wound ended and another began.

'Vicious dogs,' muttered Praetor. He crouched by the corpse. The helmet had been knocked off during the fight. Beneath it, bony protrusions that characterised the Chapter were revealed across his forehead as well as further nubs in his cheekbones. Praetor used a finger to lift the Black Dragon's lip, examining the gum and the set of needle like fangs sprouting from it. He noticed something else too. 'No tongue. What was he doing here?'

'A slave, like our brothers,' He'stan replied.

Tsu'gan clenched his fists. 'Did this *mutant* side with the xenos then, a traitor to his own kind?'

'No, I don't think so,' answered Praetor. His gaze went to the body of the Salamander, a few metres farther into the valley. 'They were allies. It seems the Black Dragons have been incarcerated here for a long time judging by their armour and trappings – much longer than our kin at least.'

He'stan nodded. 'Agreed.' He was watching Tsu'gan as he went over to the dead Fire-born.

'Brother Koto,' Tsu'gan said, tiring of seeing the dead bodies of his former company brothers. 'Stabbed in the back by a traitor's blade.'

'What makes you say it was a traitor that killed him?' He'stan asked. The serrated sword embedded in poor Koto's back was plain for all to see.

'It's no dark eldar weapon. Looks old and poorly maintained.'

'A weapon of opportunity, then?'

'Perhaps… Must've been some throw to piece Koto's armour like that.'

'Do you think the dark eldar are that strong?'

Tsu'gan looked up from the body at the Forgefather. 'They don't look it, but my perceptions have been challenged ever since we entered this place.'

'What do you see, brother?'

Tsu'gan looked down again. He stooped for a closer examination. 'His face…' he said, 'the expression is one of…'

He'stan's tone was neutral. 'Betrayal?'

Tsu'gan nodded, slow and purposeful. There was a traitor amongst the survivors. He pointed to the dead Black Dragon. 'One of them?'

'What do you think, brother?'

By now Praetor had left them, gone to rejoin the others and get Halknarr's report. Tsu'gan and He'stan were alone.

'I think not. One of our own has turned. Koto *knew* his slayer.'

'That is not an idle accusation, brother.'

Beneath his battle-helm, Tsu'gan's brow furrowed. He didn't want to think it, let alone believe it. 'And I do not make it idly. One of Koto's brothers did this to him. A coward's blow,' he hissed, clenching a fist.

'Nihilan's rot in our Chapter is not yet excised. Rage did this.'

He'stan's eyes narrowed. 'Perilous is the warrior's path if walked with anger in his heart,' he said. 'How easily his hate can be directed inwards. Do you know what follows such self-revulsion, Tsu'gan?'

Tsu'gan shook his head slowly.

'Damnation, brother.'

He'stan put his hand on Tsu'gan's shoulder and gripped it. 'You know of what I speak, and you know from whom this treachery before us came.'

Tsu'gan could only offer mute response. The Forge-father had seen to the core of him as easily as an ordinary man would see the colour of another's skin.

'Poison in a good soul is poison nonetheless – good or ill, it is no proof against it if that soul is weak, or *broken*.'

'I… I have struggled, lord. Ever since Cirrion. Ever since…'

'Ko'tan Kadai was a brave and noble warrior,' said He'stan. 'His legacy is one of honour. Don't let his death diminish you, Tsu'gan. Reward his faith with glory.'

Tsu'gan met the Forgefather's gaze. 'Death's shadow follows me.'

'As warriors, it is our constant companion. We must all endure the anvil, brother. For some of us, the hammer falls harder. That is all. But if we do not break, then the metal of which we are forged is stronger, inviolable. Pain and suffering is not the sole province of Zek Tsu'gan.'

'I know tha–'

He'stan didn't let him finish. 'Now is the time to listen, brother,' he said levelly. 'To be isolated in the void, away from my Chapter, away from my company and my brothers, it is difficult. I *crave* those bonds as you crave the respect and affirmation of your peers. It is my calling. It is my sacred destiny to endure this. All of us have a role – all are significant – even if your destiny is to end up dead, stabbed in the back on some alien world.

'I face that fate every day. I am far from home. Should I die, another will be called. I am no more special than you, brother. I merely follow a different path. Only you can decide where yours will take you. Do you understand me, Tsu'gan?'

His battle-helm hid the tears in Tsu'gan's eyes but not in his voice. It came out as a rasp. 'I do.'

He'stan had averted his gaze and was looking over Tsu'gan's shoulder. 'Praetor is hailing us,' he said. 'Brother Halknarr has found something.'

Then he walked, leaving Tsu'gan behind. Tsu'gan waited for a few more seconds before following, his steel returned, his purpose renewed.

There *was* another path – He'stan had just put him on it.

When they'd rejoined the others, Halknarr was relating his findings.

'Tracks end here,' he said, indicating the path of ground where the trail ceased.

Praetor regarded it with narrowed eyes, crouching to touch the ground with his fingers. 'This stone has been disturbed,' he said, indicating the path beyond where the tracks faded. 'Like it's been laid over the top of something.'

'Like the city itself has moved?' offered Halknarr.

Praetor looked up at the old campaigner, 'Aye.'

'There is more.' He traced back his steps to slightly

farther up the ridge, just a few metres back. He pointed, 'See the deep impressions?' A few of the Firedrakes nodded. 'Someone knelt here. In power armour.'

'A deathblow, perhaps?' suggested Persephion.

Halknarr shook his head. 'No blood.'

'Surrender then?' Praetor said, nonplussed. No Astartes, especially not a Fire-born, would even consider it, let alone actually do it.

As Tsu'gan looked on, he was reminded of He'stan's words to him.

'Are you saying the dusk-wraiths have taken a prisoner, Brother Halknarr?' asked Daedicus.

'I am, and one that went willingly.'

'Not Elysius?' said Persephion.

'It wasn't the Chaplain,' Tsu'gan asserted at last. 'It was Cerbius Iagon, my old squad brother.'

All eyes, barring the Forgefather's, turned to Tsu'gan.

'I fear he has betrayed his own.'

'Perhaps he had no choice?' offered Daedicus, more with hope than conviction.

None amongst the Firedrakes wanted to believe betrayal amongst brothers.

'This place affects the mind,' muttered Halknarr, eager to be moving on. 'Who knows what pressures our brothers were under?'

Praetor stood. His face was a stern, unreadable mask. He'd heard enough. 'Elysius lives still, we can we sure of that.'

'Their pursuers doubled back,' added Halknarr. 'Whatever route our brothers took it did not end here in this place, but nor were the xenos able to follow.'

'Then we follow those tracks and try to get ahead of them. We have to reach the Chaplain first.'

'No, Brother-Sergeant Praetor,' uttered He'stan, clutching the Spear of Vulkan in his fist like a divining rod. His eyes blazed brightly. 'I have seen another way.'

CHAPTER SEVENTEEN

I
The Enemy of Doubt

NOT SINCE HIS trials on the Cindara Plateau had Elysius fought this hard to overcome adversity. Back then, over a century before, he had been human. Now he was Astartes and still this darkling place punished his mind, body and soul to its limit.

Ba'ken was a heavy burden on his back and they had fled through the xenos wasteland for hours. Throughout, they'd been harried by mercenary bands. Whooping hellions, atop their savage sky-boards, had tried to draw down on them in a narrow defile of ruins; a pack of whelpmasters and their warp hounds had dogged them without relent until Zartath had found another escape route; the very shadows themselves hunted, gelid warriors with alabaster skin and lank hair like ocean-weed. Through guile and cunning, Zartath kept them ahead of the dark eldar's clutches, taking the survivors down new routes when others were closed off.

And as they ran, Elysius couldn't shake the feeling they were heading somewhere. An inexorable destination awaited them on the dark horizon, drawing closer with every moment, and when they arrived it would all end, one way or another. Tonnhauser acquitted himself well – the human was resourceful, strong, steeled by his experiences of the night-city. While Zartath scouted ahead, Tonnhauser became Elysius's running companion. The Chaplain was glad of it. The human's resolve shored up his own. More than once, Elysius had wanted to stop and turn, to face his foes in glorious battle and end the hunt in blood. Tonnhauser stopped him. If nothing else, the human should be given every chance to live, even though Elysius thought the likelihood of that very doubtful.

When the baying of distant beasts ceased and the pursuit horns and the shrieked goading of the slavers stopped, when they did finally rest in a small, dark place below the earth, it felt as if they'd been running for days.

'Nothing. I've heard nothing for almost an hour.' Elysius had his head pressed against the cavern wall. It was cool, but with an icy bite that pained his exposed cheek.

Ba'ken was prone in the middle of the small chamber. His breathing was so shallow his chest appeared still, as if it wasn't rising at all. But he *was* alive. For now.

Zartath regarded the Chaplain from across the opposite side of the cavern. He'd taken them deep into the bowels of the Razored Vale, away from the hunting packs and the sky-bound mercenaries that sought them. Of Helspereth and her wyches, there'd been no sign since the encounter on the ridge.

'Means nothing,' the Black Dragon snarled. 'They will come when they are ready. The xenos always do.'

It spoke of years of bitter experience and again Elysius found himself wondering at just how long Zartath and his brothers had been incarcerated. To have survived this long, it was an incredible achievement but it had broken the Astartes irrevocably.

What fate awaits you if we live through this, mutant? Elysius wondered, and his gaze went to Tonnhauser.

Despite his courage, the Night Devil looked exhausted and close to the end of his strength. He'd become an increasingly feral and ragged figure since they'd first been brought to the Reef on Helspereth's raider. It seemed like several lifetimes ago. When the hunt was on, when life or death became split decisions, governed by fate more than design, it was easy. Move and live. Stand still and die. It was a simple yet brutal doctrine. But now, in the quiet dark with only each other and their thoughts for company, a different battle for survival was being fought. It existed in the mind and Elysius knew of it all too well. He was Astartes, one of the Reclusiam, and his resilience was formidable. But lately, he had found his resolve sorely tested, in this his personal cauldron. Zartath was testament to the fate waiting for any Space Marine who gave in to the madness of the Reef.

Doubts crept in to Elysius's mind like insidious fingers of shadow. What if they were never found? What if even now his rescuers lay slain? What if he fell before he could deliver the Sigil? Then it too would be lost. The Nine would become the Ten and the Forgefather's quest made much more difficult.

Elysius crushed his misgivings in a clenched fist.

Faith is my shield. It is the wellspring of my conviction. It is water when I thirst. It is warmth when I shiver. It is vigour when I am weak. It is nourishment when I hunger. With it I am tempered and my will forged into a weapon. This I swear in Vulkan's name.

The litany did its work. For Elysius the words brought a measure of comfort but also a sense of defiance. They had made it this far.

'A few steps farther...' he said out loud.

'What do you say?' asked Zartath.

'Nothing. How long must we linger here?'

'Soon, we'll move again.'

'And to where would you have us go, Black Dragon?' asked Elysius, standing to stretch the muscles in his legs and back. A half-glance at his crozius and he saw the dullness of its haft in the reflected glow of his eyes. Hope was close to being extinguished too.

'To wherever the xenos are not,' came Zartath's laconic reply.

'And after that?'

The Black Dragon's annoyance was obvious as he eyed the Chaplain.

'We move again, Vulkan-priest. And so on, and so on, as I and my brothers have these last years. Do you think there's an alternative?' he snapped.

'Sooner or later they will catch us. By then Ba'ken will be dead from his injuries and you and I will be weakened. We should consider finding somewhere to take a stand, at least make our sacrifice a cost the xenos won't forget.'

Zartath rose rapidly like a striking adder. 'Fool! We are already forgotten. Vulkan's sons, so quick to stand and hold for glory. Your tenacity will see you dead, brother-priest. We move and do not stop. How else do you think my kin and I lived this long? Honour and nobility are concepts alien to this place. They'll get you nothing but an unremembered death. Not until I see her or him again and can kill them, will I stop moving. Only then will I have peace. Only then will a measure of revenge begin to account for the loss of my brothers.'

The close confines of the underground cavern magnified and reflected the sound. Zartath's impassioned words were echoing into silence when the grind of gears emanated from below. At once, the ground started to tremble and a thin sliver of light cracked the ceiling above them.

'What is this place? Where have you brought us, Zartath?' asked Elysius, going to his crozius.

The Black Dragon was vigorously shaking his head. 'We are moving,' he hissed.

'Up...' added Tonnhauser, his voice choked with fear as his gaze went skyward.

The crack was widening and the floor was moving underneath them.

'Sealed,' said Elysius, heaving on one of the doors to the chamber. It had locked when the gears were engaged – it was all a part of the same mechanism, a trap sprung by the movements of its prey.

Zartath tested the only other. 'This one too.'

'Up we go then,' said the Chaplain and raised his head towards the chasm of light.

It was a lifter chamber, concealed in the rock. Elysius realised that now, somewhat belatedly. The inexorable destination he had felt them approaching – they had finally arrived.

* * *

II
The Coliseum of Blades

SLOWLY, THEY WERE ferried upwards. The walls fell away as the lifter plate rose, much larger than the chamber itself. There was no way out but up into the unknown light. Elysius was shielding his eyes, crozius drawn, when they emerged into an arena.

Shadows folded upon shadows, the gloom unleavened by brazier-lanterns hewn into the flagstone floor. The lambent light from their dulcetly burning embers hinted at patches of old blood, described the outline of barbed walls. Broken weapons, the skeletons of old warriors long dead in the black dust, were limned in red firelight that gave a visceral cast to the scene.

Open to the sky, lightning revealed the mouldering battlefield in flashes of blood-tinged monochrome. The dour faces of statues glared down upon it. These were the dracons and archons, nobles of the frontier realm. They stood upon their black pedestals, titanic in stature, a testament to the egotism and vainglory of the dark eldar. Some were dilapidated, age simply eroding them; others were defaced, their reigns ended in bloody assassination or worse, forgotten ignominy. One stood unblemished, aside from the rest. He was depicted in his lamellar, insectoid armour, a long cape drawn about his broad shoulders. The effigy cradled a helm in the crook of its arms, and its eyes stared imperiously from a face drawn in cruelty and casual malice. An'scur – Lord of the Reef.

Sunken into a deep oval trench, the arena was surmounted by blades. In the darkened pulpits and stalls a gaggle of ghouls looked on.

The Parched. Elysius recognised the wretches from

before. Here they were in their hundreds, awaiting a spectacle. His gaze was drawn to the centre where a tall, lithe creature beckoned him with just her eyes. They glittered like poisoned emeralds behind a domino mask.

Helspereth.

She had drawn him here. It was not vanity on the part of the Chaplain that led him to this conclusion. Elysius knew the wych queen was obsessed with him, like a child fascinates over a trapped insect until its wings and appendages have been removed and the curiosity dies with the creature itself. Ever since the ridge, perhaps ever since they'd arrived in the Razored Vale, she had herded him here.

She *wanted* him, in her own twisted way. And now she had him and an audience to bear witness to whatever humiliation she had planned. This was Helspereth's intended theatre, the final act about to commence.

'And then there were four,' she said, in a sibilant silken voice with hidden barbs. She gave a vicious smile when she regarded Ba'ken. 'Well, soon to be three.'

A rattle of blades revealed a coven of her wyches, hiding in the shadows behind the survivors. Zartath had loosed his bone-blades but was not quick enough to react.

Elysius felt the cold press of metal against his neck and knew the others were similarly incapacitated. One thrust was all it would take...

'Welcome,' said Helspereth with mock geniality, 'to the Coliseum of Blades.' She flung her arms wide to encompass the gruesome place in all its anti-glory. 'True,' she mused, 'it has seen fairer times. The flesh trade here is not what it once was. Dysjunction is a cruel and draconian mistress.'

Eyes adjusting to the preternatural gloom, Elysius did now see how ruined the arena was. Its towers and cages were broken and rusted; cracks in some of the walls ran deep; a thick veil of dust swathed almost every surface. It was now a fallen shrine to murder, a Coliseum of Blades no longer.

Helspereth's eyes took on a fevered aspect as a tremor ran through her body. 'I have slain so many in this arena. Gutted and cleaved and hewn and sawed and devoured... it is my temple. Here I worship. Katon, the Slaver King slighted me – I killed his gene-bred humanoid, the troglodyte barely whetted my bloodlust. Katon followed...' She pointed to a spike where an impaled skull grinned macabrely. A scrap of hair clung tenaciously to the bleached bone scalp. It trembled in an eldritch wind emanating from behind the wych. A coldness came with it, a chill that Elysius felt in his marrow.

Something else was with them in the arena, something the Chaplain could not yet see.

'Morbane, mon-keigh barbarian-lord, fell to my trident,' she went on, touring the shadows, revisiting old victories in her mind's eye, 'Shen'sa'ur, one of the hated kin, I strangled with a barbed whip; the green-skinned brute, its hollow name was Tyrant, died to a thousand of my dagger cuts. I have bled them, I have decapitated, eviscerated and disembowelled. My legacy of blood is longer than ten of your lives, mon-keigh. You should feel honoured that I want you at the end of my sword.'

Then Elysius did something he hadn't done for many long years.

He yawned, a long and exaggerated gesture that ended with a curt rejoinder for the wych. 'Are you done?'

Helspereth stuttered, wrong-footed, 'W-what?'

'I tire of your rambling, hell-kite. I said: are you finished with it?'

Imperious nostalgia turned to anger in Helspereth's expression and body language.

'Face me now,' she said evenly, 'and I will release the others. Once I'm done with you, I'll give them all a head start before I follow.'

'Why me?' Elysius asked.

'Because you are not entirely unbeautiful for a monkeigh,' she snarled and her own false beauty was eclipsed, 'because I want to crush your pathetic illusions of faith and expose the error of supplication to a powerless, mortal god.' She moved closer. Her eyes were like black, pitiless coals. 'I will drink in your sorrow and despair like a panacea. Such divine and sustainable agonies I will reap from your sundered flesh,' she purred. Licking her blood-red lips in anticipation, she suppressed a tiny thrill.

'Now,' she added, 'come to fight. I have yearned for this since first I took your fleshless arm from your quivering body.'

Elysius's mouth was a grim straight line. It barely moved. 'Very well.'

Helspereth smiled without warmth, without feeling. 'Choose your weapon.' She stood aside, revealing a host of blades and bludgeons. The Chaplain recognised a defunct chainblade, even a broken storm shield amongst a mass of lesser weapons.

He looked away. 'I am already armed.'

Helspereth glanced scornfully at the crozius Elysius brandished.

'That preacher's stave? What weapon is that for a warrior?'

'It is mine, given in honour and received with belief and humility,' the Chaplain said. 'I wouldn't expect you to understand, wych.'

Helspereth made the facial equivalent of a shrug and hissed. 'Let's begin…'

She flew at Elysius, grinning savagely, and he was hard pressed to deflect her attacks. Wounds opened up in his cheek and above his left eye, and a score of deeper rents marked his power armour before the Chaplain had regained his footing and realised what had happened.

He was breathing hard when she came again. Helspereth's blade whickered, like it was fluid and not edged metal at all. Elysius parried, once, twice and again before a stab of pain tore into his side like a torch and his skin burned with his own blood.

'Too slow… too slow…' she goaded, stepping back to admire her murder-craft. The wych's chest was steady, her heartrate barely above a casual beat.

'Don't listen to that hell-bitch!' snarled Zartath, struggling against the bonds and blades that held him down. A skein of razor-edged wire bound the Black Dragon, while a pair of wyches pressed spears to his neck. Beads of Zartath's blood were already rolling down the tips and hafts due to his efforts. Tonnhauser was bowed by a sabre to his neck, whereas Ba'ken was unconscious and left alone to his oblivion.

Evidently, Helspereth wanted Elysius's companions to bear witness to his demise.

The cold came again. It fringed the eldritch wind, preceding it like a frosty veil. Something shimmered, dark on dark, like two pict negatives overlapping one another and exposed to a half-light.

'Tell me, wych,' said Elysius. 'Did your great triumphs come at your hand or something else's?' He thrust into the formless shadows with his crozius, rewarded when it struck flesh and a creature resolved itself. Impaled on the Chaplain's stave, it squirmed and shrieked in pleasure-pain. A cold thing, a white thing, a creature of lank, almost vampiric appearance – Elysius had heard of mandrakes. He grunted as he twisted the innards of this one and gutted it.

The Parched, already drooling at the arena's bloody proceedings, swooned above them.

'A simple test, my love…' Helspereth purred, her excited gaze drinking in the dying mandrake's agony, '…to see if you were worthy.'

Elysius shrugged the corpse off his crozius, the mace-like head threaded with ropes of gore. 'No more games.'

She came again, buoyed on bounding pirouettes, her twin blades a whirlwind of edged metal. Elysius ignored them. He missed with a swipe to the body but caught Helspereth across the cheek with his fist as he backhanded.

She staggered, but recovered quickly as the Chaplain pressed. An overhead strike sliced air, the follow-up shoulder barge overbalancing him. Fresh agony in his chest was Elysius's payment as Helspereth sank one of her blades deep.

The Chaplain pulled away, using the heavier weight of his body to lever himself, and the sword *shucked* free with a welter of blood.

There was a rattle in his throat, the faint gurgle of fluid. She'd nicked his lung in the last attack. It was slowly filling with Elysius's own lifeblood.

'Hag,' he spat, his sputum flecked with crimson, 'stand still so I can choke you.'

'An enticing offer.' Helspereth's reply was half serious. She leapt through a flurry of Elysius's blows, her acrobatics confounding the Chaplain's rage, cutting him as she moved.

'I will bleed you, my love,' she promised. 'Like the Tyrant, I will take from you a thousand cuts until you lie empty on the arena floor, a husk like all the rest.'

He fell, collapsing to his knees, and Elysius came face-to-face with a rictus grin. The skull was humanoid. It mocked the Chaplain.

You'll die here, it said. *Lay down, brother. Lay down, you are tired. The darkness waits. It will take you. We will take you. Let us.*

Elysius forced himself to rise. The movements were painful but this was his cauldron. Pain was nothing, only a means of focussing the mind. His faith would provide the strength he needed.

It is vigour when I am weak...

'Not. Done. Yet,' he growled through gritted teeth and turned.

'Oh, good,' said Helspereth. 'I've only just begun.'

She attacked again. This time, Elysius blocked the harder blows, letting the nicks and jabs fall where they might. Each left a jarring impact, but not so strong his power armour couldn't absorb it. His riposte struck Helspereth across the midriff. The Chaplain had to time his attacks, wait for a moment when brute force could wound her. She gasped, the air exploding from her lungs. Elysius struck again, against her shoulder. Helspereth's reply was lazy and he took it on his pauldron. He thrust an armoured knee into her stomach, a sideswipe to the neck drawing a yelp of pleasure from the wych.

Unrelenting, the Chaplain came on again. He smashed Helspereth's parry aside and punched a jab into her torso. She coughed, spitting blood. A second blow was intended to take off her head but she blocked and held it.

Harsh, edged sparks spilled off the locked weapons in a cascade. Both combatants fought for dominance but neither had the beating of the other.

'I enjoyed that,' Helspereth hissed when their faces closed during the struggle. She sucked at the blood of her lip and her eyelids fluttered lustily. 'But I'm getting bored now,' she added. Shifting her stance, she suddenly overbalanced the Chaplain. In less than a second, Elysius was on the back foot, his single arm shaking with effort as Helspereth pressed down on him with her two.

The bloodied blade of her sword was less than a handspan from his eye.

'I shall keep your face when I am through with you,' she promised.

'I have a confession to make,' Elysius said through a grimace.

'Oh?'

He whispered. 'I was faking, too.' With a roar, he threw Helspereth off. She sprang back, quickly shifting from heel to toe.

'Even with one arm,' the Chaplain boasted, 'I can still beat you.'

Apoplexy marred her cold beauty as a murderer's visage took over. She flew at Elysius. It was to be the deathblow.

'*Vulkan, armour me...*' he muttered, thrusting out the crozius arcanum. Impossibly, its mace-head and haft ignited into glorious energy-flame. Helspereth was struck by its power and faltered. Elysius used this distraction to stave in the wych's skull. She fell, a look of dumbfoundment on her porcelain face. Shattered by the blow, the domino mask fragmented, exposing Helspereth's face behind it. There was fear there in her twisted countenance. Even in death, she knew what fate awaited her. Ravening soul hunger was not the sole preserve of the dark eldar – other still more terrible beings craved too.

She Who Thirsts awaited Helspereth. Several lifetimes of torment were her fate now.

CHAPTER EIGHTEEN

I
Victory and Retreat

A SCREAM, HORRIFIC and piercing the veil separating the realms, ripped from her throat. Elysius had never heard such a desolate sound. Her blood was touching his boots when he struck again... and again. All the pent-up aggression and nerves released in a cathartic flood as the Chaplain turned Helspereth's head into a red paste. Her skull cracked beneath the third blow and he bludgeoned it to fragments before he was done. Even then, Helspereth's headless form quivered with the jolts of energy from the crozius.

How Elysius had known to thumb the activation rune then, he would never learn. How it had burned into life at all when it was supposed to be broken and spent was another mystery. Did a lingering kernel of energy in the weapon's power cell impel it to life at the crucial moment? Or was another power at work, one governed by faith?

The Chaplain was wise enough to know that some miracles should simply be, and not be subject to questioning.

Appalled at their queen's death, the wyches staggered forwards to regard her corpse, not even realising they had let their prey loose.

Zartath was quick to exploit their shock. His bone-blades sheared the razor-wire bonds and as he was still rising he cut down one of the wyches. A second fell to a gut wound from Tonnhauser's knife. The Guardsmen stabbed several times to be sure the creature was dead. The third sprang away and was about to throw its spear at the human when a green-clad giant rose up behind it and crushed its frail frame in a brutal grapple hold.

Like wrestling the leo'nid of the plains.

The bones snapped audibly before the wretch expired.

'Just catching my breath,' gasped Ba'ken, his face greying and his eyes dim. 'What did I miss?'

The sound of clapping, echoing across the lonely arena floor, forestalled Elysius's reply.

All eyes turned on the slowly rising raider as it cleared the walls and descended into the deep basin of the coliseum.

The skimmer was unlike any other Elysius had seen. It was huge, replete with banners, hellish pennants of flesh and other macabre panoply. Chains swung lazily from its segmented armour plates. The plates were daubed in red and black, layered and spiked like an insectoid horn. Skulls and other grisly totems hung from the chains. Corpses rattled against the metal flanks.

In the centre of the machine, towering over its long

fuselage and situated at the rearmost deckplate, was a throne. Two further deckplates, expansive and shielded by more layered armour like that at the prow, harboured warriors clad in black and bone. Their faces were covered by heavy helms, their armour thicker than that of the lesser kabal warriors. Each carried a bladed polearm not unlike a halberd, except all along the edge fell energy crackled.

'Incubi...' Elysius knew of these creatures. They were a lord's trusted retainers, his bodyguards and executioners without peer. In all his skirmishes against the dusk-wraiths, he had never fought them.

Upon the throne their master reclined. He was every bit the titanic statue that cast its shadow over the Coliseum of Blades.

'And you are An'scur,' Elysius concluded.

The archon nodded. He was helmed, his expression hidden behind a daemon's face wrought in metal.

Behind him, the Parched squirmed and spasmed in their stalls, part in ecstasy at the gruesome killing display they'd been treated to, part in undisguised terror at the presence of their lord and master.

An'scur turned and hissed at them in his native tongue, making the creatures scatter from sight.

'Slayer!' roared Zartath as he recognised the dark eldar lord and rushed at him across the arena.

The Black Dragon was only a few metres away when An'scur faced him and nonchalantly extended a finger. A thin line of barely visible mono-wire sprang from a tight brass ring. When the hooked barb at the end struck Zartath's body the Black Dragon collapsed, wracked by convulsive agony.

'Sit...' said An'scur, the concession to use a heathen tongue not a light one.

The point was well made. The archon had dominion here. His incubi saw to that, as did the long-nosed cannons trained on the Salamanders and their human charge.

'So you are Helspereth's pet,' he said, lifting off his helm to reveal a white-pallored face and eyes like slivers of jet. His long, alabaster hair was bound in silver scalp locks and fell back over his head and neck in a shower of tight braids.

'Amusing,' he added. An'scur's gaze went to the prone form of Helspereth.

As the drone of the hovering skimmer-machine filled the silence, Elysius thought he saw a tremor of regret in the archon's face.

'Poor, bloodied Helspereth,' An'scur said. 'I will miss your tender mercies.' He added something more in an alien dialect Elysius didn't know.

'She won many victories here,' An'scur told him.

Elysius kept his silence. In truth, he was bleeding badly and finding it hard to stand at all. Behind him, Ba'ken had slumped to one knee and Tonnhauser was doing his best to support him.

'Strange that a one-armed mon-keigh would be her undoing,' the archon continued. He looked down at her broken body again, lingered on the crimson smear where her head had been. 'Fascinating...'

An'scur looked at Elysius once more and donned his helm. 'Kill them,' he said.

All Elysius could think to do was mutter one last supplication as the incubi lowered their long, bladed staves.

'Vulkan, forgive me...'

Then the thunder came, blazing from the shadows in a cluster of bright, burning muzzle flares.

Salvation had arrived. The Firedrakes had found him. Not only that, they were led by the Forgefather.

THE FIREDRAKES ATTACKED swiftly. A raft of bolter fire took apart a pair of incubi warriors, several others weathering the sudden fusillade on their superior armour before the throne-mounted archon gave the order to rise.

Strafing dark lance fire ripped up the arena floor, churning flagstones and turning stone to dust.

Tsu'gan veered aside from one burst, hauling on his combi-bolter's trigger and clipping another incubus but not felling it before the raider lifted it from view. He advanced alongside Praetor, with Vo'kar and Persephion. The others, led by Halknarr, quickly surrounded the wounded and set about dragging them back from the battlefield.

Tsu'gan's eyes were on He'stan's back as he led the charge, screaming Vulkan's name like an invocation. A tongue of fire surged from the Gauntlet of the Forge, searing the underside of the archon's raider-skiff and melting the metal. One of the engines died but the machine had enough power to achieve loft.

The dark eldar lord was shrieking from his potentate's perch. Several of his incubi dropped lithely from the deckplate, rushing to intercede against the Salamanders.

'Firedrakes, assault as one!' roared He'stan. He slowed to let the others catch up, tearing out chainblades and hammers as they moved. Together they crashed into the dark eldar elite.

The Forgefather impaled one on the end of his spear. Praetor clashed with another, smashing aside its blade with his storm shield and crushing its skull with his thunder hammer.

Persephion fell, his flank ripped out by one of the incubus power-glaives. He rolled and groaned before Vo'kar rushed in to shield him and hold the creature at bay.

Tsu'gan ducked a savage jab. The blade's energy flare sent warnings skimming across his retinal display. A reverse swipe cut a groove in his plastron, not deep enough to fully penetrate. His heart leapt with brutal joy when his chainblade met armour and then flesh. The incubus squealed as Tsu'gan drove the grinding teeth of the weapon further then twisted. As he tore the chainblade free, Tsu'gan's opponent broke apart in a cascade of gore.

'For my brothers,' he spat, ready to move on to the next target.

There was to be none.

'Fall back, form a barricade!' ordered Praetor. The incubi released by the raider were all dead. Even He'stan was retreating.

Tsu'gan turned, initially dismayed, but saw the Forgefather had what he had come here for. Surrounded by Halknarr and his Fire-born, Chaplain Elysius was alive and carried the Sigil.

Behind him, Tsu'gan heard the raider rise still further. Desultory blasts speared from its cannon-mountings now, no more than a deterrent to further attack. Horns were blowing too and there was the baying of beasts, the cackle of the hellion and the screeching of the scourge. The archon was amassing his warriors. The kabal was rousing to his banner. Interlopers had been found in the Razored Vale. They needed to be expunged.

Vo'kar had Persephion. He was dragging him back towards the others. Tsu'gan rushed over to help him, gripping beneath the wounded warrior's arm and pulling.

Another of the Black Dragons, unconscious but not dead, was with Elysius and the others.

'Kill, acquire and retreat,' said Vo'kar. 'Now I know how the White Scars feel.' He laughed, utterly incongruously in the circumstances, and Tsu'gan smiled.

He'stan's voice came over the comm-feed in his battle-helm.

++*The Sigil is ours once more*++ he said, ++*Glory to Vulkan!*++

Praetor's strident tones followed. ++*Engage homing beacons*++

A series of dull icons from the small wrist-mounted devices locked to each and every Firedrake lit up the gloom in pearlescent white.

++*Even through the veil...*++ Praetor's voice was already fading as transition took hold, ++*...they will find us...*++

HOT LIGHT FILLED Tsu'gan's vision as a sense of dislocation swept over him. The ruins of the Volgorrah Reef faded as a new vista slowly resolved through the blaze of teleportation. It was dark and hard to see. He scented burning cinder, an acrid tang he recognised, and knew something had gone wrong.

II
Geviox Reclaimed

AGATONE'S FORCES SWEPT the Ferron Straits in a tide. All across the dusty flatland, the dark eldar hordes were in full retreat. Whatever had kept them here, warring against their natural instincts by holding ground, was gone.

The brother-captain of the 3rd Company and operational commander of the Gevion Cluster War stood proudly in the cupola hatch of a Land Raider battle tank and gave the order to advance.

'Salamanders! Forward as one. Slow and steady.'

A chorus of replies from his sergeants filled Agatone's comm-feed as affirmation was given.

From the rearline, Techmarines manning a battery of Thunderfire cannons ordered cluster fire into the panicked dark eldar ranks. They were little more than chaff now – most of the alien elite was either dead or had already fled into the webway. In the distance, hugging the horizon line, portals of dark liquid shimmered. One by one they vaporised out of existence, leaving a grimy fog that lingered on the breeze for a time like smoke before disappearing completely.

The vanguard of the Salamanders brought more battle tanks. The armoured spear was to be led by Agatone in his Land Raider, *Fire Anvil*. It had once been N'keln's and before him, Kadai's. For the first time since his promotion to captain, Agatone felt worthy of its legacy. He sank below the cupola hatch, letting it slam with a dull *clank* as the engines roared and *Fire Anvil's* tracks started to move.

On the left flank, their vantage point a set of iron hills, Lok commanded the Devastators. Their salvos of missiles and plasma bursts took apart a rearguard of grotesques ferried out of the webway to stymie the Salamanders assault. Lascannons lanced the air, scything down raiders and other, more heavily armoured skimmer-machines, before their cult troops could ascend and flee.

This planet, this entire cluster of worlds would be cleansed. Agatone had sworn it.

Rhino transports followed in the wake of *Fire Anvil*. They carried what remained of the 3rd's Tactical squads, armed and armoured for close engagement. It was the way of Vulkan.

Look thine enemy in the eye, he had purportedly said, *and let him see the fires in yours.*

Predators rolled between the armoured transports, the battle tanks sending punishing salvos from their autocannon and lascannon turret mounts.

Overhead, Assault squads burned the air with contrails of fire from their jump packs. They kept pace with the tanks, protecting their flanks and seeking out isolated enemy targets.

There was no great stratagem to it. None was needed. Agatone had fought the last of his enemies to this killing field and fashioned his force into a hammer. Now he meant to bring that crashing down upon the dark eldar, or what was left, and crush them in a decisive blow.

Supporting the Astartes were the Night Devils. General Slayte had survived the war and meant to end his part in it on the frontline with the rest of his men. Who was Agatone to deny him?

'For those who died and the glory of the 156th,' Slayte rallied his men.

Inside the dusky confines of the *Fire Anvil's* troop hold, Agatone smiled. Such courage.

The Salamanders reached the last of the webway portals swiftly, impelled by stoic fury and their long historical enmity against the dark eldar. A final few raiders surged through the inky darkness of the portals, the last to be conveyed to Volgorrah before the sons of Vulkan brought the fire and the horizon burned.

Dense explosions rocked the sky above, the conflagration unleashed by the Salamanders on the ground rising to reach it. The *Vulkan's Wrath*, strike-cruiser of the 3rd, was tearing the fleeing ships of the enemy apart. In low orbit the broken vessels flashed with incendiary flare that looked like starbursts to the warriors below.

And on the ground, amongst the carnage, a bright blaze of dislocation as the battle's latest arrivals sought vindication and vengeance. The Firedrakes teleported into the heart of the stranded xenos troops from the frigate *Firelord*. Each of them fought silently. Praetor, unhooded, appeared grimmer than the rest.

MOMENTS EARLIER, THE Firedrakes had materialised in the teleportarium of the *Firelord*.

In his heart, Praetor felt well and whole. They had recovered the Sigil and Chaplain Elysius yet lived. At times, hunting through the monster-haunted depths of the Volgorrah Reef, the veteran sergeant had doubted that outcome. Then he noticed that Tsu'gan was missing and his heart fell.

He'stan tried but failed to hide his grief. He removed his helmet, as if it was stifling him, and slowly shook his head.

'The perils of the warp are known to us all, brothers,' Halknarr offered in a small, respectful voice.

Teleportation was a highly dangerous mode of travel. It meant slipping into the empyrean and riding the tides of warp space. Fell creatures lurked in those depths, attracted by the tiny soul fires of the living. Their hunger was insatiable. Even with a homing beacon slaved to the *Firelord's* teleportarium, despite the prayers and acts of supplication made to the machine-spirits by the Techmarines, it was not an exact science. Tsu'gan had failed to make translation. His fate was likely a terrible one.

He'stan nodded but the old campaigner's words did little to assuage his obvious guilt. 'His path,' he began, 'it was not meant...' the thought trailed away. Pragmatism took over. 'We are victorious,' he said, masking a tone that suggested he felt anything but. 'The Sigil is safe and our Brother-Chaplain has returned to us.'

The arrival of Apothecary Emek and a clutch of medi-servitors and serfs prevented an immediate response.

Praetor's face was harder than the flank of Mount Deathfire. His mood was just as volatile. His thoughts were plain to all.

I have failed him, they said in the blankness of his eyes and the tightness of his mouth. *Not only that, I have lost another.*

'Bring him forwards,' snapped Emek. He rasped, his voice affected by the grievous wounding he'd received on the *Protean* during another of Praetor's missions. The Apothecary had very nearly died. He was the sole survivor of Brother-Sergeant Nu'mean's squad. It had left him scarred in many ways. Vulkan's testing of his sons was as severe as it was unremitting.

Daedicus and Invictese carried Ba'ken, the others parting to let them through. Emek hastily checked the sergeant's vitals with a bio-scanner. Unconscious but alive.

'The sus-an membrane has put him in a regenerative coma,' he muttered, interpreting the data relayed on the scanner screen. Several red areas denoted serious damage. They were focussed on the torso. Emek eyed the Firedrakes sternly. 'Fortunate given the condition of his body. It will take months to repair this damage. I cannot vouch for the psychological injury, of course.'

'Ba'ken is strong. He will heal, brother,' uttered Praetor, not in the mood for the Apothecary's bile. Though he had not known him well, Praetor knew the tragic events that had unfolded aboard the *Protean* were directly responsible for Emek's distemper. He had once been an optimistic, youthful-minded warrior. That life spark had been eclipsed the moment his injuries had near crippled him. Perhaps Praetor's fate, that which he'd felt on his shoulders ever since Scoria, was not so dissimilar – only his scars were within.

Emek held his gaze before ushering a pair of servitors with a grav-bed forwards. The Firedrakes laid Ba'ken down, the grav-bed sinking a little with his weight before the correct amount of loft was reasserted. 'Take him to the medi-deck,' he said curtly, dismissing the serfs.

'Him too,' he added, gesturing to Persephion who was being supported still by Vo'kar. That left a glassy-eyed and haunted-looking Tonnhauser. 'That one I can do little for, save sedate him and hope he recovers.'

'You're as brittle as Fugis, perhaps more so,' said Elysius, approaching the Apothecary under his own strength as the wounded were being taken away.

Emek had never seen the Chaplain's face. He guarded his surprise at it well, but there was a tremor of recognition visible in the Apothecary's body language.

'I am sorry we lost Tsu'gan,' Emek said, bowing slightly before his Chaplain. In the intervening months since the *Protean* incident the two had discussed much.

'Many were lost to bring this back to the Chapter,' Elysius replied, holding the Sigil of Vulkan aloft.

All eyes went to the holy relic at once.

The Chaplain's mood was suddenly dour. 'I only hope it was worth our sacrifice.'

'You need medical attention, my lord,' added Emek.

'In a moment,' said Elysius, turning. 'Kneel, my brothers,' he addressed the others.

The Firedrakes went on one knee. Even He'stan gave genuflection before his Chaplain.

'Loss and death is the hammer that tests us. In Vulkan's cauldron, in his forge fires are we set against the anvil. I commend Tsu'gan's soul and flame to his breast. In hope and brotherhood is the circle of fire maintained. Let us remember him, let us remember his deeds. Honour his sacrifice. He was one of us. Fire-born.'

'Fire-born,' they repeated in unison.

'Firedrakes, stand,' boomed Praetor. He held his thunder hammer aloft like a banner. 'Zek Tsu'gan.'

'Tsu'gan,' they chimed together.

Zartath, thrashing and raging as soon as he came around, dented the Firedrakes' reverie.

'Release me, dogs,' he snarled, straining as Oknar and Eb'ak moved quickly to hold him.

'Who is the dog here, savage!' snapped Eb'ak, resisting the urge to strike the Black Dragon.

'You Sons of Vulkan are insane,' Zartath spat. 'The warp is no place to walk unprotected.'

'Shut him up,' Halknarr warned.

Praetor held his fellow sergeant back. 'He's raving, brother. Calm yourself.'

'Release me!' Zartath struggled on. The bone-blades slid from his vambraces.

'Kesare's breath,' hissed Oknar.

'I thought it was just a rumour,' added Daedicus, pulling out his chainsword.

'Desist,' Praetor ordered. 'And let him go. Now.'

Oknar and Eb'ak obeyed, backing away immediately as the feral Black Dragon was released.

Zartath bared his fangs at them then looked to Praetor. 'Strange way to show your appreciation. I saved your priest and one of his flock. A human, too, though I expected *him* to die. Hath you no honour?'

'He speaks the truth,' said Elysius. 'We would not have survived without him.'

'A ship,' Zartath uttered quickly, 'I need a ship and a way back to my Chapter.'

'That's not happening any time soon,' Halknarr told him.

The Black Dragon growled. The bone-blades extended further. 'Will you stop me?' he sneered.

'Don't make me regret my decision, brother,' Praetor told him in a level voice. He tapped the haft of his thunder hammer.

Emek stepped through the throng. He'd been on his way to the Apothecarion when the Black Dragon had come around. He eyed the bone-blades with a mixture of disgust and fascination. 'Does it hurt,' he said, 'when they come out?'

Zartath exhaled and stood down. The blades slid back into his forearms, 'Aye, every time.'

'What will we do with him?' asked Halknarr. He looked to He'stan for guidance but the Forgefather seemed content to observe only.

Praetor grunted, evidently unhappy. 'He stays here.'

He addressed Zartath, who was on the verge of another outburst. 'For now. If he can behave.'

'I'll examine him in the Apothecarion,' offered Emek. 'Some of those wounds appear to be fresh.'

'I need no tending,' the Black Dragon seethed.

'Even still, you *will* go with our Apothecary,' Praetor told him, nodding.

When he saw he had no choice, Zartath acceded to the will of his new keepers. He left with Emek without further incident.

'A bizarre ally, for sure,' said Halknarr when they were gone.

'I vouch for him, though,' Elysius replied. 'If not for Zartath, the dark eldar would've caught us sooner than they did. Even so, many still died to get us to that point.'

'At least the dusk-wraiths were denied your head, my Lord Chaplain,' offered Halknarr.

Elysius nodded, but privately he wasn't so sure. Inwardly, he wondered if they had ever wanted *him* at all, that perhaps the dark eldar had a different purpose. At the back of his mind, then just a nascent realisation yet to surface, Elysius wondered if in fact he had merely been the bait to snare a different prey altogether.

'Techmarine,' Praetor's stentorian voice interrupted the Chaplain's thoughts. The Salamander at the teleportarium's controls stood ready to receive the sergeant's orders. 'Set coordinates for the Ferron Straits. Bring us to the thick of it. I want to bloody my hammer before this is done. One last time.'

The Firedrakes agreed.

A grim smile returned to the Forgefather's face as he stepped onto the teleporter plate with his brothers.

Tsu'gan would have approved.

CHAPTER NINETEEN

I
Ferro Ignis

THE GATES OF the vault beckoned.

Head bowed, He'stan handed the Sigil of Vulkan to his lord.

'Whatever lies beyond these gates,' said Tu'Shan, 'we must be prepared for it.' He took the Sigil from the Forgefather and pressed it into the impression wrought into the metal.

Almost immediately, the churning of gears sounded throughout the cavern as an ancient mechanism went to work. This was artifice of the oldest kind, from before the Great Betrayal and the Long War that still followed. Whether it was Vulkan's hands that had wrought it or older still, none amongst the Chapter knew. It was a holy place now, though its secrets, lost to time, were about to be revealed.

Tu'Shan stood back, rejoining He'stan who'd lifted his gaze as a shuddering din echoed around the subterranean chamber.

He'stan made the symbol of Vulkan over his left breast to mark the import of the moment. Tu'Shan remained still, not wishing to disturb it. They two were the greatest heroes of the Chapter, lords of legend themselves, and yet they stood humbled before the gate and the legacy it represented.

'I sense our primarch's hand in this,' uttered the Regent, his voice just above a whisper.

'His ways are strange. Now, I know why I was guided back.'

Slowly, a crack appeared in the centre of the gate. It fed down from the cavern ceiling, some hundred metres or so higher up, and snaked around the Sigil itself until meeting the ground. Dust and light, made warm and lambent by the magma glow, spilled forth.

Regent and Forgefather let the cloud, redolent of ash and cinder, envelop them.

It billowed into nothing and the gate was left open, a corona of ruddy light smudging its threshold.

Low-burning braziers lined the walls of a small, round room. The rock was smooth, veined with black fissures and deep red. Their light was cast upon a single object located into the centre of the chamber. It was a book, cradled on a pedestal of obsidian.

He'stan stepped forwards. 'From the Tome of Fire,' he said, somewhat nonplussed.

'It surprises you?' asked Tu'Shan, facing him.

Gaze fixed on the pedestal, He'stan replied, 'I had thought it would be one of the Nine. I believed that's why my pilgrim's path had brought me home. I was wrong.'

Tu'Shan didn't know what that portended but chose to keep his sudden disquiet to himself.

'Lord Vel'cona,' he called to the shadows and the Chief of Librarians emerged from the darkness. His eyes flashed cerulean blue.

'It has power,' he uttered in an awed voice.

'A lost chapter,' He'stan concluded, taking another step towards it before he faltered.

It was a plain looking thing. Leather-bound in drake hide, it was unadorned save for the icon of Vulkan emblazoned into its front and a dark gold clasp to bind it.

'As our primarch's namesake, it is your right,' Tu'Shan told the Forgefather.

Regarding his Regent for just a moment, He'stan nodded and entered the room.

Crackling brazier flames breached the reverent silence. A warm atmosphere pervaded, but it was heavy with the weight of moment.

'It must not leave this place,' said He'stan, voicing what he knew in his heart as he approached the book's cradle.

This was a temple to Vulkan, a secret chamber of the primarch. His will had brought them here, across the millennia. It seemed impossible – for the braziers still to be lit, for this sanctuary to have remained undisturbed for so long. He'stan couldn't say what had drawn him here when he and Tu'Shan had first discovered the chamber. Nor could he be certain why the primarch had chosen for his sons to find it now. All he knew was that they were here and this, a portion of Vulkan's distilled wisdom, was what he meant them to find.

Hands shaking, He'stan undid the clasp and opened the book. As he read, his face began to darken.

* * *

TU'SHAN AWAITED THEM on his throne. He'stan was close by, standing a respectful distance behind the Regent, as were his Firedrakes. Praetor was amongst them, twenty of the 1st Company as honour guard for their Chapter Master.

Master Vel'cona and Chaplain Elysius, whole again wearing a newly fashioned power fist, were the only others present. They waited in silence for the arrival of the *Caldera*. The Thunderhawk gunship had docked at Prometheus less than an hour ago. Two of its occupants had been summoned to the Regent's presence upon their arrival.

The great gate to the throne room opened and two Salamanders walked in haste through its ornate arch. The pair of Firedrakes flanking the gate eyed them both warily.

'My liege,' said Pyriel, trying to hide the shock of seeing Vulkan He'stan as he fell to one knee, 'we bring grave news.'

Dak'ir knelt alongside his master, head bowed. He felt a strange sense of foreboding but not from the revelations they were about to impart. It was coming from his brothers gathered in the throne room and he needed no psychic wit to discern it.

They'd made their return from Moribar with all speed, and though the planet was not far from Nocturne, a twist of warp fate had ensured they'd arrived *after* He'stan and the Firedrakes. Pyriel had recovered en route, he and Dak'ir discussing what they had seen in the vision.

The Epistolary related that to the assembly now. He described their 'meeting' with Caleb Kelock, how the technocrat had revealed, even in death, all of his secrets. Pyriel told of Kelock's account, that he had discovered plans for the weapon years before his death. It was a relic from before the Age of Strife and the technocrat had coveted it to his doom.

Throughout Pyriel's explanation, Tu'Shan was stony faced.

'It is an apocalypse weapon,' the Librarian said, 'the one we used on Scoria, or at least a version of it.'

'It's my understanding you weren't present when that happened,' said Vel'cona. His gaze was penetrating as he regarded his student.

'I have *seen* it, my lord,' said Pyriel, trying not to balk before his master's fire. 'In a psychic vision on Moribar, I saw it lance from the heavens and tear our world apart.'

Tu'Shan's eyes narrowed, his anger visible in the fire flaring within them. Even a threat against his world was an affront to him and the Chapter.

'It goes back to Stratos, my lords,' Pyriel continued. The next part was difficult for Pyriel to say. 'Ko'tan Kadai's death was a deception.'

'Explain yourself,' the Regent pressed, 'and do it quickly.'

'During his… *resurrection*, Kelock's mind was opened to us. We saw his past deeds and the measures he went to once he realised the destructive potential of the weapon. Somehow, Nihilan achieved the same feat. A trap was left for us on the sepulchre world and we very nearly succumbed.' Pyriel kept the part about Dak'ir's loss of control to himself, though Vel'cona looked far from deceived.

'An item, a way to break the cipher Kelock protected the weapon template with, was needed. He hid it on Stratos in a vault.'

'The Dragon Warriors were seeking it,' said Vel'cona.

Pyriel turned to him, 'Yes, master. And they suc-
ceeded. It was never about killing Kadai. His death
was... incidental.'

Now, Tu'Shan's fists were clenched. To hear that one
of his valued captains, his brothers, had been slain to
create little more than a smokescreen was galling. He
looked down at Pyriel's companion.

'And what say you, Hazon Dak'ir? Was your former
captain killed for no better reason than it was conve-
nient? You were there at the moment of his death.'

Dak'ir looked up at their faces for the first time since
he'd entered the chamber.

'Nihilan hated Kadai, my lord. He hates all of us. But
there is a greater plan than revenge at work here. We
must be careful. Nocturne is in peril, and we must arm
ourselves.'

Tu'Shan's gaze bored into him as if seeking the truth
in Dak'ir's words.

Why are they so wary of us? thought the Lexicanum. All
of their faces were stern and guarded. *Why are they so
wary of me?*

His answer was forthcoming.

'We will.' Tu'Shan leaned forwards in his throne. 'But
we have learned much, also.'

Dak'ir noticed the Regent's fists were still clenched.
Whatever was coming, it hadn't been easy for Tu'Shan
to decide upon.

'Forgefather...' Tu'Shan invited.

First bowing to his lord, He'stan advanced on Dak'ir.

'"*A low-born, one of the earth, shall pass through the gate
of fire*",' he began. Dak'ir knew the words well. They
were the prophecy, the one pertaining to him. '"*He will
be our doom or salvation*".'

'Tempus Infernus...' uttered Dak'ir, without thinking.

He'stan's eyes were upon him, pieces of flame-wreathed flint driven into his soul. Unlike the benevolence they had shown to Tsu'gan, Dak'ir found only accusation in those smouldering orbs.

'"*And so begins the Tempus Infernus,*"' he continued, the other part of the prophecy as revealed to him by the book. '"*The Time of Fire comes to Nocturne, and all trials before shall seem as nothing to this. One will become many. The Ferro Ignis shall emerge from ashes cold and wreath our world in conflagration. He is the Fire Sword. He is our doom*".'

'It is you, Dak'ir,' said Tu'Shan, his voice full of foreboding. 'You are the Ferro Ignis, or will be. You are the destroyer who will bring about the Time of Fire.'

The Lexicanum rose to his feet. All eyes were upon him now.

Pyriel tried to fashion a riposte to his Chapter Master's accusation but the severe expression of Vel'cona stopped him. The Epistolary had seen what Dak'ir was capable of. He had witnessed his nascent strength during the burning and again in the tunnels beneath Moribar. The *Caldera* would not have breached the planet's tumultuous atmosphere had it not been for Dak'ir.

In the end, Pyriel stayed silent.

'And so?' Dak'ir asked, defiant.

Had Tsu'gan been right, then? Was he just an aberration? Worse than that, was he a pariah to his Chapter?

'Until we know for certain,' said Tu'Shan, 'you will not be allowed to leave this place and your psychic powers will also be shackled. You are forbidden from using them.'

'Such measures were undertaken before, my lord.'

'Nikaea is ancient myth, ten thousand years old,' the

Regent replied. 'You will adhere to this decree, until I see fit to lift it or impose more permanent sanctions. I will not risk this Chapter's safety and that of the people of my home world.'

Dak'ir shook his head, 'I am Salamander, Lord Tu'Shan. I am part of this, let me play my role. What if I am Nocturne's salvation?'

'In your eyes, I see you don't truly believe that.'

Dak'ir was about to respond when he stopped himself. The Chapter Master was right. When Dak'ir had seen the apocalypse vision, there was a part of him that believed he was not merely witnessing it but that he had actually caused it.

'I don't know what I believe,' he murmured.

Pyriel was looking around at the assembled Chapter elite, searching for some glimmer of sense amidst the unfolding madness.

'He saved my life,' he said, exasperated. 'This is an error, this is–'

Silence!

The psychic impel hit Pyriel hard. Vel'cona's eyes blazed.

There was little more to say. Tu'Shan nodded to his second-in-command.

'Take him,' said Praetor simply. Four Firedrakes from the honour guard marched from the darkness to surround Dak'ir.

'Until we know what this means for Nocturne, you will be held here in the cells on Prometheus,' Tu'Shan told him. 'I am sorry, brother. There is no other way.'

Dak'ir unstrapped *Draugen* in its sheath and handed the sword to Pyriel.

'Keep this for me.'

Pyriel nodded, unable to find the words.

Then Dak'ir held out his hands. Shackles were placed around his wrists and neck. Wrought by Vel'cona, all three bands had psychic nullifying properties.

As the final clasp was locked shut, Dak'ir closed his eyes.

Ferro Ignis. The honorific seeped into his mind like an accusation as he was led away from the throne room and to the cells.

Fire Sword.

Destroyer of Nocturne.

II
Burdens

'I WARNED YOU, Pyriel.' Vel'cona was pacing his chambers, a room of dark cobalt with much of its arcana lost to shadow. 'I warned you of the dangers.'

The sanctum was one of the Chief Librarian's many that he had situated around Prometheus. Most were protected by psychic wards, impossible for anyone but Vel'cona to locate, let alone penetrate. It was rare indeed that Pyriel gained admittance. But then these were rarefied times.

The Epistolary saw little through the darkness. A ring of ever-burning flame surrounded him but emitted no illumination or heat. It was psychic fire and the circle which the Librarian inhabited was the only concession into Vel'cona's quarters that his master was prepared to make.

'Nothing is certain, master,' Pyriel replied. 'Nocturne's fate is, as of yet, undecided.'

Since the revelations in the throne room, the entire

Salamanders Chapter had been put on alert. Captain Dac'tyr of the 4th had assembled the fleet at once and was currently anchored in low orbit above the planet. Those companies close enough to return had been contacted by astropath. Vulkan's Eye, the mighty defence laser that watched over all of Nocturne from its perch on Prometheus moon, was turned towards the darkling stars.

None knew when the Dragon Warriors would make their assault or how it would happen, but at least they would be ready for it.

'Did you learn nothing during the burning?' Vel'cona asked.

'With respect, master, you weren't there on Moribar, in the *Caldera*.' Pyriel spread his hands in contrition. 'Dak'ir's power *is* great. It terrifies me. The truth is, even if I'd wanted to vanquish him, I couldn't. He would have overwhelmed me.'

'You are my finest apprentice, Pyriel. One day you will assume my mantle as Chief Librarian. How can I let you do that if your judgement is so flawed?'

'I'm being pragmatic. We must hone Dak'ir; help him to master his powers.'

'No. You should have taken action sooner. You should have killed him during the trials. That was all you needed to do.'

'Then why not do it now? If he is so dangerous, then why don't you and I go to Dak'ir's cell right now and destroy him?'

Vel'cona scowled, the fires in his eyes deepening his expression of displeasure.

'Because you know we cannot. Doom or salvation,' Pyriel added. 'Salvation, master, but from what? We *need* Dak'ir. He is beyond us both. There is something within him, a potential that we have to realise or Nocturne itself could be forfeit.'

'And who is to say that by realising his potential we do not damn ourselves in the process?' Vel'cona countered. He sagged a little. 'You and I have always seen alike, Pyriel. It is why I encourage you to speak your mind to me, why I tolerate your occasional lapses in respect, but in this you are wrong.'

'I believe in him.'

'Then I envy your faith.' He paused and there was a hint of lamentation in it. 'Dak'ir awaits the Chapter Master's judgement and that of the Pantheon Council. Whatever is decided, we must both abide by it.'

'And you will advocate his destruction, master, when the council is convened?' It was an impertinent question, but one Pyriel felt he had a right to ask.

'I will.'

'Then I hope the vote goes against you.'

Vel'cona sighed. He knew this was not easy for Pyriel. 'We will see. One thing I know for sure, Epistolary. War is coming. The Dragon Warriors are bent on our destruction.'

'*Nihilan* is bent on our destruction,' Pyriel corrected.

Vel'cona nodded. 'I should have killed him years ago when I first suspected,' he muttered. Then he added more assertively, 'I won't make the same mistake with Dak'ir.'

Pyriel bowed his head in supplication.

It was in the hands of Vulkan now.

ELYSIUS STAGGERED AS he left the medi-slab.

'I've got you, brother,' said Emek, his arm swiftly under the Chaplain's and around his chest.

The Apothecarion was dimly lit and smelled of the

unguents and salves Emek had applied to Elysius's battle-ravaged body. The deep muscle massage was intended to released the pent-up stress and allow faster recovery. But the Chaplain's wounds were extensive, his exhaustion hidden behind a mask of determination. It had been hard enough to get him to agree to treatment. Now Emek had him, Elysius was eager to return to his supplications before the primarch in the Reclusiam. Evidently that desire had yet to transfer to his weary limbs.

'The body never lies…' Emek said. 'No matter how strong you think you are.'

Stripped of his power armour, Elysius wore only a pair of mesh leggings, part of the armour's sub-layer that went below the ceramite, and was naked from the waist up. As well as honing his mind and spirit, the Chaplain worked tirelessly in the gymnasia. His remaining arm was bunched with bench-pressed muscle.

Elysius regained his feet and Emek let him go.

The Apothecary nodded. 'Nice,' he said, 'you're healing well, the balance will come.'

'And you, brother?'

Emek turned away, busying himself with the instruments he'd left on a counter next to the medi-slab. He adjusted the settings on a bio-scanner needlessly.

'There is pain, but I'm managing it.'

The Apothecary was wearing a light robe and medical fatigues, power armour ill-suited to deep muscular rehabilitation. It exposed some of the horrific injuries he'd sustained on the *Protean*. A xenos psyker, its mind absorbed into the ship, had inflicted them. Despite several restorative attempts, much of the crude scarification remained. It had obliterated some of his honour-markings and left him walking with an awkward gait.

'I'm not talking about your body, Emek,' said Elysius, pulling on the mesh torso layer. One of the arms had been removed to account for the Chaplain's maiming.

Emek glanced at him. 'You should get an armour serf to do that for you. I could summon one…'

'Answer my question,' Elysius pressed. 'Besides the physical pain, how are you coping?'

Emek licked his lips. He put the bio-scanner down and spread both hands against the counter, bracing himself.

'Embittered,' he admitted. 'The *Protean* was no one's fault, but I sometimes wonder if it wouldn't be better that I'd died aboard rather than being condemned to this.'

'Your role in this Chapter is vital to us all, brother.'

Emek turned quickly. There was anger in his eyes. 'I am near crippled. Damaged to such an extent that even Master Argos cannot remake me anew. I used to march with my brothers, Elysius. I had such… *hopes.*'

'You do your duty, Emek. You serve your Chapter still. What greater calling is there than that?'

'I am tired, Elysius.'

'These are trying times for all of us, brother. It will pass.'

Emek's silence suggested his doubt.

'When you are finished here, meet with me in the Reclusiam,' said the Chaplain. 'We will talk further.'

ELYSIUS HAD LEFT the Apothecarion several hours earlier and was now knelt in the Reclusiam, turning his crozius over and over in his hands. Master Argos had fashioned him a bionic replacement for his lost limb.

The Chaplain still wore his power fist into battle, but the bionic one was more practical for his duties around Prometheus and Nocturne.

Elysius had already finished his litanies, yet still he pondered the weapon in his hands. The crozius was restored, again by Master Argos's own craft. It was magnificent, the equal of any master weapon in the Salamanders' arsenal. On Volgorrah, though, it had been shattered. Upon inspection later, the Techmarines had told him it should not have worked. The Master of the Forge had confirmed it. The crozius's power cell had been breached. It was beyond function.

It was no mere thing, Elysius had decided. To ignite when he had needed it the most, it spoke of something deeper than faith. He chose not to interrogate further. It had entered the Reef broken and now it was restored – that was all that mattered.

So much had been lost. He had learned of Iagon's suspected treachery and it pained him to think of it. Elysius was glad Tsu'gan hadn't seen it and feared it would now hit Ba'ken hardest of all when he was revived from his sus-an membrane coma.

I should have seen it, he thought. *I should have noticed the canker tearing Iagon up inside.*

He'd let his own doubts cloud his mind. It wouldn't happen again.

Resolved, Elysius rose and found a shadow falling across him from the Reclusial arch.

At first, he thought it was Emek having completed his ministrations in the Apothecarion.

'Brother-Chaplain,' uttered a cold, mechanical voice.

'Master of the Forge,' Elysius replied, coming eye-to-eye with Argos.

The Techmarine was armoured, but without his

bulky servo-harness. Sigils of the Cog and fealty to the Martian Priesthood sat alongside the Salamander iconography of his battle plate.

The bionic eye Argos wore in place of an organic one glowed dully in the gloom.

'It is good to see you, brother.'

'And you.'

Argos looked down to Elysius's belt where the Sigil of Vulkan was now mag-locked. 'Returned to its rightful place.'

'It has brought much revelation and unsettlement.'

'The *Archimedes Rex* is to be reunited with the Mechanicus,' Argos told him, apropos of nothing. The Salamanders 3rd Company, led by Pyriel, had discovered the forge-ship, derelict and floating in space.

'I suppose these troubling times we live in all began in its haunted corridors,' Elysius conceded.

After wresting it from a piratical faction of Marines Malevolent, the Salamander boarding party had discovered the casket with Vulkan's mark that had led them to Scoria. It had been the first step on whatever path the Chapter was now walking. The forge-ship itself had gone back to Prometheus, where Argos could study it and hold it until its rightful owners could reclaim the vessel. That time had arrived.

'Your capture pained me greatly,' Argos said after a brief silence, the lack of inflection making the warmth of his words slightly incongruous. 'And I see you no longer hide your face behind that mask of death.'

Since Volgorrah, Elysius had chosen to no longer wear his battle-helm in all circumstances. He would go into battle unhooded from now on. His charges would see the vehemence in his face, echoed by the fire of his words. His enemies would bear witness to his hate and quail before it. But those were not the only reasons.

Elysius regarded the metal plate masking half of Argos's face. Beneath it, he knew there was an acid-ravaged mess. 'I carried a heavy burden, Argos…'

'I know.'

'My guilt–'

'Was unnecessary,' the Master of the Forge interjected. 'I forgave you long ago, Elysius. As far as I was concerned, there was nothing to forgive.'

The Chaplain's voice became a choked whisper. 'Thank you, brother.'

VULKAN HE'STAN STARED through the occuliport of one of Prometheus's viewing domes, looking at the void.

'They are out there somewhere,' he said softly to the dark before Tu'Shan emerged out of the shadows.

The lights in the vast chamber were all doused. Only the reflected glow of the stars and other lunar bodies provided the room with illumination.

Until Tu'Shan had arrived, He'stan had been alone.

'Why do you isolate yourself out here, brother? I thought you were glad to be back amongst your kin.'

'I am, but soon I'll have to leave again. The Nine call to me with one voice and I must answer. I will be alone again and must prepare myself for that burden.'

After a few moments, Tu'Shan said, 'Such uncertainty.' He too was looking to the heavens now. 'Much is unknown.'

'You are questioning your decision to incarcerate Dak'ir.' It was statement not a question.

Tu'Shan knew better than to be surprised. 'I am.'

'And you want to know what I would have done in your stead.'

'Yes.'

He'stan turned to face the Regent. 'I don't know. It was not my choice to make.'

'But if it had been?'

'Then I would have done what I thought was right, for the good of the Chapter and the people.'

Tu'Shan nodded at the Forgefather's understated wisdom. There was no right and wrong answer. All they could do was wait and hope they would not be found wanting against the anvil.

'No one can see all ends, brother,' said He'stan. 'But a great time of trial approaches and there will be blood before it's done.'

They both lifted their heads to the sky again.

Nihilan was coming. No one knew precisely what he had planned but with Dac'tyr's fleet already in orbit and the Eye of Vulkan prowling the void, surely even the Dragon Warriors weren't insane enough to attack Nocturne?

'Let him come,' Tu'Shan's voice was hard and deep with anger. 'I want to look this traitor in the eye before I crush him.'

EPILOGUE

THE PENITARIUM CHAMBER was dark, its torches doused. A cold, icy smell emanated from its walls. It was a hollow place, a solitary prison with none of the purity of the solitoriums.

Dak'ir stared at Pyriel through a vision-grille in the gate. The prisoner was stripped of his power armour but the psychic dampeners around his neck and wrists were still in place.

'Your battle-plate is secured in the armourium,' Pyriel told him. The Epistolary had removed his helmet, which was sat in the crook of his arm. His face was full of darkness. He opened his mouth, unsure of what to say next.

'It's all right, master,' said Dak'ir.

'No, it isn't. It's wrong.' Pyriel turned from the vision-grille, exasperated, then quickly turned back. 'This is a mistake, but it is the will of my master and the will of the Regent, so we shall abide.'

'Do I look as though I'm struggling to escape?'

Pyriel eyed the Firedrakes, standing sentry at either end of the access corridor. Neither had moved, except to allow the Librarian entry to see his apprentice.

'No. But what choice do you have, brother?'

A brief silence fell between them, full of unanswered questions.

Pyriel attempted to answer some of them.

'You'll go before the Pantheon Council. I don't know when they plan to convene, but it should be soon.'

'Will you be there?'

Pyriel looked down. 'I will, but my influence won't count for much, I fear.'

'What happens then?'

There was something different about Dak'ir, an inner peace and calmness Pyriel hadn't seen before as he looked at him. The answer was simple. 'You'll be judged. So too the veracity and immediacy of the prophecy.'

'Of all the Librarians you've trained, I am different, aren't I?'

The Epistolary nodded. 'There's only been one other that had your natural gifts, but even he pales next to your psychic ability.'

'Nihilan.'

'Yes. That is why my master cannot allow you free until we know what the Fire Sword means.'

'Don't you mean: what the Fire Sword is?'

'No, *you* are the Ferro Ignis. I'm convinced of that.' Pyriel smiled wryly. 'But as to what that means for Nocturne, how your destiny will manifest and affect our own. That I am uncertain of.'

'But you don't think me a destroyer.'

Pyriel snorted with dark humour. 'Oh, you are a

destroyer all right, but whether for our enemies or our world, that's what is to be decided. For what it's worth, I think you are our saviour. I must simply trust to the wisdom of my betters to draw that conclusion too.'

'And if they don't?'

Pyriel's face darkened further. 'Then they'll kill you.'

Dak'ir lowered his gaze and took a step back from the gate. 'Thank you, master. For everything.'

'I'm not finished.'

Dak'ir looked up, sensing bad news.

'Tsu'gan is lost.'

Confusion and grief warred on Dak'ir's face. 'Lost?'

'To the warp. I am sorry, brother.'

Dak'ir was shaking his head. 'I don't understand. He fell in battle? What happened to him?' His eyes narrowed. Tsu'gan was his greatest adversary within the Chapter. They had never seen eye-to-eye. Were it not for their oaths to Vulkan, they would be nemeses. Yet, Tsu'gan was still Dak'ir's brother. They had bled together. News of his demise brought nothing but hollowness. There was no sense of relief. He had wanted to convince Tsu'gan of his worth, to have him call him brother and mean it. At the very least to draw blades on one another and air their grievances in the battle cages. This only left Dak'ir feeling cheated.

Pyriel explained. 'When Elysius was rescued from the Volgorrah Reef,' he said – by now, they had heard of their Chaplain's dramatic escape – 'the 1st Company had to teleport him out. There was no other way to flee the dusk-wraiths' hell-realm. During translation back aboard the *Firelord* something went wrong. Tsu'gan did not return with the others. The warp took him.'

Dak'ir's fist slamming into the gate made Pyriel flinch.

'Calm yourself, brother,' snapped the Epistolary.

'This *reeks* of Nihilan and his bastard Dragon Warriors.' Dak'ir was incensed. His eyes blazed, but only red, not cerulean blue, with the psychic dampeners in place. 'What is being done to find Tsu'gan?'

Pyriel looked nonplussed. 'Nothing. He is dead, Dak'ir. Tsu'gan won't be coming back.'

'It's a lie, Pyriel. He's been taken, I know it.'

'How? How can you be sure of that?'

Dak'ir's fiery gaze filled the vision-grille as he came right up to the gate. 'It's Nihilan. He wants us both. Ever since Cirrion, he's wanted us.'

'For what? Dak'ir, you are raving. This makes no sense.'

'To join his brood, to sacrifice to whatever warpborn potentates he serves, who can tell what machinations drive him. But, master, please believe me when I say that Tsu'gan is not dead. He is in danger, not merely his body but his soul too.'

THE PIT WAS dark and smelled of blood. The metal collar around Tsu'gan's neck was heavy. A chill numbed his exposed skin. His armour was gone, though he didn't know how or when it had happened. His fists were clenched, tight with anger. His bare feet crushed shards of glass beneath him.

The pain was purifying.

He gazed around, interrogating the darkness. The pit was spiked around the edges, the low ceiling too. Eight rusting gates, each set in one wall of an octagonal chamber, offered a way out.

This was not the *Firelord*. But he must have been here longer than the few seconds of dislocation after teleporting. The beacon, the one he had worn on his vambrace, had been intercepted. It had brought him to this place instead.

As Tsu'gan watched, four of the gates, like portcullises, began to rise.

Eyes, wet and narrowed with malign intelligence, glittered in the gloom beyond as a quartet of creatures shambled out. The gates slammed shut behind them.

They moved on misshapen limbs, chains clanking and armour plating screeching as they ground against one another. Mutated fists clutched gladiatorial blades and bludgeons. Some of the beasts had claws already and no need of weapons. Slab-shouldered, thick-necked, grotesque with too much muscle, they were taller and broader than the Salamander. Each wore a stylised battle-helm to hide their horrific natures. A stink of offal and foulness pervaded them like a miasma.

'A fight, is it?' Tsu'gan smiled. He had fought in the Hell-Pits of Themis. Saurox, gorladon and dactylon had all fallen beneath his pugilist's blade.

He tugged on a length of chain that was attached to the neck collar. It gave him about five metres before the links would go taut. Tsu'gan scowled and let the anger come.

'Bring it...'

Tsu'gan dodged a trident lunge, using the first muto-gladiator's momentum to bring its face into contact with his elbow. The helmet dented, the nose guard crushed inwards and the creature mewled in shock and pain. The second Tsu'gan broke against the chain. He let it come, pulling the chain taut at the last moment. Ribs cracked audibly as the metal links crashed against the gladiator's body. Snatching up its fallen axe, Tsu'gan went for the third. He blocked a strong but lazy blade sweep with the purloined weapon's haft then punched the creature in the face to disorientate it before burying the axe in its head. Gore and brain matter washed the Salamander's honour-scarred body.

Leaving the axe embedded, Tsu'gan rolled from the path of the fourth. This one was a juggernaut, swinging twin morningstars in both its gnarled fists. It turned quickly, Tsu'gan ducking a blow meant for his head. He went in low, under its second swipe, and came up inside its death arc. Making fists, Tsu'gan boxed either side of the muto-gladiator's head and it yelped in agony as its ear drums burst. Strange hooting noises, resonating through its metal helmet, issued from the creature as it swung recklessly at the Salamander.

Tsu'gan took up his chain again and ran around the crazed monster until he'd circled it. As it came for him again, Tsu'gan drew the chain tight. First it snapped against the gladiator's body, then its neck. The Salamander broke it with a savage twist and the creature slumped dead.

The sound of moaning behind him brought a dark smile to Tsu'gan's lips. He'd incapacitated the first two gladiators deliberately. Turning around, he approached them, stooping once to nonchalantly pick up a fallen sword.

The first he beheaded savagely. The second he ran through, leaving the sword impaled in the body.

'Your wolves needed sharper fangs,' he roared at the darkness above, where he knew someone was watching him.

'Such rage…' A disembodied voice echoed from the shadows. An armoured figure came slowly into view, walking to the edge of a lofty platform, looking down into the arena-pit.

Tsu'gan snarled when he recognised Nihilan. There was something... *different* about him, though.

'Sorcerer,' he said through gritted teeth. 'Perhaps you'd like to come down here and face me. Or are you afraid?'

Nihilan merely smiled as if he hadn't heard the Salamander at all.

His silence infuriated Tsu'gan. 'Give me my armour and weapons!' he shouted. 'And I'll cut my way free of this pathetic prison. You'll regret snaring me with your warp-born subterfuge.'

'Such rage,' repeated Nihilan, his voice oddly resonant. 'It makes you powerful... *Malleable*. You will be a worthy vessel for me, Tsu'gan.'

The Salamander frowned, eyeing the figure of Nihilan carefully. 'I'm not speaking to the sorcerer right now, am I.'

'No,' said the thing using Nihilan's body, 'you're not.'

'Then what are you, spawn?'

'He's something else,' said another voice from behind him, 'though to call it *he* is a misnomer of huge proportions.'

Tsu'gan's eyes narrowed and the knuckles in his fists cracked as they clenched.

'Iagon?' he growled, part anger, part disappointment.

Cerbius Iagon, Salamander brother-sergeant, once Tsu'gan's second in the 3rd Company, stepped forwards into the visceral light.

'You're probably wondering how you came to be here,' he said.

'You found a way to infiltrate the beacon?' The chain pulled taut as Tsu'gan came forwards. He wanted to put his hands around his former brother's throat.

'Such safeguards are easy to circumvent,' he replied. 'They've wanted *you* for a long time, brother.'

Tsu'gan sniffed his contempt. 'But not you, eh? Never you, Iagon. Until you bartered your soul and honour for a moment of usefulness.'

The barbs stung. Iagon flashed his teeth in a snarl… then regained his composure.

'I am not the warrior you are, Tsu'gan. Nor do I possess Ba'ken's strength or Dak'ir's destiny, but I have other traits.'

'You are Salamander, Iagon,' Tsu'gan implored him, his fury eroding before a wave of anguish. 'I gave my squad to you, entrusted you with its leadership.'

'You gave me nothing – *nothing!*' he screamed at him. 'Abandonment, left to the dregs of obscurity, was your legacy. You were supposed to become captain, I following in your wake. N'keln died for this. I *killed* him!'

The shock upon Tsu'gan's face curled into hatred.

'You murdered him? You stabbed N'keln in the back? How could I have missed this madness…' he said to himself.

'I did it for you, brother. I did it to ensure your ascension.' Iagon's tone was almost pleading.

Tsu'gan's eyes were hard and cold, despite the angry fire burning within them.

'You damned yourself and in so doing became my enemy.'

Iagon laughed, but without humour. 'This is vengeance, Tsu'gan. This is *your* damnation.'

Nihilan, or the thing currently wearing his flesh, snarled.

The conversation was over. Iagon retreated back into the shadows.

'More carnage,' said the Nihilan-thing, revealing spine-like teeth and a flickering aspect of its true nature.

Tsu'gan's blood chilled.

The gates churned open again. This time, all eight. The muto-gladiators brought blades eagerly into the light.

Tsu'gan grinned ferally.

'First the dogs, then I come for the master,' he promised, before his voice dropped to a deep whisper. 'Then I come for you, Iagon.'

ABOUT THE AUTHOR

Nick Kyme is a writer and editor. He lives in Nottingham where he began a career at Games Workshop on White Dwarf magazine. Now Black Library's Senior Range Editor, Nick's writing credits include the Warhammer 40,000 Tome of Fire trilogy featuring the Salamanders, his Warhammer Fantasy-based dwarf novels and several short stories. Read his blog at *www.nickkyme.com*

THE TIME OF FIRE APPROACHES

In the depths of the warp, Nihilan gathers his war host. After years of planning, his retribution against the Salamanders is finally in sight. Renegades, traitors and the alien dark eldar flock to his banner. Tsu'gan is in chains, enslaved to the Dragon Warriors aboard the *Hell-stalker*, an integral part of Nihilan's hellish scheme. But the sorcerer seeks more than the destruction of the Salamanders…

On the moon of Prometheus the fate of Dak'ir is undecided. Is he saviour or destroyer? The truth about the 'Fire Sword' will be revealed as the prophecy unearthed on Scoria is fulfilled at last.

War is about to engulf Nocturne and every Fire-born will be tested against the anvil. Not all will survive.

Read the conclusion to the Tome of Fire trilogy in *Nocturne*, released late 2011

NIGHTLORDS

SOUL HUNTER

AARON DEMBSKI-BOWDEN

A NIGHT LORDS NOVEL

WARHAMMER 40,000

UK ISBN 978-1-84416-810-1
US ISBN 978-1-84416-811-8

BLOOD REAVER

AARON DEMBSKI-BOWDEN

A NIGHT LORDS NOVEL

WARHAMMER 40,000

UK ISBN 978-1-84970-038-2
US ISBN 978-1-84970-039-9

THRONE OF LIES

AARON DEMBSKI-BOWDEN

A NIGHT LORDS AUDIO

WARHAMMER 40,000

UK ISBN 978-1-84416-926-9
US ISBN 978-1-84416-927-6

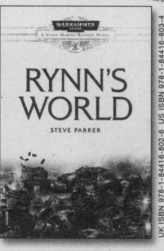

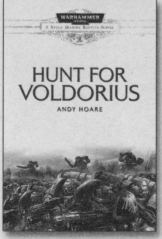